Asda Tickled Pink

45p from the sale of this book will be donated to Tickled Pink.

Asda Tickled Pink wants to ensure all breast cancer is diagnosed early and help improve people's many different experiences of the disease. Working with our charity partners, Breast Cancer Now and CoppaFeel!, we're on a mission to make checking your boobs, pecs and chests, whoever you are, as normal as your Asda shop. And with your help, we're raising funds for new treatments, vital education and life-changing support, for anyone who needs it. Together, we're putting breast cancer awareness on everyone's list.

Since the partnership began in 1996, Asda Tickled Pink has raised over £82 million for its charity partners. Through the campaign, Asda has been committed to raising funds and breast-check awareness via in-store fundraising, disruptive awareness campaigns, and products turning pink to support the campaign. The funds have been vital for Breast Cancer Now's world-class research and life-changing support services, such as their Helpline, there for anyone affected by breast cancer to cope with the emotional impact of the disease. Asda Tickled Pink's educational and outreach work with CoppaFeel! aims to empower 1 million 18 - 24 year olds to adopt a regular boob-checking behaviour by 2025. Together we will continue to make a tangible difference to breast cancer in the UK.

Asda Tickled Pink and the Penguin Random House have teamed up to bring you Tickled Pink Books. By buying this book and supporting the partnership, you ensure that 45p goes directly to the Breast Cancer Now and CoppaFeel!.

Breast Cancer is the most common cancer in women in the UK, with one in seven women facing it in their lifetime.

Around 55,000 women and 370 men are diagnosed with breast cancer every year in the UK and nearly 1,000 people still lose their life to the disease each month. This is one person every 45 minutes and this is why your support and the support from Asda Tickled Pink is so important.

A new Tickled Pink Book will go on sale in Asda stores every two weeks – we aim to bring you the best stories of friendship, love, heartbreak and laughter.

To find out more about the Tickled Pink partnership
visit www.asda.com/tickled-pink

Penguin
Random House
UK

STAY BREAST AWARE AND CHECK YOURSELF REGULARLY

One in seven women in the UK will be diagnosed with breast cancer in their lifetime

'TOUCH, LOOK, KNOW YOUR NORMAL, REPEAT REGULARLY'

Make sure you stay breast aware

- Get to know what's normal for you
- Look and feel to notice any unusual changes early
- The earlier breast cancer is diagnosed, the better the chance of successful treatment
- Check your boobs regularly and see a GP if you notice a change

Hannah Nicole Maehrer, or as TikTok knows her, @hannahnicolemae, is a fantasy romance author and BookToker with a propensity for villains.

When she's not creating bookish comedy skits about Villains and Assistants, she's writing to Taylor Swift songs. Her biggest passions in life include romance, magic, laughter, and finding ways to include them all in everything she creates.

Most days you can find her with her head in the clouds and a pen in her hand.

ASSISTANT TO THE VILLAIN

HANNAH NICOLE MAEHRER

PENGUIN BOOKS

TRANSWORLD PUBLISHERS
Penguin Random House, One Embassy Gardens,
8 Viaduct Gardens, London SW11 7BW
www.penguin.co.uk

Transworld is part of the Penguin Random House group of companies
whose addresses can be found at global.penguinrandomhouse.com

Penguin
Random House
UK

First published in the United States of America in 2023
by Red Tower Books, an imprint of Entangled Publishing

First published in Great Britain in 2023 by Penguin Books
an imprint of Transworld Publishers

A CIP catalogue record for this book
is available from the British Library.

ISBN
9781804993385

Interior design by Toni Kerr
Printed and bound in Great Britain by Clays Ltd, Elcograf S.p.A.

The authorized representative in the EEA is Penguin Random House Ireland,
Morrison Chambers, 32 Nassau Street, Dublin D02 YH68.

Penguin Random House is committed to a sustainable future
for our business, our readers and our planet. This book is made
from Forest Stewardship Council® certified paper.

To Mom and Dad,
for the hours of my childhood you spent telling me stories
and the years you spent listening to mine,
know that yours will always be my favorite.

And for all of you,
this is what I think it would be like to be the morally gray
fantasy villain's personal assistant.

PROLOGUE

Once Upon a Time…

It was an ordinary day when Evie met The Villain.

Another failed attempt at the job fairs in her village. Another day with no source of income. Another day she was letting her sick father and little sister down. Which was why her mind was preoccupied as she wandered to the trees lined like fences at Hickory Forest's edge—and walked right in.

The forest had once been frequently populated but was now the very last place anyone with common sense would choose to wander. Especially alone. Well, unless your name was Evangelina Sage and a forbidden forest seemed far more inviting than going home and admitting to your family that you'd finally found a job…and given it away.

Evie sighed, reaching out to let her fingers drift across the scratchy bark of several nearby trees as she wandered past. The forest really was quite beautiful.

The Kingdom of Rennedawn was one of the more modest of the enchanted kingdoms, and avoiding Hickory Forest when it took up so much of its land was a challenge. Still, its citizens had managed it well enough so far.

It had remained that way since a dark figure known as The Villain's emergence nearly ten years ago. There were too many rumors of him hiding out near the forest's edge to steal victims to torture. Evie knew little about the evil figure, but she was almost certain he had better things to do with his time than stalk the trees like a forest sprite. Though she'd not seen any of those, either—they tended to live farther north.

"The Villain," Evie scoffed, walking deeper into the trees and shoving her hands into the deep pockets of her simple brown dress. "Perhaps he would be less murderous if his moniker wasn't so ridiculous."

Unless, of course, the name had been bestowed upon him at birth, in which case Evie would applaud his mother for her incredible foresight.

Evie stumbled over a wayward branch, yanking her hands out of her pockets to catch herself with a nearby tree, then trudged toward the murmuring sounds of a stream.

As she walked, she sifted through her meager knowledge of the man, most of which she'd gotten from poorly drawn WANTED flyers. In them, he was always portrayed as older, with a gray beard broken up by large scars running down his face from grappling with his victims, and his teeth were often drawn jagged, like he'd rip out your heart with them—or perhaps needed to see a dentist.

So many rumors had trickled through the lands about the kingdom's greatest foe that Evie wasn't certain what to believe. She knew The Villain had burned one of the fishing villages in Western Rennedawn to the ground years ago. The kingdom had been devastated with famine after the loss of fishing for months afterward until they'd finally rebuilt. And there were many other stories of horror. Petty larceny seemed a staple of The Villain's to-do list as well, often stealing into noble homes to frighten the families and make off with their precious heirlooms.

Slowly approaching the stream—wider than she thought it would be—Evie marveled at the beauty of the sun coming in through the gaps in the trees, giving the flowers bordering it an ethereal glow. For a moment, she almost forgot about her predicament, it was so breathtaking a view. But then it all came rushing back.

Her father still didn't know she'd lost her job at the blacksmith last month. She'd been so sure she could find something else before her family noticed that the table was a little sparser at dinner or that their small cottage was colder for lack of firewood. She'd have to tell him tonight, though. They were down to their last meager food stores.

With a heavy sigh, she knelt down along the edges of the stream, her knees sinking into the spongy moss. She ran her hands through the clear blue water, then splashed some of the cool liquid against her face and neck, hoping to calm her racing heart.

She was in trouble this time. And not from some mythical villain.

No. She'd done this to herself.

The worst of it was that she'd nearly had a good position handed to her. At the fair this morning, she'd been offered the sole new maid posting for a noble family on an estate not far from her village. It wasn't ideal because of the distance, but she'd been ready to take it happily. Until, of course, she'd turned to see another woman standing beside her with such hope in her smile-lined eyes that Evie's heart had constricted in her chest. More so when she'd seen three young children standing behind the woman.

Evie had handed her the certificate of employment and watched her face light up as she grabbed Evie and kissed her on both cheeks.

I did the right thing. So why do I feel like my chest is going to cave in?

Sighing and splashing another bit of red water against her face, she began to list the other upcoming job fairs. Perhaps she could travel to one of the neighboring villa—

Wait... *Red?!*

Gasping and edging backward into the flowers, Evie felt her eyes widen in horror at the once-clear-blue water now clouded with a deep crimson color.

Blood.

She shut her eyes and tried to steady her breathing. After counting to ten, she got to her feet, nearly tripping over the hem of her long dress, and inched slowly toward the water again. It was clear to see the blood was coming from farther up the stream.

She took a step in that direction, inching one leather boot in front of the other, wholly unprepared for what she might find.

The stream was beginning to resemble a river of blood the farther she walked up it, the opaque red engulfing any remaining blue. It had to have been an injured animal, a large one if the amount of blood was any sort of indication. Certainly not something that warranted Evie's personal investigation.

And yet, here she was, in the forest that was suddenly getting darker as the sun began its descent behind the trees...following a river of blood.

Shaking her head, she felt plants getting crushed under her feet as she grinded to a halt. She was going to turn around. In fact, her body had been halfway turned when she spotted a beast with black fur hunched over and hidden slightly among the tall grass surrounding the stream and a giant tree.

Whatever manner of creature it was, the thing was alive—groans and muffled sounds of pain were coming from its general direction. Evie crouched, gently lifting her skirts to reach the small blade she kept in a sheath around her ankle for emergencies.

She'd put the poor beast out of its misery. Showing it that much kindness was hardly a burden. But the closer she inched, the less it looked like a creature at all. It almost looked like...

A human hand whipped out from beneath the black fur, which she now realized wasn't fur at all but a dark cloak. The hand circled around one of her wrists, pulling her down beside it.

"Oof!" She hit the ground hard, her shoulder connecting with the forest floor as an arm banded around her waist and pulled her against their body. She lay on her side, her back pressed tightly against something solid and warm behind her—which was when her good sense kicked in and she started to squirm and shout.

The arm around her waist cinched tighter as a hand closed over her lips. A low voice was in her ear, sending shivers throughout her entire body. "Be quiet, you little urchin, or you'll get us both killed."

Just then, Evie saw another foreboding figure across the way—several, in fact. All men dressed in silver. Carrying very large weapons, some of them glowing. *The king's Valiant Guards!*

She struggled against the hand, but the man's other arm was locking her against him and he wrapped a heavy leg over her ankles, effectively holding her still.

"Lwet meh go." She'd dropped her knife when she fell, so she felt around in the grass for it with her free arm.

"Relax," he ordered again.

Right. That was likely, considering a strange man, whom she was certain was the thing these men were hunting, had her pinned to the ground. But she'd sought this out, hadn't she? She'd followed a literal river of blood—what else did she think was going to happen?

"Em suc a fwool." Evie sighed long and hard.

Suddenly, the hand was gone from her mouth and the voice was in her ear once more. "What are you mumbling about?"

"This is just very typical for me," she whispered.

"Being pulled to the ground by a stranger?" he said in a tone that sounded suspiciously curious.

"Well, not this *exact* situation. But if I told someone about how I ended up here, nobody would think it out of the ordinary." She jabbed her elbow into his ribs, causing her captor to curse and grunt. "Oh, I'm sorry. Did that hurt?" She did it again, making her point.

"Enough!" he hissed before he pointed a tanned hand to the men searching the trees on the other side of the stream. "Those men do not care that you are an innocent who stumbled into the arms of a demon. They will kill you without a moment's hesitation, and they will do it laughing."

"A demon?" Evie chuckled quietly, attempting to turn her body to get a look at this man with such a high opinion of himself, but his arms tightened around her once more, keeping her in place.

"You know who I am, don't you?" he asked without a hint of arrogance in his tone. And yet, the casualness with which he just *knew* his reputation had preceded him made Evie's stomach do backflips.

She'd been called many disparaging things in her life. Alarmingly all beginning with the letter F. Flighty, foolish, forgetful, and, by a strange turn of events, she was finally able to add the final F.

Fucked.

She knew. She didn't know how she knew, but she did.

The Villain, King of Darkness, Haunter of Dreams, had his arms around her. Worse, even, she was not nearly as afraid as she should've been. In fact, she wasn't afraid at all, so much as she—

Oh dear. Was she *laughing*?

She was. She couldn't help it, and if she was any louder, those men would be over here in seconds. The Villain seemed to sense this, too, because she blinked and his hand was wrapped around her mouth once more.

"We're going to slowly crawl behind that tree." He pulled Evie up so she could see the large oak in question. "And then we're going to run."

"We?" she asked as she was suddenly flipped around and shoved in the direction of the tree. There was no room to argue, so, as instructed, she kept low and crawled until she was safely leaning against the other side of the trunk. Breathing heavily and startled to see blood brushing the back of her arm, Evie turned to see if The Villain was still there.

Gone.

"Where in the deadlands did he—"

"Here."

Evie spun in the direction of his voice, stunned. "How did you get over th—" But her words cut off when she saw him.

In her defense, there was a lot to take in.

Her first thought was the WANTED posters had it all wrong. This was not an older, scarred man with a gray beard. In fact, no gray laced through his thick, dark hair, either. He had high cheekbones above the two-day shadow that ran along a very hard jawline. She figured he couldn't be more than six or seven years older than she was. If she had to guess, she'd put him at no more than…twenty-eight, twenty-nine? That couldn't be right, though. There had to be a rule somewhere that evil overlords needed to be at least fifty, maybe sixty if they were pushing it.

But not young! And not, even more disastrously, beautiful.

He was, though: beautiful. His skin was tanned and smooth. As if his off time from terrorizing people was spent lying in the grass, perhaps daintily drinking out of a teacup and reading poetry with his pinky raised.

The thought brought a hysterical giggle to Evie's lips. The Villain lifted one of his perfectly thick brows that framed the darkest eyes she'd ever seen. Eyes that assessed her in pinched confusion. It seemed he didn't fully put together that she was another living, breathing human being, because he looked at her as if her very existence was a mystery.

"You really shouldn't look like that," she said and surprised herself by almost thinking the befuddled look on his face was endearing.

He's a murderer! Her conscience rebelled, but the rest of her, the part that wasn't attached to her very wise brain, found him far too pretty to care.

Taking a careful step in his direction, Evie tried to dig inside herself for the fear she knew was there. Any minute now, she'd be paralyzed with fright and run screaming in the other direction, but he was within arm's length now and she hadn't turned yet.

Hmm. No fear, but she did feel mild concern—a sound indicator she hadn't completely lost her good sense. Until, of course, her mild concern was clouded with embarrassing thoughts of what he would smell like if she leaned in close and took a whiff.

"Is there something about my face…that is displeasing to you? Or is it perhaps that I'm bleeding from three different wounds, courtesy of the men in your village?" His voice was quiet, and outwardly he appeared calm, but Evie could see a muted fury behind his dark eyes.

Did he think she was judging him?

"Um, yes— The blood's not great…but I was referring to the fact that you look like you were carved out of marble, and I just think that as a rule of thumb, inherently evil people should be grotesque-looking."

The fury winked out as if never there in the first place, his only response to blink.

"You just can't kill people and be pretty. It's confusing." Evie began unwrapping the wool scarf her little sister, Lyssa, had given her on her last birthday, stepping closer to The Villain and holding it up like a signal of peace. "For the blood, Your Evilness."

Taking it from her in a gripped fist, The Villain twisted the scarf around his middle and cinched it tight to stanch the bleeding. "You think I'm *pretty*?"

Oddly enough, Evie had the feeling he would've preferred to have been called *grotesque* for the way his face twisted with distaste.

"That's not a think scenario—that's just objective. Look how symmetrical your cheekbones are." She closed the distance between them and placed her hands on either side of his face.

His eyes widened and so did hers when she realized what she was doing.

"You're touching my face," he said flatly.

"…Yes."

"Are you happy with that decision?" He raised one dark brow again.

He's a professional killer, right? Maybe he'll murder me now if I ask very nicely.

"I was trying to prove a point." She shrugged, letting her hands drop back to her sides.

Shaking his head, a small dose of wonder in his eyes, he said, "You are chaos."

"Would you mind writing that out as an employment reference? I'd have a job within the week, and I desperately need work." Before he could reply, there was a quiet rustle in the bushes beside them that caused the hairs on the back of her neck to stand on end.

Twisting her head in the direction of the noise, she took a wary step closer to The Villain, who grabbed her shoulders quick as lightning and tugged her toward him. "What—"

She heard the arrow before she felt it.

Pain sliced through the skin of her back as the arrow skimmed her shoulders, sending her reeling into the solidness of The Villain's chest. "That hurt." The words came out matter-of-factly, like she'd just gotten a splinter.

They'd been spotted, but there was still no panic in his voice when he said, "It only grazed you. I know it hurts, but we must run." He turned her quickly but gently, and they started in the other direction, The Villain with a slight limp from his injuries.

"Put your arm around me." He winced as they dashed around several trees, Evie a step behind.

"Why?" she huffed back as he tugged her closer. "You're moving just as slow as I am!"

A flash of amusement crossed his face like a burning star, bright and beautiful for a moment, then gone beyond the horizon. "I'm going slower to keep pace with you."

It struck Evie then. How her predicament had escalated from unemployed butcher's daughter to aiding and abetting this kingdom's greatest enemy in an alarmingly short amount of time.

Good grief, maybe she *was* chaos. Had it even been half an hour?

Which suggested a very delicate question. One Evie should do well not to remind him of. But it was too late—the thought formed on her lips before she could push it back in. "Why are you bothering to keep pace with me in the first place? You could easily leave me in the dust and use the time they're dealing with me to get away."

Yes, Evangelina. Give him reasons to leave you behind and explain why you were running with The Villain in the first place. Sign your death warrant. Well done!

He held her gaze for a second, still managing to dodge an arrow that whizzed by without breaking eye contact. Evie was jealous. She couldn't dodge a dead tree if she was staring right at it.

"Such ruthless thinking, Miss…?" She was pleased to hear notes of fatigue behind his words. He wasn't a skilled runner. He wasn't perfect, wasn't invincible.

He was, however, asking her name. "Evangelina Sage…or just Evie." Okay, perhaps his voice was a little weary, but hers sounded like it had been through a cheese grater. Running had never been her friend, and running *fast*, she believed, was her mortal enemy.

"Hmph" was his only response, which was discomfiting, since he hadn't revealed if he was going to take her viciously good advice and leave her behind.

It was probable that some of the men from the village would recognize her, but the chances of them letting her live, when they seemed in such a bloodthirsty state, were slim. Especially considering she was running beside the person they were hunting, who was probably about to trip her and feed her to the wolves.

Of course, because the universe was against her, she didn't need to wait for him to do the deed himself. A stray branch hidden beneath the bramble jutted out just enough to catch the tip of her boot, and then she was falling clumsily to the earth.

The call of more male voices was nearly upon them. They were screwed.

Or rather, she was screwed. The Villain would probably take her wool scarf and ride his evil countenance into the sunset. She stared at the back of his head from the ground. At the clean, efficient way his body moved. As if the world was made to bend to his will.

She watched that ridiculously perfect head turn to the empty spot beside him and then back toward where she was helplessly sprawled on the ground. Back stinging, shoulder aching. With the addition of a large bruise forming after hitting the ground for the second time that day.

The voices were closing in, and they sounded angry. Evie attempted to climb to her feet to at least find a hiding place. But a familiar hand appeared in front of her, and she gripped it despite the shock overriding her decision-making skills.

"You fall down often." The Villain looked her up and down as he said it, seeming to catalog the fact like he was making a scientific discovery. "Let's move, Sage."

Ignoring the formality in his usage of her surname, she blustered, "The first time I fell, it was because you pulled me down!" She gripped his offered arm for support, and they moved away from their pursuers as quickly as they could manage.

"But you fell so easily. I barely tugged."

"You cannot possibly be blaming me for not being sturdy enough to withstand someone *yanking* me by my wrist?"

He didn't dignify her question with an answer, just gripped her tighter as they hustled through the forest like a pair of bandits. Eventually, the scenery of unending trees began to take on a darker tone. Not only because of the fast-fleeting sunlight, but the color of the trees was a different kind this far in. Long, twisted trunks and branches held warped leaves of a lush moss color, and the high-pitched screeching of strange birds filled the thick air, sending deep, unsettling chills through her.

"Where are we going?" she asked hesitantly. The little light that was left in the sky seemed to vanish within seconds, and night cloaked over them like an unwelcome blanket. Well, unwelcome to her, at least. The Villain looked around at the blackness, and for the first time since she had encountered him, she saw a truly wicked glint in his eyes.

He belonged to this, the night, the darkness. It was his.

And Evie…was still not afraid.

So incredibly odd.

"To safety. My home and where I conduct my business."

Evie attempted to pull her arm from his and turn in the other direction. "Safety in a place the public has nicknamed Massacre Manor? I'm okay, thank you. I'll take my chances with the village brutes."

His arm was a steel hook around hers, and she couldn't move an inch. She may as well have been welded to him. "If I'd wanted you dead, I would have left you back there."

She arched a brow. They were moving at a far more leisurely pace than before, the low buzz of voices behind them fading into almost nothing.

They'd lost them. For now. The safety in that caused Evie's

inappropriate curiosity to get the better of her. "Why were they chasing you in the first place?" she asked, angling her head at him and the pouch he gripped at his side. "Did you steal something? Weapons? Money? Someone's firstborn child?"

The Villain halted for a moment, and Evie yelped as the pouch moved. Before she could protest, The Villain reached inside and pulled out a larger-than-average-size frog, so green in color that it nearly blended against its gold-rimmed eyes. It sat peacefully in The Villain's hand, staring at her. She stared right back at it.

"Is that frog wearing a crown?" Evie asked after a few beats of silent staring.

The Villain ignored her question, holding the frog up a little higher. "I will not deny that thievery is one of my better traits. However, in this case, those men were attempting to rob *me*."

The dots were connecting, just in a way that was too strange for even Evie to understand. "Rob you of…a *frog*…that's wearing a *crown*?"

The Villain turned and continued to walk, and Evie followed quietly. "This is no ordinary frog," he reasoned. "He can…understand and communicate with humans as well as if he were one." The frog let out a healthy ribbit as if to demonstrate his fine communication skills, but The Villain ignored him. "And he is in *my* care." The words prickled over Evie's skin like a warning. "Magical animals get auctioned for quite a bit of money. The men from your village thought it would be prudent to find out how much stealing him on my daily stroll would cost them."

Evie gasped in horror. "And the crown is because…?"

The Villain paused, raising his hand holding the frog toward Evie as though the reason were obvious. "His name is *Kingsley*."

Evie blinked at him for a moment. "Are you serious?"

"Do I look like I'm joking?"

Fair point. Evie actually hoped he wouldn't attempt a joke—the shock might kill her.

He lifted the open pouch and gently laid Kingsley the Frog back inside it before turning to Evie. "Just a little farther until we reach the manor."

Evie followed, but not quietly this time. "How do I know you aren't just keeping me alive so you can kill me in a more fun way later?"

"What is a fun way to kill someone, I wonder?" His face was inscrutable, but she could tell she'd surprised him again.

"Well, I don't know! I'm sure one must find some joy in an activity they partake in so often." She reached out a steadying hand and grabbed his shoulder as she stepped over a fallen log.

His shoulder tensed under her fingers, something Evie didn't completely hate the feeling of, but his face remained impassive. "You're correct. There are a few fun ways." He stepped out of reach once she was safely past the log, and she dropped her hand back to her side. "But I hardly have need to implement them when your two left feet will be your undoing."

"For the last time, I am not clumsy. I fell once. The first time was your fault, too." She strutted in front of him, arms crossed. "I have my faults, Your Evilness, but one of them is not being prone to—"

Smack!

Evie's head reeled back sharply. *Ouch.*

She blinked at the open night air, wholly confused about what had just happened.

A heavy sigh sounded behind her as The Villain moved around her small form to place his hand against her invisible attacker. But the minute his fingers touched the space, a barrier began to dissolve around them in a flash of blue light. The corners of the scenery melted away, revealing large stone walls and a black iron gate. Behind it, high-rising cobblestone towers.

His castle was hidden by magic—that had smacked her in the head.

The gate swung open, and The Villain motioned for her to walk in front of him. As though resigned to dive headfirst into a moat of hungry sea dragons, she followed his instruction. Honestly, at this point, what else could she do? She'd exhausted any other options when she'd agreed to help him and let him help her in return. May as well see this through to its bitter, bloody end.

Massacre Manor was far too large to just be considered a manor. It could probably house her entire village, plus another two villages of the same size, comfortably. It was dilapidated and crumbling in some parts, but there was a charm to its dishevelment. The stones making up the structure were muted grays and browns, moss and vines overgrowing in the crevices and spaces between. But its disorder made it appear inviting and mysterious.

Perhaps even a little comforting.

They stepped around cracked fountains covered in more moss as Evie's gaze bounced about the surrounding garden. It was surprisingly well-kept. In fact, she was sure she saw a patch of daffodils and choked back a giggle.

But the grandeur of the space was truly the most frightening, as it somehow seemed to grow bigger the closer they came—increasing at the same level as Evie's impending doom.

In short, it was huge, and what a very grand place to die.

Swallowing hard, staring at the dark wood of a large door, Evie turned toward The Villain, signaling a question with her eyes.

"If you push on it lightly, the door will open." There was a confusing dryness to everything he said. Like he either had a secret sense of humor or he truly believed everyone else in the world was incompetent.

"I know how doors work," she said, exasperated.

He squinted, as if he didn't quite believe her. "Then why isn't it open yet?"

Ah well, incompetent people everywhere it is, Your Evilness.

"Let me get that for you, sir!" A gravelly voice sounded from the window above them, and Evie shrieked in surprise, stumbling back into The Villain.

"Hurry, Marvin. Ms. Sage seems to be having some sort of attack."

"How long has he been up there?" She pulled away from the solidness of his chest and found herself alarmed to catch the freshness of his scent. Shouldn't he smell like death? Not faintly of cinnamon, whiskey, and cloves.

"He's one of my guards. He's always up there." As if they'd timed it, the heavy door swung open with an ominous creak.

Evie followed him inside to the dimly lit entry hall. "Okay, I'm inside your lair, Your Evilness. Why have you brought me here?"

He rolled his black eyes and trudged across the massive room toward several large stone stairs against the far wall, leading to who knows where. He called out over his shoulder, "If you're going to work for me, Sage, you cannot continue to call me that."

His strides were long, and Evie rushed to catch up as they began their ascent. "Work for you?" The idea was too ridiculous. "I can't do that. You're...you're...bad."

He froze on the second flight, leaning against a stained glass window. "I am," he said, not even attempting to deny it. He walked toward her, looming. She knew he was trying to intimidate her. "But you said you needed employment."

She had? Oh yes, she had, when she was in a ramble-induced state. Evie was used to people tuning out those musings, not marking them as job applications. "I do," she admitted wearily. "But why would you possibly offer me a job? What about today has told you I'm qualified for any of the kind of work you do?"

"You have a cutthroat way of thinking I find valuable, and you helped me, despite all you've heard about my reputation." He looked down at the blood-soaked scarf around his waist.

"Your injuries!" Evie reeled back, looking at him with disbelief. "I completely forgot. Are you in a lot of pain?"

He grimaced but didn't pull the scarf from his waist. "I heal quickly. What of *your* injuries?"

The bruise on her hip was going to be ugly and purple. As for the bite of the arrow that had nearly flayed the skin off her back, it was stinging, but the worst of it had subsided.

"I'll live." She shrugged, neglecting to mention the additional knife wound on her left shoulder. Put there by her last employer.

That still hurt like a bitch.

He nodded, holding his hand out, and said, "What do you say, Sage?"

Evie paused, knowing admitting this could get her killed, but she couldn't bring herself to lie. "Would you still be offering me this position...whatever it is...if you knew that my father was once a knight for the king?"

His face remained impassive; in fact, he looked bored. "Is he still?"

"No no! It was well before I was born. It was just a way for him to save money for his butcher's shop. He retired after he married my mother." The next part was painful, so she said it quickly. "He's far too ill to work anymore anyway, and his only loyalties are to his family."

The Villain shrugged. "Then I do not see why that would be any sort of issue."

Well, that one aside, she was certain she could still find quite a few.

"What would working for you entail?" she asked, eyeing his hand like both a lifeline and a death sentence. "I have no interest in hurting people or helping you to hurt people. Or being one of your...lady friends."

Hand dropping back to his side, his lips twisted upward, almost as if he were attempting to...smile? "You're hardly the kind of woman I'd take to my bed."

Evie's face burned, and the sting on her shoulder was suddenly no comparison for the burn of rejection she felt in her chest. Which was ridiculous, because she hardly wanted to be desired by this man, but for goodness' sake, she had a little pride.

Putting his hand before her once more, his beautiful face becoming an impassive wall, void of emotion save for the slight softness around his eyes, he said, "I will be frank. I will not force you, but you know where 'Massacre Manor,' as you so eloquently called it, is located now. You know that I am not immune to the slice of a blade and, the worst of all your offenses, you've seen my face."

He stared hard at a curl lying against her forehead. She must have looked a wreck after running through the forest like a criminal.

"You are a liability, and I do not have the time to allow Tatianna to weave through your mind, removing the memories of this day. I am bleeding on my favorite shirt. You need work, and I'm willing to give you a generous position with an even more generous salary." When she didn't move, he sighed and added, "And I can assure you I have never harmed an innocent."

"But what of my village?" she blurted out before she could think better of it. "What if I help you harm someone I know?"

"That would be very awkward for you," he said unsympathetically.

She narrowed her eyes at him until he relented.

"I will spare the *villagers* from my *truly* murderous intents." His tone was agreeable, but she couldn't shake the feeling he was saying more than she was guessing.

She couldn't believe she was actually considering it, but the thought of being able to provide for her family had her heart racing in her chest. Before she knew what she was doing, her hand was clasped in his.

She'd expected it to be cold, but it was warm, and the sensation of his fingers curling around hers was making her feel drugged. "Fine,

I accept your offer. What depraved things am I going to be doing for you, Your Evilness?"

Keeping their hands clasped and their eyes locked, he let a smirk dance across his full lips. "Congratulations, Sage, from this day forward, you are my new personal assistant." He dropped her hand and turned away to continue up the stairs, but he'd barely moved three steps before he turned back toward her dazed form. "And if you must call me anything, 'sir' will do just fine."

CHAPTER 1

EVIE

Five months later…

There were severed heads hanging from the ceiling *again*.

Evie sighed, waving to Marvin as she shut the heavy castle door behind her and strode across the main hall, her low heels echoing off the stone floor in tandem with her fast-beating heart.

The Villain was in a mood.

One severed head was par for the course. A regularity that Evie had grown alarmingly accustomed to in the time she had been working here. But three male heads dangled there now, their mouths open in a silent scream, like they'd left this life in abject terror. And if she looked close enough…

Ugh, one of them was missing an eyeball.

Evie scanned the floor before taking another step, hoping desperately to avoid crushing the eyeball under her heel like she had a few weeks ago when she'd ventured into the boss's torture chamber to relay a message. The scream she'd let out then was no more than a peep, but if it happened again, she wasn't sure she could maintain such composure. She could handle a stray finger or even a toe, but eyeballs popped when they were stuck under one's foot, and that seemed to be the line Evie's mind had drawn in the sand.

She sniffed, walking forward. *A fair one, if anyone asked me.*

But it was neither here nor there. The brand of horror she came across on the day-to-day didn't ruffle her the way it should have. Her need for normalcy had whittled away, bit by bit, since her employment began, but she didn't mind. "Normal" was for those who didn't have the ability to stretch their minds past the unreachable end. It was something her mother had said throughout her childhood, and for some reason, it was the one piece of advice Evie could not ignore.

It really couldn't be helped in any case. She was the personal assistant to The Villain, after all. She chuckled at the job title, imagining the ridiculous way the employment posting would appear in a news pamphlet.

MUST BE WELL ORGANIZED.
MUST ENJOY WORKING LATE NIGHTS AND RELISH WRITING LONG DOCUMENTS.
MUST BE COMFORTABLE AND EVEN SUPPORTIVE OF ARSON, TORTURE, MURDER.
AND MUST NOT SCREAM WHEN THERE IS AN OCCASIONAL
DEAD BODY LYING ACROSS YOUR DESK.

In the boss's defense, he'd only done that last one once since she'd begun working here. After arriving at work at her usual punctual time, she'd crossed the office, immediately spying the corpse of a burly man sprawled across her desk. Slashings all over his body, chunks of flesh missing.

He'd been tortured before being killed, that much was clear, and the boss had thought to dump the man on her very organized and shiny white desk, which was set up just outside his very large, disorganized office. She'd never forget the look on his face when she walked in, saw the body, and then found him leaning against his office entryway. He just stood there, arms crossed and sharp gaze focused on her.

Ah, yes, Evie had thought. *He's testing me.*

But it helped that he didn't seem as if he were *expecting* her to fail.

She'd grown so alarmingly used to *that* look from the villagers, she'd cataloged it in her mind under things that made her want to commit acts of violence.

So instead, she'd sifted through every possible reaction that would serve her best in that moment—aka allow her to keep her job—and ultimately settled on simply being herself.

Well, herself with a mangled corpse on her desk.

She'd glanced at her boss, her chest tightening at the intense way he was staring back. It was almost like he was *willing* her not to fail, which made no sense at all. Maybe he had indigestion—from all the torturing this morning and whatnot.

"Good morning, sir. Would you like me to work around this gentleman? Or is this your subtle way of telling me you'd like this body moved to a more appropriate location?" she'd asked with a friendly smile on her face.

He'd just raised a brow, then shoved off the doorjamb and strode to her desk—and the body.

She'd bit back a sigh as black leather stretched over his thighs when he leaned across the desk—because he threw the body over his shoulder like a sack of potatoes, not because he had very nice thighs. His eyes never left hers as he'd straightened and carried the man toward the nearest window...and promptly tossed him out.

Evie bit back her gasp, determined to prove herself. Besides, this job was still going *wildly* better than the last.

Taking a large gulp of air, Evie had held The Villain's gaze, ignoring her new interest in leather attire or, more dangerously, his thighs. "Very creative disposal method, sir... Could I get you a cup of cauldron brew from Edwin?" The ogre who worked in the kitchen made batches of the brown sludge derived from magic beans every day, along with freshly made pastries. She'd never heard of the drink before, but it enhanced work productivity and seemed to put everyone in a better mood, dead bodies notwithstanding.

The Villain's lips had tugged upward, his dark eyes dancing with mirth. He wasn't quite smiling, but it was close enough that her heart pounded in her ears.

"Yes, Sage, you know how I take it."

She'd not come to work to find another dead body on her desk since then, but that didn't mean the last few months hadn't been challenging. For the most part, The Villain tended to be gone a lot, likely villainizing the nearby townsfolk in some manner she didn't care to dwell on. They'd made a pact of sorts that he'd not pursue his evildoings within *her* village—or at least she'd taken his grunt as acceptance. But still, something told her even a dead body on her desk was going to be more fun than the mood he was in today.

Because signs of excessive decapitation could only mean one thing:

one of his plans had fallen through for the third time in two months.

She heaved another sigh as she approached the endless, winding staircase. Evie stared at it for a moment, wondering why there was enough magic in the walls of this place to move objects on their own and keep the temperature comfortable, but not enough to make the stairs less, well, awful. She shook her head. It would be added to the suggestion box.

Note to self: suggest a suggestion box.

As she began her daily climb, she avoided the door that appeared to her left after the first flight. The door that led to the boss's personal rooms.

Only the gods would know what he did on his *personal* side of the expansive and decidedly gloomy stone structure.

Don't think about his personal life, Evie.

Another good rule for the list she'd been adding to like clockwork since her first day there.

Stop trying to get the boss to laugh, Evie.

Don't touch the boss's hair, Evie.

Don't find torture attractive, Evie.

Don't tell Edwin the cauldron brew is too strong, Evie.

Her breathing grew labored as she climbed the second story and rounded on the candlelit banisters to the next flight, calves beginning to burn beneath the thick blue skirt that brushed the tops of her ankles.

An echoing scream from the torture chambers in the dungeons below stopped her in her tracks. She blinked for a moment, shaking her head, then quickly continued up the stairs again.

Despite his other obviously nefarious doings, the boss had a strange and confusing set of moral checkpoints that he followed rather diligently—first of which was to never harm innocents, to her relief. His evil was very much the vengeful kind. She also liked that his moral list included treating the women of the world with the same level of respect and esteem as the men. Which, in hindsight, wasn't much to begin with, but at least the office rules were more consistent than the outside world's view.

Before she worked for the evil overlord, Evie had spent her days employed by her local village blacksmith, Otto Warsen. Organizing his tools, handing him whatever instruments he required so that he could stay hard at work on the forge. It had been a decent post, one that paid enough for her to support her ailing father and still be home in time to make dinner for him and her younger sister.

Or at least it had been a decent enough position—until it wasn't.

Evie felt along her shoulder beneath her linen shirt to the raised, jagged scar hidden there. If it had been a normal blade, it would've healed properly. But whatever magic had been ingrained into the white dagger was now living beneath her skin like a curse. One so vicious that anytime she felt an ounce of pain anywhere on her body, the scar glowed. A nuisance, since inanimate objects seemed to get in her way at an alarming rate.

If there was something to stumble over, it would surely find her.

Chuckling through another heaving breath, Evie began her climb of the final set of stairs—a lair big enough for a village and he had them working on the top floor? Evil, thy name is villain—but she continued on to the person who had altered the course of her life.

It seemed feeble to merely refer to her boss as a "person." In so many ways, he was larger than life, but her being responsible for his every want and need had humanized him. The mysterious veil that lay over him when she'd first begun had slipped away, and a far clearer picture was set in her mind.

Still, she had much to learn.

Like what darkness lurked within him that there would be *three severed heads* hanging from the ever-loving ceiling.

She reached the top step and swiped a hand across her sweaty forehead, despairing over the time she'd spent making herself presentable that morning. A mirror wasn't necessary to know that her cheeks were flushed and the wispy hairs coming loose from her braid were sticking to her forehead. Moving down the hall, she could feel the slick sweat sliding between her thighs.

A tempting thought of loose trousers danced across her mind.

The boss had made it very clear there were no rules in the way his workers dressed, meaning for the first time in Evie's employment, she was permitted to wear something other than drab-colored dresses. But she feared wearing something as scandalous as trousers would draw too much attention to herself.

Women? Have legs? Alert the town crier!

No, she already courted enough suspicion in her small village about the "mysterious" job she disappeared to each day. Best to blend in so nobody deigned to take a closer look.

If anyone asked about her work, she told them she'd gotten a position as a maid at a large estate in a neighboring village.

It wasn't a complete lie. She was always cleaning up messes around The Villain—granted, they usually involved blood.

Reaching the end of the hall, she pulled on the gilded sconce closest to the stained glass window, then stepped back as the brick wall slowly slid open, revealing the hidden ballroom that doubled as their workspace beyond. She hustled into the large room as the wall slid closed behind her and took a deep breath. The fresh smell of parchment and ink permeated the air in a comforting, familiar way that never failed to make her smile.

"Good morning, Evangelina."

And now her morning was ruined.

Rebecka Erring sat with her pool of administrative professionals to the left, everyone pausing their work to blink up at Evie now. Rebecka's eyes held Evie's gaze from behind large, round spectacles, and Evie said, "Good morning, Becky."

She smoothed a palm down the front of her high-collared dress that was two sizes too large for her. "We'll see," she said, followed by six sets of eyes returning to their parchments as they realized there would be no bloodshed today.

In all honesty, Becky was quite pretty. She was a mere two years older than Evie, but those two years must have added ten in Becky's head by ways of superiority.

Her light-brown skin was flawless, and her tight-lipped smile did nothing to take away from her striking features. Her cheekbones and jaw sat at the same width, drawing your eye to every high point of her face. If her personality reflected even an ounce of her physical beauty, Becky might be the best person Evie knew.

But alas, she was heinous.

Evie smiled sweetly, tucking a stray hair behind her ear. "Hard at work this morning?"

The other woman smiled back, laying it on so thick that they could have repaved the walkway up to the castle with it. "I was the first one here this morning, so I got a jump on things." In Becky-speak, that translated to, *I was here before you, therefore I am better than you. Behold my fearsome attendance record.*

Keeping her eyes glued forward so she wouldn't roll them, Evie pushed through the throngs of people bustling around the room at breakneck paces. The boss demanded efficiency from every person he employed, and every person here desperately wanted to prove themselves indispensable.

The hidden room was large and open, desks and tables laden throughout. Stained glass windows, depicting various scenes of evil and torture, were evenly spaced along the beige brick walls, bringing in a warm array of light over the space. The cobwebbed chandelier above them glinted as the light hit it, reminding Evie of the severed heads still hanging from the rafters below. She really hoped that scream from the torture chambers wasn't another head about to be displayed as well.

She'd only been to the dungeons a few times, but never long enough to accurately assess the room of horrors. But a few of the interns had. It was the highlight of their squeamish conversations near the kitchens.

"It smells like rotted flesh and despair," one of them had said.

Evie had promptly asked what despair smelled like, but the other girls just returned to their whispering.

She had never been very good at making friends.

For one thing, ever since her mother's disappearance when she was a child, Evie'd become far too good at letting serious matters roll through her like a tide so they never landed close enough to hurt.

She briefly thought this job might give her a more somber air. That people would look at her and see someone with sophistication and world experience. But despite every reason she had to become a dark and menacing character, Evie had remained exactly who she always was—an optimist—a terrible thing to be in a villain's office, mind you. Granted, she didn't *want* to become evil, but when you spend most of your life trying to see the sun, you begin to wish for rain.

In her most private moments, she wondered what it would be like to never smile again, to be feared the way her boss was. But Evie Sage was not a villain, and anyone who suggested she was would get laughed at in their face.

Of course, was it any wonder everyone still saw her as the same when she continued to grin and bear it all? Like with the rest of her village, Evie had told her father a lie and kept him and Lyssa in the dark about where she went every day. It was for their own good, really. Her father already worried so much because of the burdens he was placing on his daughters, being ill and unable to work since he'd caught the Mystic Illness—a sickness that had plagued the kingdom for the last ten years.

The disease attacked without any rhyme or reason, seemingly selecting its victims at random. Some died quickly from the illness—the lucky ones. Others were left too weak to get out of bed as it slowly stole their lives, like the worst sort of thief.

Her father had had it long enough that the healer assured her and Lyssa it wouldn't kill him, for now. But he was weak too much of the time to continue in the profession he'd done before.

Thankfully, he'd been a butcher, which was a boon for Evie, since she'd grown up around blood and corpses, and now that very trade was her profession. Although seeing animal corpses was very different than seeing the corpses of human men.

As she sat down at her desk and began her daily chore of balancing their ledgers, she reminded herself that at least today, her desk was clean. She'd only been working an hour when something crashed against the wall behind her—and made her jump right out of her chair, her rear hitting the floor with an embarrassing thud. Her arms had hit the papers as she fell, too, two hours' work organizing invoices falling around her like paper snowflakes.

Amateur move, Evie.

She knew she always had to be on alert with her desk so close to the boss's office.

She watched as the last paper drifted down onto her chest, not bothering to pick herself or the work up yet. Something or someone had most certainly been slammed against the wall... Another crash, followed by two softer thuds and glass shattering.

And there goes the framed picture I just rehung last week.

Still on the floor, feeling ridiculous, Evie turned over and went to her knees to pick up the papers strewn about. "Ouch," she muttered softly, rubbing at her backside.

But she might as well have yelled, given the way the black door of

The Villain's office jerked open, shaking the walls and making the rest of the workers freeze. Evie slowly looked up from the papers in her hands, her vision catching first on the tip of a shiny black boot and then moving upward. Dark pants intended to be loose but instead hugged muscular thighs that were attached to an impressive torso.

Her eyes skipped past the loose V in his puffy black shirt that exposed the strong top of his chest. Even rumpled, he looked distractingly attractive.

When her gaze finally reached his face, she had to swallow a sigh and bury it where nobody would ever find it. But how could she help it? His jaw was sharp and angled enough that it could be a weapon itself, strong enough to make her insides quiver.

Don't let the boss quiver your insides, Evie.

She used to think the hardest part of him to look at was his eyes. A startling black that pulled you in, a web meant to ensnare your soul. They were the type of eyes that begged you to look away, but Evie ignored that plea, because they were very nice to look at.

And his mouth.

Perhaps the most expressive part of his face, every change so slight but so rich in meaning that she'd begun to catalog them. For instance, right now his mouth was pulled tight. When she glanced back up at his eyes, he was staring down at her. His head was tilted slightly, and her stomach did a flip as she wondered what he must be thinking about her being on her hands and knees, like she was playing a ridiculous game of leapfrog.

Is he confused? Confounded? About to kill me for my clumsiness?

He slowly bent his knees, kneeling until he was eye level with her.

Lacking the fundamental intimidation she should be feeling, Evie instead smiled brightly at the man the entire kingdom lived in fear of. "Good morning, sir." A muffled groan came from within the boss's office. Raising her brows and angling her head to look past his, she added, "Having a busy morning, are we?"

The boss raised his brows back at her. "Quite." Shaking his head as if rattled by his own answer, he began gathering the rest of her strewn-about papers before placing them on her desk.

Evie put her foot down to stand and winced, earning a sharp look from the evil incarnate standing before her. His mouth twisted down into a frown. He was...angry? Of course he was angry. Evie had interrupted his business by falling flat on her ass.

She started to pull herself up with one hand on the edge of the desk, but the boss gripped either side of her waist and lifted her before she could protest. Not that she would've, had she had time to, because his large hands were, well, very nice.

When she was finally on her feet, he dropped his hands in an instant, clenching them at his sides. Warmth stole up her cheeks as she awkwardly tried to look anywhere but at his face, afraid she might see a smirk or worse, and landed upon the open V of his black shirt.

And her mouth, for some gods-forsaken reason, decided to produce an excess of saliva.

Evangelina Celia Sage, if you choose this moment to drool, you are never reading a dirty novel again.

Too distracted by the patch of skin, Evie nearly missed the way her boss was assessing her. Not the way her previous employers had, but in a far more analytical way. Like he was searching for inconsistencies.

"How did you fall, Sage?" His words had a smooth sophistication. A lilting accent that only made his voice more alluring.

"My chair turned on me," Evie said flatly. "And my rear end became very well acquainted with the floor."

His lips twitched upward, and Evie felt like she'd just found a treasure trove. Twisting to put the rest of the papers down, she felt another sharp ache slide down her back. She winced.

The ghost of a smile slipped from his lips, and Evie cursed her own clumsiness for causing it to disappear.

"Do you need to see the healer?" he asked, placing a hand on one side of her desk, leaning down in a way that put emphasis on his strong forearm beneath the sleeve of his rolled-up shirt.

Hmm...suddenly her mouth was completely dry.

"No, sir, I wouldn't want to subject Tatianna to my war with the chair." She leaned in, gesturing at him to come closer into her confidence. He turned his head slightly, giving her his ear, and Evie smothered her surprise at him entertaining her antics. "Best to keep this between us, or it may enlist the other chairs in a revolt."

Then the boss did something that nearly made Evie's mortal soul leave her body—he laughed. Or rather he coughed, a lot, into his hand.

It was closed around his mouth, clearly masking a smile he was having the fight of his life trying to keep off his lips.

Evie mumbled her shock under her breath. "That wasn't even that funny."

The watchful eyes of the other workers snapped them both to attention, and before the boss turned to glare a warning at their audience, the crowd scattered like ants that saw a large foot coming at them.

Except, of course, Becky, who kept her hawk eyes glued to the pair from the other side of the room.

"See the healer, Sage. We have a big week ahead of us, and I can't afford you falling dead on me."

"I don't think anyone's ever died from a bruise on the ass, sir."

His eyes went tight, and his mouth did a familiar movement that even Evie knew meant she'd pushed too far.

She took a tiny step backward. "But I'd hardly want to be the first, so I'll just—I'll just head there now." She made a wide path around him, passing his office. She spied a scrawny-looking man inside, lying underneath a brick that had come loose from the wall above. No doubt, after he'd been slammed into it.

Kingsley sat on the edge of the boss's desk, as he always did these last few months, his wide, unblinking expression taking her in before his webbed foot lifted one of his tiny communication signs. This one in red chalk, reading, OUCH.

Evie had grown quite fond of the tiny creature's presence. He mostly just sat there, observing and offering up quiet counsel with the slab of slate the boss gave him to write on. His tiny gold crown always at attention on his slimy head.

Ouch indeed, Evie mouthed back to Kingsley before returning her attention to the broken man lying on the ground.

She tried to muster the sympathy she should feel for the pain of another person, but she'd seen so many men come and go from that room that she was trying to save her sympathy for those who deserved it.

A weaselly-looking man, whom she was almost certain she'd seen throwing rocks at a group of ducks last week in her village, did not make the cut. A smile graced her lips as she struggled to remind herself the boss was most likely not beating this man to a pulp to defend a few ducks' honor. Her mind also begged the point that even if he wasn't intentionally defending the ducks in question, he had by association.

Which for some reason was just as adorable.

She forced her smile into an even expression and continued forward to the small hallway that led to the healer's quarters. For the bruise. On her ass.

Before she could throw her head in her hands at the disaster that was her morning, she remembered her boss on his knees before her, handing her the discarded papers, the sliver of his chest, *his laughter*.

Perhaps her morning was not a *complete* disaster.

Of course, there was no telling what his reaction would be when she returned to her desk and had to admit to him the discrepancy she'd found in the books that morning. She didn't know everything about The Villain yet, but she did know that he detested disorganized recordkeeping, almost as much as she hated stray eyeballs.

CHAPTER 2

EVIE

"Bend over."

Evie didn't move. "Perhaps you could buy me dinner first." Honestly, even a dinner at the nicest tavern wouldn't entice her to bare her backside to the healer. Surely magic could work through the cloth of her skirt—if she said it in her head, perhaps she could will it to be true.

She sat on the exam table and held back a wince at the pain when she shifted, her gaze holding the healer's in a game of chicken Evie had no intention of losing.

There wasn't a day since Evie had known her that the healer did not wear at least some element of pink. Today, the dainty color made its usual appearance in the form of tiny bows pinned throughout her lovely hair, making her look younger than her twenty-seven years but no less tough an adversary. The healer raised one dark brow at Evie's refusal to move.

"Come on, Tati," Evie said with a pleading grin. "I've already met my humiliation quota today, and I'm afraid revealing my backside to you would break the meter."

Eventually, Tatianna sighed and pushed a dark braid of hair behind her ear, her large brown eyes narrowing as her hands began to glow a warm yellow.

Oh, thank the gods.

The light drew Evie's attention to the gauzy sleeves of yet another lavish gown hugging the woman's generous curves. Evie usually felt too guilty to spend her wages on anything so frivolous as a new gown—but that didn't mean she didn't envy the healer's lovely wardrobe.

Tatianna moved her hands toward Evie, hovering in front of her shoulders without actually touching her, and suddenly Evie's backside felt like the time she had sat on the hot stones in the village square after a day of summer sun beating down on them.

"You've bruised your tailbone, little friend. Quite badly in fact." Tatianna's voice was like clear water, crisp and smooth, pulling her lightly from her panic. She exhaled a sigh of relief. A bruise she could afford.

"Of course I have." Evie rubbed her forehead. "And how much is it going to cost me for you to heal it?"

A long stretch of a smile spread across Tatianna's face, which to those who didn't know her would set even the most anxious person at ease. But Evie did know her—and that smile was, for lack of a better word…scary.

"Hmm," the healer said, tapping her chin in contemplation. "If you want it fully healed, I want two secrets."

"Which means you're getting two secrets, because in what world would I want to go about my day with a painful bruise on my backside?" Evie rubbed her temples and raised a brow. "How big of a secret are we talking?"

Walking toward her table of salves and potions, Tatianna chuckled as her dress swished back and forth. "Nothing blackmail-worthy but better than idle gossip you'd hear in the kitchen."

Evie dug in her brain for something sufficient as Tatianna sifted through her tinctures and moved her glowing hands over a small bowl as she worked. Sharing secrets was hardly something Evie took issue with; she was an open book for the most part. She'd often had trouble keeping overly personal things *in*, especially with Tatianna.

If she could pay everyone with her private, ridiculous thoughts and habits, she'd never have to work again.

Hopping off the table with nervous energy, Evie wandered over to the shelf by the door and found a small bottle. It was a charming little thing. Evie thought it would make a good ornam—

"Don't touch that!" Tatianna screeched, making Evie's heart race.

"What? Why? What is it?" Evie frantically looked at the bottle and the hand that had almost touched it. "Does it turn people into frogs or something?"

"What?" Tatianna shook her head, confused. "No, it's a slow-acting sedative. It's very potent."

Evie pulled her hand back as if burned, frowning as Tatianna smiled and said all too casually, "I keep my frog potions in a different cabinet."

A choked noise left Evie's throat, but before she could ask if the healer was kidding, she continued.

"A secret, if you please," Tatianna said, turning back to her brewing potion.

Evie paused in contemplation and then grinned. "I had a dream about the boss last night."

A series of crashes and a screech came from the direction Tatianna was standing, but it was so unlike her to lose composure that Evie wondered if there was some other figure in the room she could not see.

Tatianna whirled around then, knocking several more things over in her flurry to face Evie.

Evie's mouth opened, her hand going to her face as if something was written there she couldn't see. "What?"

There were not enough thieves in Rennedawn's east-village slums to steal the wicked twinkle in Tatianna's eyes. "Oh, and what did you and the boss do in this dream, you naughty little assistant?"

Evie huffed a laugh and attempted to bend over to pick up the discarded parchments but immediately straightened when she felt her injury protest. "You are very presumptuous to assume it was anything but innocent."

Tatianna scoffed in indignation, sweeping the contents back onto the table with a slight wave of her hand. A rare gift for healers but a useful one for Tatianna, who sometimes needed to use her abilities to mind-bend objects out of a wound without touching them.

"Have you seen the man? As if anything associated with him could ever be innocent." She paused for dramatic effect, hands coming up with a flourish. "He's a walking vice."

Evie circled her hand above her own head in the shape of a halo, but the healer merely laughed and began mixing contents back into the bowl, hands once again taking on their warm yellow glow.

"I adore you, Evangelina, but you are far from innocent." Turning around and handing Evie a small brown bowl that smelled sickly sweet, she grinned. "You are corrupt by association, my dear. Now, rub this on your bum and put the gloves on first or it'll warp the bones in your hands."

Hastily tugging on the gloves, she grabbed the bowl and darted behind a cloth screen in the corner for some privacy. She yanked her skirt down a couple of inches and smoothed the salve between the fabric of her skirt and the bottom of her back. As she did, Evie contemplated her precarious position working here. She'd seen truly horrific things in her time thus far, all more jarring than the last. But she never once felt the need to stop anything, just the urge to offer help where she could and distance where she couldn't.

That was neither here nor there, however. Even the most "stand-up citizens" were capable of terrifying cruelty. She would hardly feel guilty for taking money where it came. Especially from a place where she was never mistreated or looked at like a plaything.

Nausea overtook her as she began to feel the broken piece of bone melding back together, a sickly, unnatural feeling. The body wasn't meant to heal at this pace, but she didn't have time to waste on a broken bone.

After the last of the bone fragments slid into place like a puzzle piece, Evie straightened, then turned and bent from left to right to test her mobility. The sharp pain was gone like mist on the wind, replaced with a tight ache that was far preferable.

"It'll be sore for the next couple of hours, but after that, it should feel normal." Tossing the rest of the bowl's contents into the fire of the stone hearth, Tatianna rolled her sleeves up. "Just be careful—the bones are still pliable. If you sit incorrectly, they could move."

Evie wrinkled her nose, throwing her head from side to side to shake the image. "That is revolting."

Handing Evie a small capped vial, pink in color, Tatianna said, "The next time someone asks me to describe my work, that's exactly what I'll tell them."

Before Evie could ask about the vial's contents, Tatianna interrupted, her tone taking on a concerned softness. "For your father." She rolled her shoulders and looked out the window. "To manage his pain. I'm sorry I cannot do more for him."

A hot burning began in the backs of Evie's eyes, causing her to sniff lightly and clear her throat in an attempt to push it away. She carefully took the bottle and laid it in the pocket of her skirts. "So if I sit incorrectly…will my right ass cheek be bigger than my left?"

A startled laugh busted through Tatianna's mouth as she shoved Evie lightly on the shoulder. "You are too gullible, little friend. My magic is strong, and all will be fine. Now, get back to work."

Ignoring the lingering melancholy, Evie grinned wide and spun on her heel toward the door. "Oh!" she said, spinning back around. "The second secret!"

Tatianna raised a brow, her eyes flashing at Evie for just a moment. "The second?"

"Yes," Evie said boldly. "That dream I had about the boss last night." She leaned closer. "It *was* dirty."

Giggling at the shock on Tatianna's face, Evie spun back around only to halt immediately in her tracks.

Swallowing a lump in her throat, eyes wide as saucers, Evie said, "Hello, sir… Any chance you'd like to add my head to the entryway?"

CHAPTER 3

EVIE

E vie followed the boss down the hallway back to the open office area. Her face was burning like she'd eaten something spicy, and the pace at which the boss was moving wasn't helping with the redness in her neck and cheeks.

He'd just stared at her blankly. Completely devoid of all emotion. In fact, she thought she saw the little emotion that was there flicker out the minute he locked eyes with her. As if her silly comment was not even worthy enough to be embarrassed or outraged.

My stupidity is profound enough to be acknowledged, dammit.

She opened her mouth to say as much, but the boss paused in front of large wooden doors that led out to the parapet walk and opened them, motioning for her to pass in front of him. Rubbing her damp palms on her skirts, she stepped forward, feeling the rush of the midmorning sun against her skin.

Evie wasn't a particular fan of high places, so seeing the distance from where she stood to the ground below caused her to back into the stone edge of the parapet and cling there.

"You're missing the view." His voice was low and gravelly in a way that made her head tingle, like the pitter-patter of rain against a roof.

"I know what Hickory Forest looks like," she said dryly, shutting her eyes tight. But the images of the grand trees beyond were clear. She'd grown up in a village on the outskirts of the forest that took up so much of Rennedawn's lands. Trees the size of giants blanketed the area surrounding the manor, thick green foliage standing out against a cloudless blue sky. The warm, balmy weather brushing her skin was typical of their kingdom's forgiving climate, attracting all manner of beings to their modest section of the world.

Evie finally found enough strength to open her eyes and caught the tail end of a curve in her boss's lips.

Glorious.

Ugh, not glorious, Evie.

She needed to be sedated, clearly.

The Villain continued like she wasn't the blithering mess that she was. "I wanted to bring you away from prying ears." He edged closer, his dark hair curling slightly against his tan skin. "It's a matter of grave importance."

Something about the way he stood, the wind billowing his black cloak about him, gave Evie a great sense of foreboding. Of course, that perfectly rational emotion was overtaken by the less sensible part of her brain that ignored the danger in favor of how attractive he looked.

Anyone with common sense knew that the loveliest blades were always the sharpest, but for Evie there was no such thing. Her sense came and went with the wind, nothing common about it.

Drawing the tip of her shoe in nervous circles, she looked the boss directly in the eye. "Okay, before you go all brooding Earl of Darkness on me, it *was* a dirty dream, but I meant, like…dirty. You know, with dirt, the brown stuff. It was muddy and a carriage rolled by and splattered muck over both of us and you said, 'Better get this washed, Sage.'"

She could feel that awful tumble of words that spilled out every time she was nervous or an unwelcome quiet appeared, so she continued. "It was one of my more ordinary dreams, actually. Nothing explicit or inappropriate." Her arms were flailing now, full-blown wing movements like she was trying to take off.

What was worse was the heightened color tingeing the sharp angle of his cheekbones and the slight widening of his eyes at the words tumbling from her lips.

A smart person would cease speaking at that clearly taken-aback expression, but Evie was not smart. Or rather, Evie was smart, but her brain and her mouth seemed to have a swift detachment from each other.

"Nobody was naked," she said with a confident finality, rocking back on her heels.

Nobody. Was. Naked?

His eyes flashed, and her twisted imagination had the gall to see something burn there, for just a moment, before they shuttered again. He cleared his throat and scratched the back of his head, seeming a little unnerved.

Seeing him lose any ounce of his impeccable composure gave Evie far too much satisfaction.

"I was not referring to your nighttime imaginings, Sage." His throat bobbed as he walked around her to look out at their surroundings. The Manor was in a part of the forest that was so thick with foliage, no one would think to stumble this way. Every village in Rennedawn was intentionally built over natural large gaps in the trees, almost as if the gods created the map of their lands by hand.

But Massacre Manor was the exception, living encased by its surroundings, like an armor.

The boss braced his hands on either side of the stone pillars. Evie knew his shoulders and back would be tensed beneath his cloak if it wasn't obscuring her view.

"Sage?"

Oh, he'd been talking, hadn't he? She'd been too busy ogling him as if he were the last piece of pie.

"Oh yes, I...agree." She nodded emphatically, rocking back and forth, doing her best to mask her confusion with a false confidence.

"Is that so?" He whistled low and raised a hand to rub the perfectly maintained stubble at his chin. "Well, with your agreement in mind, I'll begin the arrangements to have you married off to one of the river gremlins to allow us safe passage for our shipments from the southern kingdoms."

"What?" Evie gasped "Sir, I— No, I wasn't— You can't be serious!" But he could be. Evie had seen him do far worse to other employees who weren't cooperating, and she'd arranged most of them. Her heart was pounding, blood rushing through her ears, making everything sound muffled.

Without realizing it, she'd brought herself closer to him, searching for any ounce of humanity in his black eyes. Anything that might take pity on this magicless human with a terrible attention span.

But instead of humanity, she saw his eyes squint and crinkle at the corners. Evie took a large step backward to better observe the picture. His lips were curled up at the sides, and when Evie caught sight of them, she yelped.

"Was that a joke?" She almost cringed at the blatant shock in her voice, but her reaction to something so unpredictable could not be contained.

His smile widened further than Evie had ever seen it, and a single dimple on his left cheek poked free.

"And you have dimples?"

He rolled his eyes, and the dimple disappeared. "Just the one. Now that I have your full attention—"

"Was that your first?" Evie interrupted, unable to process all this new information in an efficient manner.

The boss's head knocked back in surprise. "My first what, you little tornado?"

"Your first joke."

He grunted and opened his mouth to speak, looking quite outraged, if she were being honest. "Of all the—" He paused to pinch the bridge of his nose. "Sage, do you honestly think me incapable of humor?"

"Of course I don't think that," she said earnestly. "You hired me."

Letting loose a long-suffering sigh, he pushed a strand of dark hair meticulously back into place. "I speak to you for less than three minutes, and I'm more turned around than the interns during my favorite day of the week."

"Metaphorically speaking, of course, as I am not shooting arrows at *you*." Evie gave him a pointed look to reiterate how she disapproved of his "self-defense" training for the poor souls who came here on "internships." Cast-off noblemen's children, people who owed gambling debts, and other general reprobates alike applied for the entry position all the time.

Massacre Manor was a far cry from the kingdom's capital, the Gleaming City, where most of the interns had stumbled in from. The decadence and abundance so different than the squalor of their new place of employ, for most of them their *first* place of employ. Evie had been to the city once as a child. It had been an entire day's ride north from her village, when the forest was still considered safe to travel. She had been too little to remember much, but she recalled the contagious energy of it vibrating the air. Remembered vaguely meeting a magical specialist with her parents, and, just like the stories children in her village had told her, he had been kind and helpful with seemingly endless knowledge to share.

It was nice that quite a few interns had magic, as many of them accomplished their tasks quicker.

That sure must be useful for cleaning the toilets. Evie snickered inwardly.

But they kept applying, coming back, despite the harshness of the job.

The proof was in the pile of letters laden with words of woe and how a down-on-his-luck son of a noble found himself in deep debt to a very expensive brothel. It was always someone in *desperate* need of a second chance, and though the danger of the job was well-known in less-desirable parts of the kingdom, so was the pay.

Evie was quite certain the interns made only slightly less than she did. Which in any other circumstance might cause her some level of outrage, but she was working for The Villain. She would be grateful she held one of the only job positions that didn't call for her Scatter Day participation.

The event took place at the end of every work week, unless of course the boss was having a bad day. Then it could be the beginning of the week, the middle of the week, in the morning, during her lunch hour, or… Well, she could go on. It was, at the very least, consistent in that every Scatter Day consisted of the boss sending the interns outside and having them run from something. So far, she'd watched them try to escape a crossbow and countless magical beasts. But Evie's personal favorite was the day the boss was so fed up with their antics that he began chasing them himself across the back courtyard.

It was the fastest she'd ever seen them run.

"I'll remind you that, at your bequest, I haven't actually killed an intern in several months."

Evie shook her head hopelessly. "Sir, I hate to belittle your successes, but there are people who go their entire lives without killing *anyone*."

His face remained serious. "How dull."

"You also can't even really say months, can you? You pushed Joshua

Lightenston off this very parapet last week, and he broke his neck."

"Well, he deserved it."

She threw her hands up in defeat. "Why?"

The boss rubbed his chin and grimaced like an unpleasant memory had resurfaced. "He said something I didn't like."

"If I had that luxury, Becky would've gone over this thing several times already." Evie took a contemplative pause. "Actually, sir—"

"No."

"But what if I make a very official and organized pro/con list?" she pleaded.

"Give me one con to Rebecka Erring as an employee." The breeze picked up, tossing that rebellious dark lock against his forehead.

"She's determined to be my enemy."

His face was suddenly closed again, so suddenly that Evie heard the sharp intake of her breath. "Always keep your enemies close, Sage. Life's more interesting that way." The smile he was giving her now held no joy, only cruel promises.

Evie swallowed hard, disappointed in herself for needing to take a slow step backward. Out of his sphere and back to her senses.

"Speaking of enemies. May we get to what I brought you out here to discuss before the other employees begin to believe that I'm throwing *you* over the edge?" he asked.

Evie rolled her eyes and motioned her hand forward. "Go on."

His mouth turned down in a frown as he spun away from her, back to the forest view. "Another shipment has been compromised."

Evie tried not to groan, but the frustration was palpable. It had taken her *weeks* to organize that shipment trade-off and plan the perfect undetectable checkpoints between here and the Gleaming City. The office was run on illegal cargo coming in and out, selling it, trading it, stealing it from King Benedict directly most of the time.

"I suspected as much, since I saw the extra…" Evie tapped the top of her head lightly with her pointer finger.

"They were Valiant Guards."

King Benedict's personal guards? They never involved themselves in The Villain's business. It was a point of strangeness to her, in fact, that in all the times The Villain had struck Benedict by lifting his resources, stealing cargo of all kinds, he'd never struck back.

"So I assume we didn't make it out with any of the borrowed goods?" This trade deal was going to bring in at least four large crates filled with weapons from King Benedict's personal collection. Depleting them of not only the swords and firearms themselves but the value of the weapons would no doubt be an enormous loss to their esteemed ruler.

Or it would've been if the whole thing hadn't been blown to bits.

"My Malevolent Guards were able to make out with two of them."

The Malevolent Guards were the elite group of people who managed the more violent parts of The Villain's business—the *fieldwork*, some of the interns had coined it. The most ruthless warriors were among them, many of them magic users of varying kinds and educations. Most in the office steered clear of them, but Evie helped Edwin make them sandwiches.

Shoot, I forgot to restock the cheese. They are fiends for provolone.

"That's better than none at all, I suppose," Evie responded. She would accept any small favors if it meant not scouring a map, looking for another discreet trade from natural paths in the forest.

"Always the optimist, aren't you, Sage?" His tone was light, but his face told her he didn't think that was a good thing.

"I like anticipating the good—that way it's easier to see it...even when the bad happens."

The boss looked at her with some unreadable emotion. "If we could all see the world through your eyes."

"It would be very colorful." She smiled wide and turned her face up to the breeze. "So that's three shipments compromised in the last two months."

"Three too many." His voice was lower suddenly. A deadly tone that she'd seen make the bravest of knights shiver with fear. She, for some reason, found it comforting, which was...troubling.

Danger isn't attractive, Evie; it's scary.

Or...it's both, her brain countered.

"Aside from the little hangmen downstairs, how are you planning on handling this?" Evie was afraid of the answer, but this was becoming a very distinct pattern. Systems that had worked for them for months were suddenly failing, and the common denominator was becoming very clear.

"We have a traitor in our midst," he said in a low voice.

Evie sucked in a breath, because he stood tall and dark, promising destruction, and all she could think was...

"How can I help?"

Evie was certain the clock on the wall ticked louder when she was trying to focus. Each stroke of the small hand felt like it was grating against her skull.

Tick-tick-tick.

"Ugh." Evie threw her head down on her desk. She'd been going over the list of employees for the last two days in her favorite gold-foiled journal, writing little notes next to their names. Any indicators of suspicion or skewed loyalties had to be recorded. She'd figure out who was sabotaging them, and she'd hand them on a silver platter to her boss.

"What are you working on?" *Ah*, the other grating in her skull.

Evie picked her head up and closed her notebook, nearly taking out Rebecka Erring's wandering hand. She quickly returned her quill to her favorite tincture of ink, a gift from her father. "Nothing you need concern yourself with." Evie pinched her lips tightly into a smile, trying to keep every inflammatory word inside her head.

"Why are you making a list of employees' names? I need to know everything that goes on in this office," Becky said with a pompous sniff.

Evie considered the woman closely and then leaned her chin against her propped hands. "Does that mean you're aware of the office pixies using ink to make self-portraits of their rear ends?" The pixies handled small tasks around the office, usually acting as scribes. It was quick work for them, since there were so many, but their erratic temperaments occasionally made them get creative with the ink.

A frustrated groan escaped Becky as she straightened and shook her head. "Again?" She turned quickly, eyes narrowing behind her glasses as she caught sight of the tiny fluttering creatures. All giggling as they scattered the papers about the room.

"Get over here, you wretches!" Becky growled as she stalked away, and Evie breathed a sigh of relief. She grabbed a vanilla drop candy from the tin Lyssa had given her and popped it in her mouth.

Despite the everlasting animosity between them, Evie did not envy the woman's job. Every little drama, every conflict between the interns or any of the more permanent workers, was her responsibility to manage. When the boss had oriented Evie to the rest of the workers, he'd explained the system in which the manor worked. Every employee in charge of different tasks in different areas. It reminded Evie of a beehive. Becky's particular specialty being a resource to the humans and other beings so the boss wouldn't have to deal with the constant melodrama.

At the beginning, Evie thought she and Becky could be friends, that whatever stiff coldness lived in the woman during their first meeting would thaw. But despite Evie's every effort, Rebecka Erring was determined not to like her. It was still a mystery whether it was because she found Evie obscenely annoying or if the rumor Evie had heard from one of the interns was true. That Becky had, once upon a time, wanted to be the assistant to The Villain, and Evie had been given the position instead.

Regardless, it was very clear that Evie and Becky would never be friends, and that was just fine with her.

Closing the book once more, Evie stood from her desk with her ceramic chalice in hand, praying Edwin had brewed the cauldron of bean juice strong enough to wake the dead.

As she wandered off to the kitchen, though, Evie couldn't help the little voice in her head, wondering if there was an innocence to their feud, or if it could lead Becky down a different path.

The one of a traitor.

CHAPTER 4

EVIE

Evie spent the rest of the day drowning her sorrows in the mystical effects of the cauldron brew while warily looking at her fellow workers. *Someone* was guilty, and as much as she'd like it to be Becky, the woman was too much of a staunch rule follower for her to think she'd be capable of that kind of deceit.

Groaning as she straightened, she felt her back crack as she twisted and turned. The ache in her muscles was demanding her attention, and she'd finished the suspiciously little work she had to get done before the end of the workday.

Any minute, the large bell in the north tower would toll, and everyone in the room would scatter back to the monotony of their lives outside of this place. The pixies would return to the wood, whatever creature was wreaking havoc upon the interns would slink off to its cave, the interns would drag themselves back to whatever hovel they could afford, and the remaining employees would head home as well.

There were very few who resided in the manor full-time, Tatianna being one of them, Edwin another, and the only person keeping the dragon currently in their courtyard calm, a man named Blade.

As though thinking of him summoned the charming dragon trainer, she looked up and there he was, striding through the office, a large gash on his forehead.

"Is Tatianna available?" He grinned sheepishly down at Evie, the way he did every time he came in with another injury from the scaled beast they'd acquired shortly after her employment began.

Evie shook her head, smiling. "I don't know, Mr. Gushiken. Why don't you ask her yourself?"

Blade leaned down, exposing a large expanse of chiseled chest above his very tight vest. Evie was never certain if he did it ironically, but the dragon trainer always seemed to be wearing colors that drastically opposed each other. Today his vest was a green so bright that it hurt her eyes, and his pants were an orange that reminded her of sunsets and butterflies.

He mock grabbed his chest and said, "So formal, my sweet Evie! You wound me."

Evie giggled at the hopeless flirt, closing her catalog of names. She stood up from her desk, then walked around to face him head-on. His amber eyes were warm, much like the rest of his personality. He smiled, his full lips pulling up at the corners, softening the sharp angles of his cheekbones and the narrowed edge of his dimpled chin. Blade was the person in the office closest to her age, only younger than her by a year.

"I'm not *your* anything, you big flirt." She reached up to brush his dark shoulder-length hair off his forehead, then grimaced at the skin torn away from his scalp. "That thing is going to kill you one of these days."

When Blade had first arrived, the dragon was barely the size of her palm, and she'd even held the little creature a few times, cooing at it like it was a defenseless infant. But the beast had grown in just a few short months to an alarming size, snapping and growling at everyone. Only Blade managed to get close, but even he didn't come away from the encounters unscathed.

He was the one who'd found the egg, after all, in the mountains to the east. He'd been hiking there, ever the explorer, and found a nest abandoned by the mother. He'd told Evie after the creature hatched that it took to him immediately.

He'd bonded with the little beast, couldn't bear to be parted from it, but the upkeep was far more than Blade could afford. Fortunately, it was around that time that he came across an advertisement from someone calling themselves "The Villain," requesting any and all magical beasts. So Blade turned up on the front steps two weeks after Evie did, offering the dragon in exchange for a place to sleep and a position as the dragon's tamer. The boss had agreed to his terms, but they'd yet to have any use for the dragon, for many reasons.

One of them being that when it wasn't trying to bite Evie's head off, the animal was afraid of *everything*.

Blade's smile widened. "That *thing* is a sweet creature with the occasional temper tantrum." His eyes brightened as he caught sight of Becky moving past them, carrying a stack of papers to the board pinned to the wall. "Like you, lovely Rebecka!"

Becky froze in her tracks, turning her wide-eyed gaze toward them. "That is not an appropriate way to address a coworker, Mr. Gushiken." Her disapproval practically oozed off her, but to Blade's credit, her disdain didn't seem to faze him.

In fact, he seemed to be oddly fueled by her censure. "Perhaps we should discuss this further at the Evergreen Tavern." He somehow found the bravery to wink at her. "You can read off your very long list of complaints."

Pushing her glasses farther up her nose, Becky sniffed and looked at him like something foul she'd stepped in. "I would rather drink paint than converse with the likes of you in my free time. The only reason I'm doing so now is because I am being paid to tell you that your hygiene leaves everything to be desired."

She eyed the blood sliding down his cheek, gritting her jaw before adding, "Your blood is as offensive as your smell. Take care of both immediately or you'll find yourself without a paycheck at the end of the week."

Evie rolled her eyes as the she-demon stormed away. "Why do you press her like that?"

Blade shrugged, using one of his leather wrist cuffs to dab up some of the blood. "Because it's fun when she gets ruffled." Eyeing the closed doors, Blade lowered his voice. "I've heard there's been another bust on a shipment. How's he handling it?"

"Did you see the entryway?" she answered dryly.

"So normally, then?" Blade chuckled and then froze, remembering how close they were to The Villain's office.

"You can speak freely. He's been everywhere but here the past couple of days."

"No arson for you today?" Blade gave her a mock pout.

Evie huffed a laugh, which was unsettling because the man was hardly joking. She'd started quite a few fires since she obtained the job, figuratively and literally. "That's not my only job here, you know."

He nodded quickly. "Oh, I know. I heard from someone you've cut the boss's destructive tirades down to two a week."

"I don't let him talk to any of the interns before he's eaten breakfast—that's the key. He's crabby on an empty stomach," she said, wondering just how many of their workers' lives were saved because of a frosted pastry.

Evie leaned back against her desk, gaze going to the large clock on the wall. The loud clang of the bell rang throughout the room, startling some workers at their desks and causing others to bolt from their seats, their bags already gathered to return home to their loved ones.

A few stopped to eye the closed door of The Villain's office. It wasn't often the boss was absent at the end of the day. He usually opened his door to indicate he wouldn't kill anyone for making their daily escape.

Evie looked at them and nodded with quiet authority. "Go on. He's gone for the day." She'd reap the consequences if the boss was angry.

Without question, they all scurried toward the hidden door, the bounding of heavy footfalls on the stairs ringing in their wake. Moving to her own bag, Evie packed up her few belongings, trying to ignore the uneasiness she felt.

Where in the deadlands had *The Villain gone lately?*

"I'm sure he's fine," Blade reassured, waving to Tatianna as she ventured through the hallway into the open room. "Hey, Tati!"

"I wasn't worried about him—" Evie started.

But Blade was already running toward the healer. Tatianna studied his forehead, then gave him a long-suffering expression as she pointed him in the direction of the healer's quarters, following closely behind him.

Evie gathered the rest of her things, giving the boss's closed office door one last, longing look.

Don't care more than you should, Evie.

Sighing to herself, she headed for the stairs.

Too late.

She passed through the doorway, unable to stop herself from glancing back at The Villain's closed door again, wondering if one of these times he wouldn't return.

CHAPTER 5

EVIE

"It tastes watery," Evie's ten-year-old sister, Lyssa, muttered under her breath.

"Shhh." Evie held her finger to her lips as her father moved slowly to the table, his own bowl of soup in hand. He'd been in a spectacular mood when Evie returned home that day. Which meant he would be cooking.

Since their father's illness began, he'd found few pleasures, but one of them was that when he felt up to it, he'd cook dinner for his children. It was his way of taking care of them. So even though the things he made often tasted like liquid shoe leather, Evie would be damned if she and Lyssa didn't swallow every drop.

Because her father cooking meant he was well, and it gave them a taste of what their family was…before.

Evie looked toward the two empty chairs at the table, one at the opposite end of her father and one beside her. The seats her mother and her older brother, Gideon, had once occupied but never would again. But still the chairs sat there, like their memory was haunting them.

"How is it, girls?" Griffin Sage was a large man, with a warm smile and a full head of thick brown hair. In his younger years, he'd been the catch of the town. A man who'd built a successful butchery business from the ground up. Their mother, a foreigner from a lovely string of kingdoms southeast of their continent, Myrtalia, Rennedawn's home along with five other kingdoms. Her mother had loved her father to distraction until the incident...until she'd left them.

Evie's earliest memories were of her parents laughing together, singing and dancing in their small kitchen. Clearing her throat, she smiled at her father.

"It's delicious, Papa." Pointedly looking at her little sister, she said, "I think Lyssa would like seconds."

A small foot connected hard with her shin underneath the table. Chuckling, Evie ladled another large scoop of the lumpy liquid into Lyssa's bowl. She wouldn't hope for this lasting sense of lightness, where every living member of her family was well and happy. But there was no rule saying she couldn't try and enjoy it.

"How's your work at the manor?" Her father smiled warmly at her, a healthy glow to his cheeks that she hadn't seen in months.

Swallowing a hard lump of potato, Evie began stirring the soup with her spoon, attempting nonchalance. "Oh, it's been rather uneventful, actually."

"I wish I worked in a castle." Lyssa pouted, wincing as she took another bite.

Evie coughed, nearly choking. "It's— It's not a castle, Lyssa. It's simply a manor house."

"But it's probably as big as a castle, isn't it?" Her sister looked at her with wide, questioning eyes.

Evie loved far too much about her job—the people, the strategy. But she hated this part. The lying.

She couldn't tell her family a single truth about what she was really doing. As far as they and the rest of the village were concerned, The Villain was a vile, reprehensible creature. Anyone even hinted to be associated with him was punished to the full extent the law allowed. But even knowing she could one day be found out, knowing that the wrath of the kingdom could so swiftly descend upon her, did not scare her. If anything, it excited her.

She was as reckless as her mother.

"It's very large, yes." Evie took a bracing sip of the wine she'd purchased on her way home, doing her best to divert the subject. "How are your lessons coming?"

To her relief, that single question set Lyssa on a tirade about the boy in her class who wouldn't stop pulling on her braids. Evie sighed into the welcome distraction of Lyssa's innocent life. What she wouldn't give for just a touch of that youthful bliss.

Evie was only twenty-three years old, and yet she felt like she'd lived a lifetime. Between the way she took care of her family and the mistreatment she'd been dealt by those crueler and larger than she, it was a wonder her hair hadn't gone gray.

It's a wonder you made it to twenty-three at all with the ridiculous situations you get yourself into.

She supposed that was why she reconciled her work so easily in her mind. She had no idea what The Villain's end goal was, aside from doing everything to screw over the king. But Evie knew the important things—he didn't take advantage of his female employees, he paid all his workers fairly, and he requested his cauldron brew with at least a pound of sugar.

The last fact was not as relevant as his other virtues, but it was Evie's favorite. Every morning she'd have to sneak his preferred amount of sugar out of the kitchen along with cream from the chilled box and add both to his drink as discreetly as possible. She was uncertain why he was so embarrassed about his preference, but she supposed it wasn't good for his reputation to enjoy any such frivolities.

She loved even more that she was one of the only ones who knew, so much so that she found herself staring dazedly at the wall, smiling as her pulse quickened.

Her father finished his plate, clearing the table and placing the wooden bowls into the bucket near the stove. Evie stood so quickly, her chair wobbled. "I'll take care of those, Papa!" She smiled and patted his arm, ignoring the frown marring his cheeks.

"Evangelina, I am perfectly capable of—"

"Would you tell me one of your stories?" Lyssa tugged at their father's arm with a wide grin, then gave Evie a knowing look that made her seem much older than she was. Her sister wasn't completely untouched by the harshness of the world, no matter how Evie tried to shield her.

The two of them sat down again, and Evie stiffened slightly as her father settled in her mother's chair, Lyssa crawling into his lap and looking up as he dove into one of his many stories of villains and the heroes who defeated them. Her throat tightened as she swallowed the truth that she now worked for those he despised.

Turning back toward the bucket, Evie gripped the rag and scrubbed at a pot harshly. She felt her cheeks sting and her heart begin to pound around her shortened breaths. Feeling the water beneath her hands, she closed her eyes for a moment and began humming a light melody of a song her mother so often favored when she tended the dishes.

It was comforting to Evie somehow, despite all the pain her mother wrought. That tune was one of the last good things her mother had given her before that day, before the dandelion fields, just *before*.

Evie caught her reflection in the glass of the window in front of her, saw her father behind her carrying a dozing Lyssa toward her room. Looking back at her own face, Evie felt her lips pull up in a smile. One she'd practiced so many times before. Even when she felt like her lungs would collapse, even when her heart felt like it would give out from the strain, she'd always managed to tug her lips upward.

Her mother's voice echoed in her head. *Worry not, hasibsi. You could fix a broken world with just your smile.*

She had been wrong, of course. Evie hadn't fixed anything that day or in the days that came after.

But Evie still smiled.

Just in case.

And not for the last time hoped it was enough to keep those she cared about safe.

CHAPTER 6

THE VILLAIN

She was humming again.

Trystan Arthur Maverine, or more affectionately known to the public as The Villain, tapped his long fingers against his sleek black desk. The noise should've irritated him. It should've grated against his skull. He already had a headache after hearing laughter from the other workers outside his door. Being evil wasn't supposed to be joyful, and his migraine was proof.

But he kept his anger contained. He'd gotten most of it out at the beginning of the week anyhow on the Valiant Guards he'd happily slaughtered and hung from the rafters for all to see.

Again, the lightness of her voice flitted through the small, open crack of his office door. If it were anyone else, he was certain he'd yank the door open and demand the infuriating sound cease immediately. He'd threaten and intimidate until they were shaking with fear and his reputation was solidified in their minds once more. It was safer for him — *and* for them.

But it wasn't just anyone; it was Sage — which was the only way he could think of her. Having to work close enough to smell her vanilla scent was more familiarity than a person should need. Like a fool, he moved closer to the door and set his ear against it. He had to know what song it was. It had to be something she enjoyed often enough to memorize the tune.

Or perhaps it was —

Whack!

Reeling back, he held his hand to his nose as a bark of pain left his lips. He'd been so preoccupied by her song choice, he didn't even notice the sound moving closer.

There was no humming now, just shocked silence and his befuddled assistant standing on the other side of the open door that had just made direct contact with his face.

Her elegant nose scrunched up as she took a cautious step backward, hands fluttering in front of her. "Oops." Then her bow-shaped lips pulled into a wide smile, and suddenly the pain in his face was nothing compared to the fist squeezing his chest.

"I'm so sorry, sir. I should've knocked first." She shrugged her small shoulders as if to say, *What are we going to do with me?*

He had a few ideas.

Shaking his head, he glared down at her. "Is there a reason you barreled into my office like a wrecking ball, Sage? Or were you just hoping to assault me with my own door?"

Her light eyes widened as she stepped around him and deeper into his personal space. As if she wasn't already invading every other area of his life. "'Assault' is a bit strong, isn't it? I'm sure you've been hit harder, in far more vulnerable places."

She paused for a moment, seeming to consider the words she'd just spoken. The working of her mind was unlike anything he'd ever seen. It was almost as if every thought, every word said, made the nonsensical wheels of her mind turn until she could make sense of them in her own specific way. It was surprisingly intriguing. It was...

Disgustingly distracting, and he hated it.

And then she'd say something that would just render him speechless, like, "Not that I'm thinking about your vulnerable places! I mean, I am now because I said it, but I mean vulnerable like your—" She paused, and for some unfathomable reason, he *needed* to know how she'd finish that sentence. So he waited... "Your ear?"

That familiar, annoying buoyancy whirled through him, making him feel vile things like joy and the unmistakable need to laugh.

He stared hard at her. The delighted glimmer in her eyes, the high points of her cheeks, the slight uptick of her lip, like she was always ready to smile at a moment's notice. Blowing out a breath and running a hand up to smooth his hair down, he turned back toward his desk. He needed to regain some level of footing.

"My patience is thin this morning, Sage."

"As opposed to every other morning, sir?"

Trystan walked around his desk and seated himself in his chair, ignoring Kingsley as the frog seemingly moved closer to Sage. Kingsley had sat on his desk every day for the past nearly ten years, giving Trystan quiet, unwanted counsel with his ridiculous one-worded signs. It was incredible how the amphibian only needed one word to irritate. It was a talent.

Trystan motioned with his hand for Sage to take one of the smaller seats opposite his desk. He never mentioned that those seats hadn't been there before her employment began five short months ago. He never wanted to encourage any of his workers to be relaxed enough in his presence to sit.

But it was practical to have them now that he had a right hand to brief daily. It had nothing to do with wanting her to be comfortable.

Nothing at all.

She quirked a dark brow and settled into the open seat, her bright yellow skirts swishing around her legs. Her dark locks were pinned back in her usual braid, one lone curl always escaping to lay against her cheek. Her smile warmed when she saw Kingsley hop closer to her, nudging his green head into Sage's hand.

"Good morning, my little king," Sage said, adjusting his crown. "Don't you look handsome this morning."

Kingsley made a gurgled ribbit of approval.

Sage gently scooped the frog into the palms of her hands and nuzzled him against her cheek. Naturally, Trystan began planning the amphibian's demise at the sight. "Sage, do not make a pet of my prisoners."

"Then stop having adorable prisoners." She winked at Kingsley before placing the treacherous creature back on his desk.

"Point taken," he conceded, putting both hands up in submission. He sighed and tried to come back to who he was before this natural disaster of a person entered his hemisphere.

You are evil incarnate. The world fears the very mention of your name. A cold-blooded killer.

A sudden, small squeak came out of her, sounding suspiciously like a sneeze. She looked up at him sheepishly.

He was a puddle on the floor, and every speck of dust in that room was his enemy.

"Proceed," he bit out through his clenched jaw.

Her pale hands were on his desk then, sliding a sheet of paper toward him. "I compiled a list of every employee here, giving as much detail as I could about them. I'm sure Becky or Tatianna would have more intel, should you need it. Tatianna loves her secrets and Becky keeps records so pristine, she should work for the kingdom's council."

It surprised him that Sage should give Ms. Erring any sort of compliment; he was aware of the bizarre feud between them. Though he was loath to admit it, he found it mildly entertaining.

He looked down at the top paper in the pile. Her neat script was scrawled across the page, the names of every employee with multiple anecdotes written beside each one. It was an extensive amount of detail and had probably taken her hours.

Clearing his throat, he gave her a rare look of approval. "Well done, Sage." He picked up the rest of the papers in the pile, leafing through them slowly. "This will be a considerable help."

She beamed at him, and he felt a disgusting, festering sort of sensation begin to stir. He watched her nonsense wheels begin to turn behind her eyes once more. "Sir..."

He put the papers down, giving her his full attention. "Something amiss?"

She folded her hands together, fidgeting. "I'm just wondering, instead of doing all this back-end work...why not just *question* everyone until you find the culprit?"

And this was why he'd hired her. Well, one of the reasons. She was smart, conniving in a way she couldn't quite see, but there was a quiet ruthlessness to her that was so disarming coming from someone who seemed to dole out kindness like it was candy. "Do you mean to ask...why am I not torturing everyone under my employ until someone confesses?"

Her cheeks went red, which had a humbling effect on him. A mock look of outrage crossed her delicate features. "O-Of course not!" she sputtered.

A dry, low chuckle escaped his throat before he could cough

it back down, then Trystan leaned forward onto his elbows. "Rest assured, Sage, the thought did cross my mind. But I don't just want to find the person who's been ruining all our hard-earned plans."

He paused, watching as she leaned in, too, like she was mesmerized by him, but that was impossible. "I don't want them to see me coming."

Her eyebrows shot up in understanding, and he added, "I want them to sit wherever they're sitting in this office right now, thinking they've gotten away with it. That they'll *continue* to get away with it. All the while, we whittle away at their identity behind closed doors. I want them to feel safe, and just when they think they are truly in the clear, I will destroy them."

He waited for the fear to flash on her face. Waited for the disgust to settle in. But instead, a knowing smile spread across her lips. A twinkle formed in her eyes as she leaned back in her chair, crossing her arms. "And you know if the traitor finds out you're looking for them, they'll inform the person they are answering to. You want to take *them* by surprise, too."

He couldn't catch the drop of his jaw in time. "You— Yes, that's exactly it."

Her grin turned to one of her full, beaming smiles. Like there was a joy in understanding his mind. "We're not ruling anyone out, by the way. I'm on there, too."

This surprised him more than anything, because of course she should be on the list. Nobody was ever truly innocent. Least of all, this secretly maniacal cyclone sitting across from him, even if he knew it wasn't her.

"Take your name off the list," he said gruffly.

Sage shook her head, frowning at him. "I shouldn't get special treatment. It could easily be me; I work the closest with you."

"It quite literally cannot be you." His eyes roved the small, glittering gold mark that circled her pinkie finger and then back to her face.

Her eyes followed his, and a dawn of understanding overtook her features. "Oh yes, the employment bargain."

Bargain keepers were not easy to come by, nor was the magical ink used to make the bargains themselves. The one Trystan kept on staff cost him a fortune every time he used his services. It's why the employee bargains were typically only done in green to his Malevolent Guards.

They acted as The Villain's guards and personal spies when the situation called for it. With the green-inked bargains, Trystan was ensured that his guards never betrayed him. Once a new guard agreed to the posting with their signature, they'd be bound to Trystan's life force with the inked-on ring. If anything happened to The Villain at their hands, the green ink would turn to a poison. Seeping into their bloodstreams and killing them swiftly.

Loyalty was easy to acquire when the only other option was death.

He'd originally intended to give Sage a green ring with the little ink he had left from his last purchase. But when the bargain keeper had arrived, he couldn't go through with it.

He'd picked the gold instead.

"I couldn't betray you even if I wanted to," she said resolutely, eyeing the thing with a hint of wistfulness. "I can't say I'm upset about being eliminated from the suspect list. The work this person's ruined for me alone is enough to make *me* want to torture someone."

He enjoyed pushing her a little too far sometimes, a habit he'd like to shove under his boot. "I have a couple of poor sops in the dungeons downstairs. If you want to try your hand?" He wasn't being serious.

She pushed up from her chair, turning back toward the door, looking discomfited.

Good.

She made it nearly the whole way before she paused and glanced back at him.

"I would, you know. Torture someone," she clarified, an alarming sincerity on her face. "If I knew it would help you—if it was someone hurting you... I'd do it and I'd probably enjoy it just a little." With that, she spun on her heel, her sunny dress offsetting the weight of her words.

Trystan rubbed his chest, feeling everything she'd said break shards out of the walls he'd built. Feeling the cracks all the way to the blood roaring in his ears. He cursed, pushing back from the chair and turning to the window in the corner to stare out at the horizon.

He peeked back toward his desk, where Kingsley watched him with an almost sympathetic expression before holding up one of his signs that read TROUBLE.

No shit.

Trystan whipped back toward the window, trying to slow his breathing.

The damn organ between his ribs continued to pound relentlessly. He cursed again, gripping the windowsill until his knuckles turned white, but his heart wouldn't slow.

As if insisting on reminding him that he had one.

CHAPTER 7

EVIE

Evie was going to scream.

She'd spent the entire day discreetly walking back and forth among different sectors of the office space. Idly overhearing conversations, trying to catch a whiff of *something*. But the only focus among the staff was what tavern they'd meet at for drinks at the day's end or who was sleeping with whom in the coatroom.

The latter, Evie would admit, she was mildly curious about.

She desperately wanted to confide in Tatianna about their office rat, but to her devastation, there was no way she could rule her out as a suspect. Not yet anyway. In fact, looking over the surroundings that had become as familiar as a worn pair of gloves, Evie realized there was not a single person in this room she *could* trust. Well, save for The Villain himself, and oh the irony in that.

It was alarming. The helpless, sinking feeling of betrayal that spread through her. It all felt so *personal*. It wasn't her agenda being uprooted, but it felt like it. She'd spent so much of her precious time making sure every ounce of effort and focus went to the success of the company.

It was more than the work itself, though; it was the people she was surrounded by. There was no pretense of being "better" here. They were all flawed enough to compromise any fantasy of moralistic value in favor of survival.

It was beautifully comforting, in a world that had done its best to make Evie feel tragically alone.

Sighing and standing up from her seat, her small journal in hand, she did a loop around the room, then headed to the office's surprisingly spacious kitchen area. She gave a greeting to Edwin as she walked in, feeling a brush of warmth at the oven's heat.

"Miss Evie!" Edwin called with a jaunty bow before taking a tray of flaky bread from the oven. "Have a pastry; I insist!"

Like all other ogres, Edwin was nearly as tall as the ceiling with glowing turquoise skin. His smile was wide and friendly, and those things were only complemented by his spectacles that were just a few sizes too small. He was also smart as a whip and always said things that made Evie think for a long while after he said them, and they both loved books.

Evie nodded at the open novel propped on the table. "In a moment, perhaps. What are we reading today?"

"Oh, you'd like this one, Miss Evie." The ogre winked at her, and the metal of his eyewear moved with the motion. "It's a romance."

"Is it now?" Evie beamed at him.

"Go visit your window—I'll fill you a chalice." He nodded toward the other end of the kitchen, where soft light was peeking through. Evie smiled knowingly and headed in that direction.

There were many beautifully designed windows throughout the manor, but this private area tucked into the corner was her favorite. The tiles were haphazardly placed in a design that altogether formed the shape of a vibrant sun shining its light down on an old book. An accurate depiction in Evie's eyes, since a good book often felt like the same comfort as the heat of sunlight brushing your cheeks.

She'd spent much of her time in this kitchen, venting her frustrations to Edwin, but more so to this shining piece of art. Sometimes in the whisper of quiet, it almost felt like it answered her back. Becky would occasionally wander into the kitchen and make a snide comment that Evie would be forced to answer with one of her own. It had become part of the routine she'd grown oddly accustomed to.

Eventually, Evie stood up and headed back to the office. She'd just walked up to her desk again when she thought she heard a slight clicking coming from somewhere in the room.

Her gaze wandered to the large clock on the wall, the second hand gliding as an uneasy feeling twisted in her gut.

Evie looked around to see if perhaps someone else had noticed the sound, but the low hum of voices and heads bent toward their desks told her she was the only one to note it.

It was probably nothing.

But that swirl of unease seemed to bloom into a flood of anxiety that made it difficult for her to focus on anything else.

She was tempted to retrieve her boss. Wherever the deadlands he had wandered off to. After their briefing that morning, he'd stormed out in a hurry, not bothering to tell anyone where he was going.

Which on any other day wouldn't have bothered her. He'd always had his secrets, that air of mystery that aided his dark reputation. But lately, it nagged at her that he'd trusted her with so much and yet so little. She dared to want more of him, and that thought alone was far too dangerous to explore further.

Click. Click. Click.

Letting loose a little growl of frustration, Evie tried to tune out the rest of the room to better hear the rhythmic sound. Was it getting louder? She tested it, wandering farther to one part of the room, then the other. Waiting for the noise to go from faint to blaring where it was the loudest. If her building suspicions were correct—and they were— the noise would lead her right to her desk.

Well, not exactly, but close.

A small croaking sound permeated the air over the clicking, and Evie looked down to find Kingsley sitting beside the tip of her shoe. Wide eyes searched hers, trying to convey something he couldn't express.

"Well, hello, my lovely friend." Evie slowly knelt to the ground and held out her hand, and the frog did the smallest hop into her palm. "You must be more careful when hopping the office floors, Kingsley. If you found yourself squished under a wayward boot, how would we all go on?" She smiled at him, forgetting the clicking only for a moment before it struck once more.

Kingsley seemed to hear it, too, because the frog leaped from her palm and toward the one place Evie had hoped she wouldn't have to look. Through the doors beyond her desk, into the boss's office.

Sighing, Evie walked toward the door, now slightly ajar, and pushed it all the way open.

Her instincts were screaming at her to not move a step farther. But it was as if a string had been tied between her and the mysterious noise, one that would not be broken until she found it.

The large space seemed smaller without The Villain inside. The desk didn't give her the same heart-palpitating feeling she normally had when she saw it, most likely because a certain someone wasn't occupying the chair behind it. She should leave. She was *going* to leave.

Until Kingsley leaped onto the desk with another one of his signs. And this one showed a singular word that chilled her. DANGER.

A small voice in her head told her that she should heed the frog's warning. She shouldn't have been in this office without permission, anyway, and she certainly shouldn't be rustling through his desk for what probably was just a broken clock or…perhaps a particularly noisy weapon?

But it was too late to listen to small voices when her own was screaming at her, *LOOK INSIDE THE DESK. IT'S NOT LIKE THE FROG WILL TATTLE.*

"Ugh," she muttered, the word echoing in the quiet as she rubbed her head. When she walked closer, her nerves steeled themselves, despite the odd sense of satisfaction at finally finding the source.

She bent low, the skirts of her dress brushing the floor. Reaching a hesitant hand up, Evie grasped a small, cool object, carefully bringing it out and holding it up for inspection. The clicking was now screeching at her, though the object itself looked very unassuming.

Turning it over, Evie's moment of victory was fast replaced with overwhelming fear.

"Of course," she said, her voice surprisingly steady. Sighing a ragged breath tinged in annoyance, she said to only herself: "Of course it's a bomb."

CHAPTER 8

EVIE

Everything seemed to move slower at first. The air stilled along with her as she stared down in abject horror at the little device sitting against her palm.

Then her heart began to catch up on the moment of impending doom, and she felt it pound so hard that she gasped for breath. Her free hand flew up to clutch at her chest, begging it to slow. She couldn't think. She couldn't do *anything*.

The device was gold and rectangular, a tiny timepiece dangling lightly off the bottom. With a shaking gentleness, Evie moved her hand to turn the round timepiece over. When her eyes found what they were looking for, her already cold blood froze solid, binding her stiffened limbs tightly together.

Three minutes. Only *three minutes* before the small gold-tipped arrows pointed to the twelve on the top.

A ringing began in her ears, one so piercing that it made her want to throw the device to the ground and squeeze both of her hands to the sides of her head. A ragged breath escaped her lips along with a light sob.

She was hysterical and—

She was wasting time.

Get rid of it!

She clutched the device, peeking at the timepiece once more.

Two minutes and thirty seconds left.

She thought about tossing it out the window, but Blade and the dragon trained directly below The Villain's office window, so that option was out. Maybe if she could contain the blast, perhaps she could spare just a few people. Keep the castle standing at the very least. She looked up to see Kingsley watching her with a new word on his tiny sign. RUN.

Throwing the doors open with one hand, Evie exploded into the main office space, ignoring the people stopping to stare at her. A few caught sight of the device in her pale fingers and gasped, diving out of her way as she searched for a place to get rid of the thing.

A voice, which under different circumstances would grate at her, grounded her in its familiarity. "The parapet!"

Evie turned toward Becky, who'd swung the door to the outside open, waving her hands frantically for Evie to move.

And move Evie did.

She burst into a sprint and ran into the cool, open air, huffing a quiet "thank you" to the woman as she passed. Evie had to have been in some sort of adrenaline fog, because she thought she saw concern on Becky's pinched face.

The heat of the summer sun hit the top of Evie's head—the first time it had appeared from behind the clouds all morning. Her heart was racing, her skirts kicking up around her with each furious step. The device remained cool in her hands, despite her rising body temperature, the ticking a cruel reminder.

You want the ticking! she reminded herself. *No ticking means you're dead!*

If she could just get to the end, she could send the device over the small rise at the end of the parapet. She could save the manor, or most of it, at least. More importantly, she could save the people inside.

Had the parapet always been this long? It felt like she wasn't even close to the end. She pushed her legs to the brink and ran harder, watching her destination grow closer and closer. Still not fast enough, she impossibly pushed herself farther, nearly reaching the end when—*No!*

The stiletto heel of her boot snagged beneath a loose cement block, bending her ankle unnaturally as she stumbled.

Evie watched in horror as the bomb slipped from her fingers, sailing through the air. Watched it soar up, high, high enough that it skimmed the top of the stone rise, but it didn't make it over. It clanged down, landing far too close to keep her from the blast.

"Oh gods," Evie whispered, diving to remove her heel from the hole it was now wedged into. Her breathing was so short that her vision began to blur, the tips of her fingers beginning to bleed from scraping against the rough surface of the brick where the heel of her boot was stuck.

But it wasn't budging. Realization hit like a cool mist. She turned toward the opposite end of the parapet, toward the doors at the other end.

This is it. She'd never make it in time.

She had forgotten to hug Lyssa before she sent her off to school that morning, had of course assumed she would get another chance. She'd yelled to her father that she loved him, but had he heard her? Did he know?

A different face flashed in her mind—her boss, The Villain. Evie couldn't believe she was leaving him when he needed her most. Who would make him begrudgingly smile now?

As a lone tear ran down Evie's face, she thought that must be the saddest thing of all.

CHAPTER 9

THE VILLAIN

A little while earlier…

Trystan pushed his way through the western side of Hickory Forest. There were rockier mountains in this part of the kingdom, so it was easy to get turned around.

Even easier to hide.

Or at least that was what Trystan had thought when he'd started storing his safe houses below the mossy forest floor. His Malevolent Guards had dug small hideouts at various checkpoints along the textured ground, keeping his most valuable possessions dispersed throughout all of them.

Most of them contained stolen shipments that were sent to the king from the neighboring kingdoms. All allies looking to "aid" the king in his ongoing battle with the "dark figure" who had appeared nearly ten years ago to sabotage King Benedict's reign.

Trystan's lips ticked up in a smile. He loved his job.

When he'd started doing this all those years ago, he couldn't have imagined the empire he'd build. All the people who would work for him, help him toward his goal.

To the people of Rennedawn, that meant interfering with the kingdom's economy, slowly but surely leaving him and the rest of the kingdom impoverished. For Trystan, it meant ensuring King Benedict never got what he wanted, no matter the cost.

His Malevolent Guards had gotten better and better at intercepting shipments containing weapons, liquor, and wares, but he still sought something bigger, something that would derail everything Benedict held dear...

He shoved a branch out of the way, leaving his horse tied to a tree closer to the bottom of the hill. His magic coiled beneath his skin, like it sensed the danger he was approaching.

He hadn't wanted to, but he'd left in a hurry that morning. A missive had arrived by one of his spies, or ravens as they liked to call themselves, letting him know urgently that another vital safe house had been compromised.

The frustration roared through him as he shoved the hair off his forehead. He approached the hidden door slowly, freezing when he caught the silver glint of the Valiant Guards' armor.

Them. His anger rumbled and shook.

How had they found another safe house? The only people who knew their locations were his guards, who couldn't give away his secrets even if they wanted to; Kingsley, who wouldn't say a word for obvious reasons; and Sage, who said she'd torture someone for him.

And it was not the time to be thinking about that, not when Trystan saw one of his longest-standing guards lying face down in the copse of trees surrounding the entrance with a dagger in his back. More of his guards stood their ground, fighting the remaining knights, and he realized he'd asked them all here earlier that morning to load in extra cargo, out in the open, where they could easily be found.

It had been his fault.

Trystan's magic wouldn't wait any longer. It took on a life of its own and came out of his fingertips like water slipping through the cracks of a dam. Nobody else could see it, but he could, the gray mist surrounding the Valiant Guards that were still happily slaughtering his men and women, his guards, his people.

The first Valiant Guard was slow to realize what was happening to him, but when the gray mist circled him, Trystan saw exactly how to hurt him, his power illuminating the best places to strike in a vibrance of color amid the gray.

The glowing red around the knight's abdomen was The Villain's perfect opening; it was the guard's weak point. His magic swept in, circling the knight, and the gray mist sharpened and angled right for that spot. The knight let out a curdling scream, dropping to his knees before collapsing to the ground.

The act of killing gave The Villain strength, fed his power, made him strong. Strong enough to push the rest of the gray mist around the remaining knights, finding their weakest point and slaughtering them all. The Villain took a sick satisfaction from watching the pile of silver-clad bodies pile high until there wasn't a single knight left standing.

The head of his guard, Keeley, stood to the side, assessing a comrade who was clutching their side in pain.

Trystan walked forward to assess the damage. "Did they take anything?" he asked, keeping his face blank as he counted the dead. Four.

Three men and one woman dead, because of him.

He gritted his jaw, ignoring the burning guilt rushing through him. It was a useless emotion. There was nothing productive about feeling the pounding pressure of people dying for him, knowing he wasn't worth their sacrifice.

"No," Keeley replied absently. "But we'll have to move everything, sir. One of the knights took off to relay a message before you arrived."

He nodded, taking the information in slowly. The rest of his guards looked to him, but there was no time to mourn. They needed his instruction; they needed The Villain.

"Have everything moved to one of our more secure locations," he called to them. "Bring the dead back to the manor, and we'll—" His humanity made him stop. "We'll have them buried."

The guards nodded, looking at him with a reverence he didn't want. Another guard spoke over the silence. "What are you going to do about this, sir?"

Trystan's jaw ticked as his gaze swept over the group still standing, the guards who lay dead, and the Valiant Guards beside them. "What needs to be done," he said cryptically, giving them their final orders and then heading back to his mount.

As he swung his leg over his steed and guided him back to the manor, the question echoed in his head once more.

What are you going to do about this?

He didn't consider the question, for he already knew the answer.

As he rode south, speeding slightly when he felt a strange tingling sensation on the back of his neck, he made a vow.

There will be vengeance for anyone who has suffered in my name.

When he finally arrived back at the manor and strode past the moving wall into his office space, he knew something was wrong, could feel it, something— He didn't make it two feet before Rebecka appeared before him, an unusual dishevelment to her normally composed appearance.

"Sir!" she gasped.

An eerie feeling prickled down his arm.

"Bomb. There was a—bomb in your office— Evie—"

Her name brought him back into focus as he gripped the small woman by the shoulders. "Where is she?" He knew his voice was strangled and harsh, but this wasn't the time to gentle it.

"The parapet. She took it outside!"

He dropped his arms and began to run before the last words left her lips. He flew through the doors and didn't stop. His black cape billowed around him as he raced up the stairs and to the parapet, where he caught sight of her small form in the distance, looking forlorn and resigned.

Bomb—where was the bomb? He followed Sage's gaze to the top of the tower at the end of the parapet. His eyes found the small gold device, so close, too close.

"Run!" He pushed his legs harder, letting the panic be fuel to bring him to her.

Her wide eyes flew to him, blinking as if she didn't believe he was real. "My foot is stuck!" she called back, sounding as frantic as he felt.

He called back in disbelief, "Well, pull it out!" His words released on a growl, and he watched with bated breath as she continued to tug at her leg, not gaining an inch.

Sweat beaded along his forehead, and his loose black shirt was beginning to stick to different parts of his body as the sound of his boots echoed off the stone and cement beneath his feet. It wasn't fear— he was just running very fast.

He was nearly to her when he felt the vibration in the air. His eyes flickered to the gold device as he drew closer. The timepiece hanging from the explosive began to shake, and he felt the tower beside them rumbling. Right as he reached her, grabbing her by the waist, throwing her to the ground and pressing his body on top of hers, he enveloped them in as much magic as he could gather and yet knew it likely wouldn't be enough.

And then the world went red.

CHAPTER 10

EVIE

E vie was bleeding.

She could feel the warm liquid dripping down her scalp as she slowly blinked her eyes open. She couldn't see much. Her vision was clouded by black fabric and a muscled chest. The smell of smoke flooded her senses, but also something else. Something warm and comforting.

Her head was being cradled, and when her vision finally cleared, black eyes were peering into hers. But she was too disoriented to read the emotion behind them.

"Sage?" Her name was spoken in the smooth accent of The Villain's voice, raising the hairs on her arms.

"Hello, sir," she murmured weakly, trying to make sense of her rapidly moving thoughts.

The pinch in his brow smoothed, and he exhaled a ragged breath. One of the hands cradling her head came up to her cheek, and he cursed when he saw the blood. "Where else are you hurt?" he asked, his voice brusque, furious even.

She tried to assess where exactly the painful points were coming from, but if she were being honest, she didn't feel much but contentment when he was holding her like this. He must have taken her silence as a sign of her distress, though, because he moved them both to a sitting position.

He tore a bit of his cloak, bringing it to her head to stanch the bleeding, and looked back up toward the destroyed end of the walkway. The small tower adjacent was crumbled into nothing.

"Please speak. It's unsettling when you're quiet." His voice was steady, but something in him seemed shaken.

"I'm glad I didn't explode."

The look in his eyes warmed, and his lips pulled high, the elusive dimple making an appearance. "The feeling is mutual."

She groaned, remembered she'd almost gotten him killed when he dove for her.

"Why didn't you run?" There was nothing accusing in his voice, just curiosity.

She looked to her ankle. Her body seemed to remember it should be in a great deal of pain, and she gasped as the throbbing set in.

The Villain leaned back, placing her hand where his was to hold the piece of cloth to her head wound. He gently lifted her foot. "May I?"

Evie felt a little breathless but nodded.

He lifted her yellow skirt, dirtied from the smoke, until it was sitting just above her ankle. Carefully taking her worn heeled boot in his hand, he slowly pulled it off. Evie let out a hiss of pain, and he froze.

"I'm sorry." He grimaced, pulling the shoe all the way off along with her wool sock to reveal the angry, harsh swelling that lay beneath. His warm, calloused hands gripped her calf above her injury, and Evie worried if he let go, she'd float away.

"Can you move it?" This was a different man speaking to her, or rather the same man, just without his usual layer of pretense pushed forward like his life depended on it.

He was real right now, and that safe barrier of his otherworldly splendor fell away, leaving Evie embarrassingly breathless.

He was staring at her, waiting for her response, as she attempted to move her foot quickly before he saw too much behind her eyes. "I can, but it's painful."

"Good, it's not broken." It must have been Evie's imagination, the way his hands seemed to linger on the lines of her ankle. But they weren't. The poor man was trying to check her for injuries, and Evie couldn't stop the shivers that his touch sent through her.

After handing her the discarded shoe, he gripped Evie's hand in his. Slowly, he brought her to her feet, and she favored her uninjured foot. She made the mistake of shifting her weight to the injured one out of habit and gasped, falling forward into his chest. Gripping his shoulders in both hands.

"Sorry," she squeaked.

He cleared his throat once, twice—*oh dear*—three times before putting a steady hand to one side of her hip. "That's…all right."

Looking at the destruction around them, Evie shuddered in horror.

The smoke and dust had cleared, giving them a perfect view of the ruined tower. The top was simply gone, large pieces surrounding them while others certainly had fallen all the way down into the courtyard. Beyond the tower, a large portion of the west side of the manor's wall was completely collapsed. From this distance, Evie could see the remains of what looked like a study or perhaps a small library.

Not the books. Anything but the books.

The end of the parapet was gone. They were both about two steps from falling right over the edge. Debris covered the ends of her hair and probably the top of it, too, and when she looked over at her boss, his hair appeared nearly white from the ash.

Hot tears burned behind her eyes, and Evie felt the horror of the last few moments seep in through every pore. "Oh no, the manor."

She hated crying, especially in front of other people. Especially in front of her *boss*.

But it was too late; tears were already running hot down her face. "I can't believe this happened. Why would anyone— I wish it wouldn't— I can't believe— I'm so sorry." Evie's hands were still on his shoulders, so he must have felt them shaking, but she couldn't bring herself to look at him.

The blast had been contained. The ruins surrounding them were disheartening, but the manor still stood. It could've been so much worse. But still, part of it was gone, and it was his home, and she had been so afraid.

A sob ripped through her, and she braced a hand against her stomach to try and push it back in, but that seemed to do the opposite. Another one poured out of her. The Villain placed his hands on her shoulders, pushing her back enough to examine her face. Evie didn't have it in her to fight him.

"Are you…crying?" He was horrified, it was so plain in his voice, and she wanted so badly to shrink away from him, but of course her injured ankle kept her locked in place.

"No. I have a condition where my tear ducts produce an excess of warm, salty water when I'm tired or in distress."

But the comment went unnoticed as he calmly reached in his pocket for a handkerchief. To Evie's surprise, it wasn't black like the rest of his attire but instead a vibrant light blue. "Here." Placing it lightly in her hand, he waved an arm at the remains of the tower. "Nothing in there was worth anything, not as— It wasn't important."

There was something he wasn't saying; that was clear. But Evie was too relieved that he'd chosen to ignore her outburst of emotion to question him further on it. She sniffled, smiling slightly at him through her tears, and she thought, just for a moment, she caught a look of ruin in his eyes.

Whatever was in that tower must have meant a great deal.

Clearing his throat again, he bent an arm under Evie's legs and the other behind her back. "Hold on," was her only warning before she was lifted into the air against his chest.

"Whoa!" she gasped, gripping her arms around his neck. Which, of course, was thick and corded with muscle, and because her face was only inches away, she could see his pulse beating steadily there.

Shaking her head, she clasped her hands behind his neck, trying to take this situation as casually as she could. "No wonder you have such a superiority complex. I would, too, if I could see the world from this vantage point!"

Rolling his dark eyes, he began to walk them back toward the open doors. A crowd of onlookers had formed, and Evie saw The Villain's eyes sharpen before several gasps were heard and they scattered back inside.

"I'm hardly taller than the average man," he said flatly.

"I feel like I'm being carried by a tree." A considerably warm tree whose arms touching her legs and back made her brain turn to mush.

He adjusted her higher. So much so that her lips accidentally brushed his shoulder, and the shock of it must have repulsed him, because he stumbled so hard, he nearly dropped her.

"Sorry," she mumbled, face burning.

"Stop apologizing," he gritted out. It was clear he was angry; the situation must be intolerable for him. "You say that too often. It's irritating."

They'd nearly reached the doors, but the comment made Evie do a double take. His expression remained grim, his eyes determinedly forward.

"I can't help it. Apologizing for things comes too naturally to me."

This seemed to make him angrier. "No more of that when it's unnecessary or I'll dock your pay."

Evie sputtered as he walked through the doors, sighing at the open area of the office she truly hadn't thought she'd see again.

Keeping her high in his arms, The Villain allowed his voice to bellow out over the space, tinged with authority. "It would seem that someone misplaced an explosive in my office." A chill set over the room as he continued. "It is a good thing Ms. Sage found the device before it could cause any permanent damage."

She might have imagined his grip tightening around her legs.

"If anyone knows anything about this, please come find me. Otherwise…I'll come find you."

There was an unmistakable threat in his words. One that sent the employees scattering to their desks as he carried her past them toward Tatianna's quarters.

The bustling of papers being thrown about echoed behind them as he carried her away. She leaned into him once more, trying to enjoy these last few moments in his arms. "Someone tried to kill you."

His mouth flattened into a thin line. "Yes."

"You seem to be very calm about that," she said incredulously.

"Don't let appearances deceive you, Sage."

"So you are angry?"

He stopped just before Tatianna's doors, looking down at her, his face so close, Evie had to force herself not to look away. His eyes flashed once more to the cut on her head that was still bleeding but slower than before.

"My anger knows no limits," he admitted. "But I am also…not surprised."

Her brows shot high. "You knew this was going to happen?"

Sighing, he pushed the doors to the healer's quarters open. Tatianna wasn't in the room, so he walked over, gently placing Evie on the examination table, putting her once again at eye level with his chest.

"No, but there was a reason I was sent away, dealing with another compromised safe house, the same day that someone placed an explosive in my office. Whoever did this didn't want me here when it went off." He rubbed a frustrated hand over his face. "They wanted to strike where it would wound."

"By blowing up your desk knickknacks?"

He huffed out half a laugh, the dimple reappearing in his left cheek, and shook his head. "Among other things."

Evie wanted to know more, but before she could ask another question, Tatianna blew through the doors, her soft pink robes swirling about her ankles. "I leave for five seconds to help stitch a wound for Blade and one of the interns tells me that you ran with a bomb?"

Tatianna brushed past the boss as if he weren't there, pushing Evie's hair away from her face before pulling her in for a hug. "You brave little fool."

"The interns are very melodramatic," Evie said, her voice slightly muffled against Tatianna's shoulder.

"Her ankle is sprained, Tatianna." The Villain's voice was farther away. Evie turned to see his back heading for the door. "See it healed as soon as possible, and then I will be escorting Ms. Sage home."

At that, both women whipped their heads up to look at him with their mouths hanging open. "You mean to where I live?" Evie asked.

"That is generally what people consider a home, is it not, Sage?" He didn't give her time to respond before spinning on his heel and walking out, calling behind him, "I'll be waiting right out here."

CHAPTER II

EVIE

The carriage was bumpy and knocked against her bad shoulder, causing her to wince. Evie had been lucky, too lucky, that the glow of the scar wasn't visible beneath her dress. The pain from her ankle and head, like any pain, had lit the scar enough to knock someone out if they looked beneath the thick fabric. But Tatianna had worked efficiently, only getting to the parts where she knew Evie needed healing.

It was irresponsible to let a wound inflicted by magic sit untreated for so long, as she had her knife wound. But when one was trying desperately to move forward from something, it was quite annoying to be dragged bodily backward by useless limitations. If she had the wound treated, they would ask questions, and she wasn't quite ready to face that. She would, she promised herself she would, when she was ready.

Evie's little situation with her former employer was no more than what many young women experienced from leering employers who made inappropriate propositions. If she weighed it overall, she'd been quite lucky to escape that altercation with only a magical scratch to show for it.

That thought alone, that she should feel *lucky* for only a minor injury, not to mention that any woman should feel that way, was so horrifically ridiculous and unfair, it was like watching someone steal something precious from you and thanking them for it.

Anger pulsed through Evie so fast that she had to suck in a breath to keep from screaming. Cool afternoon air kissed her cheeks as she tilted her head back, calming her. She'd tell Tatianna when the wound was less raw, and her emotions as well. It was silly to feel embarrassed that she'd left herself in a vulnerable position. This was not her fault. And maybe it was time she asked for help.

Shaking her head, she pushed the wound from her mind and looked around for something else to focus her attention. The sleek, open black carriage they trotted down the road in was simple in design, not needing extra ornamentation to be striking—much like her boss.

The chirping of birds and other unfamiliar creatures sounded different from her morning walks to the manor—the forest was fully awake now.

After Tatianna had healed her ankle, berating Evie with a million questions, the boss had escorted her down to the front gate, where the carriage and horses awaited.

They hadn't spoken since.

It usually took Evie about an hour each morning and each evening to take every hidden shortcut off the regular pathways to the hidden veil of The Villain's castle. But they were taking the long way, down the dirt path, and Evie wanted desperately to fill the uncomfortable silence.

She hated quiet.

It was quiet the last time she saw her brother. It was quiet the day her mother left. It was quiet when her father got sick. The quiet had brought her so much pain. An instinctual part of Evie shrank from it, waiting for the next blow.

She distracted herself with the pull of the leather reins in his black gloved hands. He handled the vehicle with grim determination, his face focused on the road before them and the fast-setting sun.

Evie pulled her eyes away to look at Kingsley, who sat perched on a small stand that she was certain had been put there solely for the frog's use. "Do you bring Kingsley for carriage rides often?" she asked.

Her boss didn't look at her or their web-toed friend as he said, "Even I am not so evil that I won't allow him a little...sunlight." He paused, almost choking on the last word. "Anyhow, the more freedoms I give him, the fewer escape attempts the little nuisance makes." There was a pointed look between The Villain and the frog. Kingsley broke first, turning his tiny body back to the scenery.

"Thank you for doing this, but my ankle is fine now; I could've walked." Her braid was nearly undone, loose wisps of her black hair tickling her neck.

"I didn't realize you don't ride." He didn't look at her, and his grip on the reins tightened.

"I have. Once or twice, but there's no way my family could afford a mount. Let alone a place to house the poor creature. Besides, I like to walk."

He nodded, seemingly to himself. "Of course. Who doesn't enjoy a two-hour jaunt every day."

Evie couldn't think of an appropriate response to that, or even an inappropriate one, which meant the situation was truly dire.

But he seemed to find the silence as intolerable as she did, because he spoke before she could blunder through another sentence. "Do you still keep that dagger in your boot?"

It took her a moment to process what he was asking and how he could possibly know about her one and only weapon, but then she remembered all those months ago. "Yes...I do, though not the same one. I never picked it up after—"

He was nodding before she finished. "Good. You shouldn't be walking these woods alone, unprotected." The Villain finally turned his head in her direction, a sly smile on his lips. "You never know what kind of menacing characters you'll find."

She'd meant to make a lighthearted joke, but the words came out far more serious than she'd intended. "Oh, I don't know. It worked out well for me the first time."

It was the wrong thing to say.

The smile slipped from his lips, and any levity between them was suddenly weighted with the events of the day. "I would hardly call nearly dying 'well,' Sage."

With a light clicking from his lips, the horses trotted into a canter. He was eager to be rid of her.

"*Ah*, but I didn't die, so it worked out as well as one could hope— well, given the new job requirement and all. Good thing I was looking for employ, now wasn't it?" *Shut up, Evie.*

He seemed to contemplate his next words very carefully, tilting his head to the side as if trying to make sense of them.

"If you would like to resign… It would be an *extreme* inconvenience for me. However, given your work performance and the dedication you've given the company, I would accommodate you."

A roaring panic began low in her gut and bloomed up through her chest like a poisonous weed.

"I don't want to resign!" In her rush to get the words out, she stood suddenly, nearly tipping over the edge when the carriage hit a large dip in the road. Kingsley made a gurgled sound of outrage as Evie wobbled.

Swiftly, The Villain grabbed both reins with one hand, reaching for her arm and pulling her down. "I didn't mean to cause an upset. I was merely giving you the option."

"Well, you did cause an upset! I *need* this job, you selfish bastard." His eyebrows shot high at her words, but she didn't care; she was too upset, her heart racing at the idea of not being able to feed her family or afford medicine for her father.

"I would of course set you up with a fair amount of severance pay. Enough to keep you and your family comfortable for the next couple of years while you find other employment." He said the words too casually, like they were something he'd practiced.

Which only made her angrier.

"I am not a charity case," she said flatly.

"What did I do that gave you the impression that I am in the habit of charity?" He looked as offended as she felt. "I was giving you an option because you've done good work and have been loyal. You also saved my office and staff from a bomb today. It is not personal, so do not take it as such."

The words did nothing to quell her anger, not only at him but at herself for denying the obviously generous and lifesaving offer. With the extra money, she might be able to afford a private tutor for Lyssa, perhaps even a specialized healer for her father, but she didn't feel gratitude.

The thought of never enjoying the brisk air of the morning as she strolled through Hickory Forest, the irritating but familiar climb of the stairs, the clamor of the office space, Blade making every person in the office fall in love with him, Kingsley and his little signs. Even Becky hating, well, everything about her.

It was…home.

She needed it. It was hers. Everything else she had to share with her father and sister. But working for The Villain gave her the opportunity to do a little taking herself.

She wouldn't give it up, selfishness be damned.

"No. I appreciate the offer, but I must decline." Some cosmic force must have taken pity on her, because he didn't question her choice any further, just exhaled a bit harshly and loosened his jaw.

"Very well."

The familiar sounds of the bustling village square came into sharp focus as Evie pointed to the left of the small fork in the road. "Take that back way—it leads right to my home, and we won't be seen."

He adhered to her wishes without question, pulling the carriage into the familiar drive that led up to the small cottage she shared with her family. The yellow tulips lining the front walk looked odd from her current position: being in a carriage…belonging to a glorified murderer.

Life was strange.

When The Villain pulled to the edge of the drive, it occurred to Evie that he had driven her home. Which was *ridiculous*, because she'd known this was happening the entire carriage ride, but for some reason her mind wouldn't allow the absurdity of the situation to settle into her reality.

Oh, for the love of all that was good, her boss was looking at her *house*. Even worse, he caught sight of the clotheslines hanging from the side of her home, several of which had her undergarments blowing in the wind.

Her face burned red, and she turned to him, trying to pry his attention away. "What if you're seen?"

He tilted his head toward her, his face looking younger as it softened into an expression of genuine amusement. "Nobody, save my employees, knows what I look like. If I'm seen by anyone, they will think me any ordinary highbrow noble."

Ordinary.

The word was so far from an accurate descriptor for him, Evie nearly busted out laughing. But before she could, a thought struck her. "What about those men who were pursuing you in the forest the day we met?"

His face didn't lose any levity as he smirked and said, "They weren't pursuing me because I was The Villain. They were pursuing me because they wanted Kingsley. Remember, magical animals sell for a high price. But I had miscalculated the sorts of weaponry they wielded."

"Well, thank you for—"

"Evie! You're home early!" Her little sister's voice cut through the air, startling her.

Oh, for the love of—

Evie groaned as Lyssa came into view, black hair disheveled and covered in dirt. "Emmaline said she saw you in a fine carriage, and I said that couldn't be you but—" Her sister stopped when she caught sight of the two of them side by side.

"Oh, hello." Lyssa bobbed a curtsy, and Evie was beginning to wonder if she had died and this was some sort of torturous afterlife.

The Villain stood tall, stepping down from the carriage, turning back toward Evie to offer his hand. After both her feet were firmly planted on the ground, Evie said, "Um, Lyssa, this is my— I mean he's— Um—"

"Trystan Maverine." His deep voice was a calm, steadying sound, though hearing a name come from his lips was jarring. *How did he make that up so quickly?*

Bowing low, he continued. "I am your elder sister's employer. She had a small accident at work, so I escorted her home."

Lyssa's brown eyes widened, then she dipped into a curtsy. "Oh! Yes, Evie has accidents a lot."

How funny that her sister was about to have one as well…when Evie throttled her.

But her boss didn't seem to be as annoyed by the presence of her ten-year-old nuisance as she was, because she could see a light upward tugging of his lips. "I'm sorry to hear that."

Lyssa didn't slow. "Oh yes, she falls all the time. She fell down the well once! Can you believe it? An actual well! She was trying to save a bird and she fell right in. She was stuck there for hours, and when we finally got her out, she was soaked and pruning like dried grapes!"

Her boss slowly turned to her, a strange satisfaction on his face at hearing this piece of news.

"It was a very cute bird," Evie said defensively.

He nodded, unfazed. "I'm sure it was."

"Are you a prince?" Honestly, had her sister found a pound of sugar before they'd arrived here?

"I am not." His voice was flat. He somehow didn't seem irritated by this interaction, but then again, she supposed, he was used to dealing with her ramblings every day.

Lyssa didn't seem to hear him, staring at him with quiet wonder on her face.

Evie narrowed her eyes at her sister's bedraggled clothes. "Aren't you supposed to be at school?"

"It's a holiday," her sister said quickly, looking guilty.

"Oh, really?" Evie tapped her chin, crouching down to look her sister in the eye. "What holiday is that?"

"Your hair is a mess, Evangelina," Lyssa said, scrunching her nose.

"You're changing the subject."

"So? You do it all the time."

"Not on purpose!" Evie threw her hands in the air, abruptly remembering their audience. The Villain, or *Trystan*, was eyeing them like a zoo exhibit, a faint twinkle in his dark eyes.

"We'll discuss this later. Where is Papa?" She rubbed her temples, trying to stave off the beginnings of a headache.

"He went into the village to have a drink with some of his friends."

"A drink?" Evie asked incredulously. His mood and health had been noticeably better the last couple of days, but he hadn't had the energy or the will to venture into the village for anything other than visits to their local healer in *years*.

It wouldn't last, and Evie wouldn't let herself hope for it. But she could see the joy radiating from Lyssa, finally seeming to have one healthy parent, and she refused to be the one to take it away from her merely because of her suspicions. "That's...wonderful."

Lyssa nodded, tossing a wide grin at The Villain like a weapon. "Are you staying for dinner, Mr. Maverine?"

The magnificent horses with the carriage chuffed impatiently, drawing her boss's eye toward them.

"I cannot, I'm afraid. There is much work to be done, and the day is not yet over." He removed one of his black gloves and reached out a hand toward Lyssa. She immediately put her hand in his as he bowed over it.

"It was a pleasure to meet you, Lady Lyssa."

She giggled, and Evie felt like her chest was about to erupt for all the fluttering going on inside it.

A stray "ribbit" from the carriage caught Lyssa's attention as she leaned past both Evie and The Villain to look. Her face scrunched, but her young eyes were delighted. "Is that frog wearing a crown?"

Evie and her boss turned back toward the carriage. Kingsley was holding another of his signs, this one reading HALP.

The Villain reached back, quickly ripping the sign from the animal. "Give me that, you little traitor." His words came out on a growl, which morphed quickly into a cough when he saw Evie's and her sister's amused expressions.

After dipping into a small curtsy, Lyssa spun on her heel, then ran back toward the edge of the house, where two other little girls waited. All of them giggled as they ran off.

"She's in big trouble," Evie said grumpily.

"Go easy on her—she's young," The Villain said diplomatically.

Evie turned toward him, planting her hands on her hips, a look of mock outrage on her face. "Aren't you supposed to be evil?"

"Encouraging children to neglect their education fits under that bracket, does it not?" He tilted his head as if considering it.

Plucking a stray weed from the walkway and then another, Evie said, "Where did the name Trystan come from, anyway?"

"My mother, I imagine."

Evie straightened like a rod, slowly dropping the weeds and coming to stand, staring at him with wide, unflinching eyes. "Are you saying... the name you just gave my younger sister...is your *real* name?"

Disbelief overrode her senses even further when he squinted in confusion. "There's no need to overreact, little tornado. It's just a name."

"Like the deadlands it is!" she sputtered. Trystan. His name was *Trystan Maverine*.

"If you're having some sort of episode, may I suggest you sit before you faint and crush the tulips?"

"You're being far too casual about this. You just told a ten-year-old, who can barely lie about a fictitious school holiday, let alone the identity of my 'employer.'" She began pacing up and down the walkway, trying to regain some of her equilibrium, but her frenzied brain was buzzing, keeping coherent thoughts out of focus.

"I shared a name. One that nobody else knows me by. My identity as 'The Villain' and as Trystan Maverine have never been connected." His face was a mask of calm, his voice steady. "Nobody will know working for me means working for The Villain. Do not distress yourself."

"I wasn't worried about that," she said. "I was worried about the danger it would put you in."

His head reeled back as if she'd slapped him. "Do not take it upon yourself to worry about my safety, Sage. Your job is quite literally to 'assist' me in the areas I request. My protection, you will find, is not included on the list."

"Fine. I won't," she huffed, turning in the direction of the front door, but her anger dissipated when she replayed his name once more in her mind. "Trystan?" She spun around.

Something about his name on her lips must have triggered an unpleasantness, because she caught sight of the fist of his ungloved hand tightening, his knuckles turning white.

"It's really…*Trystan*?" She frowned.

"Do you dislike the name?" he asked dryly.

"No…it's just…not what I expected." She leaned back on her heels, noticing dark clouds coming over the horizon.

"I am going to regret this with an alarming intensity, but what *were* you expecting?" He had his head slightly leaned away, as if she was about to strike him.

Smiling crookedly, taking a step toward him, she dealt her first blow. "Fluffy."

The response was beautiful.

His mouth gaped open like a fish. Opening and closing, trying to find the right words. But of course, there were none. She clasped her hands behind her back, waiting.

After a few moments of silence that for once Evie didn't mind, he said, "Fluffy? You looked at me and thought to yourself, *He looks like a* Fluffy?"

The name in the rough gravel of his voice, which seemed to be getting higher pitched in his outrage, sent her tittering.

"Fluffy is a beautiful name. I had a dog named Fluffy once." She nodded succinctly and then deadpanned, "He used to growl at lint."

The noises coming out of him were not in any language she'd ever heard.

"I suppose Trystan is a fine substitution," she continued. "I am, however, a little offended you trusted my sister with that information before you told me."

He seemed to come back to himself then, shaking his head, looking a bit dizzy. "I didn't think I needed to tell you. My real name is on a small plaque on my desk."

Evie pursed her lips. "No it's not. I would've noticed."

He mumbled something under his breath that she couldn't hear, but it sounded like, "You'd think so, wouldn't you?"

But then Evie replayed his office in her mind, recalling the layout of his desk. In her defense, it was hard to look at *anything* else when his presence demanded every ounce of her attention. But she did recall a little black rectangle in the back corner and…

"Huh, maybe it *is* there."

"It's not a maybe," he said in disbelief. "It is."

She waved a hand carelessly in front of her. "Yeah, yeah, sure."

"I—" He paused and angled his body back toward the carriage. "I think I must leave before my head spins right off my neck."

Evie nodded. Her work here was done. "Very well. Have a safe trip back. Thank you again for the ride home—oh, and the saving-my-life part as well."

"I would accept your thanks if it wasn't being employed by me that put your life in danger in the first place." He hoisted himself up into the carriage, and Evie was surprised at the surge of melancholy that cascaded over her at seeing him leave.

"I'll be at work bright and early tomorrow, sir, to make up for the day."

"There's no need, Sage. Take tomorrow off." He pulled the loose glove back onto his hand, tightening his cloak around his neck.

"But why? I'm fine," she argued.

"I'm well aware. However, the work I need your help with won't be in the office but in the field."

The words froze Evie in her tracks. "In the field? Are you going to make me light an empty cottage on fire? Steal a litter of puppies? Or something…grosser?"

He chuckled. "Relax, Sage. Nothing gruesome. You can wipe the lurid thoughts of blood and destruction from your mind."

"I wouldn't say my thoughts of blood and destruction are lurid," she corrected, scrunching her nose.

"If you're not opposed, I'll need your help tomorrow evening at the Redbloom Tavern, eight o'clock."

The Redbloom Tavern was not the seediest establishment around, but it was certainly no palace, either. Evie had gone once on a whim with a few girls in her village on her eighteenth birthday. The beer was stale, the wine tasted of vinegar, and the people were filthy and loud. All in all, she had quite enjoyed herself.

"Very well. But may I ask what you could possibly need, work-wise, at a tavern?"

He rubbed his jaw before taking the reins in both hands. "The bomb that was planted in my office."

The mention of it brought back the smoke, the panic, the frantic beating of her heart, and she sucked in a breath.

"I recognized the timepiece. There's only one man who could make and sell that sort of watch, the kind that can be hooked and aligned with explosives."

"And he works at the Redbloom Tavern?"

His lips twisted downward, the dark clouds above casting a pallor of gray light on him. "He owns it."

He looked to Evie once more with that wary sense of expectation. Like he was waiting, wondering if this was the request that would make her turn her back, would make her run.

But her stubbornness and lack of self-preservation had carried her this far. She stepped forward and nodded. "I'll see you tomorrow night, sir."

A flash of relief shone on his face for just a moment before disappearing behind a mask of indifference. A sudden noise from his lips, urging the horses into action, and then he was gone.

Evie looked at the spot where his carriage had been. Where he'd just stood. Her front yard would never quite be the same place again.

And then it started to rain, and she couldn't shake the feeling that this was a very bad omen of things to come.

CHAPTER 12

EVIE

It was cold tonight.

Evie pulled her brown cloak tightly around her. Not the ivory one she'd treated herself to for her birthday but the one she'd had since she was sixteen.

Worn and patched over, it was essentially worthless. Which was the only wise course when entering an establishment like this. She pushed open the doors and glanced at the clock on the far side of the wall. She was early, but only by a few minutes.

The raucous yells from the table closest to her told her that someone had just lost a valuable hand of cards, and sultry laughter said that someone was about to get lucky in other ways.

Pulling out a chair on the farthest side of the room by the window, Evie seated herself and pulled the brown cloak from her shoulders. In addition to the cloak, she'd picked out her drabbest dress. The only pitfall being the corset had to be worn over it rather than beneath, pushing her small breasts up to high heaven.

Under any other circumstance, that would not bother her. She already had so little to work with in that department, it was always fun to wear a corset that gave her the illusion of it. But she was in a seedy tavern, drawing the salacious gazes of more than one person in the room, and she was trying to remain discreet.

This was a work excursion, after all.

Her heart rate increased when she saw a figure in a dark cloak enter the room, immediately exhaling when he tugged the hood down and it wasn't her boss. She saw The Villain every day without having the nerves her body was currently throwing at her, but for some reason, this was different.

It was bad enough having the man in front of her house, but now they were in a place of laughter and alcohol. With couples having trysts in every darkened corner and—

Why was she blushing?

"Here all alone, love?" The voice was painfully familiar, and when Evie looked up, her suspicions were confirmed.

"Rick," Evie squeaked, feeling her heart accelerate in her chest. Her face burned as her eyebrows shot to her hairline. "What are you doing here?"

He laughed in a way that made Evie cringe. Their short-lived relationship had been a youthful mistake born of loneliness that Evie had had trouble escaping since losing her mother and brother. It was a hard lesson to learn that sometimes it was better to remain lonely than to waste companionship and energy on someone undeserving.

"I could ask you the same thing." He leaned an arm on the back of her seat, and Evie indiscreetly moved her body away from his. Rick was not unattractive. In fact, from an objective standpoint, he was very handsome.

But his personality seemed to negate anything the outward qualities might have saved. He grinned at her in a way she knew was meant to be seductive but instead made her want to gag. "Since when do you frequent places like this, Evie?"

Sighing, losing the last strands of her patience, Evie rolled her shoulders. "I'm meeting someone." She kept her words clipped, hoping he'd hear the disdain in them and move away from her.

But to her disgust, her blatant denial seemed only to encourage him. "Oh, is that right?" He reached out and ran a finger down her cheek, then laughed when Evie slapped it away. "You didn't used to have this much bite to you, did you?" he asked. "I would've extended our *friendship* a little longer."

Evie didn't point out that she had been the one to end their courtship after realizing what a selfish little ass he was. The physical aspects of their relationship had been unimpressive, nothing like the endlessly romantic scenes from some of her favorite books. After the initial euphoria of attracting such a sought-after man's attention had faded, Evie was left feeling empty, hollow. She'd ended it with him quickly after that and was affirmed in her decision when he told her what a waste of his time she was.

"If life was built on regrets, we'd have monuments the size of giants." The cheer of the crowd half drowned her words as another patron won another hand at cards.

Rick laughed, and Evie sneered, which of course he didn't detect in the slightest. "You always say the most charming little things." He looked at her like an amusing exhibit, one you stared at in wondrous curiosity while shoving fairy floss down your throat.

She needed him gone, preferably before her boss arrived. It really wasn't necessary for The Villain to know her judgment had ever been *that* poor.

"Well, it was nice seeing you again, but like I said, I'm meeting someone." Evie sounded firm and confident. It made her feel like a totally different woman from the one who had last spoken to Rick. Like she not only knew she deserved better but believed it.

She was calm, cool, collected.

That is, she would've been, if Rick would have stopped talking. "Not a...lover?" His eyes held an astonishment that made her chafe. "I must say, I'm surprised."

"Why?" Evie's tone was sweet, even docile-sounding. But someone who knew her better would hear the danger in the question, see the quick anger building behind her eyes.

"Well." Rick angled his head at her, like the question had an obvious answer. "It's *you*." Such small, seemingly innocent words, but they had the force to knock the wind from her sails. They were pointed, with so many different interpretations, her mind began throwing words at her.

Irritating. Irrational. Failure.

If the arrogant ass would've just kept that little opinion inside, she wouldn't have looked up with such vengeance. She would've ignored her boss walking through the doors, cloak pulled over his dark head. A strong attempt to get rid of Rick before The Villain arrived at her table would've been made.

But none of that happened. Rick had in no certain terms issued a label upon her that said she was too much a burden for a lover. And nothing much mattered to her pounding emotions besides proving him wrong.

When The Villain saw her, he nodded in greeting, lowering his hood slowly. Upon spying Rick staring down at her, he frowned. He began walking toward her with such purpose, her toes curled. Evie sucked in a sharp breath, gripping the table once, before nearly exploding from her seat.

She made it to her boss in two large strides and threw an arm around his middle, snuggling into his side.

He tensed all over, so quickly and rigidly that Evie thought for a moment she might have frozen him somehow. But she felt his head move down to her, and she couldn't bring herself to look at him. Even when he questioned slowly, "Sage... Might I ask why you're clinging to me like a barnacle?"

She didn't answer him, just looked back to Rick, whose jaw had fallen to the floor. Evie reached up and patted The Villain's chest awkwardly. "This is, uh...my lov...er." She stumbled over the last words, and her boss made an unearthly choking sound.

Evie did look at him then, and his face held a frank horror. His mouth was still open slightly and his brows were so furrowed that they touched. "This is Rick," Evie said with wide, pleading eyes. "He is someone I used to see."

The Villain searched her face, and Evie forced a smile, trying to mask the panic she felt. But when her boss tilted his expression back up to Rick, his face was a mask of cool.

"Hello." Clear warning rang through the hollow edges of the greeting.

Rick sized The Villain up and had the common sense to let the cocky smile slip away. "Oh, hello."

Her boss couldn't decide what to do with the hand that was hovering over Evie's shoulder. She resisted amusement when the arm fell stiffly around her. His lips thinned when Rick tracked the movement.

"Well, Rick, it was delightful seeing you, but you should go," Evie pressed. "We have lots to do!" The look of scrutiny made her squirm. "Like each other!" She laughed, but she felt her boss jolt under her hands as if she'd slapped him.

Rick coughed before shaking his head and laughing snidely. He started to strut past them but stopped to clap a hand on The Villain's shoulder. "Good luck."

Evie felt such waves of embarrassment, she needed to sit. She walked back to the table slowly but whipped around when she heard Rick cry out in pain.

The Villain had his hand around her ex-lover's shoulder, squeezing so tightly that she could see Rick's face pinched and frightened as he tried to lean away. "*Luck* is something you will most certainly need if you ever bother her again." The dark rasp to his voice sent the hairs on her arms standing on end.

Rick nodded furiously before tripping over himself to move in the other direction.

Evie sat slowly as the barmaid arrived. "Wine, whiskey, rum, whatever you have, bring it."

"For me as well, whatever she's having." The Villain sat with a heavy sigh in the seat beside her.

Pulling a few loose strands of hair behind her back, Evie leaned forward, resting her head on her hands. "Good evening, sir. Thank you for that little rescue back there."

His eyes widened, and he coughed into his hand. "Good evening, Sage. Don't…don't mention it."

Her brows pushed together in confusion until she noticed his gaze pulled to the ceiling, like he was avoiding looking at her.

"What—" But before she could finish the thought, she remembered how much her dress revealed and pulled herself backward in the seat so hard, she nearly knocked herself over, but the boss reached out quickly to grip her seat, helping the front legs meet the floor once more.

He let go of it as soon as it rested back against the ground on steady legs. "Thank you for assisting me with this. I'm sure you have plenty else to do on the evening of the week's end."

Evie snorted. "Sure. Lyssa was going to read me a new novel she's composing called *Trystan and the Lost Princess*."

"Sounds an intriguing tale." He grimaced, taking the drinks off the barmaid's tray and sliding one over to her.

"Oh yes, and then I was going to drink tea and settle down with a real book." Evie smiled, remembering Lyssa's sketches of her boss for the cover. Grinning wider when she recalled convincing Lyssa to give him a large, feathered hat.

"What sort of book?" The Villain asked, taking a sip.

"I don't know. I like romances, usually the dirty ones." And suddenly he was choking, spraying part of his drink across the table.

He brought another brightly colored handkerchief, this one yellow, to his mouth. "My apologies—I wasn't prepared for quite such an honest answer."

She shook her head at him, *tsk*ing with disapproval. "And yet you're fully aware you're conversing with *me*."

He nodded, looking resigned. "Fair point."

Swallowing a disgusting mouthful of whatever was in the wooden cup, Evie began to search the room. "So where is this elusive tavern owner who daylights as a clockmaker...for bombs?"

"He'll be here." His mouth set in a grim line. "He always arrives a few minutes after eight o'clock."

"You've been here before?" she said, voice tinged in surprise.

"No, but my people have."

Ah, his guards.

"Not that I'm complaining, but what use am I in this situation?" It had been gnawing at her all day. In truth, over the last few months, she'd discovered many hidden talents about herself. Conversing in a social setting was, unsurprisingly, not among them.

"*You've* been here before," he said pointedly.

"How did you— Never mind. So what?" she questioned.

"So an unfamiliar face arriving here alone to see the tavern owner would arouse suspicions, and I want no strings left untied."

She thought he had to be exaggerating, but when she looked to the rest of the room, there were more than a few curious eyes on them, on *him*. Or it was possible that everyone else in the room was as obsessed with his face as Evie often was.

Don't be obsessed with your boss's face, Evie!

"But why me?" she pressed. "Surely others in your employ have frequented this establishment."

Evie wasn't certain why it mattered, but she was addicted to feeling useful. Without it, what value did she hold?

"Because there are very few I can trust right now, and you just so happen to be one of them." Any flattery she would've felt at the statement evaporated when she saw his eyes flash to the gold ring tattoo on her finger.

He didn't want to trust her—he had to. She wasn't sure why it made an unpleasant difference, and yet it did.

Plastering a wide smile on her face, she took another life-altering swig of her drink. "So people see you with me and how ordinary I am and then poof! Disinterested."

She chuckled to herself about the apt description but froze when she looked up and saw that his eyes had grown cold.

"You're chronically underestimated by people." He removed his cloak, finally, to reveal an off-white starched linen shirt. In contrast with his dark hair and eyes, the shirt was a clear effort to blend in that fell like a heavy wheelbarrow...over a cliff. "We'll use that to our advantage."

"You say that as if you're not one of those people," she said, nervously twirling a lock of hair around her finger.

"I would never make the mistake of underestimating a woman like you. It would be a fatal one." His eyes were molten, his chin hard and unyielding.

Her heart pounded against her chest. It was the best compliment anyone had ever given her.

But she was snapped out of her reverie when The Villain's back straightened, his entire body tensing. "He's here."

Evie's head whipped around, despite him hissing at her not to, only to see a man so unlike what she'd imagined that she bit her lip to keep from expressing her shock. The tavern owner was young, with a friendly face and a dimpled chin. His smile was wide and open—he looked kind.

"That's him?" Evie asked in disbelief.

"Call him over, as if you know him," The Villain said, hard eyes not leaving the man across the room, who was now greeting and smiling at patrons.

"I don't even know his name," she hissed back.

"Malcolm," The Villain said with absolute venom behind each syllable. "Just call him over casually, perhaps say—"

"Malcolm! Over here!" Evie yelled, standing slightly from her seat, cupping her hands around her mouth.

The Villain put two fingers to his temples. "I'm angry with myself for even trying."

Evie ignored the people around her looking on with annoyance that she'd drawn their attention. She stuck her tongue out at one of them, and she thought her boss might faint.

Looking up from the group with twinkling eyes as they caught on to her, Malcolm picked up a pitcher of ale and made his way across the room.

He reached their table quickly, a jovial smile on his face as he said, "Good evening, my lady!" But it slipped when he caught sight of The Villain's face. "Oh, for the love of the gods." Malcolm's eyes widened. "What the fuck are you doing here, brother?"

CHAPTER 13

THE VILLAIN

His brother stared at him with a disdainful expression, which was to be expected. Considering the last time he had seen him, Trystan had attempted to stab him with a spear.

Which was, in most circumstances, how their interactions usually went.

Even now, that urge overwhelmed him when he remembered his brother was responsible for the explosives in his office that nearly blew all he'd worked for to pieces. That he'd nearly killed—

No, Trystan wouldn't think of it.

She was still there, breathing in front of him, with wide, confused eyes and in a dress that he refused to look at another moment or the table in front of them would find itself snapped in half.

Trystan stood to his full height, towering slightly taller than his brother, and narrowed his eyes. "I thought we were due for a chat," he said sardonically.

Malcolm's brown eyes shot wide, peering around each of Trystan's shoulders. "What? No spear this time?"

"You know very well I don't need such things to inflict harm."

Malcolm's eyes darkened. "Oh, believe me, brother, I know."

The pointed sting toward the destructive nature of The Villain's magic no longer hurt him as it used to. Anger lived in its place. Sage's eyes were darting between them as she clearly attempted to do her best to catch up.

"Do you know why we are here?" Trystan asked darkly.

He realized his mistake the moment the word left his lips. *We.*

Malcolm's attention shot to Evie, who, to her credit, remained calm under his scrutiny. "I can't say I know why you're here, but I'd love to know about this lovely creature you've brought with you." His brother raised Evie's delicate hand, pressing his lips to the back of it.

She laughed nervously, and Trystan wondered how his brother would continue to sling drinks once he severed that hand from his wrist and lobbed it across the room.

"I'm Evie." Her eyes shot to Trystan, a question there, but he couldn't make it out. "I'm his—your brother's assistant," she finished finally, cautiously, like she wasn't certain that was the right thing to say.

By the intrigue growing in Malcolm's eyes, it wasn't.

"His assistant?" Malcolm turned his attention back to Trystan, who was fisting his hands at his sides in an effort not to strike him. "Business that good, then?"

Trystan's gaze scanned the busy tavern. "For you, too, it would seem."

Malcolm took a step back, spreading his hands wide. "Can't complain—all the ale, women, and cards I could ever hope for. It's as good as it will get for someone like me."

Trystan found it in himself to smile, though he was certain Malcolm could sense the malevolence through the turn of his lips. "Don't sell yourself short; your clock making is something to be marveled at, indeed."

Malcolm's nostrils flared, and an undecipherable emotion flashed across his face—guilt, or the shame at being found?

He burned to throw his brother against the wall and watch the life drain from his eyes, but he knew there was a strategy to traitors, especially when it was one's own family. He wanted his brother to struggle like a filthy rodent caught in a trap. He'd marvel in it, enjoy it to indescribable degrees.

Malcolm must have caught the bloodlust in his eyes, as he took a cautious step back. "Now, now, Trystan. I don't know what you think you know, but I can assure you, you're mistaken."

Trystan could feel the dark power pulsating in him, homing in on every weak point of his brother's body. The invisible gray mist surrounded his brother, leaving small, colorful lights behind all of the places he could inflict pain. After it curled away, he saw the blue light surrounding his knee. An injury from their childhood that, if struck in just the right way, would cause him immense, permanent pain. As always, the spot around his brother's jugular glowed black, the kill spot. He'd be dead in moments.

He shouldn't have brought Sage.

Trystan wanted to kill Malcolm, but it was unfortunate that his assistant would have to witness it if he did. He wasn't sure why he'd extended the invitation for her to come in the first place; he could have easily found a way to blend into the background of the disgusting tavern on his own. But he seemed to make better decisions when she was near, less impulsive, more strategic. She steadied him like an anchor to a wayward ship, and he couldn't resist bringing her near so that he would not drift too far into his hatred.

Daring a glance in her direction, he knew it was a regrettable decision the moment his eyes caught her face, which was devoid of any visible fear.

There was *never* fear. It was disarming and confusing, enough to pull Trystan from the smoky shadows of his power and release the veiled hold he had on his brother, who gasped and fell to his knees. The tavern remained undisturbed. To the naked eye, Trystan had barely lifted a finger.

"You were going to kill me!" Malcolm gasped, face agape in realization.

Trystan nearly spit when he leaned over his brother. "It is the least of what you deserve after the reckless stunt you pulled."

Malcolm shot to his feet, shoving against Trystan's shoulders. "I don't know what the deadlands you're talking about!"

He barely moved an inch under the push of his brother's hands. "That was a mistake," he growled, raising a fist to deal a blow. But then he felt a warm hand wrap around his, bringing it down. Disarming him with the electrical shock that went careening up his arm at the feel of it.

"Sir, if you're going to murder your brother, may I suggest you don't do it in a room full of witnesses?" There was no censure in Sage's voice, just concern and perhaps a touch of curiosity.

He looked down at his assistant, pulling on the muscles in his neck because of their height difference. A small, reassuring smile was painted on her lips, her hand still resting around his fist. His knees nearly gave out when he felt her thumb stroke, just once, over the back of his hand.

Clearing his throat, he shrugged his hand out from under hers, stretching his fingers wide to relieve the sensation. "Where can we talk privately?" he asked his brother.

"A creative way to put attempting murder, but since we're blood and you have a beautiful woman to entertain, I suppose I'll oblige." Malcolm rubbed the back of his neck, a nervous gesture Trystan had seen him do countless times since they were boys. He shrugged off the sympathy.

"This way." Malcolm nodded to the doors behind the bar. "Through the kitchen, in the back."

Trystan turned toward Sage, intending to tell her to—

"I'm coming," she said, just as he'd opened his mouth to speak. "Don't tell me to stay here. Not when you dragged me out at the week's end and didn't bother to tell me it was your brother we were coming to meet."

He reeled at the sharp tone he heard in her voice, foreign and unfamiliar. "You're...angry?" He wasn't certain she was capable of that emotion. It was an interesting development and, by the way his body reacted to the scrunch of her nose, an inconvenient one as well.

"Of course I'm angry!" She rolled her eyes, bringing her hands up to her temples, cheeks growing red. "You lied to me!"

"I did not lie," he said flatly. "I merely withheld the truth."

"That's the same thing."

"No, it's not." Trystan felt his brows pinch together in confusion. "Lying would have been to tell you we were going to a masquerade ball to meet a fairy king."

Sage took a step back, narrowing her eyes. "That was oddly specific." Angling her head, realization bloomed behind her light-blue eyes. "Do you have some kind of fairy king fantasies?"

The fact that moments ago he had been on the verge of murdering his only brother, yet now was being accused of having shocking fantasies of creatures he'd never even encountered sent an unwanted wave of laughter out of his mouth.

It happened so little that the sound was foreign, even to his own ears. Rusty and low, like a doorframe of an old house that was abandoned by the owners.

But the delight overshadowing any residual anger in his assistant's eyes, that made it feel like that door was being thrown open so hard that it shook the walls, and he couldn't begin to figure out how to close it.

"Are you coming?" Malcolm called back, seeming to break a spell that had been cast between them, one where they were just two people matching wits and exchanging smiles.

"*We* are," Evie said, smiling with satisfaction as she walked past him. He turned quickly to grab her cloak and draped it over his arm, following sullenly behind her.

Malcolm gestured a hand in front of him for Sage to pass through the kitchen doors. As he watched her dark head of curls disappear beyond the door, he moved to follow, but Malcolm brought a hand up to his chest, looking entirely too sympathetic.

"You laughed."

"I know," Trystan said, shaking his head, hoping to knock the building ache out of it.

"You're fucked."

Trystan shoved Malcolm into the doorway, hard, before walking through and calling out behind him, "Shut up."

CHAPTER 14

EVIE

Evie stared hard at the wooden planks that lined the back wall of the tavern, waiting for the two *children* to join her out in the cold.

She caught sight of her boss first, who, in the torchlight, looked like a death god come to claim her soul.

Take it and whatever else you want.

Hiccupping into her hand, she groaned internally, "Too much ale."

The Villain looked at her quizzically. "It was wine."

The corners of her mouth pulled down, and she nearly missed Malcolm coming to join them. "Oh dear."

Slapping his hands together, Malcolm motioned to the empty, quiet space around them. "Well, if you're going to kill me, here would be a good spot, I think. Just be sure I'm dead before you bury me."

Evie opened her mouth to object, but Trystan had already thrown Malcolm up against a wall, holding an arm to his throat. "Did you partner with the person trying to sabotage me, or are you behind the entire operation?"

Malcolm sputtered and began to turn purple. "I don't know what you're talking about," he rasped. "If this is about the clock I sold a few weeks ago, I had no clue what it was for."

A vein began to throb in The Villain's forehead, and his lip curled in a snarl. "Why should I believe a word that comes out of your mouth?"

"Because," Malcolm gasped, "I'm your brother."

The Villain held an arm to his throat for a beat longer. Evie reached out a hand, unsure of what to do in this situation. Other than watch her boss murder a family member she hadn't known existed an hour ago.

But before the life left Malcolm's eyes, Trystan released him, turning away with barely concealed rage.

Coughing and clutching his throat, Malcolm looked at Trystan's back with widened eyes. "You didn't— I really thought you were going to do it this time, Tryst."

"I did, too, you little shit." The Villain turned, walking toward Evie as if in a daze. He draped her cloak about her shoulders, doing the buttons up under her chin. "It's cold," he muttered, turning back to his brother.

Evie barely noticed the chill, with the mix of the alcohol and the fact that her boss had just done something so out of character that she nearly fell over.

Her boss missed Malcolm's look of bemusement, but Evie didn't.

"So you believe I had no idea where that clock was going?" Malcolm asked.

Trystan turned back to her. "Do you think he's telling the truth?"

"He's *your* brother—how am I supposed to know?" She blinked at him, noticing the unrest behind his black eyes. He needed something from her. She turned back to Malcolm, really looking at him.

He was staring at his brother with the kind of reverence someone would give to King Benedict but was trying to keep that neatly concealed behind the lift of his chin and the set of his jaw.

Evie took a step toward Malcolm, noticing now so many similarities in his features. Features she saw every day across a black lacquered desk. "That clock that you knew would be attached to an explosive? It nearly killed me."

Both brothers took a sharp inhale. She continued anyway.

"I would've left behind a sick father and a little sister with no means of support. So I will ask you to be honest, because your actions didn't just nearly cause my death, but you nearly doomed them as well."

She took a step even closer, her eyes not leaving his as her voice came out steady, strong. "Did. You. Know?"

Malcolm looked her dead in the eyes. "No. I didn't."

Evie nodded and smiled lightly. "Then please tell us what you *do* know, so we can find out who did. I have a few choice words for them."

He met her smile with one of his own, a genuine one that looked nothing like the cocky grins he'd shown her thus far. Pointing a finger lightly in her direction but looking at Trystan, he said, "I quite like her."

"That seems to be the consensus. Now listen to the lady and *talk*," he said. She tried not to take offense at the dry sarcasm in his voice.

Nodding, Malcolm began spinning a tale, but there was obvious truth lining every word. "A man came to me sometime last week. I was a little…inebriated—"

"You were drunk out of your mind," Trystan interrupted. "Go on."

Evie bit back a laugh as he continued. "Right, well, I didn't see his face. He wore a hood, and like I said, I was not in my right head. He asked if I still made my 'special clocks.' I, in my vulnerable state, told him that I had one already made in my office. He paid cash, and that was it; he was off with it before I could ask any questions.

"I awoke the next morning with a raging headache and immense regret about not asking more questions and identifying the man before I gave the key to creating such a lethal device. I vowed not to sell them anymore after the last time when these awful little boys decided to use it to play a prank on their grandmother."

Evie gasped in the face of such cruelty.

Because watching someone murder their brother is fine, but you're drawing the line at old ladies in peril? Is that where we are?

Malcolm continued. "I even asked the other patrons the next night, plus my workers, but nobody saw past his hood. He moved like a ghost."

There was a hollow, chilled feeling working its way through Evie. No answers, no name, not even a description. What's worse was that, soon, whoever was doing this would know their attempt had failed. They'd see the damage they sought to inflict hadn't taken out who they'd intended, and they'd come for him again.

Evie couldn't allow that to happen.

"There must be something else," she said. "You must remember something, even the smallest detail that might help." She could hear the pleading in her own voice and hated it, but she was desperate.

Malcolm shook his head, looking to her and then behind her to his brother. "I'm sorry to both of you, truly. Tryst, I know we have our *squabbles*, but we were once thick as thieves, you and me. I would never seek to truly hurt you. There's a reason we've tried to kill each other for years and neither has ever succeeded."

"Because you're bad at killing?" The Villain bit out.

"No." Malcolm huffed a laugh, moving closer to his brother and putting a hand on his shoulder. "Because neither of us truly ever wanted to."

"Oh, I wanted to. I dream about it nightly, as a matter a fact."

He smiled knowingly. "Then why aren't I dead yet, brother?"

The Villain rolled his eyes and turned toward Evie, who was nearly bursting. Because really, this whole scene was adorable—threats of killing aside, of course. He asked, "Are you ready to leave?"

The wine or ale or whatever that swill was had given her far too much confidence. "If you're done playing with your little brother," she said, unable to hold back a grin.

He narrowed his eyes at her and began to walk to the other side of the back wall. "Thanks for nothing, Malcolm."

"Come back and have a drink another night. I promise I won't sell any more explosives to people trying to kill you," he called out with a cheeky grin. "Lovely to meet you, Evie. I hope you'll return soon."

Evie gave him a small curtsy. "Not until your drinks stop tasting like rotten vinegar." She scrunched her nose, and he laughed as she turned to catch up with her boss before he disappeared into the night.

But she halted in her tracks when Malcolm called after her one last time.

"Evie!" She turned to face him. His eyes were wide, so wide she almost saw the thought forming. "He had bright blue ink around his fingernails. When he took the clock from me, it was glowing and all over his hands."

Her heart swelled with hope. "Blue glowing ink? Well, that *is* something."

He nodded, clearly satisfied, and once more called to his brother over her head. "We both know who sells it, Tryst. It's not a coincidence."

Giving him one last smile, she barreled after her boss, the chill of the night air invigorating her. The Villain was moving at a snail-like pace, so much so that she needed to skid to a halt to remain beside him instead of ahead.

"Did you hear?"

"I did."

"And?" she pressed.

"Ink stains are hardly a lot to go on, but glowing blue ink... I suppose that leads us somewhere." His strides became longer as he approached a cropping of large trees, his black horse waiting loyally beside it. He brushed a hand between the animal's eyes, a contented sound coming from its mouth.

"It had to be magic, right? What sort of ink would glow?" Evie paused, rubbing her chin thoughtfully. "Unless your brother was even drunker than he let on."

The Villain's jaw tensed, but he didn't turn from stroking his horse gently. "Oh, Malcolm was, but I don't think he's wrong about this. It makes sense, all things considered."

Evie tilted her head to the side. "What do you mean?"

But he ignored her question, pulling his horse farther into the trees. "Will you be safe getting home?"

She angled her head at him, curious as to the concern creeping into the edges of his voice, like words bleeding through to the next page.

"Yes, I know the way. It's brightly lit with lanterns and perfectly safe."

He nodded before mounting the creature and looking down to her with an unreadable expression. "Thank you for coming with me tonight."

She nodded, a grin pulling at her lips. "Of course, sir. It's my job."

He looked like he wanted to say more, but then his mouth shut tightly. With a sharp nod, he turned and rode on into the night, leaving her in the darkness.

But as Evie walked home, she couldn't help feeling he was still nearby, keeping an eye out that she made it back safely. Or maybe that was just the fanciful thinking brought on by too much bad wine. Either way, it lightened her step and put a slight smile on her face.

Until she got home and realized that someone wasn't just trying to kill The Villain. They had wanted to use his brother, someone close to him, to destroy him.

After she changed and climbed into bed, she lay for hours, her stomach twisting with one thought. Would this enemy try to use her next to get to him?

CHAPTER 15

EVIE

The Villain never missed a sunrise when she was there.

Evie had decided to go into the office early that morning. Her week's end had been spent in the village's very small library. The dust had gone up her nose as she sifted through page after page, looking for anything she could find on magical ink, and further, on explosives. But the limited selection only had one book on magic.

Her village was small, so informative magical texts were harder to come by as the prices increased, and few people ever developed magic. Fewer still were magical specialists, the educators of the magical world. They were charged with documenting and assisting when someone's magic awoke, helping them understand it. Evie wasn't aware of any new magic users in her own village, but she knew nowadays having a specialist was a privilege not many outside the Gleaming City received.

The book she had managed to find in the sad excuse for a library was useless. All the information was general, things she knew just from listening to the people around her. The breaking point was when she came upon the last five chapters that summarized controlling your magic before it could control you.

Evie had shut it tight, placing it back on the shelf, ignoring the lingering feeling of her mother's unruly presence. Magic hadn't just controlled Nura Sage; it had destroyed her and in turn destroyed Evie's sense of safety. Her childhood gone in the blink of an eye.

This is what you get for reading books with no naughty words in them.

The chirping of birds brought her back to her present, determined to make this day a good one.

Lyssa had spent the previous night at a friend's house, and Evie's father had been in such good spirits, she figured she could spare the extra time that morning for herself.

Her original plan was to wander for a while. The dark mist of the morning air had yet to abate, giving the atmosphere a crisp bite as she walked through it. But like a moth to a very bright flame, Evie's aimless wandering led her right where she wanted most to be—at work.

You live a sad, sad life, Evie Sage.

She'd been here this early before, to help with odd tasks or check in weapons shipments to the manor. Evie looked down at her watch when she saw shooting colors of light begin to appear over the horizon. The office was expected to be full and bustling before the clock struck nine, and hers had yet to hit thirty minutes past five. Shaking her head, she touched the glittering barrier slowly forming under her fingertips, waiting for it to recognize the imprint of her palm, and swiftly entered the place she felt the most herself.

When Evie finally made it past the stairs of doom, she found her boss where he always was this early in the morning.

The grand balcony could be found just one floor below the main offices, and to Evie's knowledge it was almost never used. Likely because it was accessed through the large training room for the guards and the rest of the staff. She imagined it was hard to find the time to enjoy the fresh air between brawls. Its large glass windows were clear, unlike the stained glass of the rest of the manor, lighting the space when the sun was well in the sky. The doors, plated against white wood, stood as tall as the high, vaulted ceilings, and unlike when she normally saw them, today they were flung wide open.

Evie had no way of knowing that *this* was how The Villain spent every morning. But the handful of times she found herself in this spot at this time, when the sun's rays finally began to brush the gray stone railing, he was there.

Not wanting to disturb him, Evie turned on her heel and began to tiptoe slowly away.

She had made it two steps before she heard, "Sage, if you wanted to sneak up on me, perhaps you should've worn quieter shoes."

Evie's brows scrunched together as she turned around to see him fully facing her, knocking her nearly breathless. His black shirt was so loose, the deep V exposed most of his chest, revealing far more than a teasing amount of hard muscle. But it was his hair that made her eyes widen like saucers.

It was tousled from sleep, and though Evie had seen it in a variety of different states, she had never seen it like this, untethered, a little wild. Not since they had first met, anyway. The stubble at his chin was slightly overgrown, and Evie quietly begged for the dimple to appear.

"People who want to sneak up on other people don't usually creep in the opposite direction, sir," Evie said, raising one brow at him. She resisted the urge to ask him what he'd done for the remainder of the week's end, after they'd met his brother.

But he walked toward her, and Evie stiffened when the golden light of the morning brushed against his cheek, lighting only half his face. "Unless they're lulling you into a false sense of security. Trying to keep you calm, levelheaded, so they can strike," he said with a slight uptick of his lip. No dimple.

Damn it.

Evie's grin widened. "Are you saying I make you feel calm and levelheaded, sir?" She tilted her head and eyed him with jovial condescension. "That is so sweet."

He shook his head, looking at her with a gravity she didn't understand. "I've never felt more turned around than I have in the entire time I've made your acquaintance, Sage."

And then the dimple appeared.

The colors of the sunrise were beginning to spread over the rest of his face, surrounding the back of him. Lighting him from the inside out.

The Villain shook his head as if from a daydream and said what Evie was certain were his four favorite words.

"Cauldron brew now, Sage."

After she placed what was sincerely just liquid sugar on her boss's desk, it was still well before the rest of the office would arrive, so Evie had taken it upon herself to do what she liked, wandering back to the kitchen. She'd been munching on one of Edwin's newest creations while sipping her morning brew. It was a confection of fried dough fashioned into a ring. He'd frosted it, and Evie was quite certain that it was the best thing she'd ever tasted.

Her next bite was interrupted by a series of crashes and Blade's cries of outrage.

The dragon is awake.

Evie grabbed a second cup of brew for her friend and made her way to the back courtyard to say hello. She spotted Blade and the dragon almost immediately.

The creature was massive, with glittering, deep purple and green scales trailing up and down the spine of his large body. The dragon's eyes were wild as he pulled and turned against his collar, while Blade struggled with one hand on the chain and the other held out to calm the poor thing.

"Hello, Blade. Hello, *Draaagon.*"

The last words were said on a shriek as the creature barreled toward her, only stopping when Blade stepped before him and said, "No! We don't eat friends; we talked about this!"

The dragon's face dipped and calmed slightly at Blade's censure, turning away from both and flopping into a large heap under the shade of one of the higher balconies, making the ground beneath them shake.

"Sorry about that." Blade gave her a wide, dazzling smile. His vest today was the color of the pinkest of roses and his leather pants a bright red that clashed in the most charming of ways.

Evie's heart had slowed back down enough to smile shakily and hand over the ceramic chalice she'd brought him, thinking it a miracle not a drop had spilled.

"You're a vision!" Blade smiled back, raising his cup in salute to her.

"What has him so on edge this morning?" Evie raised a brow and looked to the animal. She swore he looked directly at her and rolled his eyes.

Am I receiving judgment from an overgrown lizard?

"He saw a mouse," Blade said gravely, and Evie was seized by a boisterous laugh.

"Is he any closer to flying?" Evie asked lightly after she recovered herself.

Blade's face took a quick turn of panic that was washed away immediately by a haughty expression. "Oh, don't worry, he will. He's just taking his time getting there, that's all."

"What about breathing fire?" Evie questioned.

Blade's face remained unchanged, but Evie did not miss the way his fist clenched. "He sneezed enough to light a few candles last week."

Evie raised a brow and pulled her lips into an encouraging smile. "Well, that is something, isn't it?"

"Actually, Evie, would you mind grabbing my book on the subject from my quarters? I'd go, but I don't want to leave him when he's like this," Blade said, giving the animal a pointed look of accusation.

"Of course, but where are your quarters?" Evie asked, scanning the area.

Blade pointed a long finger toward a set of spiral stairs that sat edged against the west side of the manor. "Those lead right up! It should be sitting on my bedside table. It's red with gold lettering on the front."

Evie nodded, and Blade kissed her cheek. "You're a lifesaver, my sweet Evie!"

"All right. Enough." Evie chuckled, making a show of wiping his kiss away from her skin and turning to climb the spiral staircase.

A door appeared at the top, and Evie pushed it lightly open, revealing a small but homey living space.

A wooden desk sat up against the window, adjacent to a narrow bed frame that Evie knew creaked just by looking at it. She smiled when she saw a little knit dragon sitting on the night table next to a wax candle that was nearly burned down the whole wick.

Evie gave a squeal of victory when she spied the burgundy-colored book with a cover that read, *Training Magical Beasts: For Novices.* Shaking her head and picking up the large volume, Evie realized that Blade must have embellished on his résumé about his "elite experiences" with magical beasts of all kinds if this was his evening reading. She tucked the book under her arm, straightened the knit dragon, which looked like it'd had many years of being loved, and turned back toward the door.

But the light coming in from the window suddenly caught against a gold paperweight peeking out from underneath Blade's desk. So Evie walked over, bent to pick it up and place it where it belonged, when she saw a slip of parchment underneath. Angling her head and holding the parchment to the light of the window, she froze.

It was a letter requesting employment, and the name signed at the bottom sent a chill up Evie's spine.

King Benedict.

Evie's heart began to pound as she read over the certificate. Blade? It couldn't be Blade; why would he—

A hand closed around her mouth, and Evie froze.

"Please don't scream."

CHAPTER 16

EVIE

Evie didn't scream.

She did, however, pull her arm forward and slam her elbow back into Blade's stomach.

"Argh!" Blade grunted, doubling over when he released her. Evie whipped around, gripping the certificate in her hand.

"What. Is. This?" she bit out.

"It's not what you think, okay? Can I explain?" Blade's eyes darted around, panicked. "Please don't tell the boss, Evie. I'm begging you." His desperation was palpable, and she softened for a second before Blade made to dive and snatch the certificate from her hands. She quickly ducked to turn away from him, and Blade's hand ended up slapping against her cheek.

"Ouch!"

Blade pulled back, a horrified expression on his face.

"You hit my face!" Evie gasped.

"I'm so sorry; it was an accident! Are you okay?" Blade reached for her, but Evie took a step back.

"You hit my face," she repeated, holding her cheek.

"I know, I'm sorry!" Blade said, holding both sides of his head. "Okay." He sucked in a breath and leaned his face toward her. "Free shot, go ahead."

Evie looked at him with an exasperated expression. "I'm not going to hit you."

Blade looked at her with wild eyes. "No! Do it! I deserve it."

"Blade, I'm not—"

"Hit me!" he wailed.

"No!" Evie screamed back, throwing her hands in the air. "This is ridiculous. Why do you have this?" She held up the letter and waited.

And waited.

And waited.

Finally, Blade sighed and sat on his bed, which did in fact creak, and looked at her with a sheepish smile. "So, I didn't exactly find the dragon egg when I was hiking in the east."

Evie trying to piece together what he was saying, knitting her eyebrows together. "You didn't…?"

Blade picked up the toy dragon on the nightstand and started nervously picking at the frayed edges. "I grew up in the Gleaming City."

"I thought you were from the coast?" Evie's brain was churning, the spike of adrenaline leaving her feeling lightheaded as it abated.

"I lied. I had to," Blade admitted, and Evie swore she saw tears glistening in the warm brown of his eyes. "I needed a place to take the dragon, a place big enough to hide and protect him. The boss never would've hired me if he'd known the truth."

"Which is…what? You worked for King Benedict?"

"No!" Blade insisted. "No, that wasn't it at all. I grew up in the Gleaming City, and my father worked as a political adviser for the king. I never really met him, save for a few times when I was a child. I hated it there."

Evie wanted to ask more as her stomach twisted, but she waited for Blade to finish.

"My father was so involved in court, and he wanted me to be, too. Every day, he waited for me to take an interest in the kingdom's political network, take an interest in anything besides the creatures that creeped outside our townhome. But I never understood people, not the way I understood animals."

Evie crossed her arms, refusing to feel sympathy for him yet in case he had plans to harm her boss. "I don't understand people, either, but that doesn't give me permission to betray them."

Blade snorted as he shook his head. "Evie, you're great with people. Everyone likes you—"

"People like you, too!" Evie interrupted, confused.

"Sure, and I like them, but at the end of the day, people don't make sense to me," Blade said, rubbing the toe of his boot along the wooden floor. "But animals, they've always made sense. They have rules, they do exactly what their instincts tell them to do, and they never waver from it. They're honest."

Evie held up the letter again. "Oh, the irony."

"I know!" Blade groaned and swiped the palm of his hand against his eyes. "I thought my father had given up on me when it came to having a career in the king's court, but he insisted I come with him a few months ago and at least *sit in* on a meeting. So I did, and it was boring. I didn't pay attention, my focus kept going in and out, until one of Rennedawn's treasurers started talking about making the kingdom a large sum from the sale of a dragon egg to a faraway kingdom that I'd never heard of."

Evie began to understand where Blade's story was going.

He continued. "I couldn't believe they had a real dragon egg, and they were just going to trade it away...for money?" Blade shook his head. "I kept thinking, *If I had a dragon egg, I would never give it away. I would do everything I could to make sure the animal was safe and loved.* But then they brought the egg out."

Evie walked over and sat next to him, ignoring the sting in her cheek.

"I had never felt that drawn to something in my entire life, such a possessiveness. It was mine; I knew it before they placed it on the table. I knew I had to take it—I had to take it and I had to disappear."

"You stole the dragon...from the king?" Evie said, her heart beginning to pound furiously in her chest.

"I found out the day they were transporting it, and I snuck in and lied, telling them I was there on business for my father. I waited until nobody was looking and just picked up the crate with the egg and took it away. Nobody stopped me, nobody said a word, and then I was gone."

"And you came here," Evie finished.

"I knew about The Villain because of my father, so I knew he was the only person not afraid of the king. Of course, the way that group of old men spoke about him, I was a little afraid to seek him out. But this was too important not to try. When the dragon hatched, it became even more urgent to find him, and when I caught wind of the whisper network to become employed, I wrote up a résumé and the boss hired me that very day."

"Blade, you must tell him the truth. He needs to know about this. I mean—this could be why—" Evie shut her lips tight before she revealed too much and stood to pace the room.

"Why someone is in here trying to sabotage him?" Blade finished.

Evie stared at him with her jaw hanging open. "How do you know about that?"

"The interns figured it out...and they never shut up," Blade said, chuckling, and Evie went ramrod straight, blowing out a breath.

"It's not funny! I thought it was you, you fool!" Evie picked up a pillow that sat against the wall and threw it at his head.

"Me?" Blade ducked as the pillow sang by and laughed. "I couldn't pull that off if I tried."

"But you *are* carrying around a gigantic lie!" Evie pressed.

"It's not gigantic—it's a tiny lie. More like an embellishment of the truth. I never actually told the boss where I got the egg, and he didn't ask, so I think it's for the best we just keep this between us, please, Evie."

She took a deep breath and considered her options. "I believe you," she said. "I do. But we can't keep this from the boss, Blade. You'll only look guiltier if he finds out on his own, and he *will* find out."

Blade sighed and gripped the knit dragon a bit closer. "I know, I know. Can you give me a little time to do it? And maybe soften him up some before I do?"

Evie tucked the employee letter into the pocket of her light-green dress. She believed Blade wasn't the traitor, but she wouldn't take any chances by leaving the slip of paper with him. "I don't have the capability to soften The Villain, Blade. Tell him and do it soon, or I will."

Evie walked toward the door, making her way down the spiral stairs once more, but she heard Blade mumble under his breath before she left. She couldn't make out the words exactly, but it sounded like he said, "You have no idea, do you?"

Her stomach twisted as she wondered if continuing to trust her friends would be the thing that doomed them all.

CHAPTER 17

EVIE

"**N**o."

The Villain sighed, and Evie felt a soft pang of sympathy at the exhaustion in his expression. "Tatianna, I won't be asking again. Put your childish vendetta aside and get in there to talk to Clarissa."

The three of them stood in a field of plush grass and an array of brightly colored flowers, far from the manor.

The sun shone above them, bringing a warmth to the air that made Evie want to curl into the grass and soak it in like a flower.

"You're one to talk about childish vendettas, *Villain*."

Tatianna emphasized the word like something she'd choked on, the bright yellow beads through her braids catching the light. Evie stood back and watched the two pretty people about to kill each other with unnecessary amusement.

"Will one of you be so kind as to tell me who Clarissa actually *is*?" Evie interjected, watching both their heads whip toward her, their eyes sharp and blazing. She took a step backward.

She'd done her best to put her confrontation with Blade from her mind. Blade would tell the boss eventually, and when that time came, she would stand as a roadblock between them so the boss didn't murder Blade where he stood. But that was a problem for another time.

After Evie had returned to her desk that morning, she'd had enough time to sort through the documents the pixies rearranged every couple of days. Until her boss had approached her desk with the request for her company to Rosewood Meadow, the side of Hickory Forest where the most magical and healing plants grew. It was theorized that one of the gods, Ashier, had accidentally spilled a large amount of magical pigment there when he and the rest of the gods and goddesses were painting their lands. Rosewood Meadow was charged with that magic and startlingly vibrant colors.

Despite what she knew of its splendor, Evie had wanted to decline the invitation. Staying in the office was the only way she could catch wind of anything from the other workers. But when Evie had looked at her boss, she swore she saw a flash of vulnerability in his request. So she agreed, embarrassingly quick.

Evie was surprised when they'd left the manor and found Tatianna leaning against a nearby tree, looking like she would rather be ripping her eyelashes out one by one than be a part of this little excursion.

They'd all walked for more than an hour in dead silence, which for Evie was the greatest type of torture. She wanted to ask so many questions, but the air was charged with something she had no wish to ignite. Every time a word formed, she bit her tongue hard.

"Clarissa is the only person in the Kingdom of Rennedawn who sells the sort of ink Malcolm saw," The Villain said, taking a purposeful step toward the healer, hands braced on his hips.

Evie peeked around his shoulder to look at the small hut beyond, which was charming in an odd sort of way. The chipped top of the roof was taken over by vines covered in mushrooms that hung down over a light wooden door, yellow daisies painted on the front. It was just the sort of way Evie would decorate a home she had all to herself.

As she pulled back and looked up at The Villain, the question fell from her lips like drops from a fountain. "Is the ink maker a forest sprite?" She was only half joking; they were known to frequent this part of the wood.

"May as well be," Tatianna muttered bitterly under her breath, turning her head to the sky and crossing her arms.

"Stop it. We need answers from her, and I need your help getting them." That vein in his forehead made a reemergence and pulsed under his frustration.

"You're using my romantic past against me," she protested with a raise of her arms, the grass seeming to stand at the motion. "And as a shield against your own sister."

At that, Evie gasped, slapping The Villain on the arm. "You have a sister!"

He rubbed his arm where she'd smacked him but made no comment at the blow. "That's hardly grounds for shock, Sage."

"Of course it is. I'm still reconciling the fact that you didn't hatch from an egg."

He pulled back his lips, clearly having no verbal response to that, before Evie turned on Tatianna next.

"And you! You wretch! After all the secrets I've shared, you didn't tell me you had a dalliance with the boss's sister?"

There was a heated feeling climbing Evie's neck. It usually felt this way when she was excluded from a conversation or made to feel like she wasn't worthy of information, but it didn't typically nag her the way it did now. The feeling moved through every corner of her body, catching in her throat, creating a lump she couldn't clear.

"Clare is hardly a topic worth speaking of. She's a selfish, horrid little beast who will stomp on your soul and rip your humanity from your bones." Tatianna's normally level demeanor was fraying, and seeing it made Evie want to hug her just a little bit.

"She also ate dirt as a child." The Villain's mouth was neutral, but there was an unmistakable dry humor to his words that made Evie bite her tongue before Tatianna cut it out.

"I only did that once." A voice as light as fallen snow floated in their direction, causing all three of them to turn toward it. The Villain's sister was a tall woman, waiflike, and Evie thought for a moment that she had been lied to and she was, in fact, looking at a forest sprite.

Her dark hair was cropped above her shoulders, pinned back with roses adorning the sides. Her dress was minimal, a thin brown shift that hung over her shoulders, and a light-green corset was loosely tied over the front. Her feet were bare as she moved through the grass toward them, a curious twinkle in her dark eyes.

"My former betrothed and my estranged brother all in one afternoon? I'll have to open a bottle of wine," she said in a singsong voice, walking past them and pushing the door to the small home open. She hauled a basket of strange-looking plants farther up her slender arm.

The Villain strode in after her, his long cape brushing past Evie's ankles, sending goose bumps down her arms. She sucked in a deep breath before grabbing Tatianna's wrist and dragging the stiff woman behind her.

"Make yourselves at home," Clare called as they entered the small archway, and Evie's eyes widened as she got her first real look inside. Whatever enchantment was on this house, it made the structure look a significant amount smaller on the outside than the grand splendor she was currently looking at.

The room had floor-to-ceiling windows that opened on a large living space, facing a wall filled with shelves. Shelves that were stacked with an assortment of different bottles, much like the ones in Tatianna's room.

"So kind of you to say, considering this used to be *my* home." Tatianna smirked, looking around the room with a disdainful sneer. "Did you redecorate? I hate it."

"Good," Clare said brightly, a manic sort of look on her face. "That's exactly what I was going for when you left."

"When you drove me away," Tatianna corrected.

"When you decided to work for my brother!" Clare's previously soft-spoken voice rang louder, high-pitched and a little squeaky.

"I only did that because *you* drove me away, and I didn't have a choice." A chair made the mistake of standing in Tatianna's path as she moved closer to Clare. It met a violent end as Tatianna swept it away so hard that it hit the wall, a leg breaking off onto the floor.

"You brat! That was my favorite chair!" Clare shrieked before diving for Tatianna, but The Villain appeared behind her, gripping her shoulders to hold her back even as she thrashed harder.

"I'll buy you twenty of those chairs if you calm down." The high command of his voice was softer than normal.

"I don't take orders from you, you ass, and I certainly don't want your blood money." Evie watched her boss flinch as his sister dug her nails into his hands.

"All money is blood money," he said, releasing her. Clare was still thrashing when he did, and she fell quickly to her knees. Tatianna subconsciously moved forward to help her and then whipped back again.

But not before Evie caught the subtle move and smiled knowingly.

Apparently things between them were far from finished.

"Hello, Clare." Evie held a hand out for the woman and helped her to her feet. "I'm Evangelina, your brother's assistant."

Clare's eyes glittered with mischief as she looked at her brother, a knowing smirk spreading across her lips. "Of course. Malcolm told me about you."

Evie's cheeks warmed. Whatever Malcolm had said to the woman, by the wickedness in her gaze, it couldn't have been anything good. "I'm flattered," Evie bit out, clearly not. "Did he also mention why we were there to see him in the first place?"

Clare narrowed her eyes, by Evie's guess hating to give up any advantage she had over them. "Something about an explosion?" She turned back to her brother. "And someone trying to kill you?"

"Are you pretending you know nothing about it?" His voice remained quiet, but there was a dangerous edge to it.

"I'm not pretending anything. I only know what I know, which is very little." Clare patted The Villain's shoulder with mock sympathy, walking past him to deposit her plants on the large table in front of the wall.

Glaring hard, Tatianna stormed over, then braced her hands on either side of the bench. "It's not just your brother who was put in danger, Clarissa." Clare's eyes flashed between Evie and Tatianna for a moment before a shield of indifference slammed down again.

"Why should I care about that?"

"Because you've sold to this person before," Trystan bit out. What was left of his patience was clearly being ground into dust by the tightness in his jaw. "Malcolm informed my assistant that whoever bought the wretched clock off him had ink stains on his fingers."

Clarissa laughed, and it echoed off the vaulted ceilings. "So what? Lots of people in the kingdom sell ink."

"But not everybody sells ink of strange colors, whether or not it was *glowing*," Evie cut in. "Ink is expensive, and black ink alone can be difficult to find, let alone colors like blue and—" Evie angled her head at a small vial that caught her eye. "Is that one gold?"

Tatianna smirked. "Gold, Clare? Getting ambitious, are we?"

Snatching the bottle before Tatianna could grab it, Clarissa shoved it into the pockets of the apron she had just donned. "Have any bargains you're looking to make? I'd give you a fair price on a few drops."

Evie reeled, noting the unearthly glow of the bottle, before placing a healthy amount of distance between her and the rest of the group. "I'll pass for now, I think. How exactly did you acquire magical ink in the first place?"

"I can ingrain magic in any object of my choosing—ink just happens to be the easiest for me to work with." Sparks flashed over her delicate fingers as she dragged them through the air like living light.

"Beautiful," Evie said in wonder, reaching out a hand to feel the warmth of the magic. Abruptly, the light was gone and Clarissa was gripping Evie's left hand hard in hers.

"Well, well. It seems the ink I sent for your birthday didn't go to waste, did it, Trystan?"

Evie followed her view to the gold markings wrapped around her pinkie finger—her employment bargain.

"This was done with your ink?"

The bargain keeper The Villain had hired to do it was a skittish old man who moved the ink like a liquid he could bend and control. Evie had known there was magic in the bargain she'd made, but she had no idea the magic lived inside the ink itself.

Clare narrowed her eyes, a satisfied smile spreading wide across her mouth. "Indeed. I didn't realize this was the purpose he'd use it for." She turned Evie's hand over, closely inspecting the other side.

Pulling it from her grasp, Evie tucked it back into her side, feeling more than a little defensive of her boss. "It was a necessity, of course, for someone in his position."

The Villain looked at her from the corner of the room, almost appearing grateful for her assistance.

The words Evie spoke didn't seem to register to The Villain's sister. "Yes, I'm sure he tells you everything he does is necessary. Everything has a reason, no matter how nefarious."

"Nefarious is in the job title. Now, perhaps you'd be willing to quit stalling and tell me the name of every person who's bought blue ink from you in the last three months." The Villain gritted his teeth, standing to full height and practically creating shadows around him with his anger.

For the first time since they'd arrived, Clare looked at her brother like he was someone to fear, someone to run from. Evie knew that's exactly what he wanted.

"I only sold two jars in the last month, Trystan. The first was to a forlorn widower, and the other…"

"What? The other what?" Tatianna pressed.

Clare winced before pulling a tattered book out from underneath the floorboards. "I didn't know who he was until he signed his name."

The Villain's hand landed heavily on the table. "Tell me. Now."

"The man introduced himself as Lark Moray." She bit her lip and pointed to the signature below the name. "But he signed the ledger with one of the Valiant Guards' sigils."

The boss pored over the book, flipping page after page until every muscle seemed to lock at once. Then he turned on his heel and strode past them both, yanking the door open and striding out.

Clare stalked after him, gripping the black shirt on his forearms. "When is it going to stop, Tryst?" Her voice rose with each word. "When will it be enough that you'll finally stop?"

Evie and Tatianna followed them both outside, standing and watching the scene helplessly.

Her boss stood there quietly for a moment before gently prying Clare's fingers from his arm. "*King* Benedict went after you and Malcolm and everything I've built to oppose him. I knew that when this day would come, only one of us would make it out alive. I've learned to live with that."

"This last hateful decade of revenge can end—you can make it so! He'd hardly recognize you now. You can move on." The crack in Clarissa's voice splintered something in Evie's heart.

"You knew King Benedict?" Evie asked quietly.

His brows pulled down as a haunted look came over his dark eyes. "I worked for him…for a time." He sucked in a large breath, seeming to brace himself for pain.

Evie's head whipped back before she looked at him with wide eyes. "You *worked* for King Benedict? When?"

Trystan, The Villain, looked at Evie with a gravity that made her heart sink. "Before."

"Before what?" Evie said, exasperated and a little fearful of his response.

"Before I became…what I am now." There was a sharpness punctuating the sentence, like the very idea was painful.

"A monster," Clarissa snapped, a bitter, wounded expression on her face. Before Evie could assess her boss's reaction, though, Clarissa spun around and stormed back inside her home. She slammed the door, and the daisies painted on the wooden surface seemed to jump from the force.

"Sir, that's not— I don't think you're—um." Evie couldn't think of the right thing to say, so instead she settled for asking, "What happened between you and King Benedict?"

The Villain's face was unreadable as he said, "I don't see how that is important for *you* to know, Sage."

The words weren't said to be cruel—Evie could tell he meant them as a dry and logical statement. Still, it felt pointed, and it stung. The blow of it must've shown on her face, because his mask seemed to crack just the tiniest bit.

"Sage, I did not mean—"

"I think it's time to head back, don't you?" she said, then started to walk into the forest without waiting to see if anyone followed. She kept her shoulders back, ignoring the prickling along the sides of her neck and cheeks. The grass crunched under her boots as she walked, helping drown out the sound of Tatianna's calls for her to wait for them. Evie just wanted to return to the manor before one more ridiculous thing left her lips.

Tatianna's voice grew distant, but Evie still heard her say, "Were you always this dumb, Trystan? Or is it a recently acquired skill?"

"As always, thank you for your help, Tati," The Villain replied as the heavy fall of his boots caught up to her.

Sunlight brushed against Evie's cheek, but she no longer felt the heat as keenly as she did before. Branches brushed against her arms as she was suddenly struck by all the things she didn't know.

And all the ways that lack of knowledge could get Trystan killed if she didn't find a way to stop it—soon.

CHAPTER 18

THE VILLAIN

His assistant was being painfully silent.

The two of them walked slowly back toward "Massacre Manor" after another disastrous family reunion. What spiteful god did Trystan anger to endure seeing not one but two of his family members in so short a span of time?

Trystan glanced over his shoulder to check on Tatianna, but his healer, one of the only tolerable people in his acquaintance, was staring at his sister's front door with a longing expression.

He shrugged and continued bounding after his fleeing assistant. Tatianna would follow when she was ready.

More importantly, Benedict's angle was beginning to become clear, sending the traitor through Trystan's family members. To hurt him? Possible but unlikely. The king knew very well Trystan's nature didn't leave room to be hurt by petty power plays.

Though if anything stung, it was the anger Clarissa had inflicted when she'd called him a "monster." It had not been his first experience with that word—he was quite at home with it, in fact; he'd learned to enjoy the sound of it. But it had been said with Clare's face and her voice that was so like his mother's that it felt like his chest had been cleaved in two.

In Trystan's deepest, most private thoughts, he imagined what it would be like to walk into his brother's tavern a different man. Clare and Tatianna would be sitting there, hands linked, waving him over with a glass of wine outstretched for him. Trystan would sit with them all, enjoy their company, and feel a sense of belonging among his family.

But that would never happen.

More proof that emotions were a useless inconvenience he needed to shove aside at every opportunity. Because of them, things kept going wrong in every sense of the word. Malcolm seemed to think there was some sort of truce between them, his sister looked at him like the scum on the bottom of her shoe, his workers were growing more restless by the day with the impending threats, and his assistant...

His assistant was walking in long strides, swinging her arms so hard that she looked a bit like a windmill. "You're being quiet...which is unusual," he blurted out and almost smacked his palm against his forehead.

She halted abruptly and shot him an astonished expression.

Yes, I did just make an ass of myself. Thank you for noticing.

The regret he was feeling must have been a direct result of spending too much time with his assistant, for he never wasted time on it if he could help it.

Trystan blinked away from his thoughts and attempted to listen to the words spilling from Sage's lips. But her nose was scrunched, and that seemed to be a confusing source of distraction for him.

"Are you listening?" she demanded, snapping him from his imaginings.

The tip of my sword appears to be a fine place to rest.

Empirically speaking, his assistant was beautiful. It would be inaccurate for him to even attempt to deny it. He'd thought it the moment they met in the forest, the sunlight spilling over her shoulders and the sharpness in her eyes softened by misplaced kindness. But beauty was inconsequential to him. Well, it usually was.

The women he allowed himself to be intimate with, when he did seek out such things, possessed a jaded view of the world that was familiar to him. He looked at sex like taking care of an intrinsic need, like eating or sleeping. He saw no sense in affection or admiration, though he felt a panicked twinge of both things when looking at his assistant's face.

Even though now she was still looking at him like he'd kicked her.

And that, for some reason, was...intolerable.

"Excuse me." He cleared his throat. "There was a bee, and it distracted me."

There was not a chance in the deadlands, where most spent their afterlife, that she would believe him.

"I'm sure." She squinted, and Trystan began to feel a bit weathered by her stare.

He took a deep breath, ran a hand through his hair…and gave in. "The story between King Benedict and me is a long one. Only my family knows it in its entirety. It is not that I do not want to share it with you. I simply do not think I know how." It was honest, something he endeavored to be, if nothing else.

Her expression softened, and it felt as if it connected to a thread in his chest, pulling it tight. "I have things like that in my past, too. I understand."

Now *that* sparked a flare of curiosity so strong, it nearly knocked him off his feet, but he merely nodded. "Do we have a truce between us, then, Sage?" He held out a hesitant hand toward hers, and she smiled in a way that sent off warning bells in his head. The warmth of her hand distracted him, however.

She leaned in a bit, a twinkle shining from the blue of her eyes. "Now where would the fun in that be, sir?" she said in a pseudo whisper before releasing him and turning away.

Suddenly, he was more afraid of exactly how his assistant would exact her revenge than the traitor he'd been hunting. Although both would likely be the death of him soon.

CHAPTER 19

EVIE

She was going to fall.

She arched her feet up onto her tiptoes, holding an arm out to steady herself. Her other hand was outstretched, trying to knock open the vent above the boss's desk. She growled in frustration when she was short by only a few inches. The ventilation system throughout the manor was meant to heat and cool each room to a comfortable temperature, all vents leading back to the deepest parts of the stone structure.

But they were rarely used or opened because of how unpredictable the fire-and-ice wand was, a magic-ingrained wand they'd smuggled from the merfolk. They were meant to cool and heat as needed, but the object seemed to be cursed to shoot out whatever temperature pleased it, which was rarely the right one.

So the wand was locked up, and the vents remained closed. Except for this one; this one, Evie needed open. When scanning the architectural layout of the manor, she'd seen that the vent above the boss's desk was connected directly to the one where most of the other workers took their midday meal. If she could just get the damn thing open, there was a chance the information they needed would float directly onto the boss's desk.

Literally, since she was still standing on it.

The boss was nowhere to be seen when the idea struck, and since most of the workers had cleared into the mess hall, this seemed like her only chance. In hindsight, a ladder would've been wise. Something Kingsley reminded her of when he'd watched her climb on the desk from the other side, holding one sign that said BAD and another that said IDEA.

"I don't like that negativity," Evie said to him, and, with a determined jump, her stockinged feet left the surface of the desk. She felt the vent give under her fingers, and the flitting of voices began to spill through as her feet landed back on the desk.

"Whoa. I can't believe that worked."

"Nor can I."

The dry voice stalled her moment of victory, and Evie whipped around to the open office door, where the boss was now leaning against the jamb, a brow raised.

"I opened the vent," she announced, pointing to it like that wasn't already very clear.

"I can see." His eyes shot to her discarded shoes on the floor and then to her stockinged feet on his desk before landing on her face again.

"I didn't want to put the bottoms of my shoes on your desk. I thought that would be rude," she explained sensibly.

"Yes, one must observe the proper etiquette when standing on other people's furniture."

Evie nodded and pretended to take his sarcasm seriously. "Exactly. As for the vent, now we can hear what the workers say about you when you're not in the room."

"All bad things, I hope," he said as he walked toward her. He must have cleaned up since this morning, as his loose black shirt was tucked into his functional leather breeches, emphasizing his trim waist. Coughing, Evie tilted her head up at the vent, stretching onto her tiptoes to try and make out the voices.

"It's too muffled." When she glanced at him again, he was watching her with an unreadable expression. "You should get up here; you'll hear better because—" But she was cut off by her foot catching on a loose piece of parchment, and then she was falling.

She let out a little yelp, waiting for the impact of the ground to hit, but the boss dove forward, attempting to break her fall. Instead, of course, she took them both down. When they landed, The Villain was on the ground, taking most of the impact, and Evie was on top of him.

Mortification was so palpable, it was like she could touch it. Her hands landed on either side of his head, pushing herself upward.

"Whoops."

"Indeed. Whoops." His words sounded like they'd been dragged across gravel, but he didn't look injured. He sighed, and his head landed back against the stone floor beneath him. "Are you unharmed?"

"Yes, you broke my fall."

"Lucky me," he said flatly, hand coming up to brush back his hair. Evie had seen him mess with it quite often. Almost as if it was a nervous habit, but he didn't seem the type to have those.

"Is that a bald spot?" Evie asked innocently, tilting her head to the side and rubbing her chin as she sat upright.

"What?" he barked, looking so panicked that Evie didn't have the heart to keep up the jest.

"I kid, Evil Overlord. Your perfect hair is intact."

"It's just hair; it doesn't matter." But the childish grumble in his voice made Evie smile, and a sudden warmness filled the room that had nothing to do with the open vent. They stayed still for a moment before a crooked grin pulled at his lips and Evie smiled so wide that her cheeks felt like they'd split open.

"Sage?"

"What?" she said, slightly embarrassed by the breathless tone of her voice.

"Could you, umm, dismount me?"

"Oh, of course!" she yelped, throwing herself off him quickly and rising to her feet to retrieve her discarded shoes. She giggled nervously. "I almost forgot I was on top of you."

The Villain rose slowly, gripping his desk to hoist himself all the way up. He was facing away from her when he said, "How nice for you."

"I should've asked before I opened the vent." Evie winced. He was obviously very put out with her.

"No," he said, surprising her. "It was a good idea. I'm just distracted by…the past, I suppose."

Evie's chest squeezed tight, and she walked around the edge of his desk so she could see his face. "You can talk about it if you want to." She held up her pinkie. "I'm sworn to secrecy anyway, remember?"

His dark gaze held hers, lowering to her smile, then back up to her eyes. "I suppose I could tell you…"

And then Becky busted through the door.

Honestly, it was like the woman had a bell go off anytime someone was feeling joy.

"Oh!" Becky said, eyes wide and innocent as she caught the two of them only inches apart. "I'm sorry. I knocked. Am I interrupting something...important?"

"As a matter a fact—" Evie started.

"Of course not," the boss said over her, seeming to snap from whatever spell had been holding both of them. "Sage was giving her normal level of impertinence, and I was entertaining her."

Evie glared at him, ignoring the flash of remorse in his eyes.

Becky's own eyes widened for a moment, but that expression was quickly replaced with one of righteous victory. "I'm so sorry, sir. I just thought Evie would want this back. I saw it fall out of her pocket earlier." Becky held up the piece of paper, and Evie's stomach dropped when she saw what it was.

King Benedict's offer of employment letter that she'd found in Blade's room.

Evie watched in quiet horror as her boss angled his head closer, accepting the letter from Becky's hands and then reading it furiously.

· "Sage, explain this." Any humor or lightness was gone, and Evie sighed.

She didn't want to be the one to tell him about Blade's deceit, but she'd been given no choice. "Sir, that is— Well, it's—"

But The Villain cut her off before the words could come to her.

"It's interesting that you'd like to know the secrets of my own past when it seems you have many of your own." He had an unfamiliar mocking look on his face that made a bubble of anger curl so tight within Evie, the rest of her feelings needed to move over to make room for it.

"If you would just let me explain, sir. I would've told you about the letter sooner, but it wasn't my place. I wanted to give...someone else the chance to tell you first."

Evie hadn't had the opportunity to read through the entire letter, but she knew it didn't look good. The greeting at the top didn't include Blade's name, and the listing of his qualifications for the job were also incredibly vague.

With the accusations in her boss's eyes, Evie knew what sort of conclusion he was drawing, and while she knew she shouldn't take it personally, it felt like someone had grabbed ahold of her insides and twisted so hard, she wanted to double over.

Before Evie could recover herself, The Villain continued. "I should say thank you. For proving even promised trust can be broken."

Evie glanced at the gold ink encircling her finger, holding it up for The Villain to see. "How can you say I can't be trusted?"

The Villain sneered. "The magic only prevents you from doing anything to harm me. I stopped caring who lied to me long ago."

Evie gasped, her head spinning. "You don't trust *me*?"

How had one simple misunderstanding turned into this—this moment where Evie realized all the other moments she'd shared with The Villain, all the times she'd felt there was mutual respect, were one-sided? And if he didn't trust her, what *else* did he really think of her?

Evie's father had always told her she had a gift for keeping people together, had encouraged her to use that gift at every turn. He'd relied on Evie heavily after her mother had Lyssa and her magic arrived. When Nura Sage had fallen into such despair, it was Evie's job to get her out of bed, to fix it. With no help from her father or even her brother, Gideon.

Evie had thought The Villain valued her. Found her useful, too. Appreciated her help.

But look at how her family had crumbled, how it had broken, how she'd failed. Maybe The Villain had simply taken pity on her, taken her in when no one else had wanted her. She *was* the one who'd mentioned needing employment the first time they'd met...

Evie reeled back and put a hand over her mouth as anger, helplessness, and shame made everything start to blur around her. The Villain seemed to flinch. Even Becky stilled as Evie pulled in several large gulps of air.

But The Villain recovered whatever imbalance he had suffered, and his eyebrows slashed downward as he demanded again, "Well? What do you have to say for yourself?" He gripped the letter so tightly in his fist that it began to crumple, and Evie could no longer stand there and listen to another harsh word.

She held his gaze, her stomach twisting. Shaking her head, she pushed her way past him to get to her desk as fast as she could. Becky at least had the good grace to look a little apologetic as Evie stormed past.

"Where in the deadlands are you going, Sage?" her boss called after her.

"I'm going home!" she tossed back, not bothering to slow her step.

The bustle around them went deadly silent as she marched out of her boss's office, the man following close behind.

"In the middle of a workday?" he asked furiously.

"It's not a workday for me," she choked out as an awful bitterness closed her throat.

"Oh no?" he asked incredulously.

"No," she managed, poison coating her words, her heart.

"How do you figure that? When every other employee is doing as they're *told*." He was almost in front of her again, but she held up a palm, stopping him in his tracks.

And then she said words that felt like they sucked the very air from the room. "Well, it's a good thing I'm not an employee anymore." Tears burned the corners of her eyes, but she blinked them away, keeping her expression neutral.

"What did you say?" His voice was low and distant.

"I quit."

She yanked open her desk drawer and grabbed her knapsack, throwing the strap over her shoulder as she strode to the cloak rack and grabbed hers. She swallowed back a sob, her chin high as she reached the doorway—and then she took off.

Flying down the stairs, leaving nothing but pain in her wake, Evie prayed to be swallowed into the earth and perhaps reborn as a tree, where the only thing she would be expected to do was grow.

She tied her cloak about her shoulders, replaying every moment in her mind as she always did. Analyzing every move, every word said. Over and over, until she wanted to find her reflection somewhere and smash it just to watch herself break.

Tears were flowing freely now, and she used the back of her hand and swiped it against her face. Striding past the gate, she kept walking until she began to run again. Her lungs burned in her chest, and she felt the tears begin to mingle with the sweat dripping from her forehead, but she didn't care, wanting to feel the weight of her own actions.

Holding her hand up to see her pinkie finger, feeling the mark pulse underneath a broken bargain, dread pounded in her veins. She'd quit. When she'd made a vow to work for The Villain, to be loyal, she knew the consequences would be fatal. According to one of the Malevolent Guard members, the ink in their bargains could quickly become a poison, released into the body at even the hint of betrayal.

In quitting her job, Evie may have just signed her own death warrant.

CHAPTER 20

THE VILLAIN

The next morning, Blade Gushiken's voice was laced with earnest amusement. "I think you're going to wear a hole in the floor, boss."

Trystan nearly took the man's head off.

But he halted his pacing of his office floor, not caring for the nervous looks his employees were giving him through the doorway. Or did he care?

He ran a hand through his hair. He couldn't think properly under these conditions.

Without Sage, he'd had to go back to drinking his cauldron brew black, as Edwin thought he always did. The ogre had been his village's baker when Trystan was just a boy, and he was one of the only beings in this world Trystan really believed was all goodness. It's why Sage had to spend her mornings covertly adding sweetness to the brew. If Edwin found out Trystan didn't like the drink he'd worked so hard to develop, it might wound him.

Caring about other people is very irritating.

He thought of his assistant and began pacing once more. Trystan expected her to fly through the doors of his office that morning, a demure apology on her lips and perhaps a pastry for him in hand.

A sensible explanation for why she had that letter in the first place would follow, and all would go back to how it was.

Trystan had spent the night clearing his head and was prepared to meet Sage's pleading with logical and fair judgment. After all, he'd been seconds away from telling her a secret that he'd scarcely spoken aloud to *anyone*.

The worst of it was *wanting* to trust someone. If you remained indifferent, the fallible could never fail you and you would remain safe. Trystan had *wanted* to trust her, and that was not Sage's fault but his own.

In addition to that problem, the office seemed to be going to shambles.

Rebecka had reported three interns nearly brawling to the death that morning because they'd been placed on the same cleaning crew in the dungeons. He hadn't been aware Sage knew the interns well enough to avoid skirmishes among them. Clever, but not clever enough to make him rethink her obvious transgressions.

Then there'd been some sob story about one of the men's betrothed sleeping with his cousin, and Trystan had tuned out his Humans and Magical Creatures Resource Manager before the melodrama rotted his brain.

But that had only been the first issue of the day. It seemed that in the few months Sage had been here, she'd ingrained herself into nearly every moving wheel in his organization, like vines weaving through the foundation of a very old house, becoming a part of it. The Villain had had a fully functioning business before her, hadn't he? One would have no clue, since the sky seemed to be falling at nearly every point of the morning thus far.

A weapons shipment came in, but only Sage, ever the notetaker in her gold-foiled journal, had any idea which shipment they had been expecting. It had taken twenty employees away from their current tasks to open every crate so they could catalog what was inside.

Their magical filing cabinet, envy of all because of its ability to alphabetize any document that entered the enchanted space, had broken. The A's were where the X's should have been, and the L, M, N, O, and P files had simply been...eaten by the wood.

When Trystan had finally brought himself to ask if there was anyone who knew how to fix it, they replied as if they'd rehearsed it for his own torture. "Ms. Sage usually knows."

He avoided Tatianna when he could, and for good reason, as the woman traded in office gossip. But an hour ago, Trystan had found himself feeling desperate to prove he was right to distrust his assistant, so he'd leaned into the healer's domain to ask if she'd heard anyone in the office sharing an incriminating secret with her about Sage. The healer had looked at him with such venomous disdain, Trystan thought she must have been poisoning him with her eyes.

He felt like his whole body was burning.

"No," she'd replied flatly. "I haven't."

The Villain had nodded and cleared his throat and then left the healer's room feeling almost…embarrassed?

What a nightmare this was.

And as if everything wasn't already ripping apart at the seams, Blade was now occupying Trystan's attention with something he knew would turn his already sour mood into straight-up rotten.

"Don't you have a beast to tame?" Trystan barked at Blade, praying to the gods that the dragon trainer would leave him to sulk.

"That's exactly what I wanted to talk to you about—" Blade turned as Rebecka made her way to The Villain's desk to set down another chalice of the foul, non-sugared brew. "Good morning, Rebecka."

"It is, isn't it?" She nodded happily, a wide smile spreading beneath her thick frames.

Blade frowned at her back as she returned to her new desk—right outside Trystan's office. The dragon trainer walked over and closed the door behind her before turning to Trystan again. "I don't care how hard you need to beg—just do it, please. That was terrifying." He shivered, like Ms. Erring's happiness was a sign of an apocalyptic end.

"I don't beg. For anything," The Villain insisted, crossing his arms and noting his shirt didn't feel quite as soft as when Sage managed the launderers. Today, his shirts were scratchy and irritating.

"Sage is the one who made the dramatic declaration and quit. She is the one who must apologize, if I still allow her a position here after her obvious deceit with that letter."

The dragon trainer stiffened, his hands fidgeting as his eyes darted toward the extra growth in Trystan's usually cleanly honed stubble on his chin. "Rough night?" Blade asked.

"I'll cut your tongue out," Trystan threatened.

"Right." Blade nodded. "Fair. Before you do that, can you settle a matter for me?"

Trystan pinched the bridge of his nose, battling away a writhing headache. "What?"

"I would like your permission to name the dragon."

He narrowed his eyes in confusion. "Did you not name him already?"

"All the books say you're not supposed to name them until after they've completed their training," Blade insisted.

"And how reputable is this book you're taking such careful advice from?"

"Well…" He chuckled nervously, scratching the back of his neck. "I'm unsure. Mostly because everything it's told me to do thus far seems to only anger or frighten the wits out of him. But I figure I would be a little crabby, too, if I had nothing to call myself."

"I have a few things I'd like to call you." Trystan tried to add a threatening edge to his voice, but all his senses felt duller this morning, like he'd been in the dark for too long.

"Can you suggest a few for the dragon first?" The hopeful look in the trainer's eyes reminded Trystan too much of someone he needed to stop thinking about before he sent a chair through the window.

"I don't know." Trystan paused, a strange thought coming over him. "Fluffy. Name him Fluffy."

Blade's head whipped backward, mouth falling slightly open. "Fluffy…sir?"

"It's an adequate name, I'm told," he muttered defensively. Trystan didn't like the appraising look in the trainer's eyes. "Now get out of my face, Gushiken. I'm very busy."

Blade nodded, taking a step backward. "Right away, sir." He spun toward the door but stopped, his palm above the handle. The brawny man swallowed hard, then turned back to face Trystan, looking like he was about to lose his lunch.

"What—?"

But Trystan never finished his sentence, because Blade's words were tumbling out so quick, several veins in the man's forehead began to pop.

"It was me, sir! The employment offer from King Benedict—it was mine."

Trystan froze, idly wondering how his heart could be pounding in his chest when his blood had turned to ice.

"Explain," he bit out, the word so clipped and cold, he watched Blade shiver.

Gushiken stepped forward, pushing his shoulders back, clearly trying to summon bravery. His story spilled out in waves, and Trystan didn't speak until he knew the dragon trainer had finished.

Blade spoke of his childhood in the kingdom's capital, his father's political career on Rennedawn's council, Blade's affinity for animals and magical creatures. How he'd only kept the letter to remind himself that he'd made the right choice coming here.

Trystan's body went taut when Blade's story pulled in Evie. While Blade spoke, Trystan kept his face impassive, but his mind was racing, adrenaline pumping through him.

"She kept the letter to make sure I fessed up. She gave me the chance to tell you myself because she is kind and a good friend. But make no mistake, sir; she is completely loyal to you. This whole thing is all my fault. If you want to fire me or, you know…murder me? I completely understand."

I wanted to give…someone else the chance to tell you first.

Sage's voice cut through the pounding blackness that was feeding into The Villain's mind, like a rainbow slicing through the endings of a vicious storm.

I should say thank you. For proving even promised trust can be broken.

Sage had stumbled backward like he'd struck her—*because he had*. But The Villain had been too stubborn, too triggered by his past betrayals to see anything but his own hurt.

Trystan had called her a hypocrite when it was becoming glaringly obvious the only person guilty of hypocrisy was himself.

She had wanted him to have enough faith in her, to trust her, and instead he'd punished her. Trystan held Blade's gaze. "You should not have kept this from me, Gushiken."

Blade nodded, ducking his head. "If I had known the trouble it would cause, believe me, I wouldn't have."

"Believe you?" Something dark was creeping into Trystan's voice as he begrudgingly realized what it felt like to be wrong. It felt *horrible*. "I don't know what to believe right now. But believe this: if you ever find yourself lying to me again or implicating another employee because of your carelessness, you will find your head adorning my rafters."

Blade looked queasy, and Trystan resisted the urge to chuck the man through the window.

Gushiken waved both hands in front of his face. "No, no! I promise to never keep a secret from you again, sir! I will head to the healer now to have a magical oath burned into my flesh, in fact." And with that, Blade turned to take off toward Tatianna's quarters. As he pulled the door open, he sheepishly glanced back at The Villain, something vulnerable in the man's expression.

"Um, sir…does this mean I can keep my job? That the dragon and I can remain?"

It wasn't mercy, what Trystan said next, but it was alarmingly close to it. "Yes. Against my better judgment, you may remain."

"Thank you, sir!" Blade said, his voice far away as Trystan had already moved toward a stained glass window, unlatching the glass and pushing it open to let the summer air waft over him.

The sunlight hit his face, but he felt no warmth, like Sage had dragged even the power of the sun away with her.

He hadn't realized the dragon trainer was still standing in his office until Trystan heard him ask a question so small and quiet, he nearly missed it.

"Sir…what about Evie?"

When Trystan remained silent, he heard Blade's footsteps fade away until they were gone completely.

But the dragon trainer's question echoed through his mind so many times, Trystan wanted to scratch it out.

What about Evie?

CHAPTER 21

EVIE

Evie always knew she'd die at the hands of her own foolishness. She'd landed herself in far too many dangerous situations, unintentionally, for the odds to not fall against her at some point in time.

She'd straddled her boss and then quit her job, all in one day.

Groaning into her hands, she rolled over in her bed, ignoring Lyssa when she hesitantly nudged the door open.

"I have to go to school." She lightly placed something on the small table beside Evie's bed. "I made you some tea that always helps Papa... when he's feeling sick."

Flipping over immediately to face her sister, Evie rushed to assure her she was not unwell, desperate to get rid of the forlorn look in her sister's expression. "It's okay, Lyssa, I promise I'm not sick the way Papa is."

Her sister's shoulders relaxed. "What kind of sickness is it, then? You never miss work."

Evie tapped her chest with her palm, feeling the lump in her throat moving to sit underneath her hand. "It's a sick feeling here. In my heart." It was difficult to decipher her feelings on her own, let alone attempt to explain them to a ten-year-old.

"Oh, you're sad," her sister said, nodding.

"Well..." She waited, considering the words. "Actually, yes, I suppose that sums it up pretty nicely."

"You use too many words to say simple things, Evie." Her sister patted her head before grabbing a book she'd placed on the ground.

"You should only use a couple. People understand better that way."

Smiling and feeling a little lighter, Evie got out of bed and waved her sister off. She watched out the window as Lyssa ran in the direction of her school. Then she padded barefoot across the kitchen floor and pulled the spigot to get a cup of water.

She looked down to the employer's bargain on her pinkie finger, narrowing her eyes at it. She'd expected some sort of recourse for disobeying the promise. After all, she'd *quit*. Where was her reckoning? Or was it a slow death? Would she be going about her day and then suddenly her heart would stop? She'd have to fix it, or Lyssa would be left all alone and—

A rasping cough came from behind her, causing her to jump and spill her cup on the floor. "I'm sorry," her father rasped again, collapsing hard into the chair, face pale and drawn. "I didn't mean to frighten you."

"Papa." She moved to his side, crouching before him. "Have you been taking the medicine my friend made special for you?"

He smiled guiltily, taking a shaky hand to his forehead to dab off the sweat there. "I didn't think I needed it. I've been feeling so much better."

Evie shook her head, trying not to chastise him. Her father didn't always do well to give care where he should. After Gideon died and her mother departed soon after, Evie's father had fallen into such despair, he couldn't bring himself to even hold Lyssa. They'd decided as a family that Evie would continue her education at home, away from the schoolhouse and all her friends, to assist in raising her little sister.

A sacrificed childhood was a small penance for how Evie had failed her family, her mother, Gideon. She wondered if that was why she could be so impulsive, so headstrong. Every childish part of her should've had the chance to change and grow. But instead, it was stifled, like a flower cut right as it was about to bloom.

Her father's eyes suddenly widened, and he attempted to stand on shaky legs. "Is Lyssa still here? I don't want to frighten her. She's been so happy seeing me so well."

"She's off to school already," Evie assured him. She moved his arm over her shoulder and walked him back to his bedroom. "Papa, you need to take better care of yourself. If not for your own sake, then for Lyssa's."

Evie helped him gently onto the bed, pulling the covers up under his chin, then reached into the drawer of his dresser. Quickly finding the small vial of medicine, she measured out a few drops. "Open," she commanded.

After the medicine had a few minutes to make its way through his system, her father's eyes began to close. "Why aren't you at work today, dear one?"

Evie pulled the knitted blanket off the cushioned armchair beside her father's bed and draped it around her waist as she sat down.

"I had a fight with my boss," she said, pleased to be able to share at least an ounce of honesty with her father.

His mouth pinched. "Whatever it is, I'm sure it wasn't all that bad." Smiling at her, he continued. "Perhaps you might go and apologize."

Evie tried to ignore the sting that her father assumed it was she who did something wrong. "I don't think that would help the situation very much, unfortunately."

He gave her a dubious look, his eyes beginning to droop again. "If you want an old man's advice, be honest." Clearing his throat once more and placing a hand on his chest, her father got a faraway look in his eyes. "There is so much that can be fixed by honesty, if you're brave enough to use it. It's something I wish I had been more with your mother."

The mention of Nura surprised Evie. "I— You never talk about Mama."

Her father smiled sadly at her, causing a dull ache to build in her chest. "It is painful even now, to think of what your mother did to your brother. What she could've done to you and Lyssa."

"I don't think she meant to hurt us that day, Papa." After her mother had given birth to Lyssa, their mother's magic awoke in a flurry of divine light. Nura Sage had been blessed by the gods with the power of starlight. A magic so pure and rare, when the magical specialist came to assess her, he'd brought tidings of joy from King Benedict himself. But what was supposed to be a divine blessing became their family's very downfall.

The months that followed Lyssa's birth were filled with unending sadness. Their mother's magic seemed to drain every ounce of life from her; even the color in Nura Sage's cheeks had disappeared. Evie's father had urged her to distract her mother, lighten her load. Gideon had needed to focus on his schoolwork—something Evie would've liked to do as well, but Gideon hadn't known that. He was the sort of brother who would give you his toy if he saw you wanted to play with it. Evie knew he'd give up too much for her if she asked, so she never did.

And then everything got worse.

"I hate even *thinking* of that day." Her father's face twisted into a bitter expression before relaxing. "I was working when your mother dragged you three to the dandelion fields, and I regret going in early that morning every day of my life."

Evie's mother had Lyssa in a sling around her neck the day she finally got out of bed. Her eyes had been crazed, but she'd looked alive. It was why Evie and Gideon had agreed to go on a morning stroll with her to what had been their favorite spot before Lyssa was born. Her mother had looked so beautiful. Her bronzed skin glistened against the rising sun, her eyes lined with kohl and lips rouged with red.

"She wanted to play with her magic. That was all," Evie said so quietly, it was practically a whisper.

Their mother had made the dandelions glow, had made the light move like the plants moved with it. She'd held a ball of starlight in her hand and begged Gideon to go catch it.

Evie had watched her brother run past the field, seeing too late that the small ball of light was getting larger and larger. Nobody knew what was happening until Gideon's screams enveloped the field and scorched ground took his place.

"She murdered your brother, Evie," her father said with a ferocity that made her want to cower.

She had. It hadn't been on purpose, Evie was sure of it, but it happened. He'd died right there, and Evie had collapsed to the ground in a fit of shocked screams. She'd gripped the ground with both hands, not looking up until she heard Lyssa's cries. Her baby sister had been set beside her in the sling from her mother's neck.

And her mother was gone.

Closing her eyes tight, Evie sighed out a heavy breath, willing her heart free from the vise it was currently in. "Do you hate her, Papa?"

A singular tear rolled down her father's rough cheek. "Some days, I wish I did." He pulled the medallion from the inside of his shirt and rubbed it between his fingers. "She gave me this when we first met. I keep it close because, despite myself, I miss her."

"I do, too, sometimes." She missed her mother's laugh and the way the house always felt warmer with her inside it, but mostly she just missed the before.

Before life became harsher, before circumstances grew desperate, before Evie had irrevocably changed. Who was she before the last ten years?

Her father seemed to be contemplating the same question. "But it's also a reminder, Evie, to protect your heart, for it so easily can be broken."

Thoughts of Trystan, *The Villain*, clouded her mind. She wondered how long she would've kept the secret if she hadn't quit, wondered how many times she could look at the people she cherished most in this world and deceive them.

It reminded Evie of a vase Lyssa had knocked off the windowsill a few years prior, how the two Sage daughters had sat side by side, gluing the pieces back together.

But that effort had been useless in the end.

A month or two after that, Evie bumped into it, knocking it over once more, shattering it a second time.

"Can we fix it?" Lyssa had asked. "With the paste?"

"No, love." Evie had sighed. "It's hard enough to put something back together once. A second time, I'm afraid, is far too much to hope for."

They'd thrown the pieces away.

Her head and heart fixated on that moment until her breathing grew shallow and sweat stuck to her hairline. Too many lies. It was one thing to be living a double life but another altogether where she wasn't trusted, as if her opinions and her confidence weren't worthy.

Constantly fighting for a place, one that feels important, was the single most exhausting task Evie had ever given herself.

And she *was* exhausted; she felt it in the ache of her limbs and the weight of her eyelids as she laid back against the comfortable chair and closed her eyes.

Sometime later, the sound of her father's groan startled Evie awake. She bolted from her seat and leaned over him. His eyes were closed, and his complexion was dull and colorless. "Papa?"

"Worry not. It hasn't taken me yet." Her father smiled lightly, opening his light-blue eyes.

"That isn't funny, Papa." They both laughed anyway, and Evie reached for his hand, bringing it up to kiss the back of it.

Her father was strong. After her brother died and her mother left, he did his best to keep busy at the butchery, ensuring that his remaining two children never wanted for anything. They saw less of him at home, but that had been fine. He'd hired a private tutor for Evie so she could stay away from the school and avoid conversing with the other girls in her village who reminded her of her past, girls Evie no longer seemed to have anything in common with.

Tragedy did that to a family, isolated them. Her father seemed the only one who still felt comfortable among the living, his many friends in the village by his side, comforting him in the months and years to come. As for Evie, she had been content to live with the ghosts.

Lyssa had grown up to be a social butterfly, enchanting every person she set her eyes on, untouched by the tragedy she witnessed as an infant, and Evie had remained just as she was. Odd.

Always saying the wrong thing, her mind and thoughts not built for polite company. It caused Evie such pinched worry with every interaction that she'd eventually stopped trying, had stopped living.

It had only worsened when her father grew ill. More of an excuse to bury herself in a job than actually letting herself be a person. Until she had begun working for The Villain.

It was ironic that a man who dealt with so much death seemed to have brought her back to life, but now it was over. Evie would slowly regress backward until every part of her burned to ash, like blackened dandelions.

Tears burned, but Evie blinked them back and smiled wide for her father. "Everything's all right," she said, echoing the words she'd spoken to Lyssa in that field of burned-up wishes all those years ago.

Everything was all right.

CHAPTER 22

THE VILLAIN

"**W**hat in the deadlands is this?"

The small man shook as he took cautious steps away from Trystan's desk. "It's— It's cauldron brew, sir."

He gripped the silver chalice containing the foul black liquid.

No cream, no sugar, none of Sage's ridiculous attempts to make faces with the milk. It was all wrong.

"I did not ask for cauldron brew," he said darkly.

"Of course, sir, but, um, you did say to me ten minutes ago, 'Get me a cup of brew immediately, Stuart, or I will rip the skin from your bones.'"

Ah, yes, he had said that, hadn't he? He'd thought he'd forego the brew until he could sneak some milk into it, but by noon he had a splitting headache and had grown desperate.

"I do not want this swill—take it from my sight *this instant*!" He stood, shoving the cup at the terrified man, who just barely caught it before he scurried from the room.

Trystan spared a glance at Kingsley. The frog ribbited as he held up a sign that simply read: BLOCKHEAD.

For once, the frog summed things up perfectly.

Ignoring the amphibian, Trystan settled back behind his desk to focus on his evildoing plans. Surely thoughts of mayhem and destruction would calm his sour mood.

By the afternoon, Trystan was surprised the office was still standing. A fire had started in the south corridor of the manor, and it nearly burned an entire room of charted maps to ash. It started as two of the fire pixies had a disagreement that ended in fast-spreading flames, and only Sage knew where to find the irrigation devices she'd insisted they install during her first month of employment.

"You'll never see them!" Sage had said, curls bouncing with her excitement at the water fixture installation.

She'd pushed the hose made of some material she'd insisted he invest in called "rubber" back into the wall. The mechanism locked in place, the rubber tubing flipping and disappearing behind the white bricks.

"They're hidden all over the manor! When you have a structure this big, it's important that you account for fires, especially with all the lives in your care." She'd smiled and pulled her notebook from her satchel. "Now, I've mapped out where all thirty of them are, and I'll take you to each spot so you know exactly how to find them."

Thirty?

"Sage, as delightful as a tour of hoses sounds, I have actual work to do."

She'd frowned, which had given him a foreign, uncomfortable feeling in his chest. "But what will you do if there's a fire?"

"I'll ask you where the hose is," Trystan had replied flatly.

Sage's nose had scrunched, as it so often did, and she looked at him with a curiosity that was almost…endearing? He shuddered. "But what will you do if I'm not here?" she'd asked.

"You'll always be here, Sage."

Trystan blinked, feeling a sting under his eyes. He strode through his office and pushed open the wooden doors that led out to the damaged parapet. The doors slammed closed behind him, and he blinked back the wet heat in the air. The structure on the other side was covered and propped up by wooden beams that were aiding the reconstruction being done.

He stopped just short of the ruined end, the heat of the air burning his eyes again. He'd resolved to not care that she was gone. He wouldn't dare go after her, and she wouldn't dare return here after the cruel way in which he'd spoken to her.

The heat was relentless now, the moisture so strong, a drop of water was sliding down his cheek. He furiously swiped it away and looked at the wetness on his hand with disgust.

"Sir?"

Ms. Erring's voice cut through the quiet, making the wet heat hitting his eyes dry in seconds. Sniffing like he'd smelled something foul, Trystan frowned, turning his head slightly toward her.

"What's wrong now?" he asked gruffly.

The woman was always a little pinched, but right now her face was so twisted, it looked as if she were about to swallow her own tongue. She shook her head, her large glasses sliding down her nose. "One of the men you have working through the manor's finances is up in arms because he can't read the appraiser's handwriting."

Trystan furrowed his brow in confusion. "What exactly was the appraiser valuing?"

"Several crates of jewels that had been en route to King Benedict, aid from Roselia—one of the northern kingdoms. It was intercepted by the Malevolent Guards this morning."

What a brilliant plan—pity he had no memory of creating it. "Who on earth arranged for that? The northern kingdoms usually have their shipments travel with an army's worth of guards."

Ms. Erring's mouth pulled down, but she looked at him directly when she said, "Evangelina had the plans drawn up a month ago, and you signed off on them, sir."

No, that couldn't be... But he had, hadn't he? Sage had proposed that some of the Malevolent Guards wear Roselia uniforms, slowly working their way through the throng of them and plucking the real Roselia knights off one by one.

It was suicide, but she'd seemed so sure. So he'd signed off on the plan, requiring that some of his best guards carry it out—no need to send the novices to an early demise. At least his more seasoned guards would have a chance of making it out.

But they hadn't just made it out; they'd succeeded. "Well, that is excellent. But I'm still not understanding the conflict. Why can't our financial adviser read the appraiser's handwriting?"

Rebecka Erring, in the two years he'd known her, had never been without her armor of composure. Even when he'd first met her, under those unpleasant circumstances, she'd remained impassive. But she surprised Trystan when she rolled her eyes at him. "The handwriting is atrocious, sir. It would take a translator to make out even one letter of that scrawl."

His patience was so thin, it may as well have been the ground beneath his feet. "Well, how did we manage to make it out before?"

But he knew the answer before the uncomfortable look fell across her face. "Evie could always read it without any problems," she said. "Edwin used to give her pastries while she did it." By her tone, the stern woman didn't approve of the latter.

Trystan could hardly bring himself to care, however. He was currently coming to grips with the fact that he simply did not have an office without Sage. Or he supposed he did. But it was frankly an ill-functioning disaster.

The righteous emotions from that morning had turned and mutated into what it really was all along, a way for his brain to rationalize his regret. He truly hated being wrong, but he supposed if he'd defer being right to anyone, it was to Sage. Who would probably never take another step toward this place...which meant he had to go to *her*.

Trystan tried not to let his turmoil show in his words as he looked at Ms. Erring and said, "Have the finance men put them aside, and I will do my best to translate the handwriting myself."

She nodded and turned to leave, but before she did, she looked to the ruins at the end of the parapet. "Isn't it interesting that we are quicker to repair some things over others?"

There was an accusation there that made Trystan narrow his eyes at her. "What are you implying, Ms. Erring?" He noted the sharp edge to his voice, but to Rebecka's credit, she pulled herself up straight, not wavering for a moment.

"That perhaps you need to remove your pride so that you can see what needs to be fixed more clearly."

It was the boldness with which she spoke that made Trystan respect her. Rebecka Erring was without fear when she believed herself to be right. It was that respect that saved her.

"You should mind your own problems before mine, Ms. Erring. My employees are yours to counsel; I, however, am not."

She nodded dutifully, the snap of fight winking out of her in a moment, and it confused him. Rebecka Erring was implying that Sage leaving the job was something that needed to be fixed? Trystan had been certain the feud between them had been quite mutual.

"Ms. Erring, do you want Ms. Sage to come back?" he asked curiously.

She didn't look at him, just gave him her back as she turned to open the heavy door. "No, I don't," she said quietly. "But I think she deserves to."

The words were so flat and honest that Trystan leaned against the stone half wall, the slam of the door as the woman left a dull, faded sound in his ears. He brushed a heavy hand over his mouth and down until it was resting under his chin.

He looked to the wreckage one more time before returning to his office.

Fix it.

Unfortunately, Trystan didn't have the skills to fix anything. He was much better at destroying everything he touched.

Which was why he doubted, by the end of this awful day, that even the manor would still remain standing when he was done.

CHAPTER 23

THE VILLAIN

A soft knock on the door of Trystan's office was his final straw.
It was nearly an hour until the day concluded, and he couldn't wait for the sun to go down and the day to turn to night. He wanted to drown in it.

Pushing back from his chair, he walked over and looked out the window. He nearly busted out of his skin when he heard the door creep open anyway.

"Unless there is another fire, I do not want to be disturbed," he called out harshly.

The darker magic within him pulsed, aching to find a weak spot and destroy whoever dared enter his domain uninvited.

"I blew up half the parapet last week." Every part of him went stiff as a board, and yet a deep, intrinsic part of him relaxed as the voice continued. "Does that count?"

Turning, needing to catch sight of her, he froze as an uncomfortable feeling fluttered in his chest. He shoved his hands into the front pockets of his breeches and stared at her.

His former assistant looked the same, still short, still dark-haired. Still with eyes that seemed to know too much and lips that were constantly pulling up at the corners. He went longer than this on the week's ends when he didn't see her, so the reaction his body was having was ridiculous.

But he was so *happy* to see her. What an obscene, unnecessary emotion, but there it was. He was happy... How positively vile.

And the lightness in his chest only grew when she began to speak. "I don't like feeling as if I can't do something." The words tumbled out of her mouth, not practiced but honest.

"All right…" he said neutrally.

"It makes me irrational. It's like it triggers something in me that—"

"Stop." He held a hand up to interrupt her, looking over her shoulder to the open door. "Hold that thought." He moved swiftly toward it, noting the crowd of onlookers trying to peek around the doorway, all dispersing when he glared.

All but Blade, who wandered by with yet another bandage on his head, noticing Sage and turning back to Trystan with a small fist pump.

Trystan flipped him off before closing the door and turning to Kingsley, who sat unmoving on his desk. At least he wasn't holding up his earlier sign again.

"Could you go be…anywhere else?" Trystan asked, and when the creature hopped off the desk and over two feet to land on the windowsill, he sighed, then looked to Sage. "Proceed."

"I know there are things you don't want to trust me with. I even know there are things that I just can't accomplish."

He fiercely doubted that but didn't say anything.

She moved to her regular seat; he chose to remain standing, leaning against his desk. "But not being able to take care of what I need to, of the people I need to… It terrifies me."

His curiosity was piqued as his brows shot up in surprise.

Surely this woman didn't really believe herself incapable of *anything*. Besides, she knew his overreaction and treatment of her was wrong, that he'd been wrong about the letter. So why was she explaining herself?

"I know that I can't know everything, and I respect it. You're a man with many secrets, unlike me." She laughed a little at the end, the self-deprecating kind—he knew it well.

She continued, her light eyes finding his dark ones, and Trystan flexed his hands nervously at his sides to alleviate the almost ticklish feeling spreading through his limbs. "But when you accused me of being deceitful…"

Trystan's shoulders straightened.

"It hurt me. You didn't even give me the chance to explain."

It hurt me.

He wondered if it would scar her for life if he threw himself from the window.

"However." She paused. "I shouldn't have quit so abruptly. My emotions got the better of me, and it was not a decision I would have made, had I given myself the opportunity to process that hurt appropriately."

She took a deep breath, her gaze remaining steady on him. "For that, I sincerely apologize and ask you to allow me my job back."

A silence echoed as they stared at each other. Trystan realized his lips had parted as she was speaking, and he was currently gaping at her like a deranged fish. Swallowing, he moved his jaw back and forth, trying to ease the stiffness. "You want to come back?"

The eagerness in his voice needed to be squashed under his boot like a roach.

She nodded, eyes glinting as the last dregs of sunlight spilled in. "I really love working here."

He should leave it there. Both of them acknowledging he was in the right, that she had been absurd, and letting the pieces of their lives fall back together unencumbered.

It hurt me.

Guilt. He was feeling guilt in a harsh, raw way, and he couldn't stand it. To see her sitting there looking open and reasonable, a courageous hope surrounding her. It grated against his skin, caused a pounding in the front of his skull.

Trystan found his chair and sat slowly, not letting another moment of silence step in. "Sage, I…" Tatianna must have poisoned his brew— that's what it was. It was the only explanation for the feeling when he looked at her; it had to be.

Trystan's distress only kept growing when he looked over to Kingsley, who was holding up a sign from across the room that said, SPEAK.

He stood abruptly again, and they both jumped, Sage quickly standing, too. He walked slowly around the desk, eyes never leaving hers. He wondered if there was a word for when you know you're going to fail at something, one word to define that feeling where you know no matter how hard you resist that path, it will find you.

Evangelina Sage had found him.

"I'm sorry." The apology came out fast, and he was almost certain his voice went up an octave, which was not only mortifying but enough to make him want to consider the window idea again.

"You're…sorry?" Sage's jaw hung so low, Trystan wondered if it would catch the dirt from the ground.

"Dispense with the dramatics. It's not as if I told you I have a night-light."

Sage's gaze sharpened at his words, and Trystan cursed under his breath.

Her wicked eyes gave her away as she rubbed her chin like one of the older magical specialists. "Sir, *do* you have a night-light?"

Trystan shook his head and rubbed at his eyes with the back of his hand, mumbling, "I don't…*not* have one."

The giggle she let out was loud and at a pitch that should call the birds to the window, looking for their brethren, but it was adorable, and he hoped she would do it again.

Fuck.

"You have a night-light! For what? Does it burn insects? Trying to lure something to its death?" Her words were coming out so quick, her mouth could barely keep up.

He sighed and shook his head, taking this as his penance. "I use a night-light for the purpose it was assigned, to make the night…lighter." He winced.

Gods, that sounded ridiculous.

"This is the best day of my life." Sage's nose scrunched, and she chuckled as she began her little bounce of excitement, like her laughter was going to launch her into the sun. "Why do you need to 'light the night'?" She mimicked his voice.

Placing one hand on his hip and another against his forehead, Trystan felt exhausted. "I find myself fearful of the dark, particularly when I'm alone or in my bedchamber…or both."

Sage's jaw seemed to find the floor again, shocked into silence. Concerning.

Trystan bristled. "Is that a problem?"

"No. Of course it's not," she said, amusement dwindling into softness. "How long have you been afraid of the dark?"

"I am *not* afraid of the dark, Sage. I am The Villain—the dark fears me." He let his chest puff out to prove his point, which only made her giggle again.

"My apologies, sir," she said contritely. "How long have you been afraid of the dark...*particularly in your bedchamber*?" The last part, she deepened her voice again to sound like his.

"Since I was a child," he admitted but didn't mention how it had worsened over the years or why. She must have sensed it, though, because she reached out a hand and placed it on his. He stiffened at the touch, the way he always did with human contact, his head whipping down to look at her small hand laying over his.

"I'm afraid of ladybugs," she said, nodding seriously.

Trystan gawked openly, looking to the ceiling, wondering how on earth he'd gotten here. Apologizing to an employee—badly, he might add—because somehow the conversation had been diverted to insects.

When he didn't say anything, she added, "The spots scare me."

"Of course they do," he said defeatedly. "Sage, I was attempting an apology?"

"Oh, right! Sorry, go on!" She looked embarrassed as she took a step back and gestured her hands forward for him to go on.

Sighing, he continued. "You have done nothing that would indicate to me you are incapable or unworthy of my trust. I overreacted to the letter, and it was very unfair of me—"

She interrupted quickly. "The letter wasn't—"

"I know," Trystan said, holding up a hand to stop her. "Blade told me."

Sage's mouth pulled down in a frown. "Sir... You didn't... That is to say, is Blade...?"

"Still breathing."

"See, the way I've seen you torture the men you drag through here, that somehow doesn't make me feel better," she said blandly.

"He's alive, unharmed, and still has a job here." Trystan didn't want to continue speaking of his previous mercy, as it made him feel ill. He quickly added, "As do you. If you would like to start over again."

The already uplifted corners of her mouth pulled up higher, lighting her entire face. It made his rigid limbs feel softer, like she was liquifying his bones. Stepping toward him, Sage held out her hand.

Hesitating just a moment, The Villain clasped Sage's hand in his.

"My name is Evangelina Sage. A pleasure to meet you. Shall I call you 'sir'? Or 'Evil Overlord'?"

Shaking his head, he pulled a grin, and Sage's eyes darted to his left cheek, looking pleased. The woman was unnaturally obsessed with his dimple. "I will allow either, if you go get me one of those fried things from the kitchen. And a chalice of sugary cauldron brew."

"Sold!" she screeched, nearly tripping over her own feet to get to the door.

"Sage?" Trystan called, immediately regretting it when she turned, looking at him expectantly. "I just want to understand...why is it that you want my trust in the first place?"

She leaned a hand against her cheek, and one eyebrow rose thoughtfully. "I want to know you, that's all."

That's all? Like that sentence alone wasn't enough to knock him completely off his axis. Sage disappeared through the doors, and Trystan leaned against the wall, sliding down until he was sitting on the floor, arms resting on his knees.

I want to know you.

Trystan felt unfettered fear as he sat there, because for the first time in a decade, the idea of that didn't sound so very bad.

And yet, he somehow knew in his bones she was going to be the death of him eventually.

CHAPTER 24

EVIE

Things were far too quiet.

The last week and a half of work had settled back into its average, steady rhythm. The boss dragging bedraggled men through here by their ears, still for reasons unknown to her. Two imports of weapons and other stolen goods were passed from Roselia to the manor without a single hitch.

Their office informant was slipping.

Evie was enjoying a vanilla drop, standing at the kitchen window she loved so much, which she hadn't many opportunities to visit as of late. It didn't hurt that Edwin had just made a fresh batch of fairy cakes, all iced to perfection. She was enjoying catching up until Becky ruined it.

"Must be nice, to act completely unprofessional and be welcomed back like nothing happened."

Evie's eyes rolled back in her head. She looked at Becky, who was standing in the doorway, arms crossed.

"Must be nice to be a judgmental shrew and have that excuse as a facet of your personality." Evie smiled cheekily.

Smirking, moving over to the steaming cauldron, Becky held out her chalice for Edwin to fill. The ogre was twice her size and wouldn't make eye contact with her. "Better a judgmental shrew than a naive fool always getting herself into trouble."

Evie's eye was beginning to twitch. "Don't you have somewhere to be? Like stealing sweets from children, perhaps?"

Narrowing her eyes, Becky gripped her hot drink and stalked from the room, her skirts bouncing as she walked.

Blade jumped out of her path like his life was on the line as he entered the kitchen and walked toward Evie, all the while keeping his head turned and his eyes on Becky moving swiftly in the other direction.

He grinned wide. "She was damn unpleasant when you were gone. So glad to see her coming back to herself."

Unlikely.

"Oh yes, because she's just been an absolute delight all week long." Evie shuffled back over to her desk, brew in hand, and Blade followed at her heels.

"Forget lovely Rebecka. I have something amazing I want to show you." Blade grinned, the white against his tanned skin giving him a glow of health and vigor. "Can the boss spare you for twenty minutes?"

"I'm sure he won't mind, considering he's not at the manor today." Sighing, she ignored the pinch of worry. "What is it?"

"Just come," he urged, grabbing her hand and pulling her along. Tatianna appeared beside them, a bored expression on her face.

"Where are we going? It's been slow."

"No interns to patch up?" Evie inquired as the three of them began to descend the stairs. "Or the boss's sister to tend to?" She grinned wide when Tatianna lightly shoved her.

"The boss's who?" Blade asked, eyebrows raised. Wrapping a muscled arm around Tatianna's shoulders, Blade leaned in close. "Share with the class—I love gossip."

"I didn't come along on this little excursion to be interrogated, only entertained."

Evie raised her hand in the air. "I'm pretty entertained." She lowered her hand when she caught the look Tatianna was skewering them with.

They walked into the courtyard, and the excitement was pulsating off Blade in waves. "Wait till you see the progress Fluffy and I have made. Leaps and bounds over everything else we've been trying for months."

Both women stopped short in the entryway, exchanging a look of startled confusion. "Did you say...Fluffy?" Evie asked.

Blade chuckled to himself. "I know, but believe me when I say— Boss!"

Evie's heart thundered, and she became achingly aware of a formidable presence hovering behind her. Her suspicions were confirmed when she heard a low voice far too close to her ear. "Are you cutting out in the middle of the workday, you ingrates?" There was no anger behind his voice, just wary exhaustion.

Evie turned to see him standing right behind her, his expression grim, dark circles under his eyes. "Blade has something he wanted us to see." Pausing, Evie raised a hand and rubbed a finger lightly over one of the dark patches. She and The Villain must have been equally shocked by her boldness because neither of them moved. "Have you been sleeping?"

Tatianna raised a brow, smirking, and Blade seemed to find something very interesting about his shoes.

"Sleep is hardly a concern," The Villain said, eventually grabbing her hand and pushing it back to her side. She might've imagined his fingers lingered on hers a second longer than necessary.

Evie propped a hand on her hip. "You're not a machine, sir. You can still be your evil, brooding self with a good night's rest."

"I don't know. I think the tired look gives him a menacing edge." Blade nodded, patting The Villain on the shoulder, then quickly pulling his hand back to his side when he saw the eviscerating look he got as a result.

"I think it just makes him look sleepy," Tatianna said flatly, angling her head for a better view.

"Can we possibly desist with discussing my nocturnal habits so you three can start explaining why my supposedly respectable employees are away from their posts?" He raised a brow, crossing his arms as he waited for an explanation.

Blade opened his mouth but froze when wind whipped against the back gate. Turning his head, a wide grin split his lips. "Hear that?"

"The weather?" The Villain asked sardonically.

The wind whipped against the door, harsher this time. The rattling caused Tatianna and her to jump—and for The Villain to grab Evie and yank her behind him.

"What in the deadlands was that?" he growled.

Blade strutted to the back gate, sweeping one arm out as though introducing King Benedict. "That, my dear friends, was Fluffy."

CHAPTER 25

THE VILLAIN

The Villain's pulse pounded in his ears when he felt Sage's keen eyes on him. Clearing his throat, he slowly turned to her, but she was already walking past him, arm in arm with Tatianna.

The healer called out with an astonished expression, "Why would you name the poor animal that?"

Blade's gaze darted to his, and Trystan narrowed his eyes on the man. He better not share— "Oh, it was just the silliest thing I could think of! A bit of revenge for all the trouble he's caused me."

And…the perfect example of the exact wrong thing to say. Excellent. He almost wished the man had just admitted Trystan had suggested the name, given the way Sage's shoulders stiffened.

She released Tatianna's arm and marched into the courtyard, the healer right at her heels. "How dare you name that poor creature out of spite, Blade Gushiken!" The dragon trainer looked guilty at the reprimand.

Trystan followed behind them, feeling like a unicorn's ass.

The back courtyard was one of his favorite areas in the manor. The large space was covered in stone, with clumps of grass and plants coming up through the cracks. The stone archways had suffered since the creature had begun to grow, throwing daily fits as he knocked his chained neck into everything around him.

Unlike now, as he realized the creature seemed eerily calm.

Too calm. "Where is his chain?" The Villain asked, trying to keep himself level with the fire-breathing beast—who was staring right into

Sage's eyes, nostrils flaring. Trystan felt his power move over him like a dark cloud, changing his vision so that all he could see were vulnerable kill spots on the dragon's scaled skin.

On the left side of a clawed foot, there was a weak point. If he struck it just right, the dragon would topple over onto the ground, paralyzed forever. But he caught the marks from the chains around the creature's neck, which glowed with scarred-over wounds. That gave him pause.

His power receded back into himself—just as Sage reached a shaky hand up to the beast. "Sage," he whispered into the ghostly quiet. "I wouldn't."

But she kept looking at the creature in wonder, whispering, "Hey, dragon." Flinching slightly when the creature gave a huff.

"It's okay," Gushiken assured. "After I started calling him by a name, he calmed down. He's as harmless as a house cat."

"A house cat with wings…that breathes fire," Tatianna corrected, taking a careful step away from *Fluffy*.

"Removing the chain likely helped more." The Villain walked closer to the beast, subtly placing himself between him and Sage. "I'm sure that quelled him. I wasn't aware…" He felt guilt squeeze his chest. "That they were so painful for him."

Blade frowned, clicking his tongue, waving the creature over to him. Fluffy turned clumsily on his hind legs, nudging his snout into Gushiken's hand. "I wasn't, either, but even if it wasn't physically painful, it's not enjoyable for anyone to be chained down. I should've realized that sooner."

Trystan understood that better than most, but he shoved the memory away before it could fully form and tear through the fortress he'd built to keep it at bay. "I'm satisfied…that he seems to be doing better." The creature turned toward him, a deep wisdom in his slitted gaze. The Villain nearly bent at the waist to bow, granting the creature the respect he was owed.

But he kept his legs firm, trying to keep the reverence in his face hidden behind a facade of indifference. Instead, he turned back toward the manor's gate, unable to look at the creature a second longer, knowing he'd caused him harm.

"Wait, boss, you didn't hear the best part!" Blade shouted. The

Villain didn't turn, just halted in his tracks, keeping his back to the three of them. "When I took off the chains, I noticed something interesting engraved on the inside."

The clanging of metal earned a turn of his neck. Only to see the dragon trainer dragging over a large silver ring so big, he needed to spread his arms to full length to carry it. Dropping it at The Villain's feet, he pointed to the inside, where small letters were etched.

THE VILLAIN WILL FALL

He ran a finger over the words, his other hand a tight fist as his nails bit into his palms. Both women spied the writing and gasped.

Sage crouched low beside him, placing a gentle hand on his arm and immediately settling his rising magic. "We had the chains in storage before Blade even arrived. Someone signed off on a crate of weapons and equipment being delivered, and this was in it. They came in a shipment we lifted off King Benedict's trade with Groena. The kingdom to the east. It was my first week here."

Something was nagging at him, some point he was missing, but the links of this twisted mystery refused to untangle themselves. It seemed they kept coming to loose ends with no real answers, and still an agent of his worst enemy was somewhere in this castle, a wolf in sheep's clothing.

He'd known that King Benedict was behind the attacks. After all, the king was the one who began this little war between them. But though Benedict may have launched the ships, Trystan was the one who fired the first cannon, and he'd do it again. It was The Villain's job, after all.

"Benedict knew this was coming to me. He knew Blade would take the dragon, had this made and brought in by his traitor." He kicked the chains, a flare of anger driving his power to the edges of the courtyard, his magic searching for any weaknesses to claim, to kill. "He's playing with me."

His voice was hard and cold as he added, "But I will win this game, get his head on a spit."

And with that, he strode to the castle gate once more, dark purpose in every footfall. He hoped Benedict was comfortable with the meager advantages he'd collected thus far, because his string of victories was about to come to an abrupt halt.

Rubbing his neck, feeling his own chains tighten there, The Villain smiled. He'd evaporate every chance of hope Benedict and any of his supporters had. Watch them run for their miserable lives as he descended death upon them.

Benedict had been the first person to look upon Trystan's face and call him a monster, and it was to be his life's greatest pleasure to remind the king exactly what that meant.

CHAPTER 26

EVIE

"This is him! This is The Villain!" Jayne Fairmond yelped, drawing the attention of several villagers in the square.

It was a busy selling day, carts and vendors lining the streets. Colorful fabrics were draped high, the glitter of the material brought from the Lavender Seas and the merfolk who resided there catching the light of the sun. Fresh scents of bread—probably not as good as Edwin's, but she'd call it a close second—danced along Evie's nose.

But her tranquility was ruined by someone raving about her boss on her day off. Now she had to put on a performance.

"A picture of The *Villain*?" She needed to sound fearful if she didn't want to raise suspicion. It was no secret to others in the kingdom that The Villain had sympathizers, and they were considered villainous scum as well. Evie thought she should shriek when she saw the poster—and nearly did when she saw the sad portrayal of whatever this sketch artist was trying to convey.

Whoever was supposed to be represented in the WANTED flyer wasn't just old; they were ancient. The nose wasn't even close, and the hair was wrong for many reasons, one of them being it was on fire. His tongue was out and forked like a serpent, and Evie yelped when she saw a beard so long, it covered most of the bottom of the page.

"Do you have another one of these?" She pushed her smile down so hard, it made her eyes water. Coughing, she said, "I would like to make sure I never forget the face of the traitor."

Jayne nodded, eyes glittering in approval as she reached into her satchel and handed Evie another awful poster. One she was going to frame and put right on her boss's desk.

"Thank you." She sniffed, wiping an imaginary tear from her eye. "He's *so* vile."

"Don't worry, Evie. One day the Valiant Guards will catch the traitor and stop all the destruction he's caused," Jayne insisted, clutching the poster so hard that she crumpled the paper.

"What destruction, exactly?" Evie asked innocently.

Jayne reeled back, a look of astonishment on her face. "How can you even ask me that, Evangelina?" She held her hand to her chest dramatically, looking all too much like a woman about to faint. "His crimes are too horrendous to speak of."

Ah, now Evie understood. "You can't name a single one, can you?"

Jayne crossed her arms over her large bust. "Of course I can! I just have the good sense not to speak of it." Jayne glared at her, looking as if she wanted to rip the flyer from Evie's hands. "The reason you can afford to work is only by the benevolence of King Benedict. If it were up to The Villain, you probably wouldn't even have a job."

"So true, Jayne. So true." Evie nodded sagely, then whipped around before the woman could spy the smile Evie couldn't contain a minute longer. Instead, she headed off to the center of town, where the crowds would be less, well, crowded.

A few minutes later, Evie sat against the edge of the large fountain that marked the very center of their village. Another week's end was to have come and gone, and she still felt like she was drowning, like all her worries were weights on her feet, dragging her under until she couldn't breathe.

She noted her father was doing better, at the very least, as he sat with several friends in the courtyard. His complexion had a healthy glow today as he conversed happily, Lyssa's arms hooked around one of his legs, her head tilted up as though she were hanging on his every word. Together they had every appearance of a happy, healthy family, one that didn't have dark secrets circling them like a vulture waiting for the carnage to appear.

Pressing her lips together, she stood. There were still a few hours left in the day. Perhaps she could go through her notes one more time, looking for anything else she might have missed.

Jayne was now standing with a group of other girls she'd grown up attending school with. All girls who had looked at her, whispering and giggling about Evie's mother after the incident. Feigning sympathy when it pleased them.

Evie sighed, shaking her head, and turned to walk home. She didn't have it in her to pretend to be friendly anymore.

Tapping her father's shoulder, she ran her other hand over one of Lyssa's braids. "I'm heading home, Papa. Will you be okay with Lyssa?"

The men her father was conversing with gave her friendly greetings as her father nodded and patted her cheek. "Of course, my sweet. Could you leave me the coin purse? I want to buy a couple of drinks for my friends."

"Oh, um. I suppose." She listened to the coins clink together as she deposited the pouch into her father's waiting palm. "Just please don't—"

But she was immediately forgotten when her father dove into another one of his stories, making Lyssa and the group of men laugh boisterously.

Dragging her feet against the ground, kicking dirt and stones up as she went, Evie began humming to herself, imagining she was a sorceress with power those around her could not begin to comprehend.

And she'd also pretend that scenario wasn't a loud cry for help.

Pushing a curl out of her face, she huffed in annoyance. She'd left her hair loose today, hanging low on her back, then immediately regretted it every time it brushed against her face. Sorceresses probably didn't have to worry about managing their appearance; they probably looked polished and pristine with a snap of their fingers.

Did they snap their fingers?

Evie had never desired magic for herself. But sometimes when she saw the ease with which people used it, like it was a constant companion, she couldn't help but wonder if she had it lying in wait. The way her mother had. Or if it would one day consume her as well.

She didn't know if magic that was too powerful always turned on the owner or if it was just the wielder's lack of control. What about The Villain's magic?

She exited the main square, passing a lane of tall trees before she turned right into a giant field filled with daisies. She kept walking until she was standing in front of a massive tree in the middle of the clearing she'd climbed as a child. She leaned back against the rough bark, letting it hold her weight, and sighed.

She knew The Villain had a dark magic, darker than her mother's, although she didn't completely understand the logistics of it. But she *did* understand that it made him deadly. Did he struggle to keep it from overtaking him, too? Was that what ultimately made him choose such a deadly career?

Bending her knees until she was sitting, Evie rested her head against the tree and closed her eyes.

What had her boss been like before he'd become The Villain? What had happened to make him go down the path he was on? What trauma had evoked the magic in him?

Evie sighed again and shook her head. Whatever sad backstory she was building in her mind was just a distraction to keep her from thinking about the real issues.

Problem number one: She was growing emotionally attached to her boss.

Problem number two: Her boss was also the most hated man in her kingdom.

Problem number three: Someone wanted her boss dead—which would severely affect problem number one.

"You are a fool with attachment issues," she muttered.

"Are you talking to the tree or yourself?" a familiar voice questioned.

"Sir?" Evie said, jumping to her feet, heart racing. "You can't be here!" she hissed, shoving him behind the tree, then feeling surprised she was able to move his large form.

"Sage, what are you doing?" He raised a brow but continued to move back until they were both hidden.

"Have you finally lost what was left of your evil little pea brain?" She pushed him again, and he caught her hands, gently halting her. There were no gloves separating their skin, and the burn of his palm against the back of her hand sent shivers through her. It didn't help that at the angle he was holding her, she was at eye level with his lips.

Lips that seemed to tilt and move just a bit closer.

But all too quickly, he was releasing her and stepping a good two feet away, flexing both hands like her touch was offensive to him. "I haven't lost anything. I've been to your village before. Why the gross overreaction?"

He adjusted his shirt collar, the cloth obviously well tailored. Nothing audacious, but the black leather of his trousers and the pressed, clean sheen of his shirt said he had money, enough to be comfortable.

"You don't think King Benedict has connected that Trystan Maverine and The Villain are one and the same? He knows it's you, doesn't he? He'll know where and who to look for, and I'm sure he wouldn't hesitate to let every Valiant Guard within riding distance tear you apart." How could he be so incredibly careless and startlingly calm?

He merely stood there, staring at her, his dark eyes giving nothing useful away. "If Benedict wanted his people looking for me, he wouldn't be allowing posters to go about with false names and inaccurate portrayals of my appearance." Her boss pulled out the poster she'd been given earlier, somehow taking it from her satchel without her noticing.

Evie bit her lip to keep from grinning. "I don't know, that seems a pretty accurate likeness. I'd hoped to frame it."

His face went flat and unamused. "Very humorous, Sage." He crumpled the poster and tossed it aside. "Benedict wants to keep whatever games he's playing between us. So I'll follow the bread crumbs, will play the fool just long enough for him to think he's won." His smile was sinister. "And then I'll take him down for good."

Somewhere above her head, a bird chirped, with no idea of the melodrama playing out below it. "You make dismantling a well-beloved monarch sound alarmingly easy, sir."

"Well, there is a very distinct difference between King Benedict and me."

"What's that?" Evie asked cautiously.

"I don't care about being beloved, and I don't care about doing things the right way. I will blacken whatever parts of my soul I must to keep my business running and to take down my enemies." Were there thunderclouds ominously appearing behind him or was that Evie's imagination?

Leaning back against the tree again and sliding down, putting her head between her bent knees, she sighed. "I just don't understand.

You've been doing the evil thing for a decade. Sabotaging the kingdom, working as an enemy against him for almost ten years. Why is it that only recently, he's decided to send someone on the inside to take you down?"

"Perhaps I've finally come to be enough of a nuisance, or perhaps since the entire continent knows me to be a vicious, horrid monster, the esteemed king thinks that serving the public my head on a platter when it finally suits him will make him something of a hero." Trystan sat down hard beside her, yanking a bit of grass out with his fist.

"Or it took him ten years to find someone willing to go undercover against you," Evie guessed. "Someone who was willing to take the risk you'd find them out eventually."

The Villain nodded in agreement. "Whoever it is has had an extremely careful method of sharing information with the king. I've had a few of my guards keep eyes on some loose ends, but so far, no one has stepped out of line."

Unless they found a coded way to share the information.

"What could he have done to cause this war between you?" she asked almost to herself. "I have no loyalty to the crown, obviously. Look who I'm working for." She gestured to him before continuing. "But King Benedict is well-liked, even loved by some. From what I've read in the news pamphlets, he spends his days arguing with his council to make magical education more accessible to the rest of the kingdom. He's the reason women are even *allowed* employment at all. I heard that he's now petitioning the council for women's business rights. I'm not saying you're wrong for targeting him, as he's clearly targeting you back, but what started it? What could he have possibly done to deserve such wrath?"

"He stepped on my foot once. Never got over it," Trystan deadpanned.

Evie laughed and shook her head.

Trystan stood once more, reaching a hand down for her. Lightly pulling her to her feet and turning to the path leading back to the village, he said, "Now I would like to go meet with your village's blacksmith, and I would like you to introduce me as your employer who is interested in a rare sort of blade."

The blood in her veins froze, locking her legs in a vise grip. "The blacksmith?" Her hands shook so hard, she shoved them in the pockets of her skirts. "Why do you want to meet with him?"

"Otto Warsen?" The Villain said, pulling a slip of paper from his front pocket. "Blade found the name etched into the bottom corner of the dragon's collar. Lots of craftsmen do it as a way of marking their work. An advertisement of sorts, so that anyone who admires it knows where it came from and might perhaps want one of their own."

Evie swallowed a large lump, her legs finally working again, and followed him back down the path, feeling a sickly cold slithering through her. "And whoever requested the collar's creation, in person, had to have given the order to include the engraving." She concluded, "Or at the very least, the blacksmith took a bribe to carve it in by another party. It could be our traitor."

He nodded. "We'll have to be creative with our line of questioning. I don't want the man to suspect anything untoward about your employment and make things difficult for you in your private life."

That hardly seemed to matter when a moment in time that Evie desperately wanted to forget was about to be thrown in her face like a closed fist. "Very considerate, sir."

"I trust you are acquainted with Mr. Warsen?"

Evie saw familiar faces as they reentered the square, but no one stopped them to talk because of the street performances that had just begun.

"I used to work for him, actually," she admitted quietly. "Right before I came to work for you."

He must have heard something off in her voice, because his gaze turned to hers, a pinched look between his brows. "Why did you leave his employment?"

"It was just a difference of opinion," Evie said, smiling lightly. Keeping her hands in the deep pockets of her skirts, she strutted forward, eager to leave all those feelings pushed to the past and pray to whatever gods had created this world that they didn't make her do what she'd wished she'd done all those months ago—and hit her old boss in the head with a sledgehammer.

Especially in front of her new boss. But her anger was still raw, her pain twisting and curling inside her.

She was doomed.

CHAPTER 27

EVIE

This excursion was ill-advised, to say the least. The closer they came to the smithy, the tighter the invisible cord around Evie's throat grew. She should have said no—any excuse would have done. She was usually pretty good at coming up with misleading comments to dissuade even the most curious. The last couple of months of work had been amazing practice.

But some sort of shock had set into her limbs, and now she was about to walk into the last place she ever wanted to be, facing the last man she ever wanted to see again. Any conscious feelings screaming at her to run were muffled behind a thick pane of glass. She would not listen.

She could do this. For Trystan.

Taking a steadying breath and removing her damp palms from her pockets, Evie slid her hands against the sides of her skirt. But a sharp wave of nausea roiled through her when she caught sight of Otto Warsen's burly form.

His face was smudged with black soot from the forge. He had a cloth in one hand, standing in the outside pavilion of his house, polishing a beautiful-looking sword. Evie felt rather than saw Mr. Warsen's eyes as he observed her coming, her and her boss.

The Villain.

She was hardly alone or unsafe, so why did she feel like a human sacrifice?

The blacksmith's gaze was slimy, coating every exposed inch of her skin as he looked her up and down, and it took every ounce of willpower she had not to turn back home and step into a scalding bath.

It wasn't the first time she'd seen Mr. Warsen since she'd quit. Since the night he had asked her to be his companion, his breath thick with rum. She'd seen the rage contort his face after she said she wasn't interested, and she'd known she had to get up and run, barely feeling the blade slice down her shoulder as she did. But she didn't stop—she'd kept running and running and running.

She'd never told anyone and never went back. Anytime she saw Mr. Warsen around the village, he smiled and waved in a friendly manner and she swallowed down the bile and moved on.

But there was always that little glimmer, like the two of them shared a secret, and she could tell Mr. Warsen was pleased for it. She wanted to strangle him.

More than that, she pictured how she'd feel if The Villain hung his head in the entryway.

Suddenly, the smile on her face was very real as the two of them approached. "Good morning, Mr. Warsen," The Villain said, his voice seeming to become smoother. He held his hand out to shake the blacksmith's, who quickly pulled his hand from one of the leather gloves.

Evie didn't move.

"A pleasure, Mister...?" Otto asked, his bald head reflecting the sunlight.

"Arthur," The Villain said smoothly. "I believe you know one of my employees, Ms. Sage?"

Otto narrowed his gaze warily, looking to Evie. "It don't matter what she—"

Before he could say more, Evie blurted out, "I was telling my boss of your wonderful craftsmanship when I was cleaning his collection of rare blades."

There was still a wariness in the blacksmith's face, but a renewed edge of interest at the prospect of a sale joined it. "Well, of course!" He grinned wide. "Evangelina got to witness my prowess with a blade firsthand while she was under my employ."

Evie's nails bit into her palms. "I certainly did." A modicum of disdain slipped in over her false sincerity, but the two men were too busy sizing each other up to notice.

"What are you looking to have made, Mr. Arthur?" Otto gestured to a few pieces of unfinished work. "If you want it sooner rather than later, it'll cost you, I'm afraid. I have many orders to fulfill."

"Oh, I'm willing to pay whatever it takes." The words were lower, almost angry, before they lightened again. "Especially since this will be a rather large project for you, Mr. Warsen. I hope you're up to the challenge."

Evie could practically see gold coins dancing in Otto's vision. His beady gaze darted to hers as he answered, "I love a challenge." Then he turned and opened the door to the smithy, a gust of hot air rushing out from the forge. "Please come in."

The Villain followed him through the doors, and Evie tried to stay close behind him, but she froze when she felt Otto's arm slip around hers. He leaned in and whispered in a low voice, "I'm glad you're not letting what happened between us grow into a personal matter, Ms. Sage. It was, after all, only a misunderstanding."

Her pulse pounded in her neck. "Misunderstanding, yes. I told you to get away from me…" Her boss was distracted by a row of chains hanging on the other side of the room. "And you misunderstood that for 'attack me.'"

She pulled her arm from his grasp, smiling sweetly at him. "I can see the confusion."

The blacksmith had the good grace to look panicked at her pronouncement. Good—she hoped he felt like his guts were about to spill out. Hers certainly did.

If there was ever a time to lose your lunch on someone's shoes…

Pushing her shoulders back, she looked the feeble man directly in the eye. "But I can keep things professional. I hope you have the same capability."

The Villain seemed to notice their hesitation and turned toward the pair standing by the door, a question in his black eyes.

"Why don't you tell Mr. Warsen about your most recent purchase, Mr. Arthur?" Evie came to her boss's side, her gaze focused on Trystan instead of the surroundings that haunted some of her darker nightmares.

Her boss angled his head but picked up her clue smoothly. "Of course. Mr. Warsen, what do you know about the dealings of wild creatures?"

"Not much, my lord, I have to admit." Otto seemed to be taking the stance of humble shopkeeper. He played the part well. "I'm not as worldly a man as yourself, clearly." He laughed, gesturing to his shabby clothes and dirt-covered face.

The Villain smiled, wide enough that the dimple in his cheek appeared. A boiling anger was building in her gut. Otto Warsen was hardly worthy of seeing something so precious.

But her boss didn't notice her anger at all as he added, "I've had great luck in acquiring a guvre recently."

The warmth in the room seemed to be sucked out with the mention of the deadly beast, whose serpent body and batlike wings were the least terrifying things about it. It was their breath that summoned nightmares. Dragons breathed fire, but guvres breathed venom that could melt the flesh from your bones. Their bites were slightly less deadly but no less terrifying.

"A rare and elusive creature, my lord," Mr. Warsen said nervously. "They're considered nearly impossible to train."

"Yes, well, I've hired a very talented tamer of wild beasts. I have no doubt he'll be successful once the animal is delivered to me."

Evie almost snorted.

Good luck, Blade.

The boss did a double take when he spied a small desk and wooden chair pushed up against the corner. "Is that where you used to do your work, Sage?" He walked over and ran a hand over the desk, his lips pulling up lightly at the corners when he saw the little heart she'd carved into it nearly a year ago.

She ignored his question, determined to finish what they came for. Determined not to go down memory lane when it eventually led to a steep drop off a cliff.

"My boss was hoping to procure a collar for the creature, Mr. Warsen." She took a step forward and nearly gasped when she felt a shot of pain in the scar on her right shoulder. She was quickly reminded of the magic in the blade he'd cut her with, the way her skin was probably glowing, even now, beneath her clothes.

Wincing and rubbing at the wound, Evie watched Mr. Warsen's eyes follow her hand. He smiled.

She hated him.

He lifted a familiar dagger, holding it between his hands like a sacred object. Its uniquely white-colored blade gleamed and glittered beautifully, but to her it looked like a threat. "The last project we worked on before you left, Evangelina." The closer the dagger came, the more her shoulder began to throb. He must have known, because he looked smug when he saw her wince again.

The universe was granting her small favors, it seemed, because her boss remained distracted by the little etchings on her old desk, looking lost in thought.

"I remember," she said flatly, keeping the tremor out of her voice. "I told him I wasn't certain a collar of that magnitude would be something you were capable of, Mr. Warsen, but perhaps I am mistaken?"

He took the bait like a fish on a hook. "Of course I can!" The man's chest puffed up, and he threw his arms wide. "Take a look at a few of my creations, my lord!"

They both did a full scope of the room, blades and metals hanging from the walls like trophies. "Very impressive," The Villain said, walking back toward the two of them until he was standing beside Evie. His warm presence and the smell of cinnamon drove a relieved exhale from her lips. "So you think you're up for the job? I don't want to tax you, especially with such an unfamiliar type of restraint."

"It's not unfamiliar!" Otto objected before lowering his voice to a heightened whisper. "Between you and me, my lord, I once designed a collar for a real-life dragon." Evie began to have a daydream of grabbing a wooden floorboard and whacking the smug look right off his face.

"Is that right?" her boss said, trying to mask his interest.

"It was a secret project, solicited by one of King Benedict's Valiant Guards." Mr. Warsen's grin was superior, so full of esteem for himself that he didn't realize her boss was playing him like a fiddle.

She couldn't believe it, but she felt like laughing. Evie resisted a sudden urge to plant a kiss on The Villain's cheek for making this moment easier. But he had a habit of doing that, making her float when she was feeling like she'd sink.

"A special agent?" she said lightly, acting awestruck. "I wasn't aware the king had a dragon in his possession."

Otto turned to her, but his gaze snapped right back to The Villain, wanting to keep his attention. "No, our esteemed ruler would never want any part of an animal like that." The blacksmith's eyes widened as he shook his head at her boss. "Not that there is anything wrong with harboring rare beasts, my lord!"

"It's hardly a savory hobby for a leader as esteemed and benevolent as our King Benedict," The Villain said, a look of deference on his face.

He was a fantastic play actor. If Evie didn't know the subtle shifts of his expressions, she'd truly believe the respect and admiration he was showing for their kingdom's ruler, his literal enemy.

But Evie spent an inordinate amount of time studying her boss's face, so she *did* catch the slight tick in his jaw and the rumble of something dangerous behind his words.

"Perfect for a strong-willed nobleman like yourself, my lord!" Otto said, turning to grab a cloth hanging on the far side of the room and wiping the sweat from his dirty forehead.

"Maybe you should bend over so he can have an easier time kissing your ass," Evie whispered to her boss in a low voice.

"That *would* ease things a bit, wouldn't it?"

She gripped his arm, hard. "You can't make jokes on top of my jokes without warning; I may faint from the shock."

"Noted," he said dryly, rolling his eyes. "Mr. Warsen!" The Villain called the man over with a smile on his face. "I have to know—what need of a dragon's collar would King Benedict have without harboring the dragon itself?"

"It does seem a curious sort of request," the blacksmith agreed before pausing and looking around them as though to ensure they were still alone. "If one doesn't know the whole story, that is."

"And how much might it cost for a person to learn the whole story?" The Villain dug into his front pocket, retrieving a heavy-looking pouch clanging with gold pieces.

Was that the glisten of drool coming down from Otto's mouth?

"I think for ten gold pieces, I may be able to recall the tale in its entirety." He pulled on his suspenders, waiting for The Villain's response with a greedy glimmer in his eye.

"Five," The Villain said, walking closer to the man, causing Otto to tilt his head back so he could look her boss in the face. "You will do it for five, won't you?"

He asked the blacksmith a question, and yet it did not feel like one. It felt like a command, one that a person dared not refuse.

Clearing the fear from his voice with a cough, Mr. Warsen took a step back, holding out a hand. "O-Of course, my lord. So generous of you."

The pieces clicked together when they hit the man's hands, then deposited immediately into his pocket. "Have a seat, please, my lord!" The blacksmith settled himself onto a rickety stool, gesturing to another stool across from him.

The Villain gripped the stool in his fist and dragged it closer to them, closer to Evie. "Here you are, Sage." Without another word, he moved to the other side of it, leaning lightly against a wooden support beam, arms crossed.

Evie felt the leg of the stool wobble under her weight and twined her fingers together on her lap. Otto eyed the space between the two of them, giving just a hint of disdain before switching quickly back to a jovial expression.

"Where shall I begin?" He rubbed a thick finger against his chin. "It was half a year ago, if I recall."

"For five gold pieces, I should hope you are recalling everything accurately."

Evie loved watching Otto squirm underneath The Villain's censure. "Of course, my lord, yes, it was six months ago, nearly to the day! I was hard at work, hoping to finish early so that I might find company with a woman." He winked at her boss in camaraderie, but The Villain merely lifted his brow, waiting for the bastard to continue. "It was late. I'd had a few too many drinks, you see. Helps keep you warm at night."

"You must get cold during the day as well," Evie remarked innocently. "You did use that method often."

The bitterness in her words must have become more pronounced, because she felt The Villain's head dip so he could look at her, his scrutiny like a caress against her cheek.

Otto thankfully ignored her, as though her words were like the annoying buzz of an insect that could be swatted away.

"It was the beginning of the week. I was flooded with orders and repairs. But a man came in, asking for a very special order. He said he worked for the king."

A man.

There was, of course, no guarantee that the person who'd placed the order for the collar was the person who'd infiltrated their offices, but whoever it was had a direct line to them.

"Did you happen to see what the man looked like?" her boss asked, his goals and focus singularly on solving this perplexing little mystery.

"I didn't—he wore a mask. It had the king's symbol on it, the two swords crossing over the lion."

"And he requested a dragon collar for the king? When he had no need for it?" The Villain began to tap his fingers against the hilt of the sword hanging around his waist. He was itching for violence; Evie could tell. "That is exceptionally peculiar, is it not?"

"Apparently…" The blacksmith leaned closer, looking all too much like a conspirator. "He was doing some sort of undercover work. Everyone thinks King Benedict's been too passive when it comes to dealing with The Villain."

The use of his moniker had Trystan standing up at attention. "Do they?" But Evie could tell he was pleased with this development.

"Oh yes. For all his strengths, King Benedict has a good heart. There's a rumor that The Villain was once an apprentice of sorts to the king, and that's why he's been so quick to let him get away with all his nefarious doings."

"It *would* be by the benevolence of the king and not of his own merit," her boss said darkly. "The Villain doesn't have the intelligence to outsmart him."

Otto nodded in furious agreement, oblivious to the fact that The Villain was probably imagining several different ways to decapitate him. "But apparently the good king has us all fooled. I think he's had inner dealings with The Villain on his own all this time."

"Why would you think that?" Evie asked.

"Because the man who was here said that the collar was going directly to The Villain's lair at Massacre Manor. That the king found out about The Villain acquiring a dragon, and the collar was to be a subtle message to him. That his days of wreaking havoc were numbered."

And there it was. The flat truth they'd been looking for, laid out before them. And yet they were no closer to learning the identity of the traitor—or the king's ultimate plan.

Evie's heart raced. It was funny, really, that she had felt such anger and dread when she'd entered this room, and despite finding exactly what they wanted to know, she was going to leave it feeling the same way—worse, even.

Which simply wouldn't do.

The stool groaned loudly as she stood. Shoulders back and chin high, she looked Otto Warsen directly in the eyes. "You were very helpful, Mr. Warsen, thank you. Unfortunately, my boss will not be needing your services after all."

The blacksmith nearly toppled off the stool with the force of his sputtering, "You— I— How dare you speak for your betters, you insolent little brat!"

Evie imagined for a moment that she saw steam coming out of the man's ears and nose, and a small smile graced her lips.

A slip.

When Otto's eyes caught the movement of her lips, he went from enraged to explosive. But his oncoming meltdown was disrupted when The Villain stepped forward and held up a staying hand, looking at Mr. Warsen like he was nothing more than an inconvenience.

"What my assistant says is true. I have no need of your services any longer. As it turns out, I don't think you can provide me with what I require, but I thank you for your time." There was leveled calm in her employer's voice, like the stillness in the wind before the beginnings of a storm.

"Of course. I wish you luck on finding someone who can serve you better," the blacksmith sneered.

The Villain turned to Evie. "Are you ready to depart?"

She nodded, a little awestruck by the exchange. They both began for the door, but then Evie saw Mr. Warsen move toward Trystan with that all-too-familiar dagger in his hand.

And she started to scream.

CHAPTER 28

EVIE

"**S**ir—" But the word came out on a strangled gasp as she fell to her knees in all-consuming, burning pain.

It wouldn't have mattered anyway. Before Evie had said a word, her boss was spinning toward the blacksmith and gripping his wrist in his hand. Otto screamed, dropping the dagger to the ground near The Villain's boot, and her boss kicked it clear across the room.

"Please, my lord, my sincerest apologies. My temper, you see—I have trouble managing it. It's like a beast overtakes me."

Evie stayed on her knees, as if watching The Villain about to mutilate this man was a holy scene she was worshipping.

"Do you know what I find humorous, Mr. Warsen?" There was nothing jovial in his tone at all. The storm had arrived. "That you treat your actions and choices like they are not your own."

She watched, with no small amount of glee, as the bones in the blacksmith's wrist shattered under The Villain's grip. Warsen let out an anguished cry. "Please, my lord! My livelihood is my hands. I'm nothing without them!"

"See, Mr. Warsen," The Villain said darkly, hypnotizing. "This…this you can blame on me, that I just broke your wrist. I am responsible for that." Another squeeze.

Otto began to sob as his knees gave out and he fell to the ground. "I beg you."

There was a blackness surrounding The Villain now, that flare of inhumanity in his dark eyes as he looked upon the sobbing man.

For the first time since entering this space, Evie was not at all afraid.

"Blame is an interesting thing." The Villain's voice was level, calm, like he was talking about the weather. "Most people shirk blame, as though our flaws make us weaker."

"You're right, my lord!" Otto sounded desperate. "I am weak. Very weak!"

"They avoid facing their demons like they're something to fear, to be ashamed of." The Villain squeezed Otto's wrist once more, pushing him against the ground now. "And they are cowards for it."

Otto sobbed harder, his cheek pressed against the wood of the floor.

"That is the difference between you and me, Mr. Warsen." Her boss bent his knees, going closer to the mess of a man before him. Evie searched for any amount of horror at the sight she was beholding, but all she could summon was a mixture of satisfaction and relief.

And it was utterly mesmerizing.

"I don't run from my demons. I *welcome* them. I let them envelop me until I grow stronger." The Villain released Otto's wrist, leaving him sprawled out and shaking, and turned to walk toward the dagger that had been kicked to the other side of the room. He slowly bent to pick it up, then faced her finally.

He knew.

"A weak man pushes blame away from himself like a disease, to poison and spread over the rest of the unsuspecting world."

Evie tried to remain steady as she brought herself to stand. "Be careful—that blade has magic embedded in the steel," she warned, taking a subtle step backward.

But it was too late for pretenses, because the moment he held the blade up just a few inches higher, sharp pain, like fire, electrified her nerve endings. "Agh!" Her free hand clutched the back of her shoulder as she felt the room begin to spin.

She watched her boss chuck the dagger to the farthest wall, the blade burying to the hilt. Evie gasped as the pain left her in an instant, and she wobbled for a moment before her forearms were gripped in his hands.

"Why?" he demanded low, but there was a light softening the corners of his eyes.

He wanted to know what her past was here, but she couldn't admit her shame. Not to him. So instead, she did what she did best: deflect.

"Well, when you squeeze someone's wrist like you're trying to make juice out of it, their bones tend to break," Evie said, stiffening slightly at the new sensation she felt as his thumb stroked just below her elbow.

"Sage."

She sighed and pulled away, moving over to Otto Warsen's sobbing form, growing quite overcome with the desire to press her boot against his injured wrist. But the closer she got, the more she realized there didn't seem to be a point.

He had passed out, and if Evie were to ever inflict pain purposefully on another human being, she wanted them to be fully conscious for it.

"Sage," he called again. "Why did you really leave this position?"

"Are you asking because my shoulder pain tolerance is coincidentally linked to the proximity of that dagger?" she joked weakly.

"You have a death blow in your shoulder," he said. "Do you understand what that means?"

"I—"

"It means that if I hit that scar at just the right angle with my magic, you die." His tone was growing harsher; he was angry.

But Evie didn't care, as there were more pressing issues now. "I would be willing to bet a lot that whoever came in here placing the order is the inside man at Massacre Manor. Our focus right now should be finding that person and then using them for intel on King Benedict, making them *our* mole."

She could see a war behind his eyes, but it was impossible to tell what sides were fighting and which was winning.

"We know we're most likely looking at a man, based off the information Malcolm and Mr. Warsen gave us." Evie began to pace farther away from the wall with the dagger, just for safety. "But we won't completely rule out other possibilities."

"You mean Rebecka Erring?" The Villain said, seeming to give up pursuing his other question for the moment.

"It's possible."

A soft groan came from the large man still lying in a sad heap on the floor, shattering the illusion of calm that was just beginning to surround them.

"We're trying to talk—quiet down there." Evie sighed, seating herself once more on the rickety stool. "What are we going to do about him?" Her whole body was starting to feel fatigued, like she'd run a hundred miles, which was unlikely—running and her went together like lightning and a metal rod.

Only run if someone is chasing you.

"Kill him?"

"Is that your solution to every problem?" she asked, exasperated.

"No, it's just the most effective."

"Not in this case." Wrapping her hands about her waist, she sighed. "If we kill him, the entire village will know in a matter of hours. And if anybody saw us come in here, I would be in trouble."

"Very well. Then he will leave town."

"How are we going to get him to do that?"

"Kill him and make everyone *think* he left town." The mischief in Trystan's eyes caused her to chuckle to herself and shake her head as he continued. "I will have my guards come and clean up the little mess we made."

"We?" She raised a brow.

He walked over to the blacksmith and nudged him with his boot. "They will convince this wretch, in the politest manner possible, to leave this town and his forge behind and start new somewhere else."

Then he slammed his fist down hard to the right of the man's head.

Evie gasped. "Why did you do that?"

"That will keep him down until they get here. Is there a way to lock the door?" He turned to her, all business, much to Evie's relief.

"Yes, and there's a sign as well." She jogged to the front, opening the door just a crack to turn the wooden sign hanging from OPEN to CLOSED, before slamming it hard and turning the lock.

When she came back, her boss was propping the man up, gagging him, and using one of the chains from the wall to pin him there. "We can leave out the side, and I'll send the guards back within the hour. And before you ask, I assure you, they will be discreet."

"How will they know where to come?" She just wanted to go to sleep; her shoulder was aching, and the dagger on the other side of the room was making her feel more confined than any cage ever could.

The Villain pulled a small slab of crystal from his pocket.

"You're going to call them here with a crystal?" she said with blunt skepticism.

Trystan arched a brow. "It's a caller's crystal, Sage."

Evie grinned. "How'd you get one of those?" She barreled toward him, gripping her hand under his to get a look. Caller's crystals were hard to find. The jagged and colorful objects were magically made, usually one at a time but eventually resulting in a full set. Each crystal of the set was made from a piece of the largest of them, like a beacon. Evie had heard a story of them once when she was six years old and used to pick up every shining gem in her mother's jewelry box, hoping if she dreamed hard enough, someone would come find her.

"I have friends in high places," Trystan said, pulling the gem back and closing his eyes. It glowed for a moment, and Evie's brows shot up when a low-pitched melody called back. "The guards will be here shortly."

She nodded, walking toward the dagger once more and letting herself feel the sharp edge of pain.

"Is there a way to get rid of the link between the dagger and the closed wound on my shoulder?" she asked, feeling dizzy.

He was suddenly very close, lightly pulling her shoulder back and away from it. "We'll talk to Tatianna, see what she can do."

"It doesn't usually hurt like this. I didn't even know that being near the blade would cause that sort of reaction. I'm sorr—"

"I certainly hope you are not about to apologize for someone hurting you."

She smiled, sheepish and a little flattered that he cared. "You're not all bad, are you?"

He looked offended. "How dare you."

"I know killing him would have satisfied you, for Mr. Warsen's part in aiding the person trying to take you down." She nodded, knowing full well everything The Villain did worked off an angle. "But I still appreciate you caring, even if it's only a very little, as his death might cause *me* to be the one to suffer."

He didn't move or say anything, so she shrugged and walked to the back corner of the room. She reached along the wall and said, "There's a false panel here that will lead us out the back. Very close to Hickory Forest."

She enjoyed a quiet victory when the wall gave in just one spot, letting through a crack of sunlight. "I think I'll return home for the day. If there's nothing else, sir."

Following her out, ensuring the door panel was set in place behind them, he tucked the magic dagger that he'd pulled from the wall into his belt, taking a step back when he saw her wince at the closeness of it.

"Yes, of course. I'll see what Tatianna can do about this." His dark eyes found hers and she felt pinned, but not from his power, the way she'd felt before. It was a look of knowledge, a look of understanding, and it made her feel as if every cold, painful feeling seeped out of her to make room for the warmth.

"Thank you, sir." Evie headed down the path that led to her home, shocked that the sun was still shining with so much chaos happening below it.

"Whatever he did, whatever happened that you ended up harmed, you are under no obligation to share it with me," he called out, and when she turned around, he looked uncomfortable, like his clothes were too tight. "But if there is ever a time when you decide you do not want him existing in the same world as you are, I hope you know, I will enjoy destroying him."

"Maybe I will," she said lightly. "Tell you what happened sometime." She winked at him before beginning once more down the path to her home and tossing over one shoulder, "Over a disgustingly sweet cup of cauldron brew."

The echo of his laughter carried her home, made her feel safe in a way she hadn't in a very long time.

Until her shoulder began to sting again and her reality came crashing back in.

CHAPTER 29

THE VILLAIN

It was finally time.

Trystan ducked as another swamp of purple mist melted a large patch of trees directly next to him. The heat from it singed the corner of his—his *hair*. Sprinting a few yards away, he reached up to feel if the strands were unharmed, yanking his hand down swiftly when he saw Keeley staring at him with a strange expression.

Trystan lifted his chin and refocused on the rest of his Malevolent Guards ducking around the guvre, waving their arms to distract the animal. Nature was wilder and less inhibited this close to the western edges of Hickory Forest, but the overgrown trees provided reprieve from the cloying heat. The animal had been lounging around this cliffside for more than a week, the longest since Trystan had decided to start tracking it, to catch it.

He'd seen a guvre once before, long ago…

Blinking hard, he forced himself back from the past, refusing to give the blackness that lived there a moment's thought. The creature looked different from the female he'd seen then. Her features had been stronger, more defined, her rough, snakelike skin a muted brown. The male he was looking at now was created to impress.

The smooth skin of his back was a shocking array of pigment, like every time the sun hit it at a different point, a new color emerged. Trystan scanned the creature's every move, a kaleidoscope of bursting and twinkling color.

Twinkling? He'd been spending too much time with Sage.

Moving out from behind the tree, the rest of his body was revealed, color by color. The animal wasn't bigger than the dragon currently freeloading on his property, but he was quick like fire. His wings flared when he moved, the shine making some of his guards stop to stare in wonder. His long body rippled and coiled, boneless. His head was that of a serpent, and it shone brightly like the rest of him.

"Unless your desire is to spend your final moments on earth melting into it, I would suggest *you continue MOVING*!" The Villain bellowed. Something he didn't care to do as a rule, but their carelessness seemed to demand it of him. "Keeley! Do you have the sleeping draught?"

The head of the Malevolent Guards nodded, tossing him the vial. "Are you sure you want to be the one to do it, sir?"

He gritted his jaw, eyes narrowing on the beast. "It has to be me."

This was his battle. He'd been waiting for years to capture this creature, and it would be only his life in peril when he did it.

The sleeping draught was concentrated—a drop could take down a horse, two drops an elephant. A whole vial? The guvre wouldn't be standing long. The risk was in the time it would take to work. He was going to be cut to ribbons, and he hadn't even had his afternoon pastry.

But he needed the male if he was going to catch his mate.

The Villain felt a satisfying malevolence curling in his magic, the gray mist appearing at his fingertips. *Not yet*, he soothed it. *Soon*.

There were sure to be questions around the office as to why Trystan would want a guvre and, if word got out to the public, why *The Villain* would want it. But his reasons were rooted in nearly everything he'd done over the last decade of his life. If King Benedict wanted something, The Villain had to get to it first.

Once The Villain acquired the guvre, it wouldn't be long until the news creeped its way back to King Benedict, by way of his office traitor, exactly how he intended.

The Villain smiled to himself. Victory would soon be his.

Even if it meant placing his guards and himself in possibly the most danger they'd faced in a while. As if on cue, the serpent hissed another spray of venom that just barely missed his guards, trees melting as the purple goo-like substance struck the bark, the leaves disintegrating like dust.

Sighing, Trystan gripped the vial of sleeping draught in his fist, using one of his hands to remove his black cloak, watching the garment fall to the ground. He was left in the attire he reserved for his least favorite tasks. Black leather hugged his legs, and boots lighter than his usual donned his feet and shins. His black shirt was tighter than what was comfortable, but he didn't want to be encumbered by the extra fabric.

The Villain darted around his guards, who continued to wave furiously and keep the guvre distracted. The grass made no noise beneath his feet as he crept closer and closer to the creature's back. He had one shot to get it into the beast's mouth before he let out another wave of his venomous breath.

This, upon reflection, was not my most well-thought-out plan.

Of course, Blade wouldn't have been a helpful solution, either. His résumé, full of raving accounts of all the magical creatures he'd worked with, had been pure exaggeration, clearly.

With a sigh, The Villain realized that his office and its workers were beginning to resemble a badly drawn cartoon sketching. But there was no time for letting that manic imagery weigh him down.

There was a stiffness in his legs as he ran, thighs burning, heart pounding. He dove around one of his guards, Andrea, shoving her out of the way from a blast of the guvre's breath.

She rolled and landed expertly, then screamed at another of his guards, Dante. "Wave your arms higher, you fool!"

Dante's arms were already flailing so hard, he looked like a drunk ballerina. "I'm waving them! Trying not to die, Andy!"

Trystan was close enough now to leap onto the creature's back, but the serpent's head was too high, too far away. His original plan had been to come at the creature from behind, waiting for him to open his mouth so he could thrust the sleeping draught in. But he only had one shot—he couldn't waste it.

This was suicide, and it was very probable Trystan was going to die. But dying in the pursuit of revenge was every villain's dream, so he couldn't find it in himself to mind very much.

"Hey!" The Villain yelled. His power seeped from his fingers, that familiar gray mist flowing out and around him as the creature turned with a screech so forceful, it blew his hair back from his forehead. Trystan looked for weak points, but a death blow wasn't an option; he needed the beast alive. Only one weak point was visible on the creature's foot, highlighted in yellow, barely enough to give it a paper cut.

The guvre shook his magic off, and almost immediately, any sort of hold Trystan had crackled until it shattered. He wasn't powerful enough to hold a creature of this size for more than a few seconds, but those few seconds were enough.

The guvre's mouth opened wide, a swarm of purple smoke beginning to fog out. The heat of it hit the top of Trystan's forehead, and he felt his skin singeing, burning. But The Villain smiled through the pain, for he had waited just long enough. Uncapping the vial with his teeth, he threw the draught right down the creature's large throat. It disappeared into the now-aggressive wave of heated breath that was burning through his skin so fast, if he stood there a second longer, the bone of his skull would see the sunlight.

The draught didn't take as long as expected, but neither did the damage from the swamp of breath that melted the bramble where he'd just been standing. A little close for his liking, but he didn't die, so there was that. The animal teetered to the left, his head jerking and swaying, still spraying the noxious mist.

"Move!" Trystan yelled. "Get out of the way!" His people scattered, flipping and rolling away from patches of melting ground, a rankling cry ringing out as a lick of mist brushed against Dante's leg.

"Fuck!" he yelled, jumping away and gripping the back of the red leathers he wore. "That hurts!" Dante leaned his neck around to look at the burned-away fabric of his pants, revealing a sliver of his…ass.

The guvre swayed drunkenly for a beat and then finally dropped to a heap with a resounding thud. But his guards barely noticed, too busy laughing at Dante being stripped by their prey.

Trystan sighed; he was so very tired. Wincing and reaching up to feel the wound on his forehead, he added being in pain to his list of complaints, along with the fact that his orderly life seemed to no longer exist.

"When you all cease that annoying sound coming out of your mouths, may I kindly ask you to do your jobs and get the animal to the cart?" The Villain gestured toward the incredibly large, carted cage he'd had made specifically for this purpose.

As soon as his sentence was complete, his guards were already dragging the creature onto the tarp and moving him inch by inch toward his future of imprisonment, as humanely as Trystan could manage. It couldn't be helped—removing the dragon's collar had opened up a level of...compassion. It was a hindrance already, but it needed to be minded.

He couldn't believe he'd done it. Something Benedict had been trying to accomplish for years. This was and would forever remain Trystan's victory over the man who had ruined everything, had ruined *him*. A yellow flower among the undergrowth left in the forest caught his eye, and his mind conjured an image of Sage.

Ruined.

He didn't feel ruined with Evie, though. He felt reborn.

What a fucking disaster.

CHAPTER 30

EVIE

"It's crooked," Becky insisted.

Evie pushed the frame higher onto the wall, nearly stumbling from the ladder she was already precariously close to falling from.

"So is your face," Evie mumbled under her breath, feeling the burn in her biceps from pinning up the sides of the heavy artwork.

"What was that?" Becky called up. Even a couple of feet below her, she still found a way to look down her nose at Evie.

"Nothing," Evie muttered. She hated herself for it, but the normalcy of their endless display of cutting words gave her a level of familiar comfort. After all the unpredictable abnormality of the past few weeks, it was nice to have something she could count on.

"Really? I thought you said something about my face being crooked." From somewhere across the room, Evie heard an intern cough into their hands.

"Evie would never say anything like that." Tatianna's teasing face appeared below her. "She's far too moral."

"I am not," Evie said with a frown. "I can be ruthless." Or at least, her version of ruthless.

Distracted by thoughts of doing evil to Becky to prove her point, Evie felt her foot catch against the ladder rung and slide down a peg.

"Careful!" Becky yelled. "Don't drop it."

"And of course, don't fall," Tatianna added mildly.

Since Evie's return to work after quitting, Becky had taken it upon herself to bring rule following to…an obscene level.

Just last week, Becky had issued a memo that all employees must be punctual, well-groomed, and without the odious scent of dragon upon their person. Which of course meant Blade had to spend several minutes in the washroom before entering their offices each day—which he didn't—or risk being written up—which he did.

If that wasn't enough, Becky had decided that any free and idle moment must be utilized to increase work productivity. She'd cut the spare fifteen minutes they were all given each shift in addition to ten minutes of their half-hour lunch break and replaced them with an "extras" assignment sheet. Every single task on the list was worse than the last.

But it was futile to resist, for the few who did found their paychecks "misplaced" at the week's end and their desks suddenly moved to the part of the office the spiders seemed to populate.

Startlingly, at the top of the extras list was Tatianna, who'd been given the horrifically tedious task of refilling their ink vials for their office supplies. At the healer's protests, especially because of the risk to her gowns, Becky had told her this was a good opportunity to wear more appropriate work attire, since her lavish pink dresses were better suited to a ball than to a respectable organization. Tatianna had thrown a pillow at the woman. A pink one.

"Lift up the corner. It's still crooked," Becky advised, as though Evie's arms weren't shaking with the effort to hold up the large piece of art.

Sweat beaded her brow, and Evie snapped back, "Please do me a favor…and shut up." This somehow worked—Becky didn't reply.

Evie's palm burned where it slid against the metal, and she pushed the corner of the frame higher before it could cut farther into her skin. The fact that she was even doing this in the first place was a little absurd, but she didn't trust anyone else to peek under the cloth before she unveiled her precious find.

"I hope whatever you picked from storage to replace the last portrait is worthy of the front wall," Becky said, and Evie could just *hear* that she had one eyebrow raised.

It was no secret that Becky was bitter about what had happened to the last portrait. She apparently had given it to the boss as a gift. It was an ugly art piece Becky had said was an abstract work from an elusive artist, and she never failed to brag about it whenever anyone breathed in the artwork's direction.

The sudden whipping sounds of flapping wings from the courtyard caused Becky to flinch, and Evie chuckled to herself and reached out to straighten the frame one last time before climbing back down the rungs.

Blade and the dragon had been working together like a finely tuned machine, but they still had some rough edges to smooth. Still, Evie had grown fond of those edges. Seeing as yesterday afternoon the dragon, who was still growing accustomed to free range with his wings, came crashing through one of the stained glass windows. Not Evie's favorite brew companion in the kitchen, thankfully.

It was just as well; it had been an incredibly boring and unproductive beginning of their week until that point.

After leaving Otto Warsen's smithy, a sense of finality and closure following the incident, the boss had become distractingly preoccupied with an issue he didn't seem to need her for.

But Evie contented herself with the sweet bit of joy she'd get with the dangerous stunt she was about to pull with this art display.

After the dragon had plowed through the window, taking the hideous painting with him in his destruction, Evie had yelped in fear before feeling a moment's satisfaction at seeing the painting's fiery end. The abstract portrait had been staring into her soul for the better part of the last six months.

"I doubt whatever you found in storage will live up to what hung here before." Evie didn't mind the disbelief in Becky's voice—not when she was subtly winning their battle of wills.

"Nothing can live up to that eyesore." Blade chuckled, joining them for once without a wound or blood coming from some area of his body. Kingsley was sitting comfortably on his shoulder.

"Yes," Becky drawled, looking Blade up and down. "Let's take advice from the man who woke up today and decided bathing was optional."

Blade smiled widely, like her insults were the sweetest of compliments, and sauntered closer. Kingsley's eyes darted around, looking for a means of escape from the squabble. Evie watched Becky's back go straighter than usual as she took a tiny, almost unnoticeable step backward from the frog.

But Blade saw. Evie could tell by the twinkle in his eyes, but also by the way he stopped in his tracks instead of bringing Kingsley closer. "If I ever need a new cologne, I'll ask for whatever scent you're wearing that allows you to smell so lovely, even when your rules are so rotten, Rebecka."

Evie caught a flash of red glowing around Becky's cheeks and almost stepped in to tell Blade to lay off. But before she could, Becky said, "Just pull the tarp, Evangelina. I have work to do."

With a quick smile, Evie grabbed one corner of the cloth covering and yanked, revealing the canvas she'd spent the last hour framing and hanging.

There was stunned silence, quickly followed by the howl of Tatianna's laughter. An intern walked by with a tray of cauldron brews, caught sight of the newly unveiled portrait, and stumbled into the nearest desk, spilling the cups of liquid everywhere.

"It's the boss," Blade said, wide-eyed, biting his lip to hold back a smile.

But it wasn't—or it was, just the public's perception of him. Evie had been walking through the village square last night, only to find a cart selling large, hand-painted canvases of the hideous rendition of The Villain for half the price.

It was the best money Evie had ever spent.

"It's horrible!" Becky was slack-jawed, her look of horror only sweetening Evie's little play at revenge on the boss for leaving her out of his most recent plans.

It looked worse in a larger size, the flaming-haired depiction of the man clearer and the letters in bold at the bottom standing out with perfect clarity.

THE VILLAIN
WANTED FOR MURDER, TREASON, AND GENERAL VILLAINY
DANGEROUS. PROCEED WITH CAUTION.

"Add 'hideous' to the charge list." Evie and Tatianna snickered at Blade's comment. Becky threw her arms in the air, glaring at all three of them with pure venom.

"You all make a mockery of the work we do here." She pulled her chin up, then jumped slightly at Blade's laughter. "The boss offers each of us decent, though private, employ. And if each of you had any sense, you'd show just a bit more respect for it, given how rare that really is."

The entire group paused before Blade spoke again. "I'm sorry," he said quietly, concern pinching his features. Followed quickly by panic when Becky spun on her heels, walking away. "Rebecka! Hold on!" he shouted, passing Kingsley into Tatianna's hands before rushing to catch up to the fast-moving woman.

Feeling a strange sense of defensiveness for Becky, Evie realized she really didn't know much about how she'd come to work here. Had never even asked. Perhaps it was time she changed that. Maybe if she took the time to know Becky, they could find a common ground from which to build.

"Tati, can you have Marvin let me know when the boss returns? I want to see his face when he comes in and sees the new art."

"Then turn around."

Evie froze, moving slowly in the direction of the voice, knowing exactly who was going to be standing there. Even without Kingsley's eyes darting behind her and him popping up his little sign that now read TROUBLE.

"Good afternoon, sir."

CHAPTER 31

THE VILLAIN

The caricature was amusing.

But what truly caught his attention, making him do a slight double take, was the look on his assistant's face. There was a mischievous tilt to her mouth, a maniacal satisfaction gleaming in her eyes.

He had a wild thought of getting a hundred more of those hideous depictions of him hung around the room, just to keep seeing that look on her face.

Sage gasped, her eyes going wide as she finally took in his appearance. "What happened to you?"

Ah yes, he'd forgotten to clean up the blood.

"I had a small run-in with a guvre," he admitted.

Wiping at the oozing burn on his forehead, Trystan flinched away from his own hand. Catching a guvre was not easy work, but it needed to be done.

Thinking of the guvre reminded him of the blacksmith…and the way Trystan had carelessly missed how discomfited Sage was in the man's presence.

Finding small marks of her throughout the smithy's workplace had disarmed him. The carvings on her old desk were clumsy but sweet. The paper butterflies that had been left stuck to the windows, identical to the ones Sage had cut up and put all over the walls on her first day of work. They had driven him mad.

But he'd been oddly bereft when she'd taken them down.

Seeing the little touches of her everywhere in the blacksmith's shop gave him a jittery sort of joy, which was oddly distracting. Thus Trystan had missed her flinches until it was almost too late. And he found that he hated himself for that quite a bit.

That was a problem.

He could tell his assistant was fighting the urge to rush to his side and look more closely at his wound...which was not necessary. "May I speak with you a moment, Tatianna?" he said and moved to a more discreet area of the office. Far from his assistant's reach—and ears.

Glowing dark-brown hands appeared before his face, but he waved them away. "Thank you, Tatianna, but it will heal quickly enough."

He coughed, his gaze darting to his assistant, who was holding a very lengthy conversation with Kingsley, if the rapid flashing of one-word signs was anything to go by. He turned back to Tatianna and said in a low voice, "There's a dagger for you in my office."

The healer lifted a brow. "Who am I stabbing?"

"What?" But he quickly recognized the same sardonic twinkle in her dark eyes from when they were children. "It's a magical one. It, um— Ask Sage about it."

"Is this about the magic-ingrained scar in her shoulder?" Tatianna whispered, her eyes narrowing with concern.

"She told you?" Trystan asked, one eyebrow raised.

"I felt it every time I healed her. But I never asked, and she never told me." Tatianna looked to Sage, who was currently holding up her thumb in answer to a sign from the frog that Trystan couldn't make out from here. He shuddered as he imagined what Kingsley could be convincing her to do now.

"It pains her more when she's near it, the dagger," Trystan said, feeling oddly small, unable to fix this for his assistant on his own. "Can you do anything?"

A calm fierceness lit Tatianna's expression. "I will do whatever I can...to help her."

It gave him comfort, however insignificant or ridiculous, that Tatianna looked as if she would take on the whole world before allowing it to touch Evie Sage.

"Thank you." Two words he didn't say often, but if anyone deserved them, it was Tatianna.

She nodded, patting his shoulder in a friendly, familial way before she strode off toward his office, the pink train attached to her dress gliding behind her.

Trystan wandered back over toward Sage, who was looking satisfied as she angled her thumb back and forth at the painting, Kingsley ribbiting beside her. A rusty chuckle nearly escaped the back of his throat before he caught himself. Instead, he leaned down and put his head alongside hers above the crook of her shoulder. He pretended that he didn't hear her breath hitch, pretended his wasn't an echo.

"It's crooked, left side," he whispered, quickly stepping back from the vanilla smell of her that was making it difficult to form full sentences.

"Ugh, Kingsley, you were right," she said and reached out to adjust the frame.

Trystan felt his palms itch with the need to touch her, which was absolutely unacceptable.

He spun toward his office, and the scuff of his boots moving farther away caused his assistant to sprint forward until she was walking beside him. "I'm sorry. You've been out of commission basically all week, and then you just casually say that you were playing with a guvre!"

Pushing the door to his office open, he was glad to see Tatianna had already retrieved the blade and left. He grabbed the chair closest to his desk and angled it slightly toward the window. Only because it looked nicer that way; it had nothing to do with the sun hitting it at just the right angle, causing sparks of light to glint in Sage's long black hair.

He just liked the chair there.

"I wasn't playing with it, Sage." He winced as he sank into the comfort of the other chair, not bothering to go around his desk to his own. He resisted a deep sigh as his assistant sat down and the sun fell over her cheeks.

It was just a good spot for the chair.

"Oh, were you two discussing tax reform with the creature, then?" she muttered dryly, fingers brushing lightly over the notebook she never seemed to be without.

"I need the guvre because King Benedict wants him," he admitted. It was just simpler that way.

"What need does he have for that thing?" Evie asked curiously.

"I don't know. I just know that if there is something the king wants, it's imperative he doesn't get it."

"Because of the stepping-on-your-foot thing?" Sage asked rhetorically and leaned over his desk to grab the quill out of the inkpot, giving him a perfect view of a light freckle on her exposed collarbone.

He poured what was left of his water canteen down his throat to stanch the dryness.

"You really caught a guvre?" Sage began writing something furiously in her little book. "Should I research how to maintain one?"

"No time." That of course would've been the prudent course of action, had Trystan not spent the last decade preparing for this.

They'd caught it.

Finally.

It was truly the look in the creature's eyes when he'd faced him that had affirmed his fears, an emotion he so rarely felt. But when a creature of that size peered into your soul, it was chilling. He'd locked the beast away in the cell, one large enough for him to move around freely, with a keen understanding between them.

They both had someone to protect—the creature understood that.

Or he was slowly losing his mind, and the dark clouds that swept in from distant skies, dimming the light around Sage's face, were a metaphor for how he blackened everything he touched.

"That's odd," Sage noted, tilting her head at the darkness cast from the window and then jumping slightly when thunder shook the walls.

"No, unfortunately that's to be expected when you keep a guvre against their will." He pinched the bridge of his nose, clenching his fist with his other hand.

"A storm?"

"They're called 'fate's vengeful creatures' for a reason. Holding one always has some sort of natural consequence that becomes worse the longer you keep them."

"So the natural consequence for holding this guvre is a storm?" On cue, lightning lit up the sky, followed quickly by another echoing boom of thunder. Her small hand came up and gripped his forearm, her eyes wide in alarm.

Her touch burned.

Shaking her arm off, he stood up and slinked closer to the wall, trying to bring about a distance that allowed him the space to think properly.

She narrowed her eyes at his sudden withdrawal.

"It would appear that way, yes." The skies chose that moment to split open and deluge the manor in pounding rainfall.

She had to raise her voice slightly to be heard over the torrential downpour. "And are you planning on releasing the creature by the day's end?"

"No, I cannot." He needed him at least long enough for the cogs of his plan to roll together. For the traitor to inform the king.

Sage sighed, moving toward the door, a sense of purpose in her gait. "I'll send the interns for some bedrolls from the laundry room, then."

"Why on earth would you do that?" Trystan asked, an uneasiness beginning to creep around him like a stealthy predator.

"Because if the storm keeps up like this, there's no way anyone can leave here safely at the end of the day." Her gaze was pointed as another crack of lightning lit up the room around them. She paused as if she needed to carefully choose her next words. She needn't have bothered. Waves of doom were already roiling in his stomach.

Finally, she said, "We're trapped here for the night. Together."

Lightning lit up the sky once more, flickering over Sage's lips, slightly turned up at the corners. He leaned hard against his desk when the door closed behind her.

Squeezing his eyes tight, he tried to organize his thoughts.

But as lightning flashed yet again, he couldn't help worrying that his plan for vengeance had given him more than he bargained for.

CHAPTER 32

EVIE

"It's huge!" Evie gasped.

Blade turned to her then, a sly smile on his lips. "If I had a gold piece for every time—"

A loud *smack* wrenched through the air, and Blade winced and clutched the back of his head.

The Villain didn't even look in Blade's direction as he brought his hand back to his side. "It's smaller than the dragon."

Her boss had been very quiet since she'd left his office to make sleeping arrangements for everyone. After dismissing the interns and leftover workers to the guest quarters across the courtyard under heavy guard, he'd invited Evie to the back corner of the cellar to see the creature for herself.

And the guvre was horrifying.

"Yes, but Fluffy doesn't look like that." Evie tilted her head, and the serpentlike animal angled his head with her. "Stop being cute—you're supposed to be a living nightmare."

He looked like one, at least, despite the somewhat docile manner with which he was currently conducting himself.

His eyes were large and bugging out of his head, which was sloped and tapered at the nose like a snake. When he took a step closer to the bars, his bat wings flared out, the leathery membrane so like the dragon's and yet different in a way that made her feel intimidated.

"Why are we keeping this horror show in our cellar again?" Evie asked, giving the vicious animal a little wave and gentling her expression when he tilted his head again at her.

She turned to get an answer and saw her boss watching her motions carefully, something light in his eyes and a slight upturn of his lips, so small she almost didn't catch it. "Sir? Is something wrong?" she asked curiously.

He shook his head and cleared his throat, shifting his gaze back to the bars. Ignoring her question, he said, "Guvres are notoriously mated animals."

"And you thought we could assist the creature in the courting department?" Blade asked dryly, creeping a hand through the bars, clicking his tongue. Amazingly, the guvre crept closer and nudged his head against Blade's hand.

"How did you do that?" Evie's eyes widened.

Blade shrugged. "Animals like me."

"Oh yeah, you're just always in the infirmary; I forget sometimes." Evie hadn't meant the words to sound so insulting, but of course she realized this after they'd already been spoken aloud.

To her relief, Blade chuckled and adjusted his vest. "It's the less desirable part of the job, to be sure."

"I would've thought the less desirable part would've been cleaning up the creature's excrement."

Blade and Evie both stared at their boss with open mouths. "Did he just make a joke?" Blade asked her in an exaggerated whisper.

She returned her answer at the same volume. "I *know*. He's been doing that a lot lately."

"Interesting. Do you think—"

"Enough!" Their boss put both hands on his hips, looking dark and formidable. "If you two don't mind, I'd like to finish what I was saying."

"Oh, no!" Evie said with false innocence. "We don't mind—go ahead."

Quirking a brow, seeming to want to smile once more, her boss shook his head and opened his mouth to speak. "Guvres are typically mated animals. This particular guvre's mate is of value to me."

"Then why not just capture the guvre's mate? Why go to the trouble of taking this one?" Blade began throwing slabs of beef through the bars, and the creature swallowed them without chewing.

"Because it's nearly impossible to catch a female guvre; they're too cunning, too smart. The males are far easier to defeat. Besides, this female guvre is already in captivity."

"What? Then how do you expect to catch it?" Evie asked incredulously.

"Female guvres are vengeful creatures, and the best way to capture one is to lure her in with her mate."

"That doesn't explain how you expect this female to get here if she's being held behind bars."

"Do not mistake me. When I say vengeful, I mean it in the most extreme sense of the word. If a female guvre believes her mate is in danger, there are no bars in this world that could hold her." A gravity settled over the room, and the only sounds were the hums of the creature beside them.

Evie waited for Blade to return to the office upstairs before she walked closer to the cage, pointed an accusing finger at The Villain, and whisper-shouted, "King Benedict! He's the one with the female guvre in captivity!"

Trystan glanced down at her finger and lifted a brow. "Very astute, Sage."

"Why would King Benedict keep a guvre?"

A rolling noise came from the cell, stilling them both.

"Was that a purr?" Evie leaned forward and tentatively reached through the bars as Blade had. A small yelp left her mouth as two large hands wrapped around her middle, yanking her backward.

"I would prefer you not lose a hand, Sage." The gravelly voice was in her ear, sending a series of pleasant chills down her spine. "He may be cute, as you so eloquently put it, but he has a temper."

"Hmm…I think I know someone like that." Evie gazed up at him pointedly, and her boss rolled his eyes.

"King Benedict has had his mate in his possession for ten years."

"Ten years?" she exclaimed. "What sort of consequences must that have wrought?"

The Villain released her with a wry, mysterious grin, then paced away. "Regardless, tonight, that will change."

The Villain always became distant when he spoke of his vengeance, like in order to tap into it, he had to go somewhere else. Somehow, Evie knew it was best to leave him alone with it, too. Who was she to stand between a man and his need for retribution? Honestly, if he ever shared his motivations with her, she might even join him with glee.

"I need to get back to helping with the sleeping arrangements, sir," she said and ventured back to the stairs of the cellar that would lead her into the office space.

She'd nearly made it to the top before The Villain's shocked voice carried to her. "Sage...did you just call me cute?"

She opened the door, a grin on her face.

But as the heavy metal clanged behind her, a sense of impending doom chased away her good humor. Because tonight, The Villain wouldn't be the only one seeking revenge within these manor walls.

If everything went according to plan...a frightening guvre was coming for her mate. And not even The Villain was going to be able to stop her.

CHAPTER 33

EVIE

It was impossible to focus when one's eyelids had been weighted with lead.

Evie pushed them wide with her hands, commanding her body to adhere to her wishes. "You're not going to sleep," she told herself. She'd just gone through her last vanilla candy—a tragedy, since she could use the jolt of sugar right about now. The office space was ominously empty, the only sounds the roar of the storm outside. Her father was probably beside himself with worry, but hopefully the missive she was able to send out on one of the ravens made it to him without delay.

According to her boss, the storm was plaguing most of the kingdom now. His guards had informed him that everyone was to remain indoors until the storm passed. But it wouldn't, not until the guvre was set free, and that couldn't happen until her boss got what he wanted.

The heavenly smell of cauldron brew filled her senses as she looked up to see a steaming chalice placed before her. "You are my favorite person," Evie said before looking up. "Whoever you—"

Becky stood there with an equally disgusted expression.

Evie shrugged, taking a sip of the warm liquid before pulling the chalice from her lips to stare at it. "Is it poisoned?"

"Isn't it a little pointless to ask that after you've already drunk it?" Becky asked in confusion.

"I needed the caffeination either way; a little poison never killed anybody," Evie said, smiling into her mug when Becky looked frustrated to the point of pain.

"It quite literally kills everyone. That's what it's for, you ninny." The woman was almost as literal as the boss.

"You bring me brew and then insult me." Evie put her hand to her chest in mock offense, her words taking a moment to sink in. "Wait. Why *did* you bring me brew?" she asked with a healthy dose of suspicion.

"Anyone with eyes could see you were dead on your feet, and if you are determined not to go to the guest quarters like the rest of the workers to wait this out, I would rather not have to listen to you snore while I actually *work*." Becky returned to her desk across the room, completely ignoring Blade's wave of greeting when he walked past her.

Looking a little like a kicked puppy, Blade appeared in front of Evie's desk, dark hair damp from the rain. "It's six in the evening—let's go break into the boss's wine cellar and make a night of it."

"You will *not* be doing that!" Becky gasped, standing up, spilling the cup of pencils that was teetering at the edge of her desk.

"Have no fear, Becky. I won't drag you into our shenanigans. I know better than to implicate you in any kind of unsanctioned fun." Blade smirked and ducked when Becky chucked one of the pencils at his head, and it knocked into Evie with the eraser side.

"Hey!" Evie whipped around to Becky. "Didn't you lecture the boss last week about throwing rocks, you hypocrite?" She grumbled, rubbing at her head, before Tatianna appeared with two bottles and five glasses.

"I've brought wine, Blade! Let's drink. You too, Rebecka—I don't want to hear it." Tatianna placed a glass on her desk and filled it to the top.

"We can't…" Becky stared at the glass like it was filled with actual poison instead of wine.

"We can. The workday is technically over, and this wine is from my personal stash," Tatianna said, brushing one of her pink ribbon–tied braids behind her before pouring a glass each for Evie and Blade.

Evie accepted hers gratefully and took a bracing sip, feeling the warmth spread down her throat and her aching limbs.

"Can you call it 'my personal stash' if it's stolen from *my* personal stash?" Their boss appeared like an apparition, and while Blade was damp, The Villain was soaked to the bone. As was Kingsley, who sat high up on the boss's shoulder, his gold crown dripping and shiny like the rest of him.

The Villain's black shirt clung to every curve of muscle on his torso. Evie gulped as he walked toward her, a thick intensity cloying the air.

"I told them they shouldn't be drinking, sir," Becky said quickly, knocking her chair over in her haste to stand.

"Please relax, Ms. Erring. I realize being here overnight is an inconvenience I imparted on you all. You may cope accordingly." Their boss looked to Tatianna and the last empty glass. "As long as that glass is for me."

"But of course!" Tatianna said jovially, filling it to the brim and handing it to him with a flourish.

"No sign of the female guvre?" Evie asked, watching her boss down his glass in three long sips, then holding it out for Tatianna to refill.

"None." He walked toward one of the stained glass windows. Kingsley leaped off his shoulder and onto Evie's desk as he walked past. "But I'm not surprised. It'll take time."

"How will we know when she comes?" Becky asked.

He turned to the group just as a crack of lightning lit up his face. "We'll know," The Villain said ominously.

"Did you plan that?" Evie asked, nodding toward the storm.

Blade chuckled into his hand, and their boss rolled his eyes at them. "You two are incorrigible."

"I agree," Becky muttered darkly, sending her glass of wine a longing glance.

"Just drink it, Rebecka." Tatianna walked over, putting the full glass right under her nose. "The boss literally told you to relax. Where's your rule-following spirit?"

It was hard for Evie to tell if Tatianna hated Becky or deeply respected her. Their interactions had always teetered somewhere in the middle.

Taking a tentative sip of her glass, followed by a contented sigh, Becky sank farther into her chair.

"Atta girl." Tatianna gave her an encouraging pat on the shoulder that Becky nudged off while taking another sip of her drink.

"Careful, lovely Rebecka." Blade raised his glass like he was about to give a toast. "You may enjoy yourself, and your body may go into shock."

Evie chuckled when Becky lifted her middle finger back to him, making steady eye contact as she drained her glass. Evie saw Blade's throat bob as he tracked the movement.

Another bout of lightning struck down, the crashing thunder shattering a window and causing each of them to duck their heads, covering them with their hands.

Blade peeked out from under his and frowned at the shattered glass. "Who, uh—who's picking that up? Because all the interns are off for the night and my fingers are very sensitive."

"To glass?" Tatianna said dryly, pouring more wine for Evie and a slightly dazed-looking Becky.

"I'll clean it," Evie said. The warmth was beginning to settle in, making her feel lighter, the threads in her chest unraveling. She moved to the closet to grab a dustpan but was halted by Tatianna, who raised her hand. With a flick of her wrist, the shards of glass lifted and clattered into the trash bin.

Blade sighed with a mock frown. "I wish I could do that."

Tatianna's beautiful smile stretched wide. "You have your own special talents, my dear."

"Like being irritating," Becky added.

"Or getting injured." Evie giggled.

"What about his complete lack of self-preservation?" Tatianna chuckled, sipping her drink.

"I don't like this game," Blade said darkly, downing his glass.

"The color blindness is also something to be admired."

All heads turned to look at their boss, who was watching the interaction from just a step away, like he didn't want to fully immerse himself with the living. His wineglass was empty, and Tatianna moved to uncork another bottle to top him off.

Blade looked at The Villain with betrayed outrage. "You too, sir?"

Their boss shrugged, a blank look on his face, making his comment all the funnier for the seriousness with which he'd delivered it.

"We could do the boss's talents next?" Tatianna looked gleeful, the wine making her eyes brighter, her face glowing.

"No, you will not—" But the boss's voice was drowned out by Evie's and Tatianna's tittering.

"His inability to smile at anything that's not related to death or torture." Tatianna cackled, and Evie laughed with her.

She gripped her stomach, tears burning the corners of her eyes. It was the kind of laughter that was difficult to stop, and the more you tried, the more intoxicating the urge became—the best kind, her favorite.

"The obsession with his hair," Evie added, wiping her eyes.

"What about his talent for heaving bodies out of windows!" Blade added.

Kingsley held up two signs: BAD and JOKES.

"Making the interns cry just by looking at them for too long," Becky added quietly, warily.

They all laughed even louder, Tatianna tilting her chalice toward the woman in a silent toast. Becky looked around, the smallest, almost indetectable smile appearing on her naturally downturned lips.

Evie's laughter finally died down to something more manageable when she looked toward her boss, who was watching them all, watching her, with a strange look in his eyes. He was at ease, peaceful. That eternal lock on his jaw seemed to have come loose, and there was a relaxed feeling to him as he said, "I am not obsessed with my hair."

That was what did it. All of them spiraled into a second, larger wave of hilarity. It was like medicine, healing all the broken pieces and forging them into something new, something different. Belonging was such a foreign concept to Evie, something she quietly longed for but had never figured out how to achieve, but here it was. Her moment, her people. It was worth the wait—

A flash of light and a thunderous boom shook the walls, sucking the levity from the room like a leeching.

The Villain's jaw went back to its rigidness, and he walked over to look out the window.

"Sir? Not to pressure you, but do you have any idea when the female guvre will arrive?" Evie asked tentatively, walking up to his side.

A piercing screech wrenched the air.

"Was that…"

"Yes." The Villain nodded, keeping his gaze on something outside the window. "She's here."

CHAPTER 34

THE VILLAIN

"**G**et back up there!" The Villain thundered from a sheltered alcove in the courtyard, reeling backward when his assistant appeared behind him with a large net. "And what in the deadlands is that for?"

The rain was coming down even harder now, the sounds of the creature's screeches piercing his eardrums. The dragon shuffled his feet in the opposite corner, ducking under one of the large castle archways in the open courtyard. The guvre hadn't arrived yet, but she was close. Sage appeared beside him in her dress that was so wet from the rain that it was wrapped tightly against her soft curves.

"It's a net!" she yelled back, holding it up and looking at him like he was the one who'd lost his mind.

"Yes, I've gathered that!" It was amazing that even with the roar of a violently dangerous creature heading straight for them, it was this conversation that was giving him the pounding beginnings of a headache.

"How else are you going to catch it?" she said, confusion pinching her thick brows together, a charming crinkle appearing there.

And now is certainly not the time for me to be noticing charming crinkles above my assistant's eyes.

"I had something a little more concrete planned," he said, gesturing to the open grate on the other side of the courtyard. "That leads right into the cellar, next to the male guvre."

"Will she fly through on her own?" Sage asked, a drop of rain trickling enticingly down her cheek. His fingers itched to brush it away.

He nodded, turning his head back to the sky, waiting. "Nothing will keep her from him, remember?"

"Then why hasn't she flown into the hole yet?" Sage yelled over the rain that was now coming down impossibly harder than it was before.

"She's not a fool!" he roared back, lightly pulling her arm to bring her back under the eave when she arched her neck out to get a look at the guvre. "She knows she'd be flying into a trap. She's trying to see if there's another way to get to him."

Light flashed in the corner of his vision, followed by more glass shattering. Sage gripped his arm like a vise and used her subtle strength to yank him closer to her. Just in time for one of the archways to collapse right where he'd stood, a cloud of debris coming over them.

Trystan became unexpectedly aware of his hands, which were somehow on the curve of her hips after Sage had pulled him closer. Feeling himself now breathing heavy for reasons that had nothing to do with his near brush with death, he lifted his gaze from his hands to her lips.

She was breathing heavy, too, both her hands gripping his forearms. "Thank you," he said finally. His voice had gone embarrassingly hoarse.

Another screech snapped him from his bewitchment with her face. Separating awkwardly, he noticed that Sage seemed unshaken by the exchange. Which did not bother him in the slightest. Why would being near him have any effect on her at all?

"Oh, no problem. You getting crushed by a few blocks of cement would've been a very anticlimactic way to go."

"Have you thought very much about how I would die?" he teased, hoping to clear the air of tension with a jest.

But as always, his tone was a little off, because Sage's eyes widened in offense. "Of course not, sir!"

Sighing and pinching the bridge of his nose, he tried to correct her. "Sage, that's not what I—"

But she surprised him when a mischievous grin overtook her wounded expression. "You're so easy." She laughed, another raindrop trailing to the tip of her nose.

Mirth climbed into his chest and made a home there as he smiled wide and free. "That is the first time I've ever been accused of that."

But the moment was shattered when the roof above them began

to crumble. Gripping her damp hand in his, Trystan pulled her along until they narrowly avoided being crushed once more.

Now out in the open, wholly exposed, he felt a moment of panic. "Go back inside," he ordered Sage.

"Only if you will," she argued, the outline of her figure clearly visible through her soaked dress. He peeled his eyes up to one of the towers, ordering himself to keep them there.

"I need to be here to close the grate once she flies inside!" he argued.

"Why can't you have one of your guards do it?" She was exasperated, he could tell, because her hands were flying around like a manic butterfly.

"I will not delegate a task this important." He hadn't done it when catching the male, and he wouldn't do it now. His plans were just starting to come to fruition, and no doubt the traitor in his office was scrambling, along with King Benedict, now that Trystan had the upper hand.

"You are aware that being a control freak is going to kill you?" she shouted over the rain, rolling her eyes before they widened in horror. "Duck!"

They both ducked then as a brownish-gray blur flew over them, swooping down near their heads, almost knocking them from their necks. This guvre was as horrifying as he remembered.

She was large, larger than the male. She could have shadowed the sun, were it making any appearances.

"She's beautiful," Sage said in awe.

"She's horrifying," he corrected.

Sage shrugged, eyes taking in every gruesome part of the guvre's body. "Oftentimes, it's the same thing."

He felt his knees bend unwittingly, like his body was attempting to bow. The creature's flight pattern was becoming clear as she moved closer to the grate with every dive. The guvre would realize soon, the only way to be with her mate was to allow herself to be trapped inside with him.

When it comes to the thing one loves most, Trystan thought before running out in the open toward the grate, the sounds of Sage's screaming protests behind him, *it is always better to be trapped together than free and apart.*

CHAPTER 35

EVIE

"**W**hat are you doing?" Evie screamed into the storm, but there was no way Trystan could hear her above the noise. The guvre howled when The Villain swerved into her line of vision. Evie watched him crouch slowly, picking up the edge of the grate lid, ready to slam it shut at the right moment.

A helpless feeling seized the blood in her veins, her stomach bottoming out as she watched the lethal animal dive closer and closer to her boss. The guvre's taloned feet were splayed and ready to pluck prey from the ground. Evie screamed when the guvre raked a claw over her boss's shoulder, a bright spray of blood visible despite the murkiness of the rain.

To her relief, her boss straightened, seeming unaffected by the wound save for a slightly more hunched stance. *It's only the venom in their breath that's lethal*, she reminded herself. If her boss steered clear of the creature's mouth, he'd live to see another day.

And then Evie would pulverize him.

"Come on!" she heard him yell. "He's waiting for you!" The creature had landed at the top of one of the towers, her slow huffing and stillness casting an eerie calm over the scene. "You were too weak to get to him before. Are you still?" He was baiting the beast, like she could understand him.

Whether she did or not, she was angry. And Evie's boss had grossly miscalculated. She could tell by the flash of panic on his face when the creature flared her wings and opened her mouth wide before going in for one more dive. Her intent was clear.

She was going to kill him.

Evie didn't think much after that, but she noticed things, of course. Her heartbeat in her ears, her boots beating against the pavement. Her dress, heavy and wet, making her steps slower. Trystan's eyes when he looked to Evie's fast-approaching form, putting up a staying hand, enraged. The creature closed in, and Evie saw rather than felt her fingers come up to her mouth, and she whistled loudly.

Her mind wandered back to her first year in school and how she'd won a contest for being the loudest of all the whistlers. She'd gotten a medal, and now probably all she'd get was sliced in the face by an overgrown flying snake.

Adulthood should be illegal.

The creature reared up, angling itself at her with the same expression of fury as before, perhaps even angrier. Evie took a slow step backward, then another.

"Sage!" Trystan yelled in her direction.

"I got it, I got it!" She took one more step before swallowing hard. "Run!"

And she did. Through the ruined back archway and then through the large open doors. Around the corner of the entryway, nearly to the stairs. But then a dark shadow came over her, and she realized the steps above her were melting before her eyes, the stone liquifying into a dark goo.

Freezing and spinning around, Evie fell to the ground when she realized the creature's head was less than a foot from hers, venomous breath permeating the air, making it difficult for her to breathe. "Oh no, no, no, no." She repeated the word like a prayer, like a mantra that this couldn't possibly be happening to her. Throwing her hands over her face, just the touch of the hot, cloying breath skimmed her palms.

She screamed.

It burned like acid, eating her flesh alive. She prayed she'd pass out soon, as perhaps then she wouldn't have to be fully conscious for her imminent death.

Evie cracked her eyes open, noticing a small alcove underneath the stairs. Rolling toward it, she desperately tried to ignore the persistent stinging in her hands the minute they touched the ground. Tucking herself in as small as she could, she hugged her legs to her chest and lowered her chin.

The creature screeched again, only this was not the cry of attack but a wounded sound. It was followed by a loud, creaking *thud*. Evie carefully untucked herself and moved just her head outside the alcove to see if her suspicions were correct. And they were.

Smiling despite the pain she felt, Evie pushed the rest of her body away from the space. The female guvre lay on her side with her scaly eyelids closed.

"That took a while. Did you slip on your way in?" she asked.

Her boss stood there, chest still heaving with the force he'd used on the battering ram that he must have ripped from the wall display. "Are you critiquing my rescue?" He wiped the water dripping from his forehead and shook out his shirt.

"No, I'm critiquing the time in which it took you to execute the rescue," she said before narrowing her eyes in realization. "And this wasn't even *your* rescue—it was mine. If I hadn't distracted her, you would've been an evil pancake."

He tossed the battering ram aside with the same effort Becky had used to throw her pencil before walking to the female guvre's side and putting a hand to her neck. "She's alive. I just hit a vulnerable point. She'll be out long enough for my guards and me to take her to the cellar."

"Are we changing the subject because you're embarrassed that you were an evil overlord in distress?" Evie walked to his side, feeling a moment of pity for the felled creature. "It's nothing to be ashamed of. Happens to the best of us."

"I'm not ashamed—it's just untrue." He always played right into her needling. To the point where Evie wondered if he did it on purpose, just to entertain her. But she nixed that theory, because really, why would he care about her entertainment?

"You cannot be an evil overlord in distress," he continued, "if you save the hero immediately after she saved you."

"So I suppose we saved each other, then." Evie smiled, wholly unaware of why the sentence shut something off in her boss's eyes.

"Head back up to the office." He nodded in the direction of the ruined stairs. "I'll take care of this."

"Um, sir?" Evie asked.

"What?" The Villain said shortly, his eyes finding the ruined stairway covered in molten liquid. Eyes flashing to the unconscious animal, he muttered, "Did she—"

"Yes, sir."

"Damn it."

"I'm sure it's fixable," she said, patting his arm. "In the meantime, you need to find a way to get this winged lady to the cellar downstairs. And try to stop getting yourself into trouble in the meantime; I can't keep saving you."

It was meant to be a joke, to lighten the moment, but it sure didn't feel like one when The Villain's molten gaze landed on hers.

CHAPTER 36

EVIE

The storm cleared the next morning, as she suspected it would. The creature's vengeful magic had run dry—he was reunited with his mate and the clouds had gone.

Evie stared at the mirror, seeing herself in a borrowed dress of Tatianna's. It had been a little too large when she'd first put it on, but as soon as the buttons up the back were secured, the bodice slowly tightened around her until the dress fit like a second skin.

"Well, that's a fun trick," Evie said, inspecting the blue velvet in the large mirror on the other side of the healer's quarters.

"I got it from a magicked dressmaker when I was visiting a friend in Verdelana." Tatianna smiled, walked over, and turned Evie's hands to inspect under the bandages. "All the best magic comes from the south. He said a dress should be worn to fit you, not the other way around."

"So, no matter what…?"

"It'll always fit like a glove." Tatianna narrowed her eyes, clearly looking at the dark circles underneath Evie's. "Did you sleep at all?"

"A little. Your extra bed was comfortable." And it had been. Evie's hands had just ached, even after Tatianna had worked every bit of magic on them. Growing back skin in places where blisters had formed was no small task, and in some areas Tatianna had admitted they were so badly damaged, it would take several magic sessions to fully heal. For those areas, Tatianna applied a salve, but Evie refused a bandage of any sort, in case The Villain were to notice the damage and ask questions.

She'd seen his reactions to her being harmed before, and the last thing Evie wanted or needed was for him to begin to think that she was incapable.

So she'd barely slept.

Of course, the healer did all that after forcing the entire story out of Evie as payment. Including the fact that she'd hidden her ruined hands, by some miracle, from her boss at the time of the injury.

The clanking of glass snapped Evie's attention back to Tatianna, who was already at her worktable, crunching leaves and all sorts of funny-looking plants into jars. "What's it like? Living with *him*?"

Tatianna snorted and continued working, the sun just beginning to come up over the horizon. "I wouldn't say I live *with* him. I only ever see Trystan in the office or on the rare occasions his wounds need tending. If I desire company, I go to the nearest pub and find myself a beautiful woman to pass the time with."

"What about Clare?" Evie said slyly, ignoring the daggers Tatianna glared at her over her bowl of herbs. "It seemed like things might not be finished there."

"Oh, they're finished," she grumbled, mashing the herbs harder than before. "She made sure of that."

"I think you'd feel better if you talked about it," Evie said in a singsong voice, ducking when Tatianna chucked a spoon at her.

"I deal in secrets, darling. I don't give them away for free."

"Even to a friend?" Evie asked, a little vulnerability slipping through.

Tatianna huffed, but then her face softened. "Oh dear. We are friends, aren't we? How did I let this happen?"

"Because I'm irresistible." Evie spun around, running her fingers through her hair, laughing when she nearly lost her balance.

"Oh yes, that must be it." Tatianna smiled.

"Well?" Evie urged, nodding to the small clock on the table. She still had twenty minutes before the boss would expect his first cauldron brew of the day on his desk, and in truth, she was eager to hear about how the two animals in the cellar were faring. "I've got time."

"It's a long story." Tatianna groaned, like talking about her personal life was an offense against her character. "The short version is, I grew up down the road from the three Maverine siblings. Clare and I were inseparable ever since we were children."

Evie's eyes widened, both delighted and a little flabbergasted at what this development meant. "Does that mean…you knew The Villain—I mean Trystan—" She didn't know why, but she'd never once thought of her boss as anything other than being born fully grown.

"Yes. I knew Trystan since we were very young." Tatianna shifted, looking uncharacteristically uncomfortable in her own skin. Like she was unsure of herself. "It's not really something I should be talking about with you."

Sighing and dragging a chair closer to sit right across from the healer, Evie said, "How many of *my* secrets do you know?"

"You get hurt a lot, so…many," she said apprehensively.

"So," Evie pressed. "Don't you think you owe me at least one? *Friend?*" She said the last word with wounded innocence in her eyes.

Tatianna groaned again and put her head in her hands. "You are a conniving little manipulator." She pulled her head up, looking at Evie with a disbelieving smile. "You've been here too long."

"Oh please, we're just getting to the good part." Evie grinned, leaning forward, and gestured for Tatianna to continue.

"What do you want to know?" A wicked look crossed the healer's face, followed by a quirk of her brow. "Why *do* you want to know?"

The quickening beat of Evie's heart was certainly just because it made her uncomfortable to be scrutinized so directly.

"Who wouldn't?" Evie rationalized. "It's hard to picture that man as anything but that…uh…man." *Why is it suddenly so hot in here?* She stood up and walked toward the windows, pushing one out until fresh, cool air brushed against her warm cheeks. "I mean, was he always so…" She weighed her words before turning back toward Tatianna, who finished for her.

"Brooding? Grumpy? Terrible at feeling and exhibiting normal human emotions?"

"Yes." Evie nodded.

"To which?" Tatianna asked, a confused look passing over her face.

"Yes," Evie repeated flatly.

Standing up from her chair, Tatianna walked toward the door of the quarters. "If you must know anything, know he was hard to read even then. He always kept to himself, always doing his best to keep any attention off him."

Evie stared, absorbing every word like precious nutrients, as the healer continued. "He had a quiet kindness to him, though." Tatianna smiled then. "He never was around much when I would come to be with Clare. He was a few years older, so I always thought it was because he didn't want two annoying little girls bothering him."

"But?" Evie asked, sensing the word before it was spoken.

"But on my tenth birthday, my mother had a party for me. My healing magic had shown up a year before, when I'd nearly been crushed by a passing carriage. Everyone was thrilled; they thought I could be a core healer."

Evie couldn't believe the absurdity because, from her meager understanding, core healers were so rare, they were practically myth. It was normal for magic to be ignited in someone by something painful, but very rare for that person to have healer's magic—much less *core* magic. But that was what core healers were. They could heal minds, bodies; some said they could heal your very soul to your core.

A myth, she thought.

Tatianna continued. "Clare and Malcolm were my dearest friends, but it suddenly felt like I was a toy everyone wanted to play with.

"My mother had made my party an open invitation, so hundreds of people were there to witness my magic being born. It was terrible. I was dragged around by my arm throughout the entire party, people asking me to heal cuts, bruises, even dire sicknesses. I hadn't seen a specialist yet, so I had no idea, really, what I was doing or the cost. I was only ten." There was a moment in her words where Tatianna began to look like the little girl from her story, lost and overwhelmed.

"That's terrible, Tati." Evie wanted to hug her friend, but she continued her story like Evie's words hadn't registered.

"It was this birthday that showed me that no matter what I accomplished in life from that day on, I would always be defined by this one, singular ability. Nobody would ever see *me*. When the party ended, I wanted to cry. I didn't even get a piece of my own cake. But Clare and Malcolm stayed behind to celebrate with just me, for me." The sadness on the healer's face slowly shifted into mirth as one corner of her mouth tilted up. "We had fun, but they couldn't dispel the heaviness in my heart no matter how hard they tried."

She looked at Evie then, her remarkable brown eyes glittering with a grace so humbling, Evie could only stare in awe.

"And then Trystan arrived."

This snapped Evie from her near worship. "He came? To your birthday?"

"I was as surprised as you." The healer shook her head and rubbed her arm. "He hadn't attended any of my other birthdays. But he came immediately after everyone left. He baked a cake."

"He baked?"

"I *know*. But he was always fond of it. Edwin used to teach him how." Tatianna chuckled.

"Our Edwin?" Evie didn't realize the ogre's history with The Villain went back that far.

"He was our village's Edwin first—ran the bakery. Was usually who Trystan spent most of his time with—he didn't like being around the rest of the family." Tatianna shook her head. "I understand why he keeps him here. Edwin was the only one who—" Clearing her throat, Tatianna dropped the words like she'd never said them and continued her tenth birthday story.

"Anyway, Trystan stayed the whole time. He even sang when we lit the birthday candles. Very off-key, I might add."

"I would sell my soul to see that," Evie said with a deadpan expression.

The healer laughed. "He told me that 'the opinions of others are ever-changing.' And to 'never care quite so much of the world's perception of you.'"

Tatianna stood there, looking the same as she always did. Beautiful and emboldened, but now she had a subtle glow to her that wasn't there moments before. "He never brought it up again. It was one of the kindest and most thoughtful things anyone had ever done for me, but the next day, he was back to his quiet gruffness. Like it never happened. Like he didn't want to be acknowledged for an act of true goodness."

That hadn't changed much, Evie supposed. She knew her boss repelled praise like it was claws against the skin.

"What happened after that?"

Tatianna beamed, her arms going wide, and warmth spread in Evie's chest. "I decided after that birthday that if someone was going to pick one thing about me to notice, I would get to choose what it would be."

Slow realization dawned as Evie looked up with wide eyes, noting the bright pink ribbon around Tatianna's wrist. "The pink."

She nodded, gesturing to the worn cloth. "I bought my first pink bow the next day, and it's been my comfort ever since."

"Well, it looks wonderful on you, so that worked out rather nicely," Evie said before asking hesitantly, "and what happened with Clare?"

Tatianna's eyes shuttered. "All I will say is, Clare never forgave Trystan for the events that turned him into The Villain, and I did. It wasn't a problem in the beginning, but it became one, and then it was over."

"I'm sorry," Evie said gently.

The healer patted her on the shoulder and smiled tightly. "Let me get to work, my friend. We can't keep The Villain waiting."

CHAPTER 37

EVIE

"**O**ne of the maps is missing from the cartography closet." Evie's boss didn't even bother to look up from his own maps strewn haphazardly across the table in the small alcove at the end of the hall.

"Could it be because I am holding a few of them?" he asked dryly, still not looking up.

Rude.

"No, smartass. It's one of the maps that details the Valiant Guards' regular routes into the city. It's not there—someone took it." When she'd seen her boss coming out with a handful of maps that morning, an idea sparked. The Villain was getting hit through his shipments, so if any of the maps weren't accounted for...

And they weren't. Evie had spent her entire morning scouring the closet, checking each one off as she went until one box was left unchecked.

He finally looked up, brow furrowed. "I don't understand. You need a key to get into that closet, and the only people who have one are you and me."

Evie placed her hands on her hips and glared. "What are you implying?"

"Be calm, little tornado—it wasn't an accusation. Just an observation." His use of the nickname made her raised shoulders relax. "I have my key here. Where is yours?"

Evie pulled it from the pocket of her skirts and held it up, twirling it between her fingers. "And the lock wasn't broken. Could it have been picked?"

The Villain shook his head, standing up from the chair he'd been sitting in. "That lock is unpickable—it's warded with magic. I—" He paused, his face going white.

"What?" Evie practically yelled.

"There was a third key," he said, squeezing his eyes shut and pinching the bridge of his nose.

Evie waited for him to continue, feeling as if she were about to spring outside her skin. But he didn't speak, just stood there, not moving an inch. She waited one more beat before speaking, because really, this wasn't a melodrama. "*Hello!* Who has it?"

He shook his head. "It matters not." When she started to argue, he held out his hand. "Believe me, Sage. Let it go."

Because she was so very good at doing that.

But she obliged anyway. For now. She was tired more than she was curious, and that was jarring enough that Evie took a step back.

It was nearing late afternoon, and she needed to go home. Needed to let family know she was well and assure that Lyssa was still being taken care of despite how much better their father was doing over the past few months.

Shaking her head, she held up her hands in surrender. "Sir, I'm exhausted. I need to go home. Make sure it's still standing and all that, and then I need to take a nap, preferably with a toasty fire in the fireplace and the pitter-patter of rain against my roof."

The surprise on his face melted into what almost appeared to be concern. But every reaction was always such a subtle shift of emotion, it was next to impossible to interpret some days.

"Yes. I suppose we can continue this the day after tomorrow." There was no way to tell by his voice if he was angry or upset. It was too even, an almost practiced sort of steady. "I was going to announce at closing time that everyone has the day off tomorrow."

Evie blinked. "But it's the middle of the week. Why?"

"Until we find the person giving away our secrets, I'd like to have the office formally searched without anyone here to interfere. If the spy left even a scrap of a clue, I want to find it before they have a chance to get rid of it."

She nodded and scanned the lines of stress across his face. He probably needed a nap as well, but that was hardly her concern.

"I'll see you the day after tomorrow, I suppose."

"Actually, Sage, now that I've considered it, you're not getting the day off. I need your help in the search."

Evie frowned, her brows furrowing as she said, "Why am I being punished because someone is trying to blow *you* up?"

The Villain lifted a brow, ready to respond, but his head whipped to the side. The sounds of whispered giggles came down the hall, and both Evie and The Villain waited for a moment so they could greet the two wanderers. Until the echo of two voices reached them—one most likely a man and the other a woman.

"I wonder if the boss will give a reward to anyone who knows information regarding the mole." Evie could tell by the tone that it was one of her least favorite interns.

"He might…" But Evie didn't hear the rest because in her panic, she'd thrown open a panel of the wall that lay before one of the hidden rooms and threw her boss—who was apparently so shocked that Evie touched his person that he moved without protest—inside with her.

The space was not made for two people—in fact, it was hardly fit for one. Evie's entire body was pressed tightly against her boss's, his low voice hissing in her ear. "Why the deadlands did you do that?" he grumbled under his breath. "Little tornado."

"Hey," she warned, ignoring how close together their faces were. "That time 'little tornado' sounded like an insult."

"When were you under the illusion it was a compliment?" he whispered back incredulously.

She held up a hand to silence him and nodded toward the wall.

Muffled words were being spoken, but Evie couldn't quite make them out. Pressing her ear against the cold stone panel, she squeaked when the wall gave a little under the gentle pressure of her head. Before she could fall through it, making an absolute ass of herself, strong hands wrapped around her waist, bringing her back into him.

The wall stopped moving, and the continued conversation flitted through the crack, thankfully distracting her from the large male body pressed against hers.

"Whoever's screwing The Villain over better be counting their calendar days."

"Did you see the way he carried Ms. Sage in after the klutz almost got herself killed? If I knew being a charity case was all it took to get The Villain's attention, I would've made up a far better sob story in my application letter."

A cruel laugh followed the words, and Evie felt a numbness settle over her. It was freeing, in a way, that words such as those did not sting and fell her the way they used to. Despite her many moments of doubt, Evie knew who she was. She didn't always get things right, but she worked hard, and she always kept trying, even when she failed.

Those were good things to be, good things to have around.

And if Evie was able to choke down one more breath, perhaps she'd begin to believe that was true.

"Sage," The Villain whispered.

"Shhh!" she shushed back, turning toward him and pointing her finger to the door. *Listen*, she mouthed at him.

"It has to be someone higher up in the company," the man said.

"Oh, most certainly. I'm sure the boss already knows who it is. He's just giving the fool time to sweat while he comes up with the perfect plan to dispatch them."

Evie felt his hands tighten on her waist ever so slightly. She wondered if he was trying to figure out a polite way to get past her, but his fist tightened at the mention of his team. He was getting angry. She couldn't see his face, but there was a palpable energy in the air.

"Could you imagine if it was Evangelina?" the male voice said, and they both cackled at that.

Evie clenched her fists so hard, she thought her bones might crack.

"As if that woman is capable of any kind of deception. She looks like she'd get lost in her own home."

Embarrassed heat flooded her cheeks as she remembered who was currently pressed up against her—and how her boss was now hearing what the staff really thought of his assistant.

It occurred to her that many people would love to be in her position as the fly on the wall. Getting to hear the words people spoke of you when you weren't around to defend yourself. But as it turned out, it was awful. Absolutely horrendous.

What a wonderful day I'm having.

"I'm going to—"

Evie whirled around, which caused her shoulder to graze The Villain's chest in the cramped area, and put her small hand over her boss's mouth before he could say another word.

"You're not going to do anything," she whispered. "Now hush, or we might miss something important." It was quite literally torture to hear every disparaging word—but they'd stand here and listen if it meant saving Trystan's life.

Evie couldn't explain it, but she had the strong feeling something important was about to happen, like a large object was hovering overhead, waiting to drop. She just hoped they weren't standing under it when it fell.

"Did you hear what the other interns were saying?" The woman's voice was haughty.

"No, what?"

"They found a mask with King Benedict's emblem on it. In a corner of the stairwell the day of the explosion."

"What?" the male voice said, astonished. "Why didn't anyone report it to the boss?"

"My guess is they didn't want to give it to him and then be deemed a suspect for coming across it in the first place."

"Makes sense." The male voice chuckled. "Have you seen the way the man handles slights against him? Look at what he did to Joshua Lightenston."

"Oh, no." The female's voice became a conniving whisper. "I heard he did that because of what Joshua said about Ms. Sage."

Evie narrowed her eyes at The Villain, who'd gone rigid underneath her hand, black eyes looking everywhere but at her.

"We better stop this, Saline. Unless we want to be next."

"All hail saintly Ms. Sage." Saline chuckled as their footsteps faded into the distance.

Evie realized her hand was still over The Villain's mouth, his soft lips a soothing contrast to the stubble tickling her fingers.

Dropping her hand back to her side, Evie awkwardly apologized. "Sorry, sir."

Then she quickly shoved the hidden door back open and stumbled into the light, a burning sensation prickling along her skin.

"Is your hand bleeding?" His already low voice seemed to have dropped an octave. When Evie turned back to address his question, she enjoyed the sight of his back muscles stretching his shirt as he pushed the heavy wall panel closed.

"Um," she mumbled, looking down to see her nails had scraped one of the blisters that still remained on her palm. "Oh, look at that. I suppose it is."

"Is it from the burns you got last night?" He said it so casually, Evie nearly missed the implication of the sentence.

She exhaled hard, taking a step backward to have a better look at him. "How did you know about that? Did Tatianna rat me out?"

The Villain rolled his eyes, moving back to the table where his maps were. He took a seat and picked up the charcoal pencil. "Hardly. Tatianna is a vault. I knew about your hands last night."

Evie was confused and tired and still a little wounded from being raked over the coals just now by people who were meant to respect her. "Why didn't you say anything?"

"Because you were quite obviously trying to hide it. I didn't see a need to draw attention to it against your wishes." He kept looking down, his voice about as emotionless as a brick.

Well, Evie seemed to have enough emotions for them both. "Well, it's not from the burns. Not exactly," she grumbled. "I squeezed my palms too hard, which happens sometimes when I'm feeling…stressed."

This caused him to jerk his head up and look at her, too directly. "Because of what those nitwits said?" He looked in the direction they had walked, back to the office space.

"I prefer the word 'nincompoops,'" Evie said thoughtfully.

"Why?" The Villain angled his head at her.

"Because it sounds funnier."

He sighed like he was exhausted. "I don't have a response to that."

"Excellent." She nodded, itching to leave before his scrutinizing gaze burned a hole through her. But something occurred to her that gave her enough courage to look right at him as she asked, "What did Joshua Lightenston say about me?"

Evie tried not to flinch when his eyes darted away from hers and found something interesting out the window beside the table. "I don't recall."

"You don't recall?" Evie said skeptically. "You, who recalled during an inventory the other day that you'd only fired seven arrows at some knight last *year*, can't remember what an intern said a few weeks ago?"

She watched The Villain clench his jaw, and suddenly, she wanted the ground to open up and swallow her. Because, whatever was said about her, it must be unbelievably bad if even someone with as evil a heart as Trystan couldn't bear to repeat it.

"Never mind," Evie said quickly, her stomach twisting. "I really don't want to know."

He sighed. "Joshua Lightenston was impertinent. Let's leave it at that, Sage."

"All right." Evie swallowed, wringing her hands together.

"That's it?" He looked at her suspiciously, and his knowledge of her notorious stubborn streak sent a pang of familiar comfort through her.

"That's it." Evie offered what she hoped was a convincing smile. This wasn't the first time someone had said something mean about her. It certainly wouldn't be the last. "I'm tired, sir. I think I'll head home."

All of a sudden, the exhaustion from the last several days nearly buckled her knees. The guvre, her injuries, the gossip. It all just seemed too much, and she wanted to go home. To go to sleep. As if to prove her point, a large yawn escaped her mouth as she rushed to cover it with her palm.

"I'll take you home," he said, stretching his shoulders.

"That's not necessary, sir," Evie said, feeling herself sway from the exhaustion.

He put a hand on her arm to steady her. "Yes. It is."

As he gathered his maps and guided her away, Evie couldn't help but remember why she'd sought him out in the first place. Someone had stolen a map.

And Trystan knew who it was.

CHAPTER 38

EVIE

The carriage ride was silent.

It seemed the only thing that could stop the track of Evie's mouth was bone-deep tiredness, and her boss looked concerned. He kept subtly glancing at her, careful not to move his head, but Evie saw it anyway.

"You'll have to drop me off far enough from the house that Lyssa doesn't see you, or she'll never let you leave." Her voice was quiet, a rarity.

She saw him nod in her peripheral vision. "But how will she get more material for her next installment of *Trystan and the Lost Princess*?"

"I suppose she'll just have to get creative." Evie bumped her leg against his, playfully, hoping he'd bump hers back. He was still for a moment, but his thigh eventually moved toward hers, lightly tapping it.

Evie smiled and settled into the cushioned seat, staring off to her side at the passing trees, trying not to get nauseous. They were moving at a leisurely pace, the carriage rolling slowly down the dirt road, neither of them in a hurry, it seemed.

She leaned her head back but snapped up immediately when she saw something that made her heart bottom out to her feet.

Off in the distance. A lone figure walked through the trees, far away from the path. She squinted when she couldn't make out their face, only to realize there was no way to see their face, because they were wearing a mask. The mask with King Benedict's emblem on it.

"Oh my—" Hiking her skirts up, she stood in the carriage, ignoring her boss's questioning look.

"Sage?"

But she didn't answer him. Instead, she took a deep breath—and jumped out, stumbling off-kilter for a moment but then sticking the landing. And then she ran.

"Sage!"

Evie sprinted toward the figure in the woods, holding up her skirts. She heard the furious shouts from The Villain behind her and ignored them. The spy would get away—she knew they would, because the masked figure had spotted her before she even left the carriage and had started to run, too.

But she wouldn't let them get away—she *couldn't*. She picked up her speed, kicking her heeled boots harder. Closer and closer she came to the running figure until she leaped through the air, slamming into the spy and both of them tumbling to the ground.

They rolled, each trying to get the upper hand. The masked figure took a swing and Evie dodged the small fist, wrestling the figure beneath her as her gaze locked on to her assailant's *very* familiar eyes.

Her lips parted when she realized who it was beneath her, quickly accompanied by horror. She could hear The Villain fast approaching behind them, but Evie reached up before he arrived, yanking the mask from the figure's head.

She gasped and scrambled to her feet, fearful she'd empty the contents of her stomach right there.

"Becky?"

Her nemesis stared, glasses gone and brown eyes squinting up at her. "Evangelina?"

"You're the spy?" Evie was still breathing hard from the footrace, but the shakiness in her voice was all betrayal.

When she looked up, The Villain stood there, staring at them both, looking a little lost.

"What?" Becky said, realization lighting her face as she bolted to her feet. "No! Of course not!"

Evie held up the discarded mask, and Becky pulled her glasses from her pocket, placing the large circular frames against her pert nose.

"How do you explain this?" Evie asked. "What the deadlands are you doing out here?"

Becky sighed, rubbing her elbow, which must have gotten hurt in their tumble. "That's none of your business."

Evie faced her boss—who did not look as surprised by the situation as she did. "Why are you not livid? Did you know about this?"

"No," he said without emotion. "I didn't. But I think I know what she's doing with it." He looked to Becky, shaking his head in disappointment. "I told you not to give stock to the rumors."

"How could I not even try? One of the interns dropped the mask in my lap, and I thought if they assumed I was part of the guard and—"

"You thought they'd give you the cure to the Mystic Illness because you were wearing a mask?" The Villain asked incredulously.

"I thought I could at the very least sneak into the Gleaming Palace with it," Becky said, with more emotion than Evie had ever seen her express. Her own primary emotion now was confusion, along with pinching hope.

"A cure? There's no such thing," Evie said, thinking of her father, how much easier life would be again if he were well.

"You're correct," The Villain said angrily.

"But you don't *know* that," Becky insisted in a plaintive voice. This wasn't a version of her nemesis Evie knew. She sounded desperate—and a little sad—and Evie felt a swath of sympathy, an almost tenderness.

"Let me see if I understand this," Evie said, crossing her arms as she finally gained control of her breathing again. "You took the mask from one of the interns, thinking you were going to traipse into the Gleaming City and steal a cure that may or may not exist?" Evie shook her head, feeling incredulous. "Are you believing this?" she asked The Villain, who looked very much like he was believing every word.

"She is being truthful, if naive," he said, shaking his head.

When the last dregs of shock finally faded, *all* of Becky's defense finally registered. "You know someone with the Mystic Illness?"

The bespectacled woman nodded stiffly, her gaze locked on something in the distance, but her chin remained high. "One of the interns left the mask on my desk last week. They were afraid to give it to the boss. I had planned to turn it right over to you, sir!"

Evie was still wary, but the initial adrenaline had worn down and the tiredness seemed to be settling back in. "How do we know you're not lying?"

The look on Becky's face when she turned to stare at Evie would remain in her memory for the rest of her life. It was one of such pain that Evie began to feel ridiculous for questioning her in the first place, feeling worse still when Becky began to speak.

"If you knew anything about me, which you do not, you'd know I would rather hang my own head in the office entryway than ever step foot near the Gleaming Palace. Unless I *had* to."

Something told Evie she wouldn't learn those things about her, at least not today. But The Villain knew; she could see it in his eyes.

Becky tossed the mask over to their boss, who caught it and tucked it into his pocket. "I'm sorry," she said in defeat. "It was foolish."

The Villain nodded, looking back toward the abandoned carriage and the startled horses. "I need to see to them." He looked at Becky with a measure of respect and just a drop of gentleness when he said, "If we ever receive concrete evidence that the king is harboring a cure, I *will* retrieve it." He looked to Evie, too. "For both of you."

He strode back to the horses now shuffling their hooves in agitation, and Evie felt Becky's owlish eyes seeing through her. "You have... someone with the illness?" Becky asked.

Evie straightened her skirts to give herself something to do with her hands. "My father."

Becky's expression was a mixture of shock and understanding. "My grandmother."

They both stood there, silently appraising each other. It was strange. "You were really going to walk all the way to the capital?" Evie asked.

"I got the map of their usual route from the cartography closet. I thought I'd pretend to be one of them and hitch a ride right into the Gleaming Palace." The third key—now it made sense.

Evie whistled. "Terrible plan."

"As if you could've thought of anything better," Becky scoffed, rolling her shoulders.

"I never said I could. I just said your plan was terrible." Evie shrugged and smiled, self-satisfied.

"I can't stand you," Becky said, but there wasn't any heat to her words.

"Back at you." Evie rocked on her heels.

They both were silent again until they heard the boss call them over to get in the carriage. To take Evie home and to return Becky to the manor.

Before either of them moved, Evie said quietly, "I'm sorry about your grandmother."

"I'm sorry about your father," Becky said just as softly.

They both began walking, still keeping a healthy silence between them.

Evie broke it before they arrived at the carriage. "I don't like that we have something in common."

"Me either." Becky shuddered. "Let's never speak of it again."

"Agreed."

CHAPTER 39

EVIE

"**W**here have you been?" Her sister's screech filled the airy space of their home as Evie came through the door.

Her tiny arms wrapped around Evie's middle, shaking slightly. A pang went through Evie's chest as she knelt to wrap her arms around her sister. The Villain, as requested, had dropped Evie a healthy distance from her house, Rebecka frowning in the back seat. Evie had waggled her fingers at the woman before leaping out for the second time that day and running to her home.

To her family.

"I was trapped at work because of the storm. Didn't the raven make it here last night?" Evie smoothed down the back of her sister's braid, willing her to calm.

"It did, but Papa couldn't get out of bed yesterday, and I couldn't get the door to latch." Lyssa pulled back, wiping her nose on the back of her sleeve. "It was unlocked all night, and I was afraid a bandit would come steal me and trade me for treasure."

Smiling through the mental assault of imagining her little sister desperately shoving at the door, Evie brushed a tear off Lyssa's face. "Oh, you silly goose. A bandit would never sell you for treasure." Evie paused dramatically. "They'd almost certainly trade you for something more fun, like a giant bee."

As desired, the sadness disappeared from her sister's face and her eyebrows shot up, one side of her mouth quirking. "Can someone own a bee?"

"No, but I think you can rent them." Evie began laughing as soon as Lyssa did.

They both doubled over onto the floor, rolling to their backs, side by side. Evie reached out a hand and placed it over Lyssa's smaller one. "I'm sorry I wasn't here."

"That's okay. I know your work is important, and we need food, after all."

"Lyssa!" Evie laughed through a gasp. "That is a terrible thing to joke about."

Her little sister nodded, looking satisfied. "That's why I said it."

Evie laid her head back down, trying to keep the pride from her face. "You are so my sister."

"Evie?" her father's weak voice called out from his bedroom. "Is that you?"

She scrambled to her feet and rushed into her father's room.

Griffin Sage lay pale in his bed, with a stillness that sent fear spiking underneath Evie's skin. "Father?" She shook his shoulder, letting out a deep sigh when she saw his chest move.

The man, who looked far older than he had a day ago, smiled weakly. "Evangelina? You're home safe."

"Shhhh. You need to rest."

Sighing and sinking farther into his pillows, her father reached out his hand for hers. He seemed so grateful to see her, so she squeezed his hand back and added, "I'm sorry, Papa. I would've tried to get home, whatever it took, if I knew you were feeling ill."

"My sweet girl. It wasn't your fault." Her father tensed for just a moment, as though he wanted to say more, but then he relaxed again. "I think you're right. I need to sleep. I'm glad you're home, Evangelina."

Evie lifted his head gently to give him his medicine, then laid him back onto the pillow, brushing sticky sweat from his forehead with a damp rag. She watched him fade into sleep, the steady rise and fall of his chest a small comfort to her guilty conscience.

Creeping to the door, Evie inched back to her own bedroom, lying flat on her bed.

The nearly set sun glimmered one last ray through the pane of her window, catching on something gold sitting on her desk. Rising against the ache of her muscles, she walked over to the table and picked up the envelope with foiled lettering on the outside that read:

Evangelina
I thought this would be of interest
X You know who I am.

Evie nearly dropped the note as her head whipped around the room, expecting whatever intruder had placed it there to be standing in a darkened corner or lurking under her bed.

"Lyssa!"

"What?" Her sister peeked her head in the room, looking irritated.

"Did you put this on my desk?" Evie held up the envelope, freezing when she saw that the lock to her window was unlatched and there was a slight gap between the frame and the glass.

"No. That wasn't there when I checked your room this morning. What is it? Can I see?" Lyssa bounced through the doorway, and Evie felt a shaking of her nerves that wouldn't calm.

"Not right now, Lyssa. This is for work; you can look later," Evie said kindly. Her sister rolled her eyes and shut the door.

The envelope was torn before she heard the click. Her fingers ripped out the parchment, bold letters etched to the front.

To Evangelina Sage
Looking for a cure?
Briar's Peak
Tonight
Dress for a formal celebration hosted by the core healer
This invitation permits one person and one person only

Evie placed the invitation down on her desk and ran a hand through her hair, tugging at the strands. Someone had broken into her room to give her something that would help her. Help her family? It must have been the spy—why else would they be so secretive? And for that matter…so creepy.

And the core healer? Was this a myth come to life? Or a trap?

With your luck, it's probably both.

Her mind was racing, her stomach reeling and nauseous from

the thought of a dangerous stranger in the same home as her family, standing so close to where she lay her head at night. Across the hall, her father groaned in pain.

Damn it.

Running to her bed, Evie bent and pulled a large box out from underneath it, throwing it on the bed and ripping off the lid. She gripped the fabric in angry fists, pulling it up and out with none of the satisfaction she'd had when she bought the dress.

Evie had seen it in the window at the seamstress a town over and had allowed herself this one indulgence. She'd been making more than enough to support her family at that point, so there was no reason not to allow herself some luxury. At the time, she had no idea where she'd wear it, but now was as good a time as any.

The fabric appeared white, but when the light hit it, it shone every color, like a walking rainbow. It shimmered, the bodice hugging, and the thin sleeves draped off her shoulders in an enticing fashion. She maneuvered around, somehow managing the clasps without falling over or breaking a wrist. After pinning her hair back with her mother's butterfly pins, she stared at herself in the mirror.

She did one twirl and laughed before collecting herself into a serious expression. It wasn't every day she wore such a pretty dress.

She sighed at the small pot of rouge sitting off to the corner of her desk. It had been her mother's favorite lip shade. She'd given it to Evie on her last birthday before she left, but Evie hadn't been able to bring herself to touch it since then.

Sucking in a deep breath, she gripped the small pot in her hands, dipped a finger into the red, and gently applied it to her lips. They stood out bright and vibrant, and Evie had the strange sense that this person in the mirror was who she was always meant to be.

She smiled.

But then her smile faltered, her brows knitting together as she realized this dress might be what she was buried in if she wasn't careful tonight.

She sighed. At least it was sparkly.

CHAPTER 40

EVIE

Evie had no idea how or why the spy had targeted her, but if there was any hope of saving her father, surely she had to take it.

After leaving Lyssa tucked into her bed under the care of their family friend, Evie tied her white cloak about her shoulders, trying not to fiddle with the butterfly pins pulling back different sections of her hair. Briar's Peak was on the other end of town, the end good people from the village tried to avoid. Despite its lovely view over Rennedawn, it was far too close to Hickory Forest.

But since Evie had nothing to fear from The Villain, she walked along the outskirts of town nearest the forest without worry, striding toward Briar's Peak. Passing a tree and standing underneath a lantern in the corner of the square, Evie rubbed her temples, careful not to smudge the makeup she'd put around her eyes.

"Reckless. You are reckless, Evie Sage." She sighed as she slumped against the bark, her heart racing as her gaze tried to make out any shapes in the dark. Not for the first time since setting off on this adventure tonight, she wondered if she should have contacted The Villain.

Truth be told, she half expected her boss to appear anyway, the way he'd done a few days ago when she was feeling deflated and a little defeated. Besides, even if she wanted to get a hold of him, it's not like she could send a messenger pigeon at this hour—their offices closed before sundown.

She looked down to the gold band around her smallest finger.

"What good is an employment bargain if you can't talk to the person who has employed you?" She stared hard at her finger, willing the mark to obey.

"Evie?"

The familiar voice made Evie smile. She turned to face Blade Gushiken, the lantern illuminating his tan skin and the light-blue satin vest for once sitting against the fabric of a shirt—a white one.

She walked over to him and punched his arm lightly. "Why are you lurking in the dark tonight?" Evie noted the emptiness of the space around him. "You didn't bring Fluffy, did you?"

Blade chuckled and straightened his vest. "No, I did not bring Fluffy. Gods help the poor creature. Although the name seems to suit him, in a ridiculous, 'you've been hit in the head' sort of way."

Her favorite way.

"You got one of these, too, huh?" There was a crinkling sound as he pulled out a gold-foiled envelope, the paper the telltale craftsmanship of merfolk-made parchment.

Relief filled her that she hadn't been the only one singled out by the spy. It was never good to wish someone the same pain or discomfort you were feeling, but it was always very nice to not be alone with it.

Evie adjusted one of the pins in her hair when the wind knocked a curl loose, holding out her arm. "Shall we?"

He smiled wide before linking their arms, and they continued down the path together. "Do you think anybody else received an invitation?"

"No, because the world obviously revolves around you two." The sardonic voice was scathing and comforting in the most confusing conflict of emotions.

"What did I do to deserve this?" Evie asked the sky as Becky stepped into the light. Her brown hair was down from her usually tight coiffure, gently curling just past her shoulders. A soft pink dress swirling into roses at the hem sat delicately against her light-brown skin. A delicate flush of the same pink appeared at her cheeks when she saw Blade's blatant appraisal.

"I was about to ask you the same thing," Becky said, adjusting her glasses on her nose, another gilded envelope sitting between her fingers. "I suppose you both got one of these as well?"

"We did." Evie frowned, noticing the writing at the top of Becky's invitation. "What does that say?"

Becky handed it to her reluctantly.

To Rebecka Erring

Looking for a cure?

Briar's Peak

Tonight

Dress for a formal celebration hosted by the core healer

This invitation permits one person and one person only

She handed it back to Becky, and they glanced at each other with knowing expressions before looking away.

"It would appear whoever left us these sought to lure us with individually compelling reasons," Blade said, studying and then holding out his invitation for both to see.

Both angling their heads closer, Evie and Becky looked at the invitation Blade held.

To Blade Gushiken

Briar's Peak

Tonight

Dress for a formal celebration hosted by the core healer

This invitation permits one person and one person only

"That's it?" Evie pulled the invitation closer, reading it over one more time to be sure. "Yours doesn't have a reason the way mine and Becky's do. Why would you come at all, then?"

Blade shrugged, looking sheepish. "It said 'celebration,' so I thought there would be free food."

Becky shook her head at him. "You are a reprobate." She smoothed her invitation carefully. "This is obviously a ploy to get us all to this place. I say we go inform the boss immediately."

Evie urged them both to the side of the gravel path, hidden from view of prying eyes. "We're almost there—we may as well go investigate whatever this is together and then report back to the boss what we find."

"I don't like it," Becky grumbled, uncomfortably pulling at the sleeves of her dress.

"Shocking." Blade smiled, offering each woman an arm. Evie wrapped her hand around his upper arm, and Becky stomped forward beside them, refusing to meet either of their eyes.

"We're walking right into a very obvious trap," she grumbled, pushing the hood of her cloak up over her head.

"True, but at least we know that going in," Blade said, then raised one brow at Becky. "Why are you even here if you thought it could be a trap? Why didn't you take that right to the boss?"

Rebecka looked for a moment like a cornered animal before glancing away. "Because...there was a chance it wasn't. And I had to know."

Evie smiled sympathetically, showing her invitation to Becky. "Me too."

Becky nodded stiffly. "Do you think anyone else from the office received one?"

"We're about to find out," Blade said, gesturing to the glow of light and noise coming from farther into the wooded path. "It seems the festivities have already begun."

It was the first time Evie had heard the word "festivities" as a threat. In fact, it sounded a bit like death.

CHAPTER 41

EVIE

There were lights everywhere.

Briar's Peak was seated at Hickory Forest's cliff ledge. There was a steep clearing on this side, far enough of a drop that there needed to be a flimsy wooden bridge connecting one side of the forest to the other. The bridge—a generous word for it—had enough planks missing that it may as well have just been two thick ropes tied together. But the rickety thing was hardly the focus.

Not when the decadent opulence spread before Evie's eyes was demanding all her attention.

The trees surrounding the peak were decorated in floating candles, orbed in light to keep them from incinerating the leaves and branches around them. Music and laughter sprinkled the air like confetti, and warmth brushed over Evie's bare shoulders as she removed her cloak.

Blade whistled low. "You clean up well, my friend." His smile was warm, unlike the daggers Becky glared at Blade before slipping off into the fray of people swaying to the sounds of the musicians' chords.

Evie *tsk*ed at Blade, lightly shoving him. "Why didn't you say anything about the way Becky looked? Your mouth was open for a whole minute when she showed up."

Blade sighed and rubbed a hand through his thick black hair. "Because the things I was thinking when I saw her in that dress weren't fit for mixed company."

Evie ducked away from a drunken couple stumbling past her, no doubt to do some of the illicit things Blade was talking about. "That was more information than I needed, to be honest."

"You asked." He smiled suggestively.

"How rude of you to point out things that are absolutely true." Evie turned away from him, catching sight of Becky before she disappeared into the crowd once more. "Well, I hope she knows what the deadlands she's doing, because I sure don't."

They passed by a long table of unfamiliar dishes, the shapes and colors of the food almost seeming from another world. Even the wine was a thick silver, unlike anything she'd ever seen.

"Magic has some perks, doesn't it?" Blade smiled, grabbing a glass for each of them.

"Should we be drinking that?" Evie took a whiff of the liquid, amazed that she felt intoxicated just from the fragrance. "We don't know who's behind this whole thing—what if these are poisoned?"

Blade took a large gulp of his, and Evie jumped in protest. "You fool!"

He nodded toward the rest of the crowd. "Everybody is drinking them, so unless they are all being poisoned to dance in sloppily drunken circles and show blatant public displays of affection, I think we're safe."

Evie took a careful sip, resisting a moan from the euphoric flavor coating her taste buds. "How can anything taste this good?" She made for another large sip, but Blade stayed her hand.

"Careful. It's not poisoned, but it's strong. Now, to find the core healer." Blade searched the crowd, eyes narrowing hard. Evie looked in the direction that he was and smiled knowingly when she saw a handsome blond man kissing Becky's hand and looking very appreciatively at her figure.

"I'll be right back," he growled before stalking toward the two of them.

"But—"

It was too late. Blade was off, nearly throwing himself between Becky and the stranger, leaning down to furiously whisper at Becky. Who, in all fairness, had pure murder in her eyes as well at being interrupted.

"Fine, I'll do it myself," Evie muttered, examining the crowd once more for any familiar faces. There was every manner of creature here, from humans to pixies. Pure-white unicorns stood tied to trees, forest sprites dancing around them. Every breath Evie took was magic, living in the air and filling her with warm happiness.

She'd quietly hoped to see Tatianna among the splendor, flitting over with an invitation of her own. Evie had made light of writing out the list of employees who could be traitors for The Villain, but every name she'd neatly cataloged for her boss to review had dug a pit so deep in her stomach that she could still feel it now, weeks later. Such an innocent way to rip apart the people she claimed to care for. She exhaled hard, pushing against the boning of her corseted torso.

These things weren't built for people with high levels of anxiety, but at least she looked pretty.

A tap on her shoulder caused her to jump and spin with her fists raised. An older man stood there, shoulder-length red hair hanging in his face. He held out a hand, dark robes covering his body. "May I see your invitation, young lady?"

Evie narrowed her eyes in suspicion, tapping the toe of one shoe against the knife she had tucked into the sheath at her ankle to assure herself it was still there. "Of course." She handed the envelope over, hoping Blade and Becky would return soon.

But the older man simply smiled after reading the envelope, not bothering to pull the invitation from within, then handed it back to her without issue. "Wonderful. Happy you came, dear."

"Do I know you?" Evie asked suspiciously, trying to place the man's face.

"No, I wouldn't expect you to." He laughed, the sound warm and soft like liquid sugar. He held out his hand again, calloused and blistered. "My name is Arthur Maverine. I believe you work for my son, Trystan. I am the core healer."

Evie was certain her body was going into shock, because she froze, unable to remember how to use words to communicate, and instead kept her mouth open and her eyes glued to the man before her. "You— I— Um, hello?"

Arthur chuckled and dropped his hand back to his side when he realized hers was too heavy to move. "I must say, you seem surprised to be here for someone who so insistently requested an invitation to tonight's festivities."

Evie shook her head and reeled back, finding her voice. "Excuse me? I didn't request anything. This invitation was left in my bedroom with an ominous note."

Arthur frowned and gestured to two wooden chairs away from the crowd. She reluctantly followed, keeping her hand out, ready to grab her dagger at a moment's notice.

It wasn't as sharp as the one she'd had the day she met The Villain.

The one tucked away with her now was something she'd purchased at the week's end merchant market for far more than it was worth. Especially considering the horrible dullness of the blade, but she digressed.

It was sharp enough to stab someone—that's really all she required should the situation call for it.

"I can assure you, Ms. Sage, it was you who invited *me* to tonight's festivities." The older man held her gaze. "You sent a letter this morning."

Evie shook her head, battling a wave of confusion. "I never sent you a letter, Mr. Maverine. I have no idea what you're talking about."

Arthur stood, pulling a piece of parchment from one of the folds in his robe. Opening it while he reseated himself, he began to read.

"'Dear Arthur Maverine, I realize you do not know me. But I know your son. I work very closely with him. Considering our connection, I would truly be so grateful if you are able to provide me an invitation to one of your illustrious celebrations. It would be of great import to not only me but also your son. Signed, Evangelina Sage.'" When he finished reading, he looked up at her expectantly.

Evie shook her head furiously. "No, no. I did not send you that letter, sir. I'm not sure who did, but it was not me." Evie searched the crowd for Blade and Becky, but the two had disappeared.

Arthur's face was pinched with concern. It was fatherly, and Evie almost asked him for a hug—almost.

"I assure you, Evie." He tested the name out like he wanted to be sure he was getting it right. "When I received this missive, I was intrigued. I felt I had no choice but to attend and seek you out."

It was at this moment that she wished she had the ability to tell truth from deception. Her naïveté chose the most random times to appear, and she never saw it coming until it bit her in the ass.

But he looked so sincere.

"Do you—? Are you aware of—?" She struggled to delicately ask if Arthur knew of his son's chosen profession.

"Who my son is?" The man folded his hands, smiling through a painful expression. "Yes, I'm very aware of what life Trystan has chosen for himself."

"Oh," Evie said meekly. This really wasn't going the way she had planned it. She felt no closer to finding her answers. In fact, they felt further away. Like she was running down a long hallway to a door she could never seem to reach. "Well, that's good, I suppose."

"You work closely with him?" Arthur asked, nothing but kind curiosity in his expression.

"Yes." Evie nodded. "He is a wonderful boss."

He cleared his throat, adjusting the buttons sitting under his chin. "I'm glad he has someone who cares for him."

Evie sensed he was implying a closer relationship, and she fumbled over her words to set the record straight. For posterity and all. "I am his assistant, so of course I must care for his needs…his *work* needs. You know, as his work assistant should always do."

"I concur."

The deep, resounding voice caused them both to jolt in their seats before she watched Arthur's eyes widen, his face going white with shock.

Evie watched Arthur stand slowly, reaching out both of his hands. "Trystan," he breathed.

"Hello, Arthur."

Evie turned around and saw The Villain's black-clad form.

His dark eyes found hers, palpable anger there. "Hello, Sage."

Eyes wide in disbelief, she said, "By the gods, sir! If you insist on continuing to sneak up behind me like that, I'm going to force you to wear a bell." *Honestly, this is growing a little ridiculous.*

But her good humor was quickly diminished by a shiver that raced down her spine as she realized the trouble she'd caused. Because of her not taking the invitation to the boss in the first place, he was now having a *very* public reunion with his father. A reunion, she was almost certain, he had never intended to have. At least not now, not in front of her.

As her gaze darted around the packed gathering, she began figuring out the easiest escape. To run away from this disaster.

CHAPTER 42

THE VILLAIN

Keep your fury calm.

It was a sentence that replayed in Trystan's head so often, he figured it was branded inside his skull, a permanent part of his being.

But it was difficult to be calm when so many things were spiking the pressure in his head like a teakettle ready to screech. For one thing, his father, a man he swore to himself he'd never look in the eyes again, was staring right at him. One of his guards had informed him of a suspicious meeting among a few members of his closest circle of employees, and Trystan was out the door before Sage's name left Dante's lips.

He knew it was one of Arthur's gatherings the moment he heard the music, saw the lanterns. The opulent decorations were everything he remembered them to be from his childhood, and he hated it.

Not to mention the dancing until dawn while Arthur used whatever magic was in his arsenal to heal the hearts of every person who asked, which was quite a few. He'd thought Arthur had retired these little soirees, but a tightness in his gut told him this was far from coincidence when so many things already seemed to be going wrong in his life.

This was planned; this was betrayal. The question was…by whom.

The twinkling sound of Sage's chattering cleared his mind of all distraction, and he finally allowed himself to look at her. His reaction to her was…startling. It wasn't like her dress was a far cry from the other bright and ostentatious colors she normally wore, but it was the way in which she wore it, like she was shining. From the pins in her hair to the black line around her eyes…and her lips. They were painted red as blood.

Clearing his throat, cursing himself for losing some of his composure, Trystan pulled his back straight, willing himself to hide whatever thoughts were running through his mind about his assistant.

Agony. This is agony.

"Sir?" Sage waved a hand in front of his face. The firelight caught against the jeweled butterflies in her hair, making the dark strands look edged in starlight.

"Arthur, would you excuse us? My assistant and I need to have a conversation," he said, unable to keep the thin edge of anger from his tone. He watched Sage's delicate neck tighten as she swallowed her breath.

"Now, now—" Arthur began, but Trystan didn't have time. He could tell by the wideness of his assistant's eyes that her imagination at what "The Villain" might do when he fired her for this recklessness was running wild.

"I'm sure your guests would like your attention." He waved at the people hovering around them, desperation lighting their eyes.

Arthur stood slowly, the familiar lines of his face causing his chest to tighten. "Promise you'll sit down with me before you leave, Trystan?" The hand his father placed on his shoulder nearly made him growl, but he bit back any response and just nodded stiffly.

As soon as he was out of earshot, The Villain whipped around to Evie, only to find her slowly creeping in the other direction. "Where do you think you're going?"

"Oh, I was just going to…" And to his surprise, she turned hard and sprinted through the crowd.

"Get back here, Sage!" Trystan hollered, feeling ridiculous as he chased after her like a fox on a hunt. He bumped into a couple wrapped in a passionate embrace and rolled his eyes at their protests of outrage. "Evangelina!" He dove for her hand, but she slipped out of his grasp and ran onto the rickety bridge, farther into the darkness.

She couldn't make this easy for him—of course she would run. Trystan used to like when people responded to him that way, once upon a time, but right now he hated it.

He followed close behind, determined, despite the heavy feeling in his heart that he must have frightened her. He wanted to kick his own ass at how he'd handled seeing her there—so close to his father. Fear was not an emotion Trystan was used to feeling, and clearly Sage was determined to make him suffer it often.

The bridge groaned and wobbled underneath his weight, and the darkness that lay beyond threatened to swallow him, but the moon once more caught on the gems in Sage's hair. Trystan kept his gaze there, knowing he'd follow that light wherever it went.

He'd never been this sentimental, and it was all her fault.

When he reached the other side of the bridge, the trees whipped in the cool night air, and, without the fire to warm it, the air was frigid. She was probably cold.

"Sage, come out. You're going to catch your death, and then I will have to hire Rebecka in your stead."

She stumbled from the bushes, twigs sticking from her hair. "That was evil." She glared.

He looked at her sardonically, raising a brow. "That's kind of the point."

She walked closer to him, nervously pulling a curl between her fingers. "All right, go ahead. Yell at me."

"Oh? Am I supposed to yell?"

"I know you're angry because of something to do with Arthur—" she started.

"I'm not angry," he interrupted, pushing a drop of sweat from his forehead. When she just cocked one brow at him in challenge, he admitted, "Yes, I am very angry, but not because of Arthur right now."

Her eyes widened. "Oh, so you *are* angry with me...that I didn't come to you before I went to the gathering thing? But I swear I didn't know it was going to be hosted by your—your, um...father and that I would upset you." She said the last word on a wince, and he had to swallow a laugh, a problem he didn't seem to have until recently.

"I'm not upset, Sage," he said, gathering his thoughts along with his racing pulse.

She gave him a scrutinizing look and motioned to the grip that his other hand had on the hilt of his sword.

He released it immediately, feeling slightly sheepish, perhaps for the first time in his life. "It's a habit," he grumbled.

"Right." She nodded, exaggerating a pout, as she walked around him to sit on the cliff's edge. The glow of the fire lit the planes of her cheekbones even from a distance.

"I'm not angry with *you*," he said, awkwardly bending to sit beside her. "I was notified by my guards that my employees were here. I knew it wasn't a coincidence, but there was never a moment where I thought not to trust you." The Villain wasn't sure why it was so important that she know this, but it was.

She seemed to believe him, peeking down at the golden band around her pinkie finger. He looked away, feeling guilty.

"I'm glad you trust me," she said flatly.

"Oh yes. You sound it," he replied, sarcasm dripping from his words.

Trystan looked to the candles decorating the trees around them, glowing, perhaps, brighter than when they'd first arrived on the other side of the bridge. The music floating gently set a lovely scene. The Villain didn't know what contentment felt like—he'd spent so long living uncomfortably in the world that he'd begun to rely on that emotion, never allowing himself to settle.

But in this moment, he thought perhaps he could. Quite easily.

"I'll say this for my father: his parties always have good music."

Sage's gaze turned to his, and his face was close enough that he could see the candles' reflections in her eyes. "Does he do things like this a lot?"

"I don't know." Trystan sighed, pressing his middle and pointer finger against the bridge of his nose. "I haven't talked to him in years."

In all fairness, Trystan had spent most of his life not talking to Arthur. It wasn't just that Arthur had spent most of Trystan's childhood traveling to different places, using the core healer abilities where he was needed. Trystan's mother, Amara, had told Trystan and his siblings that it was selfish for them to keep Arthur with them when there were so many who needed his help. It was comical to Trystan now, how that need never seemed to matter if it was coming from Arthur's children.

By the time Clare was born, Arthur had begun to slow down, spending more time at home in their seaside village. Trystan was older, so most of Arthur's attention was spent on Trystan's younger siblings. Amara Maverine was not a cold woman, but she was not an affectionate one, either. She did not see the sense in hugs or comfort when the world was so much harsher than that. It was something that Trystan was grateful for—it saved him from the feeling of rejection.

Arthur had taken a softer approach with Clare and Malcolm upon his return, but he must have assumed it was too late for Trystan. At the beginning, it had stung when Trystan would try and bond with Arthur only to be met with disinterest. But Trystan slid back into the patterns he had been raised with quickly, almost to preserve himself. He didn't need affection; he didn't need people to show they loved him; it was a waste of time. It was wasted on *him*.

In the end, it hadn't mattered anyway. By the time Arthur made tentative steps to build a relationship with Trystan, it was too late. But that hadn't stopped Arthur from trying, over the years, to send letters, to attempt meetings. Trystan had ignored every single one.

At least his siblings' hope of redemption for him had finally died, and they were far more tolerable to be around. His mother's hopes, he knew, had died, too, but that was a whole other brand of torture to subject himself to; later, perhaps. No, right now he would allow himself this small sliver of happiness, if that's what the warmth creeping through his chest felt like.

In fact, he'd wring this moment of every ounce of joy he could.

Quickly standing, Trystan watched Sage's face turn up toward his, eyebrows raised in confusion. "What are you doing?" Her eyes widened when she saw him reach out a hand for hers.

"Would you like to dance?"

Her eyes widened even more, but a small smile graced the red bow of her lips.

"With whom?" She looked around theatrically.

Trystan smirked, because in all truth, she was very funny. "With me."

Sage gripped his hand and let him pull her to her feet. When he bent his neck to take her in, he was knocked breathless by her joy aimed at him full force. It was so foreign to have someone so happy in his presence, or even *because* of his presence, that he almost missed a step.

"I'm not really certain how to dance with another person." She scrunched her nose and stared at their clasped hands. "Usually, I just spin in circles until I get dizzy."

"Well—" He'd miscalculated. The music, which had been a lively and spritely tune, had sobered into something slower, more intimate. He'd tortured many men over his ten years in this business. For information, for making him angry, for trying to kill him, and he'd been loath to admit it…but he even did it once because he'd seen a man being cruel to a duck.

It had been a bonus to find out the man was a retired Valiant Guard, but that was neither here nor there.

This was a different sort of torture, one he'd never experienced before. He'd become so good at not wanting anything above what he could take—but this woman was not a possession. She was a person he greatly admired and respected. Someone he relied on more than he'd ever thought possible.

Someone to whom he would never admit any of this.

You get this one happy moment, he reminded himself.

Without hesitating, Trystan placed his other hand on the small of her back, guiding her into his embrace. Her breath hitched, and Trystan could feel the warmth from her skin through the silken fabric of her dress. Clearing his throat, he brought their clasped hands up and began gliding them in slow steps.

"So, you dance?" Sage asked, her face tilting up to his. It was closer than he thought, and when he looked down, he saw why: she was dancing on the tips of her toes.

"I learned years ago when I worked for—" He cut off, not because he didn't want to finish his sentence but because just then, Trystan caught sight of a familiar face in the crowd across the bridge.

"What is my sister doing here?" The Villain asked in confusion.

"Clare's here?" Sage whipped her head to where he looked, but neither of them stopped swaying or staying linked together. The wheels of her brain were turning a mile a minute—he could tell by the look in her eyes. "You don't think the traitor could be…"

He interrupted before she could get the thought out. "I've had my guards tailing both of my siblings since the bomb incident. They have both been accounted for at the traitor's every turn. They hate me, certainly, but it is not either of them trying to take me down."

"I don't think they hate you," Evie said quietly as he moved them into a gentle spin.

"You can't know that." Trystan wouldn't look at her. Instead, he found one of the lights behind them and kept his gaze glued there.

"But I do." She pressed the tip of one shoe onto his until he looked at her. "I know that love between siblings. They have it for you; it's quite obvious."

"It's not like what you have with Lyssa," he said, sweeping her out into another spin.

She laughed, deeply, before spinning back into his arms. "Our relationship's a little different, yes, but the fundamentals are the same. I used to endlessly annoy my brother when we were children, often on purpose. But at the end of the day, we'd do anything for one another."

"I didn't realize you had a brother," Trystan said softly, acutely aware that Sage was the sole provider of her family.

"He died." There was a lifelessness to Sage's voice that startled him.

"That must have been very difficult for you." Their dancing had slowed, but they were still moving, still spinning.

"It was more the abruptness of it." She remained looking at him, but her eyes were blank. "It was an accident...with my mother's magic. Life never stopped changing after that. Gideon was gone, then my mother. I left school to take care of Lyssa and then had to stop my schooling to begin working after my father fell ill. I feel like my life keeps happening to me, rather than me living it."

It was a sad story; Trystan had heard many of those. That wasn't what affected him. It was the way she'd delivered the words, looking right at him. Her gaze open and honest as she laid her weaknesses bare, like they were worthy of every part of his attention.

She had it, all of it.

"I've felt like that, too." He paused. "Like life is just happening to me. Many times."

At the declaration, a startled look came over her face, which nearly made him stop, but he didn't.

"I wasn't prepared to see my father this evening."

"That was my fault. I'm so, so—" But she stopped when he gave her a mock glare. He wanted to rip that godsforsaken word from her vocabulary.

"It's difficult for me to be around him. It reminds me of my childhood. He...he wasn't there very often. Being a core healer required travel, a lot of it. There was always someone who needed him more, and it made me feel...unimportant."

That was all he could give for now. But it was enough, by the way Sage gazed at him with a kinship that he hadn't known he was waiting for. "I understand," she said, smiling lightly because she did understand him; he could see that now. "Life is sometimes just...exhausting."

A bit overcome still, he remained silent.

Sage's eyes went wide when he didn't speak, and her cheeks were tinged red. "Not that *working* for you is exhausting... It's more like..."

"Taking years off your life?" he supplied helpfully.

"I wasn't going to say that." She frowned at him. "Out loud."

A rusty laugh escaped the back of his throat. "If the work isn't tiring enough, I could have you join Scatter Day with the interns?" He widened his steps and swooped her into a long spin.

"As the one chasing them?" she asked, something scary in her expression.

"I'm not *that* evil." He arched a brow and froze when he saw a gleam in her eye. "Why are you smiling right now, Sage?"

"I was just thinking that we are worthy of a stage performance."

"As if anyone would ever want to watch you and me argue." The Villain scoffed.

"I don't know..." Evie said with a twinkle in her eye.

He shook his head, spinning them around in one more sweep.

It was a nearly perfect moment. And then the screaming began.

CHAPTER 43

EVIE

"What in the deadlands?" The Villain muttered, angling his dark head up to the night sky, toward whatever was screeching loud enough to nearly burst Evie's eardrums.

"Move!" she cried, recognizing the piercing shout in the sky and the purple hue to the cloud of smoke coming down toward them.

Her boss shoved them both out of the way and let loose a hard gasp when they hit the ground, eyes widening in realization before rolling them both over, away from another venomous cloud of breath from—

"They escaped?" Evie looked up over his shoulder at the dark guvre-shaped figure hovering in the sky. Because what else did this night need, if not a wickedly dangerous beast crashing the most awkward family reunion since the dawn of time?

And the most magical dance of her life.

She hadn't even moved her feet; she'd just glided while he—

Another screech filled the air, accompanied by the screams of a scattering crowd. *Right. Probably not the best time to ruminate, Evie.*

The dirt bunched over her heels as her boss pulled her to her feet, cursing fast and angry when he looked to the other side of the bridge. Half of Briar's Peak was gone, melting under the venom of the guvre's breath. She flinched, bile rising in her throat when her eyes found the fast-decaying body of a man, still alive, still screaming in agony. Skin melting away from his bones.

"Oh, that is so sickening." Evie covered her mouth with her hand.

"You've certainly seen far more grotesque things during your time in my employ," The Villain said, far too matter-of-factly, not taking his eyes off the guvre.

"That doesn't make that *less* grotesque," Evie said incredulously before shaking her head. An awful feeling prickled along her skin. "The guvre, sir. Shouldn't we—"

"Yes! Obviously," The Villain said, seeming surprised and annoyed by his moment of distraction. Grabbing her arm and thrusting her in front of him, he yelled for her to move. "Go!"

"All right!" Evie yelled, rolling her eyes in annoyance. She could direct herself, despite public opinion. "How did one get out?" she called back. She tried to catch the beast's coloring, but it was impossible to tell which one this was in the darkness.

What if they'd *both* escaped?

She could feel The Villain following closely behind her, yelling at her to move faster. The moment she heard the creaking snaps of old wood, she knew why. The guvre's breath was eating up the bridge behind them, plank by plank. Until the whole thing creaked, and then they were falling.

Gripping the plank like it was a ladder, Evie felt splinters break off under her grip as they fell, then slammed against what was left of the cliffside, the ropes on their end clinging for dear life. Evie looked down, exhaling in relief when she saw her boss clinging to a plank farther away but still there.

"Are you okay?" she yelled down, trying not to flinch when she felt the freshly healed wounds on her hands reopen in a couple of places.

"Fantastic. I think I'll have a picnic while I'm down here," he called back with his normal dryness.

Oh yes, he was fine.

Evie nodded and turned to climb the rest of the way up. When she reached the top, her smile disappeared as the putrid smell of rotting flesh permeated the air.

It was a massacre.

Bodies were strewn about, corpses rotting down to the bone. The few still alive were screaming as the skin dripped from their flesh. Evie forced herself to look, begging one of the faces not to be Blade or... Fine, she would prefer one of them not be Rebecka Erring.

"It's the male," The Villain said at her shoulder, looking to the sky with a quiet rage, eyes narrowing when something large clattered to the ground. He stalked over toward the fallen silver item. It was the guvre's ankle cuff, the clean lines of the break in the chain a clear indicator it had been cut free rather than broken. "Someone's released him."

"The person who got us here." Evie sighed.

"It was a setup." The Villain sneered.

But there was no time to speculate who had done it when first they had a creature to catch. "Why isn't the male staying with the female?" Evie asked, seeking cover under a giant fallen tree that was lying at an angle, one end stuck in the branches of another tree.

Her boss quickly joined her. "The females are smarter, more strategic. The males often work off pure instinct. Right now, all he knows is that he's been caged. Things will be even worse if his mate is still caged." He seemed to think better of that statement because he added, "Worse is relative. Two guvres are also as bad as one male overcome with rage."

"So destruction is his solution?" Evie rolled her eyes, pushing her loosened hair out of her face. "Men," she scoffed.

"Yes, we can discuss the obvious weaknesses of my sex later." The Villain's eyes glittered. His black shirt was ripped at the shoulder, giving him a roguish dishevelment that made Evie's stomach flutter.

At an obviously horribly inconvenient time.

"Gushiken!" he yelled with such deep command, Evie felt her back straighten at attention, her head nearly bumping the tree trunk they were hiding under.

Blade appeared out of the darkness and scrambled under the tree with them, blood running down his arm, panic in his amber eyes. "Hello, boss. When did you get here?" he asked, his casual tone a stark contrast to the chaos surrounding them.

"Could you perhaps dispense with the small talk? Any ideas on how to recapture him?"

"How much help was I the first time?" Blade asked bluntly.

Another screech and flurry of screams caused them all to jump. "None," The Villain growled.

"Then I believe you have your answer, sir." The cocky ease with which Blade composed himself wavered when his gaze flashed to a movement Evie caught out of the corner of her eye.

"I told you to stay hidden!" Blade said, an unusual steel to his voice.

Rebecka Erring appeared beside Evie under the tree, startling her so quickly, it knocked her back into her boss's chest. "My gods, make a sound!" Evie held her hand to her chest, waiting for her heart rate to slow and then quickly realizing it wouldn't while the guvre hovered dangerously above them.

"I wasn't any safer behind the trees where you left me," Becky muttered, nodding politely at The Villain and then turning to glare at Blade.

But The Villain didn't notice as his gaze darted around the screaming party guests rushing past. "My sister. My sister was here. Before he attacked." And then he took off running—leaving the shelter of their hiding spot.

"Sir!" Evie screamed, moving to follow, but she was jerked back down by Becky's rough grip on her shoulders.

"Sit down, you fool. He doesn't need to worry about you killing yourself while he looks for her. Just stay here and don't get in the way."

The words burned like the guvre's breath against bare flesh, but Evie knew they were true. Unless she could find a way to make herself a resource, she would quickly become a nuisance. Perhaps she already was one.

She couldn't be that self-deprecating now. When she finally made it home later, hopefully in one piece, she'd check on Lyssa, feeling guilty for leaving her alone once more, then flop nearly lifeless into bed. Then and only then would she allow herself to delve into all the things her brain liked to tell her she did wrong or poorly.

"We've got to get the guvre," Blade said absolutely, pulling a corded leather rope from his pocket. "Found this threaded through a few fallen lanterns—I think it'll do the trick!"

"How the deadlands did he catch it the first time?" Evie asked, raising a skeptical brow as Blade knotted a large loop at the end. "That was used to string up lights. You think it's going to hold a giant wild animal?"

"Have you got a better idea?" Blade asked, smiling roguishly. "The boss had his guards track the male for days before he had Tati mix a sleeping draught. They struggled, but they got him down instantly after they managed to pour it in the thing's mouth, from what Keeley told me."

"Then by all means!" Evie gestured wildly to the sky after another screech rent the air, slowly melting the tree next to them. The creature's wings flapped overhead, and a gust of wind knocked them all back as he soared in the other direction, far enough for them to pause and catch their breath.

"I don't have the sleeping draught now!" Blade yelled, all three of them backing up as a group of people ran past them, screaming, most of them bleeding or injured. Evie had backed up until she felt her dress catch against something behind her. Turning quickly, she saw a body slouched against the tree, hood pulled over their face.

Blade looked confused. "Is that man…taking a nap?"

"Or he's dead!" Becky said, slapping Blade on the arm. "Poke him and see if he moves."

Frowning, Blade bent low, picked up a twig, and reached out toward the drooped figure.

He crouched and moved his head toward the person's shoulder. Then jumped three feet in the air when the figure moved before the stick could poke him, a rusty laugh coming from the dark shadows hiding his face.

"I'm not dead, just a little less alive." The voice rang familiar the moment Evie heard it. Which was why she was unsurprised when the figure pulled his hood away and revealed Arthur's bloodied face, his beard matted together in red. "I'll be all right. Where is Trystan?"

"Who's that?" Blade asked, looking uncomfortable. "Oh, and who are you?"

"He's the host of the party." Evie rolled her eyes.

Blade frowned sympathetically. "Oh, well, other than the melting people, I think it's going really well."

"Blade," Evie said, crouching beside Arthur, tearing off a piece of her shining skirt and wrapping the fabric around his head. "Shut up, would you?"

"Sure, sure," Blade said quietly from behind them. "I'll go try and, um, get the… Well, you know," he said, before running away from them and into the fray.

Arthur coughed lightly, a trickle of blood coming from the corner of his lips. Panic shook Evie at the sight, worried for a man who had once cared for Trystan and very apparently still did. And he mattered to her boss, whether Trystan knew it or not.

Ripping off another clean scrap of fabric from her dress, Evie held it gently to the corner of Arthur's mouth, praying that whatever ailed him could be healed.

"You're brave." Arthur smiled at her lightly, dirt mixing with the blood on his cheeks.

Evie snorted. "Hardly." She was impulsive and headstrong on her best days, but brave? It seemed too heavy a word for the vision she had of herself.

"You must be to work for—" He paused, eyes taking in Becky behind her. He seemed to be weighing something carefully before he turned back to Evie with a different course in mind. "To work for *The Villain*."

Arthur winced around the last two words, like calling his son something sinister was more painful than any of the wounds he'd suffered.

"He's not so scary." Evie smiled, feeling a small sort of glow inside when she pictured Trystan's softer moments in her mind.

"Oh, but he is." Arthur winced again but smiled. Finding humor in his pain.

"I've never been more afraid of anyone in my life."

But Evie could hear the feelings behind his words. That his fear wasn't of Trystan but of where the life he'd chosen would lead him.

He was afraid *for* him, and Evie was so touched, she vowed she would keep this man alive, no matter what she had to do.

Just then, Becky gasped, and Evie spun around to see—

She froze.

They were surrounded by Valiant Guards, swords drawn with ruthless determination.

And they didn't look like heroes at all...

CHAPTER 44

THE VILLAIN

After a mad dash through the ruins of the party, stepping over unrecognizable bodies, some of them still groaning, Trystan spotted Clare. Tugging his sister hard by the arm, Trystan ducked them both into the shadows in one sweeping move.

She was shaking, her dress torn and her left shoulder bare where the strap was missing. It made him think of their childhood, when Clare was reckless and Trystan would feel pinches in his chest at what might happen to her.

But they were grown now. He'd learned quickly that neither of his siblings needed his worry or concern.

"Tryst?" Clare's voice shook, as though she was unsure her brother was really here to rescue her. But then she seemed to collect herself and shouted, "Father. We must find Father!"

"What in the deadlands are you even doing here, Clare?" He was feeling so many things, too many. Emotions had never been easily processed through the dark confines of Trystan's mind.

He worried for Evie, he worried for his sister, he was infuriated at whoever caused this mess, and there were not words to describe the anger he felt toward King Benedict.

"Father invited me!" Clare yelled, her usual temper flaring and melting away any trace of fear he thought he'd seen in her gaze. "What in the deadlands are *you* doing here?" Her eyes became horrified saucers. "Did you do this?"

"Of course not," he growled, freezing when he saw Blade sprint past him. "Gushiken!"

The dragon trainer halted in his tracks, swinging a looped rope, sweat pouring down his face. "I almost had him—just need a little more height." Blade peeked over at Clare and smiled like they were meeting over brunch. "Nice to meet you."

"My sister." Trystan claimed her, even though it was unwise. No one at the office, save for Tatianna and now Sage, knew of his familial connections. Or even his identity.

"Oh." Realization lit in the dragon trainer's eyes. "Oh, you're—Hello." The man obviously knew something he shouldn't, because he looked like a cat who'd found a mouse to play with.

Trystan was out of patience, as usual. "Clare. I'll find Arthur—just stay out of the way."

"I don't take orders from you." She rolled her eyes and turned to Blade. "You need a sleeping draught to take that thing down, don't you?"

"I—" Blade looked to Trystan, uncomfortable to be caught in the siblings' squabble. "That would be good. Can you make one?"

Clare curled one side of her lips at the trainer. "Yes, I can. There are some herbs I can use growing nearby—give me five minutes."

They both turned in the direction of the shrubs, but a familiar scream wrenched the air and a horrid, hollow feeling knifed its way through his heart.

Sage.

"I have to—" But then a sharp pain sliced through his head. He saw dark spots as he fell to his knees, and his last image was of Sage waiting for him to come save her, but he'd never reach her in time.

CHAPTER 45

EVIE

"**P**ut them with the rest," a Valiant Guard called over to the one hauling Evie toward a handful of people crowded together, some of them clinging to each other and sobbing as they were gathered in a clearing not far from the original party location. Arthur stumbled and groaned behind her, and Evie quickly turned to help him.

"Stay in line!"

"He's injured!" she yelled back, yelping in pain when the bigger knight gripped her by the shoulder, hard.

"Dayton!" one of the others called. "Stay your temper; these people are innocent." The voice was kind, and despite the helmet he wore, Evie felt calmer.

But then she spotted another group of people and the unconscious man lying beside them. Taking in his torn black shirt and his too-still face, Evie swallowed back a scream at the thought that he was dead. But then she saw the blood trickle from his forehead as he shifted and she nearly passed out from relief. Not dead, just unconscious.

Evie pushed through the throngs of people, ignoring the calls from a knight to stay where they told her. She dropped beside Trystan and brushed a blood-soaked lock from her boss's forehead. "Sir?" she whispered. "Are you all right?"

He groaned lightly underneath her touch, eyelids fluttering before going still once more.

For once, Becky's appearance was a welcome sight. "Is he okay?" Her eyes were wide and her breathing heavy. "Where is Blade?" she asked, whipping her head around to look at the few other people standing with them. He was nowhere in sight.

"How are we getting out of this?" Evie winced when a knight threw another screaming woman into the group. "What are they doing here?"

"It had to be a setup," Becky hissed. "There's no way they're here by coincidence. Whoever King Benedict has working for him, they wanted us all here for this."

"Then why aren't they taking us away?" Evie asked, looking around at the group. They bore the painted silver armor on their shoulders and chests. Most of their faces were hidden behind painted helmets, each inscribed with King Benedict's insignia. But there was confusion playing among them. Whoever had organized them here had apparently abandon them, and with the guvre hovering nearby, each of the knights shifted nervously.

Evie could work with nervous men; they usually came by the dozen.

Arthur hobbled over, crouching beside her, and brushed a hair from The Villain's face. "They don't know what The Villain looks like, and whoever did is nowhere to be found," Arthur whispered. "I'm too weak to heal anyone, but—" Feeling the pulse at Trystan's wrist, Arthur turned warm eyes to Evie. "He'll be all right. His lifeline is still strong. Do you have a plan?"

Becky was looking at her, too. The other people still conscious around them shuffled nervously, not paying attention to them as much as the guards. Evie found herself panicked—the person who gave the orders was unconscious. Evie's job was to follow direction and follow it well. What was an assistant to do when her ruthless boss was out cold?

It was obvious, really. Whatever ruthlessness this situation required. Evie would have to become a villain herself, because they were not going to die here. Not today.

Evie flew to her feet, forcing a dramatic scream from her lips. "Please," she sobbed. "Help me."

One of the Valiant Guards was by her side in an instant, taking her forearm in his hand. She could see his green eyes through the slit of his helmet; they looked uncomfortable.

"What ails you, miss? You have nothing to fear from us."

"Oh, I know." Evie gave a watery smile as she gestured to The Villain, still unconscious in the hands of his father. "But my hu-husband." She made the word seem forced, like she was seconds away from shattering.

The discomfort in the knight's eyes increased tenfold.

A man terrified of a woman's tears? I never would have guessed.

"He's hurt. I fear for his life; I must take him to a healer immediately." She wiped a tear from her cheek and then gripped the knight's armor in her fists. "I beg you—let us go."

The knight slowly removed Evie's hand from his armor and then took a slow step away, like her hysterics were contagious. "My knights were instructed to return every civilian here unharmed. We found your husband unconscious already, my lady."

Evie wanted to throw him a suspicious look, but she restrained herself. It was very clear he thought her quite gullible if she was supposed to believe the knights just found her boss with a small dent in the back of his head—if the guvre had done it, she was certain he'd no longer have a head at all.

"Of course." She sniffed. "You all are valiant and brave. I should've known better. You see, I have my monthly cycle."

One of the knights choked, and she was pretty sure another dropped his sword on his foot.

Women's tears scared men, but the functions of the female body clearly sent them into apoplectic fits. She continued, resisting a chuckle. "My husband and I, we've been trying for a baby, you see." The Villain groaned behind her, but Evie ignored it and kept her eyes forward. "It's why we came to see the core healer. And then my husband heard The Villain had arrived to terrorize the core's good work."

Suddenly, every knight near her was on alert, their gazes darting around those captured, obviously trying to discern if The Villain was among them now.

"Oh, that dastardly evildoer isn't here, kind sirs," she insisted, blinking up at the soldier. "He took off after the sky serpent's first attack like the coward he is."

The knights chuckled nervously, turning to the one she was speaking with for direction.

"Please, sir, I do not have the supplies necessary for my *monthly courses*…and my dress is white."

Every man within earshot winced. The guard before her nodded once, decision made. "Very well. I suppose you all may—"

A loud groan permeated the air, freezing everyone and everything around them. Evie turned her head slowly toward the groan, horror dawning like a fiery sun.

The Villain was waking up, and when he saw the knights around them, his reaction would be to ruin everything, and by ruin she definitely meant start murdering their captors. Instead of being let go and left alone, they would be outnumbered, and the guards would capture The Villain.

Or worse, they would *murder* him.

She had to do something...

Her heart pounded so loudly, the force of it nearly knocked her over as she made her way over to her *husband* on shaking legs. Dark eyes appeared as his lids blinked open, brows scrunching together in pain and confusion as he began to sit up.

His gaze settled on the group before him for only a moment, long enough for Evie to recognize the murderous rage in his gaze begin to take root, and she flung herself in front of him, gripping his collar in her fists. She watched him blink twice before his eyes widened.

It was the last thing she saw before she settled her lips onto his.

CHAPTER 46

THE VILLAIN

Trystan was dreaming.

Which surprised him, because he thought he'd lost the ability to dream ten short years ago. But here he was, having a dream, and it was a pleasant one.

He only saw Evie's face for a moment before he felt soft lips press to his. His imagination made her taste like vanilla. Probably because of the ludicrous amount of vanilla drop candies the woman ate throughout the day.

It was comical to him that a trait he'd previously inwardly chuckled at was now something that was arousing him beyond belief. Enough that his eyes drifted shut and thoughts of gruesome, horrible things faded away.

If it's just a dream anyway…

He sat up quickly, arms whipping around her, fingers pulling lightly through the soft locks of her hair. He tugged gently, nearly groaning when a gasp escaped her lips, and angled her head so he could taste her fully.

He licked at her lips, one of his hands coming down to her waist and squeezing, trying desperately to bring her closer. The small sounds she was making in the back of her throat nearly undid him. He'd never thought himself a man with a particularly good imagination, but the way she was holding on to him, sweet but fierce, and the passion behind her kisses… It ruined him.

How could the reality of kissing her possibly surpass the euphoria that was pumping through his veins at what his own imagination had conjured?

In a devastating moment, her lips pulled from his just an inch before the Dream Evie whispered, "Sir, they think—"

"Shhhh," he whispered, pulling her in for one more slow touch of their lips. She resisted for a moment before settling once more against his mouth and gripping his cheeks in her hands.

He thought he heard someone cough, which was quite rude of his subconscious, but he pulled back anyway and watched as her lips drifted closer, wanting to bring her back to him.

"What were you going to say, love?" he whispered, smiling crookedly as he ran a hand down her soft cheek.

Her eyes widened with something like…hope? Before it vanished and was replaced with realization. "Oh," she whispered. "You heard my lie to the knights about us being married? That's why you—"

"What?" He tilted his head, the dream no longer making sense. He didn't want to, but he looked beyond Evie to the crowd surrounding them. Valiant Guards were standing at attention, watching them with laser focus. Civilians were gathered around, and Arthur was leaning off in the corner, covered in blood.

It was all so—

Deadlands, this is real.

Before he could think, he stood, bringing Sage up with him, and shoved her behind him. His power boiled beneath his skin, wanting to destroy, needing to eviscerate. But before he could strike, one of the knights stepped forward.

"We mean you and your wife no harm. She explained everything." *My wife?* He looked toward Sage and read the quiet communication behind her eyes.

"I told them about our troubles with conceiving, dear."

The Villain was almost certain that if there had been an attempt made at conceiving with Sage, he would remember. Vividly.

"Yes. I see."

Sage looked relieved as she closed her hand in his. He refused to enjoy it.

"Everyone may go." The knight with the kind voice emerged from the crowd. "We're sorry for frightening you further. And I assure all of you, we are doing our best to catch the guvre and capture The Villain."

The crowd clapped lightly at the pretty speech, as did Trystan. He'd enjoy watching them try.

As the crowd dispersed, Trystan noticed for the first time since he woke that he no longer heard the guvre's calls overhead. Either Blade and his sister had succeeded, or King Benedict had won yet another round of the battle between them.

He was determined to find out, but he was caught off guard by a shorter Valiant Guard hoisting Arthur up by his shoulders. "You need to see a healer as soon as possible, my lord. Please follow me this way."

Rebecka followed as well, beside Arthur, holding a scrap of fabric that looked suspiciously like it had come from Evie's dress. Both Rebecka and Arthur disappeared quickly in the darkness of the trees, and Trystan stepped forward to follow, mistrustful of anyone who answered to the king.

But he was interrupted by the knight who'd dismissed the crowd. He was speaking to Evie. "What did you say your name was, my lady?"

Trystan stepped quickly toward her and swept his arms about her shoulders, tucking her into his side. "She's taken," he said flatly.

The knight chuckled and began to lift his helmet but stopped when two other knights swept over.

One of the new arrivals removed his old helmet, revealing a crop of red hair. "I can take you to see the other healer as well, my lord, to look at your head."

"I don't need—"

"I insist," the redhead said smoothly. "I'll show you and your wife the way." He turned toward the darkness of the wood, in a different direction from Arthur. Trystan would wait until they were nearly to the healer, and then he'd dispatch this man.

With reluctance, he followed, keeping Sage close to him, still feeling the tingling burn of her lips against his. He wanted to touch them to quell the sensations, but it would give too much away, and he was already horrified that his feelings had been on such public display.

The buzz of people leaving the peak faded into the night, and Sage's gaze kept darting around like a cornered animal, looking for any means of escape. Another knight appeared, walking toward them from the darkness.

His helmet was off as well, and he had a weathered face, accompanied by gray peppered throughout his hair. "There you are," the man said, smiling. "The healer's this way, my lord. Let me help you." Trystan wasn't about to allow that, but the man's arm snaked around Trystan's before something hard slammed into his back, knocking him to the ground.

"No!" Sage screamed. Trystan reacted violently to the sound, turning over and moving to stand before freezing against the tip of the redheaded knight's blade. The Villain nearly moved anyway when he saw the other knight grab Sage from behind, closing a hand over her mouth.

"Release her," Trystan said darkly, feeling his power begin to surge.

The redhead pressed the tip of the blade into the skin on Trystan's upper chest, drawing a drop of blood. "Erix!" he called to the other knight. "Be gentle with the lady." But he was smirking when he said it.

Trystan's breathing hitched when he saw Erix lean toward Sage's ear and whisper, "Yes, real gentle, of course." He made a puckering sound against Sage's cheek, and Trystan clenched his teeth so hard, they nearly shattered. But Sage did not wither or cry beneath the words; she began to thrash wildly. Muffled screams of outrage came from her covered mouth.

Erix tightened his grip, his arms struggling to hold her. "Be still, wench! Fredrick and I simply want to ask you both some questions."

"And how do you expect her to do that with your disgusting hand wrapped around her mouth?" Trystan had had enough of this little charade; his power was done waiting. It was time to slaughter these fools, but he halted when Fredrick said something that chilled Trystan's blood.

"They have the core healer in custody. Your little wife over here was with him when we found him. We're just being sure you are not accomplices."

"What are the charges against him?" Trystan asked, his eyes darting back to Sage, who had not stopped thrashing and trying to break free for a second. The blade Fredrick was holding was still pressed to his skin, but The Villain would allow it, let the knights think they had the advantage.

Fredrick sneered and pressed the sword even deeper into Trystan's skin. "That's none of your—" He stopped when Erix began screaming behind him.

"Bitch! She fucking bit me!" The knight was shaking his hand out, faint teeth marks in his skin. All heads turned to Sage, who used her freedom to bring her booted foot up between Erix's legs—hard. The man screamed and toppled over.

The other guard turned his head slowly to look at Trystan, still using the sword to hold Trystan down.

The Villain smiled at the man, enjoying watching the knight falter as The Villain's hand gripped around the blade and squeezed. The sharp cut into his palm was nothing.

Blood dripped down Trystan's hand as he used all his strength to push the sword in the other direction. By the grace of surprise and by the weakness of the other man, Trystan was able to knock the sword completely aside and spring to his feet, slamming his bloody fist into the knight's face. He fell to the ground with a *thud*, and Trystan was on him.

He never understood why people would say their vision went red from their anger. His vision was often the clearest and the most colorful when he was feeling a powerful fit of rage.

He struck out with his fist, snapping Fredrick's head back with a sickening *thwack*, blood spurting from the man's nose and mouth in a satisfying bloom of red. The knight fell backward, unconscious before he hit the ground.

The Villain stretched his neck from side to side and drew his sword as he stood to look at Sage and the other knight, who was still on his hands and knees.

Erix looked up, first at the bloody face of his companion and then between them. "We—we were told we'd caught The Villain. The core healer! We were just—just following orders, my lord!" The man stuttered over every word, shaking as Trystan stalked closer. "No! No, my lord. We just wanted a reward!" The man sobbed. "For catching The Villain."

Trystan chuckled as he moved the tip of his sword to the man's taut chest. "Oh, but I'm afraid you didn't catch The Villain."

He whispered the next words so quietly, even Sage wouldn't hear. *"The Villain caught you."*

Erix's eyes widened, and he pleaded, "No, no, sir, we meant you no harm. Please, please let us go."

"You meant *her* harm," Trystan bit out, his power surging around him. "And that is enough for me."

And then he shoved the blade into the man's chest, piercing his heart and killing him instantly.

Trystan watched as the man's lifeless body crumpled to the ground. Chest heaving, The Villain felt his power ache beneath his skin, wanting to be used, the rush of adrenaline pumping through him.

But when he finally looked up, Sage was staring between the body Trystan was hovering over and the unconscious one a few feet away. He stepped to the side, suddenly very aware of the blood covering his clothes and the spatter of spray marking her once immaculate dress.

There was a metaphor in there somewhere, and he had no desire to find it.

"Evie..." Her name sounded rough and awkward on his lips, instead of soft like he'd intended. His last wish was to frighten her any further.

But she surprised him when she threw her arms around him and buried her face in his neck. "Thank you," she mumbled into his shoulder while his arms remained stiffly at his sides. He wasn't sure what to do. The last time someone had hugged him—well, to be quite honest, he didn't remember the last time someone had hugged him.

He'd forgotten how unnerving it was. "Um," The Villain muttered awkwardly. "I don't know what to do now." He meant about the danger they faced, but instead she moved his hands in a light embrace. Leave it to his assistant to completely disarm him in her misunderstanding.

"You just put your arms around me," she instructed, returning her hands to his neck. "It's not hard." She was breathing fast. "You ruined my dress."

"I'll buy you another," he said, slowly bringing his arms up farther to circle her warmth, feeling frustrated and a little embarrassed at the stiff unsureness of the gesture. He was an intelligent person—figuring out the mechanics of affectionate touches shouldn't have been so difficult.

"Good." She exhaled into his neck, no doubt soaking her dress even more on the red dripping from his own shirt. Sage pulled back to look at his attire and smiled lightly, scrunching her nose. "I think you'll need a new shirt as well, sir."

He stared at her, wholly unfazed by the gruesomeness surrounding them. Acting as if he'd just closed a business deal rather than murdered a man in front of her.

And she was smiling at him.

The Villain came to an unbidden realization then, so completely tragic that his mind tried to reject the words. But they were there, so plainly it was almost comical.

He was in love with her.

Of all the foolish, horrific things he'd ever accomplished, falling in love with a woman he so completely didn't deserve made the top of his list.

But he did love her. It wasn't a question or even a sudden realization. He'd known, hadn't he? He'd known from the moment she'd called him pretty. It was like a tether was between them, wrapped directly around his heart, that she had the power to push and pull at her leisure.

Evangelina Celia Sage was woven into his being; in the blink of his eyes, in the crinkle of his smile, in his rusty unused laughter, she was there. From the moment he'd met her, he thought of her like the sun. Bright and vibrant, untouchable.

But he was wrong.

She wasn't light; she was color. Every single one, dancing otherworldly and bright over his unworthy eyes. She was the explosion of the vivid gleams and glows of the world around him, like a constant rainbow, shining not after the rain but during.

She was everything he never deserved but longed for anyway.

He remembered the blood on her clothes, the employer who had hurt her before, the unjust way she'd been treated, and the final nail in the proverbial coffin was that echoing, agonizing word.

He was ruined.

But he loved her anyway.

He knew she might feel the same, by the way she responded to him, but he couldn't encourage this, couldn't give her any idea that they had any sort of future. At least not together. His future, more likely than not, would eventually be six feet under the dirt, and he refused to drag Sage there with him.

But just for now…

Trystan allowed himself just a moment to angle his head into the crook of her neck before he made a vow.

That he'd never tell her.

CHAPTER 47

EVIE

Trystan dropped his arms and took a step back, and they both seemed unable to do more than stare at the other. Each was limping and worn, covered in blood.

"Oh, yuck." Evie scrunched her nose, angling her head away from the blood on her dress. "I wasn't aware you could kill so...efficiently." She tapped her chin. "I thought you'd prefer more of a dramatic flair... like your little head collection in the manor's foyer."

Grinning and shaking his head, The Villain turned toward her, a devilish glint in his eyes. "Evil is an art form."

The Villain then turned and strode back toward the edge of the party clearing, grabbed one of the twinkling magical lights, and affixed it to the end of a fallen branch, creating a makeshift torch. "Shall we?" he asked.

Evie pushed her arm through his and gripped it. "Yes. We have to find your father." His biceps flexed under her touch, and he halted his steps for a moment before collecting himself and walking forward.

Evie had always been very physical with the way she communicated. Hugs were her very favorite thing in the world, or hand-holding, or even a kind pat on the shoulder. Evie had always felt very different from people in the twists and turns of her mind, but touching she could never get wrong. Hugs meant you cared about someone, hand-holding meant you wanted them close, and—

She'd done practically all of those with her boss...including kissing.

The Villain must have been horrified to have to go along with such an embarrassing ruse. The guilt she felt for throwing herself at him, the discomfort she must have caused him, made her stomach twist.

But Evie had to admit, despite the horror, just allowing herself for a moment to remember…The Villain was *very* good at pretending. If she turned away from the awkwardness for a second and just focused on the kiss itself, her toes began to curl in her shoes.

He was a good kisser, but of course he was. Attractive murderers were always good kissers; she was pretty sure she'd heard that expression before. Or maybe she made it up in one of the many daydreams in which she'd imagined that happening.

Don't daydream about kissing your boss, Evie!

She also promised not to reflect on the fact that she had nearly swooned like a storybook damsel when she watched him annihilate those disgusting knights, had even enjoyed it a little.

Evie had worked for Trystan for nearly six months now, but she'd only had small glimpses of the violence he was capable of, that he contained so well.

But even after having it quite literally spray at her, disgusting pun intended, she didn't feel differently toward him.

Perhaps she should, but she didn't. And it was ridiculous to do anything just because you thought you were supposed to. So, she held tight to his arm, waiting for him to shake her off, searching desperately for wherever the other knights had taken Arnold.

They continued through the trees, but he never pulled his arm away.

"We're lost."

"We are not lost."

Evie deepened her voice and pushed her shoulders back to make herself look taller. "I'm a man. I can't ask for directions."

The Villain quirked a brow, looking like he was on the verge of something unscrewing inside his head. "You're right, little tornado. I should simply find the nearest individual in Hickory Forest, in the dead of night, and say, 'Greetings! My assistant and I are looking for my estranged father because he was taken into custody by the Valiant Guards. You see, they think he's The Villain. When The Villain is, in fact…me.'"

Evie opened her mouth to respond tartly, but he continued.

"'Oh, and have you seen a rare, fatally dangerous beast known as a guvre? We lost one.'"

Evie laughed, squeezing his arm, and The Villain abruptly stopped walking. He swung around to face her, the torch in his hand illuminating his face, and her stomach sank. He started to say something—by the way he didn't quite make eye contact, Evie knew the words had something to do with their shared kiss—but she wasn't ready to hear he regretted it just yet.

So she rushed in with, "Did your parents have you in plays growing up? You're quite *theatrical* when you want to be."

Now he looked flabbergasted as Evie clicked her tongue and walked on. "Your horse must have gotten away—we should've found him by now."

"He wouldn't leave without me."

"It's a horse. They like food and water." Evie felt an unevenness to the ground underneath her feet and quickly grabbed the torch from The Villain's hand. "Hoof prints." A lot of them, as in more than just one horse. There were human footprints as well.

"They took my fucking horse." The Villain pinched the bridge of his nose.

"It's okay, sir." She said it because she knew this wasn't really about the horse, at least not completely. She watched him bend over and pick up a scrap of Arnold's robe. "We'll get him back and make them pay."

"I suppose we should be concerned for Ms. Erring, since she was with them as well."

Evie waved her hand dismissively. "Oh, she'll be fine. Evil never dies."

The Villain snorted, and they continued deeper into the wood. "From your mouth to the gods' ears, Sage."

A rustling in the bushes beyond halted them. The Villain drew his sword and held it up in a defensive stance. "Stay back."

"It's probably a rodent or something," Evie whispered.

Suddenly, the branches parted to reveal Becky, disheveled and stumbling through with a wild, frantic look in her eyes.

"Oh, look at that. I was right," Evie snarked, but then gasped as she took in the woman's state. She rushed to Becky, quickly placing a careful arm around her shaking shoulders. "What the deadlands happened? Are you okay?"

Becky gripped one of Evie's hands, terrifying her further. What had they done to her? And why did the thought of anyone hurting Becky make her want to break things?

What a strange day.

"They—" She swallowed hard. "They heard the guvre, and they took off with the core healer on two of the horses. The one they put me on wasn't moving fast enough, so the knight that was holding me just threw me off."

Evie's eyes widened as she took in the dirt and tears on Becky's dress as well as the bruising on her face. "While it was moving?" she yelled.

She bent over and grabbed the knife from her ankle sheath, then stomped in the direction Becky had emerged from. Evie made it about three steps before one of her boss's arms snaked around her waist, pulling her backward.

"I think one assistant against several well-trained royal guards is a bit of an unfair fight. Don't you?"

"I can handle myself just fine." Evie narrowed her eyes as he spun her around to face him.

A twinkle shone in the dark depths of Trystan's stare. "I wasn't worried about *you.*"

Evie harumphed, but it was impossible to keep one side of her mouth from quirking up as she held his gaze. Becky coughed, and Evie realized her sort of nemesis was watching her make moon eyes at her boss.

Heat blistered up Evie's cheeks as they faced Becky, a mix between bemusement and disgust on her face. "What is going on between you two—" Her eyebrows shot into her hairline as she gasped. "Gods help me. Is this all because of that little *kiss*?"

Evie and The Villain both sputtered, stumbling over themselves, denying the claim.

"Absolutely not!" Evie blurted.

"That was all a part of an ongoing and brilliant strategic plan." They both knocked into each other with the way they were waving their arms.

Becky's expression didn't change as she limped over and leaned against a tree. "I think I've had enough of both of you."

The Villain raised one imperious brow. "I beg your pardon, Ms. Erring?"

Becky sighed as she sank to the ground, her head falling onto her hands. "They took off with the core healer. Their mounts were quick, so they're long gone by now. Probably already back to the Gleaming Palace, by my guess."

"You're just full of good news today," Evie said without bite, looking around for something to warm Becky's bare arms. "We need to get you to Tatianna, and we need to find Blade."

Another rustle in the bushes had them all straightening, and a dark head with equally familiar dark eyes appeared. Clare. She looked frightened and, like the rest of them, hopelessly disheveled. "Well, we caught it."

The Villain gaped at her. "How in the—"

"Don't give us too much credit," Clare said, sounding drained. "It got itself tangled in a tree, so we had an easy shot at it. The leaves I found are more powerful when I ingrain them with my magic." She flexed her long, skinny fingers and pushed a strand of hair from her face.

He pulled the caller's crystal from his pocket, waiting for it to glow in his hands before speaking. "Bring the cart, and do it quickly!"

"Where's Blade?" Becky asked.

"He's watching the guvre, over there." Clare pointed to the side. When she turned back, she looked to the three of them with a quizzical expression. "Do you know where Father is?"

Trystan's face went blank, except for the muscle in his jaw clenching ever so slightly.

"Where is he, Tryst?" Clare said, panic prickling her words.

A few heartbreaking beats went by before her boss finally said, "He was taken, assumed as…as The Villain."

"You bastard!" Clare shouted, running toward him, then pounding her fists against his chest. "How could you let this happen! Our father could be *killed*, and it will be all your fault!"

Evie's heart broke, watching him stiffen and take every strike of his sister's fists against his chest. His arms remained pinned to his sides as he waited for Clare to slow. Her fists came softer and softer until her head collapsed onto his chest. "What if he dies, Trystan?" Clare's voice broke. "What if he dies?"

"He won't." It wasn't reassurance; it was a vow.

Clare backed up, lips still pouting, eyes still brimming with tears.

When she remained silent, The Villain nodded toward all of them but didn't look any of them in the eye. "I'm going to see if I can scrounge up some horses. I'll remain with Blade until the Malevolent Guards arrive."

The Villain reappeared ten minutes later with two horses. "You'll all spend the night at the manor," he said. Evie noticed Clare didn't even attempt to argue, just robotically mounted a horse and held out her hands for Becky, whom The Villain lifted next to his sister.

"Will she be okay?" Evie asked, trying to appear unbothered either way.

"She'll be fine, Sage," he said sincerely.

Evie nodded, wishing she could go with them to the manor, wanting to stay near Trystan while he struggled with how to rescue his father. Those wishes were followed quickly by chest-splitting guilt. Her own family needed her more.

"I have to go home." Evie sighed.

Her boss frowned for a second. "Do as you wish, Sage. Just—" He swallowed hard, then reach out and hoisted her up onto the back of the second horse in a rush of strength. "Just be careful."

Evie nodded, suddenly not sure what to do with her hands. She nervously reached down and fiddled with the reins. "I will. And don't worry, sir. We'll save your father."

He looked disappointed when his eyes met hers. "Sage, villains aren't particularly adept at saving people."

"You saved me," she whispered, but he was gone, already striding away into the night, slipping into the shadows like they were welcoming him home. Her chest tightened, and she mumbled to herself, "I suppose he didn't like the idea of sharing a horse with me."

As Evie motioned her horse onto the road toward her house, she thought she heard Becky mutter under her breath, "Fools. All of you."

The woman was nothing if not truthful.

As she rode home to her family, she felt a tug back in Trystan's direction, and she wondered if that pull between her two worlds would be the thing that finally tore her apart.

CHAPTER 48

EVIE

Evie's pillow wasn't under her head.

Birds chirping in the window signaled morning had come, but she wasn't in her own bed. The events of last night came rushing back, along with the fact she'd passed out on the small sofa in her family's comfy sitting area, with a small blanket and a pillow that had decided it no longer wanted to be under her head at some point in the night.

Groaning, she reached around for it and almost yelped when she felt a human head.

Eyes shooting open, Evie saw her sister standing next to her, a mug of steaming liquid between them. "I made you some tea," she said so proudly Evie's heart cracked.

She sat up slowly, her body screaming in protest. Her thigh muscles ached from the short ride home, not used to the motions of riding. When she'd returned, the cottage was quiet, her neighbor knitting on the couch. After Evie had sent the older woman home with a grateful thank-you and a quarter of Evie's pay from the week prior, she hadn't possessed the energy to make it to her bed.

She'd collapsed on the couch, still in her dress from the night before, torn and covered in dried blood. Evie's face heated when she realized, and she clutched the blanket up toward her, but it was too late. It had slipped low enough that Lyssa jumped, her dark head of curls bouncing with her.

"What happened to your dress, Evie?" Her sister's eyes were wide with horror.

"I ran into a little trouble last night, but I'm okay, and so is everyone that matters," she said, hoping that was enough.

Lyssa still looked worried, making Evie wince, but she nodded and handed Evie the steaming mug.

"Is that okay?" Evie asked fearfully. Because in all honesty, she was doing her very best at being her sister's only parent, and she wasn't sure that was a very good job to begin with. She knew her father tried, but he'd only been lightly involved with Lyssa's upbringing before he grew ill, and now he just seemed to be a figure to slip in and out to give her entertainment.

"Yes, it is," Lyssa said, eyes clear.

Evie smiled as she sipped the tea—and immediately spit it out. "Lyssa, this is awful." She hacked and coughed the bitter vinegar taste of it off her tongue.

"Oh! I cleaned the teakettle yesterday. Could that be why?" her sister said with false innocence.

"Did you use vinegar?" Evie narrowed her eyes, holding up her hands as if she was about to pounce, and Lyssa began to giggle.

"No!" she screeched as Evie bent over to tickle her. They both laughed until they were crying and rolling to the floor to get the upper hand. Evie was bigger, but Lyssa had the relentless determination of a child that believed she could accomplish anything; it was enough for Evie to concede.

"I surrender! You win!" Her voice was hoarse from the joy, and she sat up, her smile slipping when she saw Lyssa staring at the blood on her dress once more.

"You promise nobody got hurt?" Lyssa asked skeptically.

"Nobody that you care for." It was as close to the truth as she could concede, because a lot of people had died last night—but telling Lyssa that was pointless; Evie would never allow her sister near that sort of danger. She thought of the traitor leaving the note for her, in their home, in her bedroom, and shuddered.

Lyssa saw the subtle move and frowned, asking, "What's wrong?"

Evie bit her lip, attempting to find the right words. "There's a rat loose in the manor house I work in, and it's terrible. It's eating the food, breaking things, riling the cat, and for the life of me, no matter what I do, I can't seem to catch it."

Lyssa tapped her chin with the tip of her finger. "Have you been looking in all the right places?"

"Everywhere they would be," Evie said, nodding.

"What about everywhere they *wouldn't* be?"

The words rang like a bell.

Was Lyssa right? Was Evie too focused on looking in all the most obvious places? Too focused on making lists to truly look at what was in front of her own eyes?

"I think you need to stop going to school. It's making you too smart. I don't like it." Evie bumped her shoulder against Lyssa's. "Have you looked in on Papa this morning?"

Lyssa picked up the mug of foul liquid, and Evie followed her into the kitchen, where she dumped it out the window. "He left for a walk about ten minutes ago. He said he was feeling fresh…or maybe it was refreshed? Anyway, he didn't want to wake you."

Evie's heart felt lighter at that piece of news. "I'm glad." She turned her head and did a double take at the clock. "Does that say ten o'clock!" Evie yelped, remembering that while the rest of the office had been given the day off while The Villain searched for the traitor, Evie most certainly had not.

"I'm late for work!" she screeched, bolting for her room to change. Evie was halfway through the door before she turned to look at her sister. "And you're late for school," she said in a singsong voice, making Lyssa groan.

She smiled. Maybe she was doing a good job as a replacement parent after all.

But her smile faltered as she pulled the soiled and damaged dress from her shoulders, exposing a massive bruise on her upper arm. She shuddered as she recalled those who had fallen last night under the guvre's venom—their flesh not just bruised but melted from their bones.

Her stomach twisted as she hurried to dress, unsettled that the traitor kept besting them—and there was no telling what sort of damage they would inflict next.

CHAPTER 49

EVIE

When Evie stumbled into the office, her hair a mess, Becky was already sitting at her desk, scribbling furiously, probably signing the death warrant on a litter of puppies. The woman moved her elbow forward and winced, holding her stomach, and Evie felt a quick rush of sympathy.

She walked over to Becky's desk, wringing her fingers until the bespectacled woman looked up.

"What?" Becky asked.

"Are you okay?"

"I'm fine," Becky said, looking back at the stack of checks she was signing for payroll. "Tatianna fixed it."

"She usually does," Evie said, feeling wobbly.

"Always." Tatianna's warm voice carried over as she glided in and put an arm around Evie. The healer looked like a confection—a light-pink dress hugged her curves and fell into flouncy ruffles below the waistline. Her braids were tied back by the largest pink bow Evie had ever seen.

"You look—" Evie started, but Becky finished.

"Pink."

Tatianna frowned. "I always wear pink."

"And very pretty," Evie added with a supportive smile.

"And *so* pink," Becky said, staring at Tatianna's dress like it was a contagion that would spread to her drab outfits.

"Can't a girl look nice without such skepticism?" The healer frowned and stiffened when Clare exited the boss's office, looking forlorn.

Both Evie and Becky followed Tatianna's eyes to the waifish woman. "*Ohhhh*," Evie said, dragging out the word, scanning Tatianna's outfit again. "Now it makes sense."

The healer narrowed her eyes at both of them. "Nothing makes sense when that woman is here. I want her gone."

When Clare glanced their way, Tatianna murmured quickly and mindlessly, "Is my bow straight?"

Evie laughed, and Becky had to press her lips together to keep from smiling. When the healer realized what she had said, she looked at them both angrily. "Say nothing."

Clare glided toward them, looking ethereal in a light-blue dress that complemented her dark eyes and hair. She halted in front of them, giving Tatianna a once-over and then looking away, as though disinterested. But Evie didn't miss the red tinge to Clare's cheeks.

"Hello," Clare said, her voice soft. "I was hoping to speak with you two." Her pale hand gestured to Evie and Tatianna. "Perhaps in your quarters, Tati?" Clare gazed at her with a firm, purposeful expression.

Tatianna's eyes widened like she was realizing something, and she said, "Oh yes! Let's go, Evie."

There was suddenly a nervous energy in the air that made Evie uneasy, like perhaps these two should work things out alone... "Are you sure you want me to—"

Tatianna gripped Evie's arm, her eyes clearly saying, *If the ship is going down, you're sinking right down with me.*

Evie blinked back. *Stupid boats.* Then said out loud, "Okay...let's go."

Tatianna kept her arm linked in Evie's as they moved toward the hall that led to the healer's quarters.

Clare entered the room before both of them, like she owned it, like it was hers. Tatianna's response to that was exactly what Evie would have expected: blistering anger. Rolling her eyes, the healer pushed past Clare to a small rectangular box in the corner of the room.

Evie looked at them both, confused. "What's... What's in there?"

Tatianna smiled at her, but it was a grim one. "I'm afraid this will hurt, my dear."

And then it did.

CHAPTER 50

THE VILLAIN

Well, the office search turned out to be useless, but that was hardly the problem now. Trystan stared at the crossed-out names and blinked. It had to be wrong.

Over the course of the last month, he'd been periodically removing names from his full list of employees. First eliminating any of the Malevolent Guards, then Sage, then Blade, quickly followed by Rebecka. He knew from the start it couldn't be her, but he was not a man prone to easily trusting anyone. Except Sage.

The leather of his chair groaned as The Villain leaned forward over his black desk.

His siblings, included in a brief "acquaintances and non-enemies" section of the list, were also crossed off. A few of his guards had kept a watchful eye on them since the explosion, and neither had committed any suspicious acts. Malcolm had apparently not left his tavern since that night, save to stumble out to the bushes to empty his stomach. The list had narrowed further when a confidential shipment was compromised. All ten people who had known about it had been accounted for except one. And when the guvre escaped, everyone on the list was accounted for. All except the same name.

Tatianna.

No, not her. Not one of the few reminders of his past he didn't mind having nearby.

She knew so many secrets, but how many of those many secrets belonged to her?

Trystan wouldn't sit here and ruminate on it. He *knew* Tatianna. He would simply go ask her where she was during the guvre's escape, which was what he would've done if he hadn't been comforting his sister most of the night.

He pushed open the door of his office and strode out, his boots echoing down the hall as Trystan tried to shake away his doubts. This was Tatianna—there was no way that she was any sort of traitor.

Nearly to the door, he took a deep breath and assured himself there was nothing to worry about.

A familiar scream rent the air, causing the breath to seize in his chest in a flash of hot pain.

Evie.

Trystan flew the last couple of steps to the door to Tatianna's room, wrenching the handle—it didn't budge. He began pounding on the locked door so hard it shook.

Sage's pain was surrounding him as though he could see it. It was stinging his skin, burning him so deeply he felt faint. Trystan rammed his shoulder against the hard wood of the door, but it wouldn't give. "Open the door, Tatianna!"

Another scream.

Frantic. He felt frantic. It was almost like he could see her pain in front of him, her crumpled on the floor. Her agony.

"OPEN THE DOOR!" Wood was splintering under his fists, tiny, sharp pieces sliding under his skin painfully. He didn't care.

His magic pulsed, but something was blocking his power—a ward. Clare had painted a ward on the door. Trystan pounded against the wood now with the fury of a thousand storms, fear seizing the breath in his chest.

A weak voice called out, Sage's voice: "Trystan."

It was then that he became blind with rage and panic and all the thousand things that could be happening to Evie... It only took one more strike after that before the hinges flew clear off and the door gave way to slam against the floor.

The Villain crossed the threshold slowly, chest heaving, fists clenched. The gray mist of his power snaked across the room, landing on Clare and Tatianna, who looked horrified, fearful. Breathing heavily, he took in the rest of the scene.

The room appeared as it always did, not an herb out of place. His sister and Clare stood near each other, Tatianna holding up a small box toward Sage...

His eyes softened when he saw her, relief searing through his blood that she was in one piece. But she was lying on the ground, on her side, her sweet eyes looking to him, pleading.

When another wave of screams came out of her mouth, he squared his shoulders, sending out his power to find who was harming her—and preparing to slice their flesh from their bones.

The gray mist of his magic pulsed, but instead of twirling around Tatianna and Clare, it swirled around Sage. Her eyes were closed now, her delicate hands pressed tightly to the ground, and her whole body was alight in colorful agony. Trystan didn't hesitate. He raced toward her, sliding onto his knees and cradling her head in his arms. Her fists came up, gripping his shirt, tears falling from her eyes.

His gaze never left her face as he bit out, "Tatianna, whatever you're doing to her. STOP." The graveled boom of his voice sent her scrambling, and she slammed the box she was holding shut, latching it quickly and putting it aside.

In an instant, Sage was limp in his arms, her grip softening a sigh easing from her lips.

"Little tornado?" he asked, desperately trying to keep the worry from his voice.

"Present," she mumbled into his chest, making it constrict. She was okay. Hoisting her up gently in his arms, he carried her over to the examination table before turning toward the guilty-looking women on the other side of the room.

"I will give you both the courtesy of ten seconds to explain yourselves before I rip out your throats," The Villain said, pure rage laced through every word.

"Don't do that, please," Evie muttered weakly beside him. "I'm already nauseous."

There was a short, silent pause before The Villain rephrased his words. "Fine. You both have ten seconds to explain now, and *later*, I will rip out your throats."

"Don't jump to conclusions, Tryst." Clare had the gall to sound irritated, and Trystan wanted to wring her neck. "We were helping her."

"By torturing her?" he said darkly, looking to Sage, whose breathing was shallow. Her normally vibrant skin was pale, sweat beaded at her forehead, and her face was streaked with tears.

But Sage's small voice cut through the volatile tension in the air. "They're telling the truth." They all turned to look at her as she sat up slowly. Trystan reached out a hand to steady her, and she smiled at him gratefully. His face heated.

"The dagger is in the box." She nodded toward the box on the table. It was made of simple wood, no longer than his forearm.

"I don't understand." He shook his head.

"Well, if you would stop nearly breaking your neck jumping to conclusions, I could tell you." Clare rolled her eyes and cocked a hip. "The dagger is imbued with a rare kind of binding magic. It absorbed her blood when it cut her. That's why it hurts whenever she's near it."

"And?" Trystan asked, feeling his pulse rising again.

"Clare said the only way to break the bind was to expose myself to the pain until it didn't hurt anymore," Sage said, still sounding weak. He felt ill.

"So, you...you wanted them to do this?" He furrowed his brow, head reeling.

Sage flexed her hands after squeezing them. "I wanted to be free of it, the pain."

His lips parted as he looked at her, unable to keep the fear from his gaze. "That's very brave," he said hoarsely.

Clare and Tatianna eyed them both, but when their gazes turned toward each other, they both swiftly looked away. Still both stubborn as ever.

Clearing her throat, Clare spoke again. "Tatianna allowed me to look at the blade this morning because the steel was made with ink much like mine," Clare said, not looking at Tatianna at all. "The blade is almost sentient because of it, and when it gets a lick of your blood, it steals some of your essence."

Trystan nodded; he'd heard of it before. "It's not uncommon. Warriors in battle can greatly benefit from having a blade that is connected to them, like it's an extension of their very being." He smiled to himself.

"Warrior" seemed an apt description for the small woman in front of him already moving to stand.

"I want to keep going," Sage said, color returning to her cheeks. "Clare says there's something about this magic—something dangerous and unpredictable. I prefer not to have wild magic embedded in my shoulder, waiting to take me out like a ticking time bomb." She paused and added, "I've had enough of those."

Trystan wanted to tell her no, wanted to insist that she not proceed. But what if his sister was right? What if the magic of the wound could harm her without warning? "If that is your wish, then I'm sure Tatianna and my sister wouldn't mind working together to help you."

He looked pointedly at them both, and each gazed at the other before eventually nodding at him.

"Of course," Tatianna said.

"Happy to assist." Clare nodded demurely.

The list.

"Tatianna, where were you the night the guvre escaped?"

The healer widened her eyes before taking a step back, looking at him, and proceeding to howl with laughter. "Did you think it was me? The spy!"

Clare chuckled, too, and Evie put a hand over her mouth.

These women were taking years off his life. "You laugh, but you are the final person I couldn't rule out as a suspect."

"If I were the traitor, you'd be dead already, Tryst." Tatianna reached up to pinch his cheeks, and he swatted her hand away. "The night the guvre escaped, I was at the Evergreen Tavern. You can ask the barkeep."

His head was pounding with that deep ache that had settled there when the traitor first started complicating his life.

"Then I'm out of options," he said, defeated.

Another voice floated from the direction of the open doorway. "What, uh… What happened to the door?" Blade walked in, grinning from ear to ear.

"What do you want, Gushiken?" This day was getting worse and worse.

"The guvres are doing a thing," Blade said, giving The Villain a pointed look. "Seemed like they needed some privacy."

"What sort of thing?" Clare asked.

"An, um—well, they're reacquainting themselves with each other,"

Blade said, waving his hand in a small circle.

"Oh," Sage said matter-of-factly. "They're fornicating."

A strangled sound left Trystan's mouth as he swung his gaze to Evie's, his eyebrows nearly reaching his hairline. Her lips were curved into a soft, knowing smile...

Think about it. And die, his mind threatened.

"Fantastic," Trystan said sarcastically, looking away from Sage. "And you need me there for that...why?"

"I thought you could use your magic to keep the office from crumbling. They're very...um...enthusiastic."

His eyes squeezed shut. "I'll be right there."

Blade nodded at all three of them, grinning again before disappearing behind the ruined doorway.

Trystan started to follow but stopped short. Without turning around, he said, "Is my assistant still going to be standing when I return?"

"She's safe with us," Tatianna assured.

He nodded and kept moving. But when Sage's screams began again, he wasn't entirely sure he could keep his power from eviscerating *someone* until she stopped. He just hoped it wasn't a guvre. Or Blade.

The dragon trainer chose that moment to give Trystan an encouraging thumbs-up, which was followed by another one of Sage's screams.

Actually, he did hope it was Blade.

CHAPTER 51

EVIE

"**N**o more."

"Just one more try," Evie pleaded. They'd been at this for what felt like hours, but she was growing tantalizingly close to being able to stand while the dagger was within inches of her. A vast improvement, considering when she first started this exercise, she was nothing more than a fetal ball on the ground, nearly swallowing her own tongue.

"We can try it again tomorrow. You need rest," Tatianna insisted. The daylight was beginning to fade, and the boss still hadn't returned.

"Yes, I suppose." Evie smiled sadly. "I better get home. My sister will need dinner, and I want to check on my father."

"Oh! That reminds me!" Tatianna sprang into action, pulling out jars and tonics from her small cabinet compartments. "I found a new type of pain potion for him in one of my old books! I'll mix it up for you before you leave. Now, sit and rest for a moment."

Tatianna turned a knob and ignited the small stove she kept in the corner, the smell of medicinal herbs crowding the tight space.

And Evie smiled lightly, dabbing the sweat on her forehead with the back of her hand. She was close now to overcoming the pain well enough to use the dagger for its purpose, as a weapon.

Massaging a crick out of her neck, Evie smiled as Clare sat down beside her. The woman was wringing her hands lightly while toeing the ground with her foot.

"I'm sorry you have to go through all of this."

"Oh, that's okay," Evie said sincerely. "Bad things happen to good people sometimes."

Clare nodded, staying silent for a few moments before speaking again. "I'm very stubborn."

"And not very good at segues, either, apparently," Evie quipped.

Clare nodded and smiled. "Precisely." Her laugh sounded like the little bells Evie imagined fairies must sound like when she was younger. "I'm also sorry if I was less than cordial when we first met. I'm not good with new people."

"Oh." *Ever so eloquent, Evie.*

"I was so ashamed. That I had unwittingly helped King Benedict." Clare looked up and around to Tatianna, who was intensely focused on her task. "I don't approve of how Trystan conducts his business or his little vendetta. But I hate the king."

The words made Evie feel a sort of kinship with the woman. She understood complicated family dynamics better than most. "How could you have known?"

"I didn't realize the man was a Valiant Guard until after he'd signed my purchase log. I didn't think twice about it. I was distracted that day." Clare rubbed her eyes. "One of my regulars—the sweetest man—his wife left him. The blue was her favorite, so he always went out of his way to get it. He was overcome when he came in for his regular order, and the knight followed right after."

"Almost done," Tatianna called over just as something began to burn. "Shit. Okay, not quite yet."

Clare smiled when Tatianna's back was turned, the crinkle around her eyes the same as The Villain's.

"What sort of properties does blue ink have, anyway? Why would someone specifically want it?" Evie asked.

"Nothing spectacular, to be honest," Clare said, shrugging. "My regulars who preferred it mostly used it to read what others had written with it."

"How does that work?" Evie angled her head.

"When you use ink from the same vial, with one drop, any word that was written with that inkpot can be made to appear on the page before you."

"Any word?" Suddenly Evie's heart was pounding, like she was slowly tipping over the edge of a cliff.

"Any word that was written with it, yes. When I enchant the ink, it becomes like a body. Even when the drops are separated, they can be linked again by the words. Think of it like if one of your fingers was cut off but you could still move it. Because it was once a part of you."

"So the ink will always reveal the truth?"

"Until it runs out."

Evie nodded, her mind racing.

Clare snorted, looking around the room. "It's actually most useful in office settings. Whenever you write with that ink, it takes just a drop of it to copy what you've written."

"Don't tell the pixies that. They'd be out of a job." Evie smiled and pressed a finger into her temple, exhaling slowly. "Magic ink, magic scar, magic dagger. It really is a part of everything, isn't it?"

"I'm sorry." Clare smiled. "Having magic is one thing, but I know being around it without fully understanding it can be confusing, even frustrating."

"When did you get yours?" Evie asked quietly.

"When Trystan became The Villain," Clare said, a haunted, faraway look in the beautiful depths of her eyes. "It was a...hard day."

Evie nodded, unsure what to say, which in and of itself was cause for concern. Words rarely failed her; it was the ones that came out that usually did it.

"Got it!" Tatianna walked over, looking between them like she knew she was a welcome interruption. "Here you are. Let me know how the poor man likes it—I can always switch back to the other mixture."

Evie pushed up on her toes and kissed the healer's cheek. "Thank you, my friend." She turned to smile at Clare. "And thank you, too."

The Villain's sister eyed the vial in her hand with a sympathetic expression. "Your father has the Mystic Illness?"

Evie nodded and placed the medicine in the pocket of her skirt before moving over to the table to pick up her cloak. The last few hours had been such a blurry mixture of pain and relief, she couldn't begin to recall how it had made it in here from the hook beside her desk.

"Evangelina, before you go!" Clare called, and Evie turned to meet her eyes. "I'm making another batch of different inks this afternoon. Would you like some?"

Evie shrugged, grinning lightly. "Why not? I'm sure I can find a use for a blue."

"Great!" Clare called. "I was making another order for East Marigold, anyway."

She froze, her blood chilling. Tatianna snorted. "Great name. Is your customer a flower?"

Evie's smile didn't fall from her face somehow as she turned and left the room, a renewed sense of purpose in her steps and more than one vial in her pocket.

Of all the fancy bottles on the shelves near the door... Yes, Evie had good use for this one.

CHAPTER 52

EVIE

It was late by the time Evie finally made it home that night. The light in Lyssa's room was already out, but when she entered the kitchen, there was her father, standing over a pot, murmuring to himself. The pungent smell of two spices that were clearly never meant to be mixed filled the air.

She tried to keep her heart calm, her breathing even, tried to act normally. Swallowing a lump in her throat, she forced a smile to her face.

"Good evening, Papa. What are you making?" Evie asked.

"Why is this so difficult?" her father replied quietly instead, sounding pinched and frustrated. Evie knew he meant well, and she felt a painful jab in her gut from the guilt of having missed dinner, missed putting Lyssa to bed. She pulled the vial from Tatianna out of her pocket and handed it to her father, hoping he didn't see the shaking of her hands.

"Please at least try this potion, Father," Evie said. "My healer friend said this is a new type of pain tonic and it's been seen to be very effective."

He placed a large hand on Evie's cheek. "You always take care of me." The pang in her chest turned into a crater. "So like your mother."

Excellent. Right now, when she was on the brink of a mental break, it was certainly refreshing to also be reminded of her worst fear.

"Right," Evie said in a hard voice. "Except I'm still *here*."

Her father dropped his hand from her cheek, and there was a sudden chill to the room. "Yes." He coughed. "Of course." Looking like he needed something to do with his hands, her father uncapped the vial and downed it in one gulp. In that, at least, Evie felt some relief.

"Lyssa's in bed early tonight," Evie observed, not mentioning that she was happy to not have to worry about her sister in this moment.

"She wore herself out with the neighbor girls. How was work today?" They both sat at the table, Evie pressing her palms gently into the familiar wood before folding them nervously in front of her.

"It was...productive," she said, not having a better word.

"As all work should be." Her father smiled at her. "It's good you keep busy. Idle hands lead to nothing but trouble." She knew he was thinking about her mother again by the way his other hand reached for the medallion at his neck.

"Papa... Did you know what a hard time Mama was having with her magic, all those years ago? Did you understand how she struggled? Or was it all a shock in the end?" she asked, unsure of why she needed to know the answer. Why it mattered.

He looked caught off guard by the question, but to his credit, he answered her, and she was sure it was the truth. "I knew when it was too late."

Leaving him to his "cooking," Evie moved toward her bedroom. She checked in on Lyssa, who was sleeping peacefully in her bed. Then, passing by her father's office, she saw light spilling out from under the door. Had he abandoned his culinary disaster already?

When she pushed the door entirely open, though, the room was empty.

She entered slowly, feeling wrong. This room had been off-limits to her as a child, and despite her spiral into adulthood, it still felt like breaking a rule to enter without permission.

The crackle of the fire was dwindling, offering the room the slivered ends of remaining light. There was a small bookshelf pushed against the wall, with a few thick volumes and a few thinner—clearly children's books Evie had loved as a child.

Staring back at the door with just a little bend of her neck to see into the hallway, Evie crept farther into the space, walking around slowly, assessing.

A candle flickered, and wax dripped onto a piece of parchment angled off to the side. Parchment that looked like it had been crumpled into a ball and then uncrumpled a good ten times before it was laid flat again.

Evie pulled a pin from her hair and flung it as close to the desk as it would fall. "Oops," she muttered quietly to herself. After jogging over lightly and bending to grab the pin, Evie straightened just enough to peek at the words on the paper. Some of the ink was blurred, but what was etched at the bottom was clearly visible, and it caused a deep shudder of horror.

It was a letter—a long one.

Signed "with love" at the bottom…from the last person she'd expected.

Nura Sage. Her mother.

CHAPTER 53

THE VILLAIN

"I think they're done," Gushiken whispered above the dripping quiet of the downstairs cellar, just a floor above the torture chambers. This time of day, his prisoners were exceptionally loud in their dramatically painful-sounding moans.

Trystan was unsure of how the guvres slept so soundly through the noise. It was as if they were lulled by the agony of others. In all fairness, he often was as well.

"As long as they're content, their magic should stay mild enough to keep them contained," Trystan said. His thoughts were not nearly as focused as his words. They were a tangled riot, reviewing all the events that had transpired in the last few weeks and the chaos they had wrought.

But at least both guvres were back in his possession. Blade's leather ropes had proven shockingly useful...even if the man himself wasn't.

How he'd ever thought this man was a certified animal trainer was beyond him. He really needed to fact-check résumés before hiring going forward.

"Is that why you had me remove the wall in there?" Blade asked, tapping his chin and nodding toward the cage.

"Why else?" Trystan asked sharply.

"I don't know." The dragon trainer adjusted his vest. "I thought perhaps you took pity on them."

"I don't feel pity. Ever," he said, trying to sound authoritative, but he knew how juvenile it came out.

The male guvre curled closer to the female, and they sighed quietly together.

"I just—" Trystan paused.

Last night, he had heard the male give off a low-pitched cry and watched as he raised his clawed foot and lightly scratched it against the wall separating him from his mate. As if he knew any attempt to get to her would be futile but he couldn't find it in himself not to try.

The Villain was still in denial that he possessed a heart, but if he did...it might have cracked. Just a little.

"How is Ms. Erring?" Trystan asked, changing the subject and walking toward the stairs that ascended back into the office space.

"She's fine. Back to breathing fire with the best of them."

"That was a joke?" Trystan was doing his best to appreciate humor in others rather than rail against it.

"Yes, sir." Blade smirked, walking up the stairs beside him.

"Very good."

"Thank you?" Blade asked hesitantly.

Trystan walked into the office, which had been completely cleared. Sage's desk was empty, her cloak and bag gone.

The sun had set beyond the trees, and the last rays of light shone through the window, painting the room with a warm glow. It didn't feel quite right when she wasn't sitting there.

Tatianna appeared around the corner, his sister following closely behind her, and suddenly, it all flooded back.

Him outside the door, hearing Sage scream. It was the sound of nightmares, of all his fears coming together to brutalize him.

And therein lay the problem. He was The Villain. He couldn't afford to fear anything. Least of all be afraid *for* someone. His feelings for Evie would surely fade with time, as most things did. His heart began to quicken, as if telling him what a lie that was.

"She went home," Tatianna said. "She needed to rest."

Yet again, his fear flared like a fast boil. "Was she all right? What did—"

"She was fine. Little progress was made, but she didn't seem discouraged. I sent her home with the dagger."

"What?" he roared.

"In its box!" Clare added, rolling her eyes. "You are worse than when we were children, with this mother-hen thing."

"I am not...a mother hen," he gritted out.

Blade's ears looked perked, but he became very distracted when Ms. Erring appeared, moving across the floor to her desk, her severe bun yanking her features tight.

"Evie was fine." Clare put a hand on Trystan's arm. The warmth from their childhood came through in the gesture, right past his skin and bones and shooting straight for his soul.

Tarnished as it was.

Gods, he was turning into a sap.

"You should tell her what the gold mark is, Trystan," Clare murmured quietly.

Tarnished indeed.

"It's not right to have her agree to something like that without understanding what it is."

"It doesn't affect her at all," he argued, fearing that the first good thing he'd done in years was an atrocious overstep.

He'd sincerely intended to give her the employment bargain, which, if she broke the bonds of his trust, would seep into her body like a poison. He'd only known her a day at the time, so there was no reason to veer down any other path...but then there were her eyes.

They were so honest, so open. They made him feel...*afraid.* So many things could happen to her, so many people she could trust who could turn around and destroy her. He'd hated at the time that it mattered, couldn't figure out why this woman with a loud voice and a plethora of energy could evoke such strong protectiveness.

So instead of the green ink used in employment bargains, he'd used the gold, because unbeknownst to the public, its main purpose was protection. It warded against the strongest of evils, and when she'd face them, he'd know. He'd had the same gold ring placed around the circumference of his biceps, so that when she faced any true threat of death, it would tell him one way or another. Gold ink was a fickle sort of magic; it catered to its own rhythm, letting him know in different ways when she needed him. The unpredictability was inconvenient, but it was better than nothing.

His gold ring had burned him both times she was exposed to the dagger, when they were menaced by the guvre, and when she was on the parapet with the bomb ticking away, though the effect there was delayed—the magic in the ward was more unreliable after he'd just used so much of his own. Protection magic wasn't very fond of his. A popular opinion. Each instance of Evie's peril caused a burning sensation in his arm so great that he felt her pain with her.

He'd justified the practicality, telling himself that knowing when his assistant was in trouble was essential.

And he'd live in that denial if he could.

"No, it doesn't negatively affect her, but it is permanently on her body." Clare raised a brow, waiting for Trystan to understand her point.

But he already did, and he knew he was a bastard.

"That aside." Tatianna leaned closer. "Are you any closer to determining who here is selling you out?"

"It's nobody in the manor," he said flatly, feeling more lost and frustrated than ever.

His guards, who had the best kind of loyalty—forced—hadn't uncovered a single ounce of guilt among his one hundred and two employees. There wasn't much else to do but turn to his other conclusion: that someone was getting in and out of the manor right under his nose. And it didn't escape him that the person who'd been doing this always struck hard when he wasn't there to sense them, to find them, to eviscerate them.

There were just too many variables, and they were no closer to answers.

"I'll simply murder King Benedict, and then I won't have to worry about it anymore." Trystan seemed to be chronically accompanied by a headache lately, and the one person who helped to relieve that symptom had gone home for the day.

"Sounds good to me," Tatianna said cynically, rolling her eyes when Clare glared at her.

"Killing someone is never the answer." Clare frowned.

"I admire your moral heart, little sister," he said. "But killing is often my favorite answer."

Clare remained quiet for a moment, assessing him with such familiar eyes. "I was surprised to see how much you care for your...*employees*." She used a plural word, but they both knew she was referring to a single person. "At first I thought Malcolm was exaggerating."

"He wasn't." Trystan didn't have it in him to lie. "In fact, I'm sure he understated it."

Clare nodded. "Well, I hope that—" She halted.

"Sir!" Marvin—Trystan's favorite, if he had favorites, which of course he didn't; he was evil—his *not* favorite guard barreled through the doors, sweat from sprinting up the stairs running down his forehead. "A missive came! Keeley told me to give it to you urgently!" Marvin reached out to hand it off but doubled over his knees to suck in a breath.

"I know." Blade walked over and slapped Marvin on the back. "Those stairs are their own form of torture."

"Funny," The Villain said dryly, reaching a hand out for the message, then quickly sliding the envelope open and scanning the page. The words etched there froze every muscle in his body.

"What?" Clare pressed. "What did they find?"

"Clare…" He trailed off, confusion numbing him. "The knight who bought the blue ink, who bought the timepiece from Malcolm…"

"Yes?" Clare said, sounding nervous. The rest of the room stood at attention, Marvin included.

"He's dead."

"What?" Clare staggered, pulling a hand through her short, dark locks, perhaps even pulling out a chunk. "So someone got to him first?"

"No, you don't understand," The Villain said. "The knight, Lark Moray, perished a day after purchasing your ink. He couldn't have been the one to get the clock from Malcolm. He was already gone at that point."

Trystan felt like he was outside his body, like he had separated from himself while his mind filed through what this meant. "We've been following the wrong trail this whole time."

"It wasn't him, then, who set the bomb," Clare said incredulously. "But then—" Clare threw her hands over her mouth in shock. "East Marigold."

"Who?" The Villain pressed.

"He always asked so many questions about me, about my family. He was so kind, though, I never thought." Clare's eyes watered.

"I don't understand," Blade cut in. "So it's a different man? What's the big deal?"

"There's more, isn't there?" The Villain pressed further, feeling like a disaster was looming right over them.

"Y-Yes." Clare stiffened her lip, looking haunted. "The man who comes to see me, he uses a fake name. I mean, we all knew East Marigold had to be an alias. It's ridiculous. But he came drunk just the other night and accidentally gave me the real one. After he left, I checked the town registry to be sure he wasn't some sort of criminal, and it was there."

The room was so quiet, a strand of hair could fall from his head and they'd all hear it brush against the stone. "And…" Trystan didn't recognize his voice; it was higher pitched than he thought possible.

"I…I." Clare looked at him, visibly holding herself to keep from shaking. "I didn't think it mattered, I swear!"

"Spit it out, Clare!" Tatianna said, exasperated.

"His name was Griffin Sage," she said finally.

Sage.

No.

But there was Kingsley at his feet, holding a sign: FATHER.

And suddenly it whooshed through him like a wave. The horror.

Tatianna finished his thought for him. "That's… By the gods, that's Evie's father."

"Oh my—" Rebecka's head whipped up from her desk. "Her notebook." She stood and stalked over to Evie's desk. "Where is it?" She ducked down, digging through her drawers.

"She always takes her notebook home," Tatianna said, confused.

Becky pulled an ink vial out with a determined strike, nearly shattering it. "Evie and I were having one of our…friendly chats. I may have said something about her ordering subpar office supplies, and she bragged about her father gifting her this special ink."

The vial was a vibrant purple, almost artificially so.

"When was that, Rebecka?" The Villain stalked over, grabbing the vial out of her hands and passing it to Clare.

"About a week after she started working here, sir."

"When the ink was purchased," Clare confirmed, hand once again wrapped around her mouth, eyes wide with surprise. She turned the bottle over and nodded, tears watering her eyes. "This ink has been dyed. Someone mixed a few drops of red ink in here to make it look purple, but it's blue and contains all the magical properties."

Becky nodded, looking right at Trystan. Her hazel eyes were serious and resigned. "Whatever Evie wrote in her book, her father was able to see it. Our plans, our safe houses, even how to get in and out of the manor undetected. She was always writing everything down."

"Her father tricked her," Trystan said, his voice devoid of all life, though in his heart, a tiny flicker of hope that Evie *had* been unaware of her father's machinations started to grow. "He knew she worked here all along, and he used her."

Since The Villain had met Evie, he had felt himself changing in new ways, perhaps even better ones. But now he didn't feel better. He felt destructive.

"Let's calm down," Clare said, putting a hand on his tensed arm. "He's her father, Trystan. Perhaps there's another explanation."

"He put a bomb *in my desk*." He attempted to keep his words level, but the last three came out in a roar. "He nearly killed her— *He would have killed her.*"

And now she was there, alone with him.

"Fuck," The Villain growled, breaking for the stairs just as thunder roared to life outside. He halted in his tracks for a moment, listening to the rain whip against the window. "One of you go make sure this isn't because a guvre once again found themselves outside of their cage. Tatianna, you're with me."

He continued quickly for the exit as Tatianna called after him, "And what are you going to do?"

The Villain gripped the door, taking a deep, aching breath. "I don't know yet." He tore it open and stomped out, whispering harshly under his breath, "But I know who I want to kill."

CHAPTER 54

EVIE

Evie stood frozen over the parchment, blinking at the words. But no matter how many times her eyes shut and reopened, her mother's name remained. *Nura Sage.*

She picked up the parchment with shaking fingers, the paper crinkling under her grasp. The ink was smudged, so there were few words she could make out, but the ones she could see were devastating.

Sorry. Please. I miss them.

When she saw Gideon's name, she threw the paper down, unable to take any more. It knocked over her father's inkpot, spilling the contents onto his desk.

Evie cursed under her breath as she picked up both inks that had spilled, one red and one—

Blue?

"What are you doing in here, Evangelina?" Her father's smooth voice carried in from outside the door.

She froze, head hovering over the desk, ink staining her fingers. She had been caught literally red-handed. "What is this?" Evie whispered quietly, picking up the letter and the nearly empty inkpot.

"It's ink for my letters," he said flatly. "You shouldn't be in here."

Something in his tone had changed, and when his large frame moved into the office, for the first time in her life, Evie felt nervous in her father's presence.

"But it's blue ink," Evie pressed, feeling like the room was spinning suddenly. "It's incredibly rare; why would you want it?"

"It's useful for reading documents." There was a coldness in his words, and though his mouth was tipped up in his normal friendly smile, Evie saw a flat, lifeless glimmer in his blue eyes that turned her blood cold. "What are you trying to say, my dear?"

"If I look in this desk," Evie said, hand hovering toward the drawer, "what will I find?" Even as she asked it, she scoured her mind for any other explanation. This was her *father*. There had to be one.

"Evie." Griffin Sage laughed, but it was a sound she'd never heard from him before. A laugh with no humor.

"What. Will. I. Find?" she pressed.

Both their eyes darted to her hand on the top drawer. Evie moved quickly.

She ripped open the drawer just as Griffin barreled toward her, knocking into furniture on his way. Evie shoved the large chair toward him as she reached in to rip the papers out. She ran for the door, but she only made it halfway.

Her father yanked on the back of her hair, prickling pain burning her scalp as she cried out. "Let them go," he hissed in her ears. "Do not make me hurt you, child."

"You're already doing that," Evie cried out, the pain nothing compared to the betrayal coursing through her. Evie shoved the heel of her boot into his shin as hard as she could, the small stiletto hitting bone and making a satisfying crack. He released her on a howl of pain as he crumpled to the floor, and she leaped for the door once more. Throwing it closed behind her, she managed to bar it with a chair in the entryway just in time for it to begin shaking under her father's pounding fists.

"Let me out. This instant!" he ordered.

"Shhh," Evie called, anger coming hard and fast. "You'll wake Lyssa. And I know you'd never want to harm one of your children, would you, Papa?" She swallowed down the hurt, the betrayal, and returned her eyes to the papers in her hands.

But they were *her* papers, *her* handwriting, from her notebook.

"You've been using the ink to spy on me," she said, tears burning her eyes as she looked at every piece of damning evidence. She leafed through the pages of her words, so carefully written. She had been so innocently oblivious to the fact that her father was reading every word.

But she froze again when she found another letter in the mix. This time in an unfamiliar hand, but the name—oh, the name, she knew.

"King Benedict," Evie whispered, her heart falling to her feet, her face heating and black spots appearing over her vision. "You've been working for the king?" This would drown her. This most horrific of truths would bury her in a sea of despair with a current so strong it would drown her brutally.

The other side of the door was quiet for a moment before her father said, "Open the door, Evangelina, and I will explain."

Evie hesitated for a moment, but she needed to investigate his face when her father, the one person she trusted above all to keep her safe and protected, told her that he had damned her.

She said only one thing after moving the chair and opening the door carefully. "Did you plant the bomb?"

He looked stunned by her question before backing slowly into his office, finding the pushed-aside chair, and taking a seat.

Evie stalked in after him, moving to stand over in the corner closest to the door. "I'll ask again. Just in case you did not hear me," she said coldly. "Did you plant the bomb that almost killed me."

Her words were sharp, fit to kill, and her father knew it. He looked at her like he didn't recognize her—well, that made two of them.

He took a deep sigh before pressing his hands to his temples. "Yes. I did."

"How—"

"You had the entry points written in the cursed journal. I relayed to King Benedict where to attack when necessary, to ensure your... employer...didn't interfere."

"With killing me!" she screamed.

"Hush!" the man she was beginning to no longer recognize hissed as he started to stand up, but he halted when he saw the flash of fear in her eyes. "*You'll* wake your sister."

"Afraid she'll see what a monster you've become?" Evie asked, disdain dripping from every word.

Her father began to shake. Like every emotion was coming at him at such a pace that his body could not contain or manage it. "Me... the monster?" He was back to a whisper, but he said the words with surprise before a sneer came over him. "That vile human being you have disgraced yourself with—he is the monster, not I."

"That 'monster' is the reason we've been able to stay in our home! The reason you're likely even still alive, thanks to his potions." Evie tried to keep her words level but found that she could still angle them at her father like knives. "And he…he has reasons for what he does. And so do I. I did what I had to do. For this family." She shook her head, pushing her shoulders back and standing tall. "I am not ashamed."

"You wouldn't have had to do *any* of this if you had just agreed to Mr. Warsen's offer!" Her father's shoulders moved up and down, his eyes glazed over, unseeing.

But Evie felt her own widen at what her father was saying, what he was admitting to. She was falling into a yawning abyss of darkness, and nothing would catch her.

"You knew." Her voice cracked, and she hated it. "You knew that Mr. Warsen was going to attack me?"

"It wasn't as dramatic as all that, Evangelina." Her father waved his hand, disgusted. "He came to me and offered to give me a little extra money in exchange for a few nights a week of your company."

"Do you even hear yourself?" The tears were flowing freely now, and as she wiped one away with her hand, Evie noticed her fingers had gone numb. "Do you even care that that man nearly assaulted me?"

"You always do this."

There had been many times in her life when Evie felt like she was being looked down on, being made to feel childish, or silly, or frivolous with her thoughts and feelings. To the point where even if she felt completely strong and valid in what she wanted to say, she went ignored, unheard.

*In*validated.

"You blow things up in your head to make everyone else the bad guy." Her father spit into the still-lingering fire. "Your mother was the same."

"Don't talk about her," Evie said, barely able to hear her own voice.

"Oh, so now your mother's a saint?" Griffin Sage laughed, paused for a moment, and then laughed once more. "She killed your brother."

Evie flinched.

"She left you and Lyssa." She watched him smirk, satisfied in asserting his point.

"Was that the first letter she sent you since she left?" Evie asked, bringing her eyes right up to his.

Her father froze.

"That's what I thought." This made Evie laugh, despite the sad smile that followed. "And now you have alienated not only your wife but your elder daughter." Evie clapped slowly. "Congratulations." She walked over to the windowpane, listening to the pitter-patter of the evening rain, and allowed herself a moment of amiable silence. Or more like unamiable silence, since she wanted to rip her father's head from his neck.

But she was certain that would upset Lyssa, so she decided not to cause her little sister more trauma than she had accumulated thus far.

"That was not my intention."

"Really?" Evie said, shrugging. "If someone's willing to trade me for sexual favors without my consent and also places a bomb in my workplace, knowing full well it could kill me… I don't think those are the purest of intentions, do you?"

Her father stepped closer to her, and she let him. His shadows cast over her face as his light eyes, so like her own, glared. "I lost you the moment you tainted yourself with that man. What happens to you now, while devastating, is out of my hands."

Evie sniffed and laughed again. "You not only betrayed me, but you somehow find a way to blame me for it. The only reason I did any of the things I've done was to help you, because you were sick!" she exploded.

"I was never sick!" he screamed back, his eyes bloodshot.

Evie froze. The words seeped into her brain slowly as she breathed them in. They felt like pain. They felt like poison.

"What do you mean…you were never sick?" The crackle of the fire seemed overwhelming as Evie took another step toward him, noting a touch of shame, just for a moment, in her father's worn face.

"I never had the Mystic Illness. *I lied*."

There was a clawing feeling in her chest, like a flame was trying to burn through her skin. The smoke of it got into her lungs, laboring her breath. She couldn't have heard him right.

"How could you have—? I saw you sick. The healer came and assessed you." Evie's soul was beginning to detach itself from her body, perhaps to preserve what was left. Because if this was her new reality, that her father faked an illness that was devastating families across the kingdom, that had devastated their family for the last three years...

"The healer was paid to tell you and the rest of the village that I had the illness so I could have an alibi." He tucked his hands behind his back, and Evie took a step away. "The butcher's shop was supposed to be a front, but it was beginning to interfere with my *real* profession."

"And what is that?" Evie's voice was a strangled whisper.

Griffin backed farther away from her until he was behind his desk. He reached to a compartment underneath and pulled a false board out of place. When he stood back up, he was holding a helmet. A knight's helmet.

One that gleamed of silver.

"Is that—"

"I was, and still am, one of King Benedict's Valiant Guard." He said it proudly, holding the helmet like it was the most precious possession in the world. In *his* world.

"How could you?" There was a crack in her voice as she spoke, looking at her father through a blur of unshed tears. "You made Lyssa and me think you were suffering. Put the entire financial burden of our household on my back."

"We never suffered for money. I had plenty." Her father showed no remorse.

"That you kept for yourself!" Evie felt the tears spill hot down her cheeks, the pain cracking her chest open as the words spilled out. "Why would you do that? Why would you try and offer me to Otto Warsen? Just *why*?"

"My particular brand of work for King Benedict has always been secretive, covert. It was why I had to lie about my retirement. No one could know I was a Valiant Guard. I needed to remain anonymous in the world but still be able to disappear when I needed to. Something that could confine me for long periods of time, about which no one would grow suspicious. When I saw one of our neighbors catch the illness, I was inspired."

"You're disgusting," Evie snapped.

Her father's head whipped up, and he stared at her. "Watch your tongue."

"No."

Griffin's eyes widened at the darkness in her voice before narrowing. "You should be begging my forgiveness. Otto Warsen wanted to marry you, and you denied him."

Evie let out a dry, humorless laugh. "I don't suppose you ever thought to ask what *I* wanted?"

"I think you've well proven that you are not fit to make those sorts of choices for yourself." Her father sneered. "Just like your mother."

"What did you do to her?" So many lies—too many. It was like sifting through sand, trying to find one grain of truth.

"When her power came, she was meant to work for the king. She ruined that all on her own." He looked Evie up and down. "And now you're ruined right along with her."

"You're not telling me something." The crackle of the fire drew her eye as she watched an ember spark off and land on the ground before fizzling into nothing.

The helmet clanked as her father placed it carefully on the desk. "You were meant to marry Otto so I could have one less child to worry about. Eventually you would all be off my hands and I could retire, after I told everyone I was miraculously cured."

"There is no cure." She exhaled.

Her father paused and smiled. "Not yet."

"And The Villain?" Evie said, his name renewing her horror that all the destruction done was because of her. It had been her father, but Evie had led him right to her boss's quarters. "When did you find out I was working for him?" Evie had been so incredibly careful, even more so at the beginning.

"I didn't at first. I was working on something else for the king, a project of sorts." He turned to grip the fireplace mantel, his face illuminated by the dancing flames. "But when Lyssa was at school and you were *there*, King Benedict had a letter delivered, detailing an incident observed by some of his other guards. Of a young girl traipsing through the forest with The Villain before they disappeared. A girl they identified as my older daughter."

His disappointment was unfounded, but it was palpable, impossible to ignore.

"I began reporting to the king that very day, and you became the key to The Villain's downfall."

Evie felt sick.

"No." She was cracking like a vase that was about to be thrown away.

"Yes." The memories of her father's gentle smiles would be tarnished forever by the one pulling at his mouth now, what it meant. "And now you will help me get the mated guvres back for the king."

"What does he need them for?" Evie narrowed her eyes, noting her father's face growing pale, a sheen of sweat building on his forehead.

"The greater good."

With a small smile of resolve, Evie dug deep inside herself with the last of her strength. "I don't want to be good." The last word was spoken with a malevolence Evie hadn't been certain she possessed. But hearing it now—it felt pleasant.

More, it felt *right*.

Griffin Sage limped toward her, gripping her shoulders, painful, bruising. But Evie didn't move—she just stayed there, staring at a man she'd once trusted, believed in. Who she always thought believed in her. She wondered if she'd ever adjust to this new reality. One in which the man who'd told her stories of made-up heroes named East Marigold, who'd checked under her bed for monsters, threw her love and loyalty away like garbage.

"You don't even care that you ruined your life." His voice cracked, and she realized her father looked genuinely devastated.

"No, I didn't," Evie whispered, finding pity for this broken man. "If anyone ruined anything"—she leaned closer to him—"it would be you."

His grip on her shoulders loosened, eyes going unfocused.

"I wanted to be wrong." She swallowed a lump as he released her and stumbled into his desk, knocking things to the ground. "But I knew I wasn't the moment I heard that name."

His chest started moving up and down at a rapid pace, and he was opening his mouth but holding his throat. Like his words were trapped.

"I didn't notice the ink, or the invitation to see the core healer in my room, or the notebook you gifted me my first week." Her voice cracked, and she turned away to wipe her eyes. "But when I heard the name of a story you made up as one of Clare's clients, I knew it was you."

Her father collapsed then, staring up at the ceiling, eyes glazed over in shock. She knelt beside him, taking his limp hand in hers. "That pain medication I gave you earlier, the one Tatianna made. It didn't taste different because it was the new one she'd made—it tasted different because it was a slow-acting sedative." Her voice sounded like honey, dripping, sickly sweet.

Her father rasped out just one word. "You."

"Yes, I knew. I knew before I even walked in the door." She shook her head. "I'd hoped that I was wrong."

Evie shook as her father reached out a helpless hand for her.

"But I wasn't, Papa." She swiped at the unwanted tear on her cheek, her face remaining unmoved. "There is no room in my world for someone who hurt me the way you did. You do not belong walking on the ground I walk or breathing the air I breathe. You don't get to move on or be redeemed. Your story is finished. Whatever happens to you now is of no concern to me."

She sounded stronger than she felt as she watched her father open his mouth one final time. "He's…a…monster," he rasped out.

She knew who he meant.

Evie let go of his hand and placed hers on his cheek. "We're all monsters in the end. At least mine lives in the light."

And then her father, the traitor, closed his eyes.

CHAPTER 55

THE VILLAIN

Trystan was soaked to the bone.

He rode furiously through the woods, jumping streams and boulders, barely able to see under the downpour of rain. The familiar fork in the road appeared, and he was relieved to see the lit cottage, light coming softly from each corner. Nothing bad could possibly happen in a home that looked so inviting.

By the gods, will he kill her?

He wouldn't; he couldn't. But the man had literally planted a bomb, knowing it could easily destroy her. With that thought burned in his mind, The Villain leaped from his horse, tucking it quickly underneath the pavilion at the bottom of the drive and then kicking the front door open.

"Evie!" he called, realizing that if there were any secrets left in this house, he was about to uncover them inch by terrible inch. But there was no answer, just a small-sounding sob coming from the hall. Trystan raced in that direction, halting hard when he saw who sat there.

Lyssa Sage was short, with hair that stuck out in every direction. He was sure there was no one on earth he had less in common with, but she looked up at him like she trusted him when she cried, "Mr. Maverine, I think my papa is hurting my sister."

He knelt fast, leaning away so he wouldn't scare her. A strange thing, when that was so often his goal, especially while trying to get answers. "Where are they, Lyssa?" The Villain asked, pushing soaked locks out of his face.

"His office." She pointed to a door on the right, closed and quiet. "I heard yelling, and then Evie was crying, and it sounded like someone fell."

He cleared his throat, trying not to let his panic show. "I'm sure it was just a disagreement." He turned to Tatianna, who trudged in behind him, shaking the rain from her cloak and then her braids.

"Take Lady Lyssa back to the manor," he said, holding out a hand to the little girl, which she readily accepted. The Sage women seemed to keep courage in large supplies.

"But what about—" Tatianna could've said a hundred different things. What about Evie? What about kidnapping? What about taking a child back to a place that deals with stealing, murder, and torture? Not to mention deadly creatures and salacious company…with severed heads in the entryway.

"Take her through the back entrance. Just be sure she's covered from the rain," he said.

Tatianna pulled her own water-repelling cloak around Lyssa, who instinctively snuggled into her side.

"I'm a friend of your sister's. You're going to come stay with us for a while," Tatianna said kindly, leading her out the door and into the lightning and rain.

"Evie's not a maid there, is she?" The little girl's voice, unbelievably, brought a small smile to his face, much like her sister's so often did. But the smile lasted only a second before he remembered his mission and crept closer to the office door.

He leaned his ear against it, but there was no noise. The silence made his heart pound.

Trystan put his hand against the knob and twisted slowly, pushing it open on a groaning creak. When he could survey the full scene, he stopped, his mouth dropping open.

She was there, alive. He let out a soul-shuddering sigh of relief before taking in the rest of it. The body of a man, who Trystan assumed was her father, lay prone on the ground.

Evie's eyes went to his, sad, bloodshot from her tears. Her hands were shaking. "I figured it out."

His entire body seemed to sag from pure relief.

She sucked in a hard breath. "He's not dead. But I gave him a sedative, so he should be out for— I don't know, how long do sedatives last? Maybe I did kill him." She sounded robotic, like she was reasoning everything out to herself rather than him.

He started to walk toward her, but she stood, moving up to him, holding out her hand before he could speak. After taking a deep inhale, Sage said quickly, "I know he was the traitor. I mean, I didn't know before tonight—"

"I know you didn't," he interrupted.

"Shhh," she scolded him.

He complied, feeling his back go straighter under her scrutiny.

"I didn't know, but I did earlier when I left, and I knew you'd want to take him into custody, torture him for information. But I also knew you'd be conflicted because he's my father."

Now *that* he had to object to, really. "Sage, I don't mean to burst whatever sort of morally gray bubble you've put me in. But this man sabotaged shipments and my revenge, not to mention he's the reason that many of my guards are dead. I would've had no qualms about hurting such a man."

"You wouldn't have done it, though." She sounded so absolute, he began to doubt it himself. "You would've given me the choice."

And he knew then that she was right. It would've been agony not to capture him, not to kill him, but he would've left it up to her. This betrayal no longer belonged to him alone—they shared it, the burden of it now tethering them together, and he would defer to her wishes. Because what she wanted mattered to him.

"There wouldn't have been many choices," he grumbled.

Her lips turned up—not quite a smile, but that little glimmer in her eye was still there.

Thank all in existence for that.

"I wasn't sure how long the sedative would take to go into effect, so I suppose I got lucky." Sage sighed, moving toward the open office door and walking over to the kitchen. She pulled the cork off a bottle of wine and took a large swig, then another, then another.

"What are you supposed to do after you sedate your father, who also happened to betray you in every conceivable way? What's the protocol?" She scrunched her nose adorably, and he hated the fact that he found anything adorable. Especially when Sage seemed so far away from herself.

"I don't know. I've never had the pleasure," he said dryly. "I think you have to improvise on this one."

He watched her grip the sides of her head, nodding at two of his best guards coming in fully uniformed through the still-open front door. He gestured toward the office. "Take Mr. Sage out the window if you can. She shouldn't have to see him a second time. To the cellars. A clean one, if you please."

"It doesn't need to be clean," Sage called, taking another large swig. "I felt dirty for weeks after Mr. Warsen attacked me. I still do sometimes." Her eyes went somewhere out of reach, and it scared him.

"Mr. Warsen?" He angled his head at the bottle, curious at the alcohol percentage.

"My father 'offered' me to him." She began to laugh, and as the words sank in, he slowly realized what they meant.

He spoke carefully. "Are you saying that your father is the reason Mr. Warsen hurt you?"

The story spilled from her lips in slow waves, about how Otto Warsen had made it very clear he wanted her and how she had made it very clear she didn't want him. How he lunged for her anyway and in her attempt to run, he'd ripped her sleeve, then run that dagger down her back. She recalled how she'd stolen a cloak off a clothesline to cover herself when she went home.

She sniffed and recounted how she'd gone upstairs quietly and washed the blood away.

As she talked, Trystan listened, keeping his fury contained, not wanting to frighten her. This wasn't about him.

She looked at him finally, her beautiful eyes glassed over with pain and cynicism. "He didn't succeed in whatever he'd been planning to do, since I got away. But I still feel little moments of fear."

She brought out the papers and the inkpot her father had used to trick her, the letters from King Benedict that showed how he'd played her father and her as his pawns, how desperate he'd been. Trystan nodded through it all, taking the information with a calm gentleness he scarcely knew he was capable of.

"And now I've imprisoned him. My own father." She stalked back toward the kitchen, a manic look in her eyes as she took another large gulp of wine. "Does that mean I'm evil now?"

Trystan shook his head, unable to keep up, but Sage continued. "Oh my— My father is a monster, and my mother's abandoned me. Of course I'm evil now! That's, like, every villain's origin story, right?"

He shook his head, wanting only to reassure her. "You're not evil, Sage," he said flatly. "You made a difficult choice."

Another swig.

"Er," he interrupted. "Should I take that—"

"Would you like some?" A bit of the sadness was sweeping off her face, and her eyes even looked brighter…but he should still probably try to—

"Evie!" he said, bewildered as she appeared to have downed half the bottle.

She stopped, frozen in shock or disbelief, at his use of her name.

"Sage." Trystan cleared his throat uncomfortably, loosening his collar, trying to get more air into his body. "I realize this situation has been…stressful."

She looked up at him like he had three heads, and why wouldn't she? He'd just referred to her knocking out her father and his betrayal like a heavy paperwork day, or perhaps how Trystan felt after a bad haircut.

"More than stressful," he rushed out. "What you're experiencing must be devastating and confusing and…" Gods, he was horrible at being comforting, and she knew it, too, sensed that fundamental weakness in him.

But she smiled, and he thought, *I can't be that bad, then.*

But then the smile disappeared, and a pinched look of accusation fell upon her face. "I asked him, but he wouldn't tell me. Do you know?"

"Know what?" he asked, feeling in that moment that he'd give her anything, confess to anything, if only it would put that smile back on her face.

"What the king wants with the mated guvres?"

Fuck.

CHAPTER 56

EVIE

They both sat down on the worn sofa, Evie fidgeting with her hands, squeezing then releasing, squeezing then releasing.

Silence permeated the air, the only noise the creaking of the old foundation.

She wasn't sure why her heart was beating so fast, but she felt like something big was going to happen.

Her boss looked like he was in great pain, the pinched look of his mouth making her chest hurt. He crossed his arms, then uncrossed them, finally settling them on his thighs. Evie wouldn't mind having her hands there as well.

Focus, you absolute nincompoop.

But instead of speaking, he froze, turning in a flash and grabbing something over Evie's shoulder. She gasped at the nearness of him, the heat and scent of him, but his body left hers quickly, returning to his side of the couch with something in his hand.

"Kingsley?" She had no idea the little frog had come, too.

The animal's only response was to ribbit as he looked to both of them with a blank expression.

"Little stowaway," The Villain growled. "He must have slipped into my saddlebag when I wasn't looking. You could've gotten yourself killed, you fool."

Evie leaned over and straightened the crown that by some miracle never seemed to leave the frog's head. "He was worried about us, you little darling." She fawned over Kingsley, and her boss's eye twitched.

The Villain placed the frog on the small table before saying, "Stay put, for *once*." Kingsley didn't seem to have his signs with him, because all he did was nod. Her boss turned back toward her with an expression of dread as he started speaking.

"I found out about the guvres when I became an intern for King Benedict, almost ten years ago to the day."

Evie was knocked speechless. She literally couldn't think of a single thing to say, something that hadn't happened to her in— Well, that hadn't happened to her ever. He looked at her, but she kept her gaze forward.

Should she be angry he hadn't told her this sooner? She didn't feel angry, but she'd already been through a lot that day, so maybe her brain had shut down her emotions out of self-preservation.

It didn't feel like something he'd kept from her on purpose, but it was obviously painful for him. Speaking even that first sentence looked like he'd just pulled metal spikes out of his mouth.

"If you don't want to—" Evie started. She didn't want this from him if he felt he had to. But he held up his hand to stop her.

"I just… I haven't spoken of it aloud since it happened, but if there was anyone I would share this with, it would be you."

"Okay," Evie said kindly, placing a careful hand on his shoulder. "But only tell me if you want to. I don't want you to feel like I'm holding you down with a knife to your throat." She was going for sympathetic, but then the words were out in the open and Evie realized too late how explicit they sounded.

His dark brows furrowed together, and his lips squeezed tight.

"I meant because— I meant I wasn't going to pin you down— You know what?" She fake-locked the corner of her mouth with an imaginary key and opened her boss's hand, placing the key inside his palm.

His hand nearly curled around her fingers, their eyes whipping up to each other's, but then they quickly returned to their original positions on the sofa.

"I met King Benedict when I was nineteen years old." His jaw tightened, and he pressed his fingers into the couch. "I had been considering attending the university near the city, and on one of my visits I caught the attention of a magical specialist. My magic hadn't awoken yet, but he sensed something in me."

Evie wanted to ask how a specialist could sense magic that hadn't awoken yet, but she kept her mouth shut, knowing she needed to allow him to finish.

He looked at her, sensing the question in her eyes anyway. "My magic is very distinct, which makes it easier to detect. The specialist then referred me to someone he thought could 'foster' my abilities to their fullest potential."

Another silence followed, and Evie knew he was gathering himself to tell her the worst of it, the reason he dragged men through the office by their hair, the reason she was greeted by severed heads so often on her way to work, the reason he looked uncomfortable at any sign of affection.

The reason her boss had become The Villain.

"The king met with me the next day." Evie couldn't see his power, but she could feel the air in the room change as it thrummed underneath his skin.

"He offered me a position with him at his summer home, as his personal apprentice." Trystan sighed, pressing his eyes closed once more, scratching at the stubble around his jaw. "I agreed so quickly, too quickly. But the king knew exactly what words to say—his words were like webs, and by the time I realized I'd been caught, it was too late. He told me I had potential, that I was capable of great things."

There was a sheen to Trystan's dark eyes as he stared at the crackle in the fireplace. "No one had ever said that to me before." He chuckled. "And no one has since."

That infuriated Evie, picturing a young and vulnerable Trystan looking for scraps of praise because he was so unused to it.

"The first few weeks were…incredible. My mother and father were hesitant to let me go, but I wouldn't be deterred. I had become obsessed with pleasing the king, with making him happy. I did everything he asked of me. *Everything.*"

Evie found herself overcome by his words, as she knew that feeling well. Being desperate to make others happy, to feel like she'd earned her place in the world by the standards of another.

They looked at each other, and Evie realized the comfort she found in every part of his face. The crinkles in the corners of his eyes; those rare times he smiled; his subtly expressive mouth, which drew her attention far too often.

And as what he was saying truly sank in, she realized what exactly he meant by *everything*. "The guvre?"

He nodded, his hair finally dry after the rain, curling against his forehead. Sighing, he said, "I helped him capture the guvre. There were theories that the venom of a baby guvre acted as a sort of cure-all. He kept telling me the end justified the means. I didn't know what he meant then, and I never had the chance to find out." Evie stood, her skirts tangling around her ankles as she paced away from the couch. "Why? What happened next?"

The Villain was very still for a moment before saying, "Would you mind sitting...for the next part?" He remained rigid, but there was a vulnerability there that knocked Evie silent. She walked back over and slowly sank beside him, and he exhaled hard.

"The king had me working with a magical specialist in the month that I was with him, and with each session the specialist grew more and more timid. I tried my best to make him comfortable in my presence, but something was unsettling him, and after another odd session, I finally had enough."

Evie's hands formed into fists. "What happened?"

"I asked the king—demanded, really—to know why every servant in his summer home seemed to cringe away from me, why the Valiant Guards walked in the other direction when they saw me coming down the hall. What I had done wrong."

"And?" she pressed.

"He told me that my magic was dangerous." He stood then, startling Evie, and he walked over to the fire, stirring it with the poker. "I had spent weeks and weeks with the man; he'd built me up so high I felt like nothing could touch me. When he told me that whatever was dormant inside me could hurt people, it shattered me."

"But your magic hadn't awoken yet—why would King Benedict do that?" Evie asked, starting to see the tangles of the story unwinding.

"He claimed he brought me there to see if the problem could be managed before it was too late. But after observing me carefully, there was no hope. The king told me that if he allowed me to go free, I would be a danger to myself and everyone I loved." *No.* Her heart broke for that defeated young man only looking to belong.

"He told me his priority had to be the rest of the kingdom and it wasn't personal. It was for my own good."

"What was?" Evie asked carefully.

"The Valiant Guards taking me into custody then and there." The Villain had a steel to his voice as he turned back toward her. "I begged the king, I told him I would try to be better, but he wouldn't listen. They took me to the cellars below and locked me in the dark. There were no windows, no torches. I was trapped with the darkness, and it was trapped with me."

Evie was gripping her dress tightly in her hands. "How long— How long did they keep you down there?"

"A month."

A month. A month of darkness with no hope for its end, with no way out. "It took them a month to let you out?"

"They didn't." His lips lifted a little. "I let myself out."

CHAPTER 57

THE VILLAIN

Sage had an unfamiliar look on her face. It wasn't pity, nor was it horror, but whatever it was, it made him feel good, which was unbelievable, considering he was reliving his worst nightmare. Trystan walked back toward her and took his seat once more on the sofa.

"You escaped?" she said incredulously. She shook her head back and forth, and the silky strands of her hair brushed against his arm, making him shiver.

"The king didn't anticipate that his efforts to protect the public would unleash me upon them." He smiled then, a real one, and Sage did, too. "One day, the guards grew particularly sick of me. I'd spent an embarrassing amount of time begging to be released, and I think they'd had enough."

"What did they do to you?" she asked, hesitant, like she didn't want to ask for more than he was willing to give. She didn't realize everything he was already belonged to her.

Licking his dry lips, he continued. "They had a way of seeing through the darkness in the cellar. I never knew when they would next beat me. I just felt their fists against my body, the pain."

Sage took a sharp inhale, her face open, honest. She didn't move an inch, and yet he felt her physical presence like a deep warmth. "I hope you made them suffer."

There was a wicked disposition melding with the kindness in her heart, and it was wildly intoxicating.

He felt his eyes widen at the crooked grin that pulled at her lips, dripping with a lovely malevolence. By the gods, she would kill him. "My magic awoke then. I felt it pulse underneath my skin, and it lit up the entire room—it healed me. I could see the door of the cell, the light coming from the guards… And I slaughtered them all."

She bit her lip and wrung her hands together. "Good."

"I escaped out a tunnel that led me to my first drop of light I'd seen in weeks: the sunrise," Trystan said darkly. "I vowed then that if the king believed me a villain…that was exactly what I would become."

He remembered staring at the colors of light as the sun rose above the hill, like it was illuminating his purpose before his eyes.

"It's a hat you wear well," Sage said, kindly, sadly. "But why would King Benedict wait so long to try and end you, if he really believed you to be so dangerous?"

"Who says he hasn't?"

Evie was rocked by a sudden realization. "Oh my— The men in the dungeon. The ones you torture. There must be over three dozen at least."

"All sent by our benevolent king to capture me or end my life. It's a mystery why he went to all the effort to come at me through your father," Trystan said, realizing too late how thoughtless the comment was.

Because at the mention of the man, Evie's once-calm face went chalk white and her eyes went dark. "Why *would* he do that?" She stood, pacing back into the kitchen, taking another large swig of wine, and he followed helplessly behind her.

"Sage, I apologize. I shouldn't have mentioned—"

She bent over like she was struggling for breath. "Oh gods," she choked out. "You're trying to tell me about your trauma, and I'm hyperventilating like a selfish ass." She held up a hand, keeping her head down. "Give me a moment. I'll be right with you."

"It was a long time ago, Sage. I believe you're allowed to be upset by the your father's betrayal, which happened literally an hour ago."

"Too many things happening. My brain can't process." She moaned, flipping her head up. Her hair was wild, teased like she'd just been—

He would *not* finish that sentence.

"What can I do?" he asked sincerely.

Sage nodded to herself, pushing a hand through her dark locks, tossing them over one shoulder. "I think... I think I need a hug... please."

It was the slight *please* at the end, lighter than her other words, that absolutely destroyed whatever might have been left of him. "Sage, I'm not good at hugging. That time in the forest, you caught me off guard—I do not and cannot make 'hugs' a regular occurrence."

"But you did it so well before." The little tornado's eyes scrunched in confusion, and he resisted the gratified feeling that she enjoyed their hug so much that she thought another was well-advised.

"All right. Fine. A hug." He lifted a brow, seeing no other possible recourse. He smoothed the still-damp front of his cloak. "Like this?"

He walked closer to her, and her stormy eyes widened. She stepped toward him, looking like she was beginning to doubt how to go about the act herself. Which he knew wasn't true; he'd seen her throw out hugs like they were hellos to everyone in the office. He'd never wished to be on the receiving end of one of those hugs, but... All right, he was a liar.

There was no distance left between them, and if one of them didn't move soon, Trystan was sure that every ounce of self-control he'd gathered over the years would evaporate and he'd do something truly unforgivable.

It was both appallingly horrific and devastatingly wonderful that this small wisp of a woman had undone years of building pillars of protection around himself. That he would take apart any wall that kept him from her.

His tornado, his— He sucked in a sharp breath when she raised her arms up and around his neck, straining slightly because of their height difference. He'd always thought being tall and large was a point in his favor, but he'd never thought of the distance it would keep him from her embrace.

He felt her fingers brush against his hair, and he leaned into it, feeling no better than a house cat desperate for attention. But the worst had yet to come. Because when he felt her body press against his, he thought he finally understood true torture. Not the kind he inflicted on the men in his chambers, but real, to the core of a person, life-altering torture. He'd never felt anything as sharply or acutely as feeling every curve nestled into his body, which was quickly responding.

As broken and black as his soul likely was, Trystan had never once felt like there was anything missing from himself. Not until now.

His body, his power, settled in her presence. There and still deadly, but it welcomed her. In fact, he was certain it would rear and flare when they inevitably separated. The thought gave him the courage to lift his arms and wrap them carefully around the small of her back.

His chin tucked on her shoulder, and he fully let himself settle against her. His body let out such a deep, contented sigh, it was almost a growl. Like it had been waiting for her, and now that she was here, it would only live half as what it had been before, forever waiting to be whole again.

Fuck.

Well, he knew how the guvres felt now.

She spoke against his neck, sending a shiver down his spine. "You're a good hugger." He felt wetness against his skin and realized she was crying, and he tightened his arms around her, thinking if anyone dared come near her in this moment, there was nothing and nobody that could stop him from slitting them in half.

"I'll admit, I'm out of practice, so that's good to hear." Did he sound normal? He didn't want to frighten her with the yearning that was pulsing through him. No need to burden her with his lack of self-control.

"You're telling me you haven't been giving the interns hugs after Scatter Day?" Did she realize the effect of her fingers playing with the locks of hair at the nape of his neck? No, she couldn't, or she'd shove away from him and slap him. He was inches away from slapping himself.

"I cut it back to once a month."

"The hugging?" She smiled against him; he couldn't see it, but he knew.

"Scatter Day," he said flatly.

She snickered, and he couldn't resist burying his head farther into her neck, scrunching his eyes like it was almost painful, and in a way it was. But for now, he'd enjoy it, and try to hold this memory in his heart until the day of his inevitable horrific death, which wouldn't matter because he'd gotten to hold her.

"Can we do this a little bit longer?" Evie asked, her lips nearly brushing against his neck again.

Forever, he thought. But instead, he coughed uncomfortably and said, "If that's what you want. I'm sure I can endure it for a little longer."

Kingsley appeared over Sage's shoulder, looking so small against the doorway, but the little shake of his crowned head might as well have been screaming at Trystan.

As they pulled away slowly, Trystan was knocked breathless by how close his face was to hers. Evie seemed to be as well, by the way her light eyes widened. But she didn't move back farther, and neither did he. After the harrowing night she'd had, she still was so achingly beautiful, with the smell of vanilla candies on her breath.

He took a sharp inhale as her face drifted closer, like she couldn't help it, like they were drawn together. He angled his head down, gripping the back of her dress, lightly urging her near. Their lips hovered so close, he could almost taste her.

A crash broke them apart, both breathless as they looked toward the source of the noise. It was Kingsley, who'd crashed into the kitchen table, knocking a plate to the ground.

I'm going to kill that frog.

But his anger was replaced by gratefulness, for if he kissed Sage again, there would be no coming back from it.

He looked at her sheepishly, as she did at him, before she mumbled, "I'm going to...go grab some of my and Lyssa's things." She turned quickly and started up the stairs, leaving Trystan and Kingsley alone.

The Villain looked upon the frog with a different lens, and for the first time in ten years he found himself relieved that Kingsley remained a frog...and not the kind and noble human prince he'd been once upon a time. For if Kingsley *was* a prince once more, The Villain knew how stark his inadequacies would feel against his old friend's benevolent chivalry.

Trystan had just wanted to enjoy that moment with her, where he could pretend that he was good, that he was hers. He could still feel her warmth around him, and he savored it, the memory of it, knowing it was all he was allowed to have. Because women like Evie Sage didn't end up with The Villain.

She startled him from his thoughts, appearing with two large bags. "Ready to go?" she asked hesitantly.

"Ready," he said with a slight upturn of his lips. She headed for the door first, scooping Kingsley up as she walked. And The Villain followed her, leaving the memory behind.

Where it belonged.

CHAPTER 58

EVIE

Half an hour later, Evie was dismounting the horse, The Villain's hands gripping her hips as he hoisted her down. It was bad enough being pressed against him for the entire ride there, but now she was eye to eye with him as she slid down his body.

She should've kissed him. She'd wanted to. The minute she'd touched him, it felt like a slow-burning flame had lit underneath her skin, making it hard to breathe, to think.

They'd stood there together for what felt like forever and yet still not long enough.

She made sure to pack all her sister's favorite toys, her coloring parchments, and even one of the pillows from her bed. Perhaps it would soften the blow just a smidgen when Evie told Lyssa the truth, the whole truth. Something Evie had never been given.

She had no regrets, however. Maybe that did make her a monster, but she was quickly learning that it took more to make a monster than a monstrous act. She had no idea where her line of morality was anymore, but she'd protect herself however she could.

Her father had thought he was doing his duty, and that didn't make him a monster. But the means in which he did it, the way he sacrificed her for the sake of himself… She shook her head, happy Lyssa would never be subjected to that sort of cruelty.

She followed Trystan inside the manor, pushing away the absurd urge to reach out and take his hand in hers like it belonged there.

They were halfway inside, the satchel around her waist heavy with the dagger, when: "Oh no," she said, feeling around the bag.

"What is it?" Trystan turned to her. It was still too early to see the first rays of morning, but the night wasn't as dark at this time; the sky seemed lighter. But she had plenty of time later to panic about the fact that she would be seeing him at all hours of the night *every* night, now that she'd be living there.

The real horror was just beginning.

"My notebook. I left it in my father's office."

"I'll purchase another for you, and before you say no, consider it part of your supply budget." He was being kind.

"I need that one. It has important things." She smiled to herself, remembering the hearts she'd drawn. "Sentimental things."

"Very well. We will return to retrieve this *sentimental* notebook of yours." He shook his head, raising a brow. "Marv, take these to the west side of the manor." He dropped the bags into his guard's waiting hands and turned to pull Kingsley from the riding pouch. "And make sure this one stays put in my office." Kingsley gave a croak of outrage but went willingly with the guard.

"We're staying on the west side?" Evie's jaw nearly dropped open. "The side you live on?"

He was already walking back toward the open gates, without his horse. "Shall we walk?"

Trystan kept a long stride back into the array of brightly colored trees, and Evie followed quickly behind him. "No, no, wait. I get to see where you live. Oh my gods. What do you even do in your free time? Do you have hobbies?"

"Little tornado," he grumbled under his breath before leveling his voice back to his normal volume. "Don't make me regret this, Sage."

"Can we play board games? Lyssa loves board games." She nodded wisely beside him. "Perhaps a tea party. Lyssa loves those, too."

"Why would one need a party for tea? Don't you just drink it? What on earth is the party for?" His confusion caused a bubble of laughter to leave her lips.

"I'm sorry. That's not funny." She snorted, and his mouth cracked wide open, his dimple making its graceful appearance.

"I realize once I find out what a tea party is, my ignorance will most likely be very amusing."

She scrunched her nose, giving him a final grin before dancing ahead of him. "I actually think if we cut across the stream up ahead, we can shave ten minutes off the walk."

A low, strangled sound halted her suddenly. Evie whipped around and gasped when she saw her boss crumpled on the ground. Tossing her heavy satchel away, she ran over to him.

"Sir!" His eyes were open, but his face was pinched in pain.

He gripped her arm, hard. "Run," he rasped.

"What?" Evie shook her head, confused, but then the rattle of horses brought on the swift quickening of her heart. She put a hand on Trystan's shoulder and leaned her body slightly over his to shield him. Six riders on large horses appeared, circling them, one of them with a hand raised toward The Villain.

"Stop!" she screamed, looking around for any weapon. But the only thing she had at her disposal was the dagger that she could barely be near, not to mention her satchel was outside of the little barrier within which they'd blocked her.

"Stay put!" one of them yelled. She couldn't see any of their faces with their metal helmets on. A carriage rattled closer, with a large compartment linked to the back, and Evie felt panicked. She assessed every escape, every means of bribery or deceit. But she didn't know what they wanted, and there was no telling what they knew.

She looked down to Trystan, still pinned by whatever power the knight closest to her was using. Her hand remained on his shoulder, and she squeezed tight when the carriage rattled to the middle of the circle, the horses that had moved reclosing the gap behind it.

The driver of the carriage, a large-set man dressed in silver and white, rushed toward the carriage door.

After opening it, he bowed deeply. All the knights dismounted their horses in a wave and dropped to their knees.

"Son. Of. A. Bitch," Trystan gritted out, sitting up, wincing through the pain. His face was turning red, and the veins in his eyes and around his forehead were splaying.

Evie knew immediately, even though she'd never seen the man in person. So, it was technically just a guess when he descended the small steps of the carriage and Evie said in quiet horror, "King Benedict."

CHAPTER 59

EVIE

"Ms. Sage!" A wide, perfect smile spread across the king's handsome face. He was certainly into his late forties if not his fifties, with sprays of gray through his thick, sandy-colored hair.

"At last we meet." He walked toward her, tucking his fur cape behind him. "Chain up The Villain, would you?" The king nodded to one of the knights. "With the *special* cuffs."

"No." Evie threw her body in front of his.

"Sage, move," Trystan gritted out, sounding strangled.

"No," she said, panicking.

The king shook his head sympathetically, nodding toward another knight. "It would do you well not to struggle, my dear." Such kindness in his voice. Evie would've trusted that kindness, in another place, when she was another person.

The knight reached down in a flash, gripping her by the waist and hoisting her off Trystan. "No! Get off me!" she screamed, kicking and flailing, swiping her hands out. The knight dropped her for a second and raised his arm high before backhanding her. She fell.

"Stop!" It was The Villain's voice, not Trystan's, that cut across the clearing. It was cold and deadly. "Step away from her!" he roared, the clinking of metal following his every movement as he pulled against his cuffs. Evie rolled to her side, looking at him, feeling a tear slide down her cheek.

She pulled herself up, blood dripping from her lower lip, leaves tangled in her hair.

"Yes, stop. The brutality is hardly necessary. He's chained. He cannot hurt anyone, and if you cannot handle that woman without harming her, perhaps we should rethink your position as one of my guards," the king said firmly.

Trystan didn't look to be in great pain anymore, but he was obviously weakened. From that minute of torture or from the cuffs, she was unsure.

"I didn't want it to come to this, really." The king *tsk*ed. "I was hoping to keep this clean, but you've really left me no choice. You've simply interfered too much. I was content to let you play your little fairy-tale role for as long as you desired." He walked closer to The Villain, the well-formed smile disappearing into coldness.

"But now you're trying to ruin my plans. And that, I'm afraid, I cannot allow."

Trystan was breathing heavily, nostrils flared, eyes glazed over with rage. "What...are you talking about?" he gritted out.

The king clicked his tongue as he looked down at her boss. "So much potential, yet how disappointing you were." Benedict knelt beside him, putting a hand on Trystan's cheek that he tried to shake off. "The guvres—I have a great need of them. To aid in Rennedawn's very...*bright* future."

Trystan narrowed his eyes before saying in a pinched, breathless voice, "Fuck. You."

"I second that," Evie said from the ground, drawing the attention of every man surrounding her.

"And that brings me to you, Ms. Sage!" The king turned around and started walking toward her.

"Don't touch her, Benedict." Trystan's voice was raw as he pulled once again at his chains.

"You were supposed to be my sweet little savior, but it turns out you're just as rotten as your father said."

She glared at him. "My father was a liar. But you..." Evie slowly stood, brushing the leaves from her skirts and the blood from her lip. "You're a coward."

The king smiled at her. Not the charming one he'd arrived with, but a sinister one, a vindictive one. It didn't look natural; it was almost... villainous.

"I'm afraid I need my guvres back, Ms. Sage," he said. "You see, without her mate, my guvre was unable to produce any venom in all my time with her. But now, it would seem, she does."

"You'll get them over my cold, dead body," she said, smiling. "Or yours."

"I'm so glad you said that." The king's cape swept behind him as he returned to Trystan, who was still being held back by two knights. "I'm afraid you're going to need to come with me. It would seem you're of more use than I originally suspected."

The king turned to Evie with a sad tilt of his head. "You, my dear, are not."

Evie felt large arms close around her and a familiar vile scent flood her senses.

"No! Benedict!" Trystan was going wild, tearing at the chains and the knights so hard, a third had to join in restraining him. "Let her go, Warsen, or this day will be your last."

"Such pretty threats!"

Evie was disgusted to find her suspicions confirmed when she heard Otto Warsen's voice in her ear.

"Thank you for the cuffs, Mr. Warsen. You've been most helpful." The king nodded at the blacksmith.

"I'm going to kill you," Trystan vowed calmly. "I am going to rip your heart out of your body, and I will watch the life leave your eyes."

"I believe I'll see the light leave yours first," the king said in a mock whisper before turning back to Evie and Mr. Warsen. "You may finish her off as you please; just be sure to save the body. I'll have use for it after she's gone."

Evie began to shake, the panic at finding herself once again in this situation with Otto washing through her like a fast-acting poison.

"No, Benedict, no! Please." The Villain's voice cracked, pained, shattering his composure.

Evie felt tears burn before flowing down her face.

"Please, I beg you. I will do anything you ask, anything you want. Anything, if you'll spare her. Just please—I beg you to spare her."

When Trystan, The Villain, dropped to his knees, Evie cried.

"I. *Beg*. You."

Stop, she wanted to scream at him, *don't lower yourself for me.*

Don't bend your will. I'm not worth it.

The king for a moment had a genuine look of emotion—surprise. With wide eyes, he lowered on his haunches to look Trystan in the face. "I believe I underestimated your attachment to this woman. I merely believed her to be someone who worked for you.

"But I see now. I understand." King Benedict smiled, placing a hand on Trystan's cheek. "No, I won't do this." He stood up and motioned to one of the knights, who brought a large syringe forth.

Mr. Warsen's hand closed around her mouth before she could warn him.

"I won't make you watch."

Trystan's eyes widened at the words, and he opened his mouth to yell, but the needle was already thrust under his skin, the liquid being pushed into his blood.

Evie screamed on the other side of Mr. Warsen's thickly gloved hand, thrashing and squirming, trying to get free.

But Trystan's eyes rolled back into his head, and he hit the ground with a *thud*.

"Take him to the back cart and lock him in—that should keep him down until we return to the Gleaming Palace." The king nodded to Otto, and Evie couldn't believe that mere minutes ago, she had been laughing with Trystan, planning an office tea party, thinking that things might end up okay.

"You stay behind." The king motioned to two of his knights. "Allow Mr. Warsen to kill her himself, but then ensure he returns the body to me promptly."

"Yes, Your Majesty," one of them said.

Evie watched as the rest of the knights dragged Trystan away and threw his body carelessly into the cart. And Evie knew, with a certainty that flooded her with ice, that this was the last time she'd ever see him. That her last memory of him would be him lying limp and broken, alone in a carriage.

It was too tragic, too unfair. And all because she wanted her ridiculous notebook, with her ridiculous dreams inside. Dreams that would never come true.

The carriage rattled away, and Evie said a quiet goodbye to the man who had become the focal point of her heart. The one who'd changed her whole world—a world she would no longer be a part of.

When just she, the knights, and Mr. Warsen remained, she stayed stock-still, part of her merely awaiting the inevitable. She had truly never felt so low in all her life. Once again she was trapped under the control of someone stronger, someone who took. And took and took and took. This man had robbed her—of her comfort, of her security— and she was now to be robbed of her life.

Do the right thing, Evie. Do the kind thing, Evie. Be good, *Evie.*

Otto held her there, chuckling quietly in her ear. And something about the sound galvanized her, made fire stir low in her belly.

Where the fuck did being good ever get her?

What would The Villain say? *Make this man pay, little tornado.*

And so she did.

Evie moved her foot, jamming her heel into his shin, similarly to how she had with her father, except this time she gave a rough elbow to his middle as well. When Otto doubled over, loosening his grip as he reached for his stomach, Evie slipped out and ran as fast as she could. But the other two knights surrounded her, clearly trying to follow orders and not get involved but also loath to let her leave. And she knew she was sorely outnumbered.

I'm sorry, Trystan, she thought. *I tried.*

Suddenly Mr. Warsen was upon her again, red-faced, clearly still in pain but recovered enough to let his rage take over. He picked her up and slammed her against the ground.

He held her there, pinning her arms down with his knees and wrapping his hands around her throat. This was it, she knew. She struggled and tried to move her arms, but she was overwhelmed by a wave of pain that had nothing to do with her rapidly depleting air supply.

She moved her eyes over and saw her satchel spilled open, the box with the dagger in it turned on its side, the dagger lying there on the ground, so close it could kill her.

Except it hadn't killed her. Not yet.

Looking up at Mr. Warsen's face, one that used to cause her so much fear, she knew she didn't want to fear him anymore...

She wanted to be feared.

The blacksmith loosened his grip for a second, smiling above her with yellow-stained teeth. "I'm serving the kingdom by ridding the world of you. You don't belong here. After debasing yourself the way you have, this death is a mercy."

Evie narrowed her eyes, and Mr. Warsen did not notice her right hand slipping free. He kept his grip around her throat as he leaned in close to her face. "What could be better…for The Villain's whore."

Evie closed her palm and her eyes, feeling the burn of pain in every pore, feeling it pulse in her blood.

"Actually," she rasped out.

She opened her eyes.

"I'm. His. Fucking. Assistant," she whispered and smiled, before whipping the dagger up and slitting his throat.

CHAPTER 60

EVIE

Blood sprayed her face as he fell, eyes wide. She stood up, soaked in blood, breathing hard, an ache in her neck.

The dagger pulsed in her hand. But the pain was gone.

She smiled in relief, staring at the weapon like a lost friend, and it almost seemed to answer her.

"You witch!" one of the two remaining knights yelled, sprinting for her. Evie held up the dagger to fight, ready to destroy him, but the knight halted when a large sword was shoved through his middle.

Evie gasped as the sword was tugged out and the knight fell. The other knight behind him stood there with the dripping sword.

"What the— Why did you? I mean, I'm not complaining, but why would you help me?"

The remaining knight, her unlikely hero, did not say a word. Merely stood there for a moment, assessing her, his whole face covered by a silver helmet, save for his eyes. Evie took a careful step closer to him, but the move seemed to startle the knight into action. Grabbing the reins of his horse, he quickly hoisted himself up, giving her one final glance before riding away.

What in the deadlands was that?

But she didn't have time to ask more questions. Not when she spotted a strip of Trystan's torn shirt laying against the grass.

He was gone. Taken. By *them.*

She breathed heavily. The burn of tears threatened, but she couldn't cry; not yet. The dagger pulsed in her hand like it felt her distress, like it didn't want her to be alone with it. Her heart had been nothing but in pain for the last few hours, but this, this was unbearable. She picked up the strip of his shirt, clenching it in her fist. Her feelings were too erratic. She could not tame them.

The thought of him trapped, in the dark, reliving his most traumatic past moments... No, she would fix this; she had to. If they hurt him, the man who she was almost certain possessed part of her soul, she would destroy them.

The dagger pulsed in her hand once more, and she gripped it, becoming a mask of calm, as she turned toward Otto's dead body.

She smiled.

She returned to the manor quickly, in case the knight who'd saved her had a change of heart, but she felt sick as she walked through the manor gates without Trystan. After alerting the guards of what had occurred with a composure she was proud of herself for, she made her way up the stairs.

Evie immediately peeked in on Lyssa, who was asleep on Tatianna's extra bed, Blade's knit dragon held in her tiny hands. Evie gave a watery smile and then went to the hallway, and as soon as the door shut, she cried. She cried and cried until she was hiccupping, until she sank down slowly to the ground, until her face was sticky and puffy from the tears and she was burying her face in her knees.

Her sobs faded slowly, and when Evie finally looked up, only anger remained.

A little while later, Evie found herself in the entryway corridor. She'd bathed and changed, and with it came a renewed sense of purpose as she watched Marvin following her orders. Catching her reflection in the mirror hanging across the way, her eyes stopped on the red of her lips, from her mother's rouge, then passed to her hair, unbound. She pushed it behind her ears as her loose pants swished against the stone floor.

"Lift it higher, Marv," Evie instructed as she let a wicked smile settle on her lips. Becky appeared like an apparition beside her, looking forlorn and lost.

"He's really gone?" She removed her glasses as she spoke, wiping the lenses against the thick fabric of her skirts.

Evie felt a strange kinship with her for just a moment. She gave

Becky a reassuring pat on the shoulder. "We'll get him back. I'll make sure of it—whatever it takes." And despite all that had transpired between them, all the insults and jabs and mistrust, Becky looked at Evie with something that veered precariously close to respect.

"What did you have in mind?"

Evie stared down at the gold markings circling her smallest finger. "Well, first—" She paused, smiling to herself. "I'm going to need you to kill me."

Becky's lips pulled up into a wry grin as she began speculating. "I thought you'd never ask."

"All done, Ms. Sage!" Marvin called, and Evie looked to the opulent ceiling and what had just been added. Her heart pounded in satisfaction at Becky's quiet gasp behind her. Otto Warsen's head dangled there, eyes frozen forever in an expression of fear and surprise.

Stepping back, leaving him behind, Evie made her way to the stairs down to the dungeon. Quietly vowing to herself that she would save The Villain…

Or become one trying.

The End.
Well…for now.

ACKNOWLEDGMENTS

As much as I love words, it is difficult to express them here, with so much emotion weighing them. I am so incredibly thrilled that I finally get to share this story with the rest of the world. From the time I was small, I loved fairy tales, storytelling, and the simple magic in laughing so hard a snort comes out your nose. I dreamed of this moment so many times, but I truly didn't do any of this alone.

Brent Taylor, my incredible agent, was the first person to believe in me and this story. I cannot thank him enough for all his patience, support, and kindness as he guided me through publishing my first novel. Liz Pelletier, who edited this book and made it the very best version of itself, all the while talking me through every moment of doubt and making me a better writer. Thank you so much to Lydia, Hannah, Stacy, Rae, Jessica, Heather, and everyone at Entangled who worked tirelessly on the story with me and made it absolutely shine.

Thank you so much to Elizabeth Turner Stokes for creating the incredible cover of the book and capturing the story so perfectly, as if you plucked it from my mind. But mostly, thank you for Kingsley—he'd be nothing without you! And thank you to Toni for formatting it so beautifully. Big thanks to my team at Kaye Publicity and Meredith for getting this book and me in front of so many readers.

This book was created from so many things. From every story my mom and dad created for me before bed (Say hi to Mark and Jolie, everyone! They're crying as they read this). It's made of every laugh I had over the years with my brothers and many, many, *many beloved* cousins. My characters are the kindness in my Sitto Georgann's smile and the strength in my Grandmother Rosalie. Their wit I'd like to think came from me, but I must credit my Grandfather James, who helped pioneer a whole new generation of quick-witted grandchildren (some of the many beloved cousins). It's made of my Giddo Richard, who passed away long before I could pick up a pen but whose dreams of being an author I carry on for the both of us.

I am lucky in the way that I can think of so many people to include here, who supported me that uplifted me, who made me feel like the things I created mattered. People like the wonderful artist Brittany Torres, who was one of the first people to bring my character to life. Every person on TikTok who followed this journey, whether you were here from the beginning or jumped in at the end, thank you. To everyone who ever told me I made them smile, you all made me smile every day, even when I thought I couldn't. It's a priceless gift I could never repay.

I found someone else who made me smile along this journey: my Michael, who not only loves me through every up and down, but also freely offers his back every time I want "The Villain" for a video. He carried me away, every time I asked, without a complaint. I love you.

A huge part of writing this book was about feeling less alone in the world. My characters became my family, my found family. What I didn't anticipate was finding a group of outrageously talented women that made me forget what loneliness was. They cheered me on through every victory. To Stacey, Kaven, Amber, Maggie, and Sam...thank you for destroying my loneliness and replacing it with a lifetime of warmth. You were all well worth the wait.

And finally, thank you to Evie Sage. I found her and this story when I was in one of the lowest places with my mental health, and she became my safe space. Every moment of doubt, we shared. She made me braver, bolder, stronger, when I didn't think I had any strength left. She made me want to fight, want to feel, want to laugh. Evie Sage saved me, and so did all of you. Thank you to everyone who picked up this book. I hope it made you smile.